# Br
## Bachelors
### Perfect & Available

# British *Bachelors*
## COLLECTION

January 2017

February 2017

March 2017

April 2017

May 2017

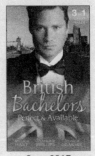

June 2017

# British
# *Bachelors*
## Perfect & Available

Jessica
HART

Charlotte
PHILLIPS

Jessica
GILMORE

Published in Great Britain 2017
By Mills & Boon, an imprint of HarperCollins*Publishers*
1 London Bridge Street, London, SE1 9GF

BRITISH BACHELORS: PERFECT & AVAILABLE © 2017
Harlequin Books S.A.

*Mr (Not Quite) Perfect* © 2014 Jessica Hart
*The Plus-One Agreement* © 2014 Charlotte Phillips
*The Return of Mrs Jones* © 2014 Jessica Gilmore

ISBN: 978-0-263-93068-9

09-0617

Our policy is to use papers that are natural, renewable and recyclable products and made from wood grown in sustainable forests.
The logging and manufacturing processes conform to the legal environmental regulations of the country of origin.

Printed and bound in Spain
by CPI, Barcelona

# MR (NOT QUITE) PERFECT

**JESSICA HART**

*For John, perfect for me, with love.*

**Jessica Hart** was born in west Africa, and has suffered from itchy feet ever since, travelling and working around the world in a wide variety of interesting but very lowly jobs—all of which have provided inspiration on which to draw when it comes to the settings and plots of her stories. Now she lives a rather more settled existence in York, where she has been able to pursue her interest in history—although she still yearns sometimes for wider horizons.

If you'd like to know more about Jessica visit her website: www.jessicahart.co.uk

# CHAPTER ONE

MAKING MR PERFECT by Allegra Fielding
*You've met a new guy. You're hot, hot, hot for each other. He's everything you ever wanted. But have you noticed that the infatuation phase never lasts? 'Fess up, ladies. How long before you're out with the girls and you find yourself saying, 'He'd be perfect if only he talked about his feelings/cooked occasionally/arranged a surprise mini-break/unfriended his ex on Facebook/insert peeve of your choice? He's still hot, you still love him to bits, but he's not quite as perfect as he seemed at first.*

*Are we asking too much of men nowadays? In a fairy tale, Prince Charming's task is clear. He has to hack his way through a thicket, slay a dragon and rescue the princess. Easy. In real life, we want our men to do a whole lot more to deserve us. Here at Glitz we've been conducting our own super-scientific survey over a few cocktails (pomegranate martinis, anyone?) and it seems that we want it all. The perfect boyfriend, it turns out, can fix our cars and dance without looking like a total dork. He looks good and he'll get rid of that spider in the shower. He'll sit through a romcom without complaining and*

*be strong enough to literally sweep us off our feet
when required.*

*But does such a man exist? And if he doesn't, is
it possible to create him? Glitz gives one lucky guy
the chance of the ultimate makeover. Read on and
see how one unreconstructed male rose to the challenge of becoming the perfect man. Meet—*

ALLEGRA LIFTED HER fingers from the keyboard and flexed
them. Meet who?

Good question. Funny how the world was full of unreconstructed males until you actually needed one. But as
soon as she had started asking around, it turned out that
nobody wanted to admit that their boyfriends were anywhere near imperfect enough to take part in her experiment.

With a sigh, Allegra closed the document and shut down
her computer. Had she been too ambitious? But Stella had
liked the idea. The editor in chief had inclined her head
by an infinitesimal degree, which signified enthusiasm.
Now Allegra had a big break at last—and it would all fall
apart if she couldn't find a man in need of a major makeover. One measly man, that was all she needed. He had to
be out there somewhere…but where?

'Ouf!' Allegra threw herself extravagantly into the armchair and toed off her mock-croc stilettos with a grimace
of pain. The needle-thin metal heels were to die for, but
she had been on them for over twelve hours and while
they might be long on style, they were extremely short
on comfort.

Max didn't even look away from the television. He was
stretched out on the sofa, flicking through channels, looking oddly at home in her sitting room. He had been tidying

again, Allegra registered with a roll of her eyes. You would never catch the magazines being neatly lined up on the coffee table when it was just her and Libby. The radiators would be festooned with bras and thongs and the surfaces comfortingly cluttered with useful stuff like nail polish remover, empty shoe boxes, expired vouchers, cosmetic samples and screwed up receipts. She and Libby knew to check down the back of the sofa for chargers. They knew where they were with the mess.

There was no point in trying to tell Max that, though. Libby's brother was an engineer. They said cosy sitting room, he said tip.

She massaged her sore toes. 'My feet are *killing* me!'

'Why do you wear those ridiculous shoes?' Max demanded. 'It's like you put yourself through torture every day. Why don't you wear trainers or something more comfortable?'

'Because, Max, I work for *Glitz*,' said Allegra with exaggerated patience. 'That's a *fashion* magazine and, while I realise that as Mr Hasn't-got-a-clue you don't know what fashion is, I can assure you that my editor would send me home if I turned up in trainers!'

'They can't sack you for what you wear,' said Max, unimpressed.

'Stella can do whatever she likes.' Such was her editor's power and personality that Allegra found herself glancing over her shoulder and speaking in hushed tones whenever her name was mentioned.

'That woman's a monster. You should tell her where to get off.'

'And lose my job? Do you have any *idea* how hard it was to get a job at *Glitz*?' Cautiously Allegra wiggled the blood back into her poor toes. 'People kill for the chance to work with Stella. She's like the high priestess of fashion. She's totally awesome.'

'You're terrified of her.'

'I'm not terrified,' said Allegra, not quite honestly. 'I *respect* her. *Everyone* respects her.'

Everyone except her mother, of course, but then it took a lot to impress Flick Fielding, as Allegra knew to her cost. She suppressed a little sigh at the thought. She had been so hoping that Flick would approve of the fact that Stella had given her a job in the face of such competition, but her mother had only raised perfectly groomed brows.

'*Glitz?*' she'd echoed as if Allegra had boasted of a first journalist job with *Waste Collectors Weekly* instead of a top-selling glossy magazine. 'Well, if you're pleased, then of course…well done, darling.'

Allegra would never have applied to *Glitz* in the first place if she had known that Stella had once mocked Flick's choice of outfit for an awards ceremony. Flick, a formidably high-powered journalist, had not been amused.

Still, Allegra wouldn't allow herself to be downcast. She just needed to make her mark at *Glitz* and a good reference from Stella would make her CV stand out anywhere, whatever her mother might say. And *then* she would get a job that would really make Flick proud of her. Sadly, that would probably mean boning up on politics and economics rather than shoes and handbags, but she would worry about that when the time came. For now the important thing was to impress Stella.

'Well, I think you're mad,' said Max. 'It's bad enough having to wear a suit to work every day.'

Allegra eyed the striped polo shirt that Max changed into the moment he got home with disfavour. 'Thank God they *do* make you wear a suit,' she said. 'Even you can't go too far wrong with a suit and tie. The rest of the time, it's like you've got an unerring sense of what will be *least* stylish.'

'What do you mean?'

'Well, take that…*that*,' she said, pointing at his top and Max looked down at his chest.

'What's wrong with it?'

'It's hideous!'

'It's comfortable,' he said, unbothered. 'I don't care about style.'

'You don't say,' said Allegra sarcastically.

It was quite incredible how lively Libby had ended up with such a stuffy brother! Max didn't have a clue about music, or clothes, or anything other than engineering, as far as Allegra could tell. He didn't look *too* bad in a conventional suit, but his taste in casual wear made her wince every time.

'I wouldn't even use that thing you're wearing as a duster,' she said.

'You wouldn't use anything as a duster,' Max countered. 'You never do any housework.'

'I do!'

'Where does the dustpan and brush live?'

There was a pause. 'Under the sink?'

He made a bleeping noise. 'In the cupboard under the stairs.'

'There's a cupboard under the stairs?'

'I rest my case.' Max shook his head and returned his attention to the television.

Gingerly, Allegra tested her feet and decided that she could manage a hobble to the kitchen to find something to eat. She was starving. Like the sitting room, the kitchen was so tidy nowadays she hardly recognized it.

Max had moved in a couple of weeks earlier. Libby's three-month placement in Paris had coincided with the

break-up of her brother's engagement, and she had offered
him her room while she was away.

'Would you mind?' she had asked Allegra. 'It's only
for a couple of months before he'll get a chance to go out
to Shofrar, so it's hard for him to find somewhere temporary. And I'm worried about him. You know what Max is
like; he's not exactly big on talking about feelings, but I
think he must be really gutted about Emma.'

'Why did she break it off, do you know?' Allegra had
been shocked when she heard. She'd only met Emma a
couple of times, but she'd seemed perfect for Max. An engineer like him, Emma had been pretty, nice…the word
*boring* shimmered in Allegra's head but it was too unkind
so she pushed it away…practical, she decided instead. Exactly the kind of sensible girl Max would choose and the
last person Allegra would have expected to have broken
it all off six months before the wedding.

'He hasn't told me.' Libby shook her head. 'Just says
it's all for the best. But I know he was planning for them
to go out to Shofrar together and now that's all off…well,
I'd feel better if you were around to cheer him up. As long
as you really don't mind.'

'Of course I don't mind,' said Allegra. She'd been at
school with Libby and had spent many holidays with her
friend's family while Flick was working. Max was the
brother she had never had, and over the years she had
bickered with him and relied on him almost as much as
Libby did.

'At least I know he's not a serial killer or anything,'
she'd said cheerfully. 'I'll stop him missing Emma too
much.'

In fact, she didn't see much of him. Max left for work
early in the morning, and she was out most evenings.
When they did coincide, like now, Max grumbled about

her untidiness and Allegra criticised his clothes. They fought over the remote and shared the occasional take-away. It was all perfectly comfortable.

And why wouldn't it be? Allegra asked herself as she opened the fridge and studied its contents without enthusiasm. This was Max, after all. Libby's brother. Allegra was fond of him, when she wasn't being irritated by his wardrobe and that way he had of making her feel like an idiot a lot of the time. Max wasn't ugly, but he wasn't exactly a hunk either. Certainly not a man to set your heart pattering.

*Apart from that one night, of course. Don't forget that.*

Allegra sighed as she picked out a low-fat yoghurt. Did everyone have an irritating voice in their head that would pop up at the least convenient times to remind them of precisely the things they most wanted to forget?

And it wasn't a night, she felt compelled to argue with herself, rummaging for a teaspoon. It had been an odd little incident, that was all. Not even an incident, really. *A moment.* And so long ago, really she had almost forgotten it.

Or she would have done if that pesky voice would let her.

No, it was all very comfortable. It was *fine.* Allegra was glad Max wasn't gorgeous or sexy. It made it easy to be relaxed with him. Which wasn't to say he couldn't make more of an effort on the clothes front. He didn't seem to care what he looked like, Allegra thought critically. That shirt was appalling and he *would* fasten it almost to the neck, no matter how often she told him to undo another button. He had no idea at all. If he smartened himself up a bit…

And that was when it hit her. Allegra froze with the teaspoon in her mouth.

*Max.* He was *perfect!* Why on earth hadn't she thought of him before?

She'd pitched the 'create a perfect boyfriend' idea to Stella at an editorial meeting the previous week. It was the first of her ideas that she'd been given the go-ahead to follow up, and Allegra had been fired with enthusiasm at first. But she had begun to wonder if she could make it work without the right man.

And now she had found him, lying in her own sitting room!

Already Allegra's mind was leaping forward, all her excitement about the project refuelled. She would write the best article *ever*. It would be fun, it would be interesting, it would tap into every woman's fantasy of making her man perfect. It would win awards, be syndicated worldwide. Stella would gasp with admiration.

At this point Allegra's imagination, vivid as it was, faltered. Stella, gasping? But a little strategic tweaking and the fantasy still worked. All right, Stella would look as enigmatic as ever but her words would be sweet. *Allegra*, she would say, *you're our new star writer. Have a massive salary.*

*I'd love to, Stella*, Allegra imagined herself saying in reply, super casual. *But the* Financial Times *has made me an offer I can't refuse.*

Surely her mother would be impressed by the *FT*?

Sucking yoghurt thoughtfully from her spoon, Allegra went to the kitchen doorway from where she could study Max without being observed.

He was still on the sofa, still flicking through channels in search of the news or sport, which was all he ever watched. Definitely not the kind of guy you would check out in a bar. Brown hair, ordinary features, steady blue-grey eyes: there was nothing wrong with him, but nothing special either.

Yep, he was perfect.

Max played rugby so he was pretty fit, but he didn't make anything of himself. Allegra mentally trimmed his hair and got rid of the polo shirt only to stop, unnerved, when she realised that the image of him lying on the sofa bare-chested was quite…startling.

Hastily, she put the shirt back on in her imagination. Whatever, the man was ripe for a makeover.

All she had to do was get Max to agree. Scraping out the yoghurt pot, Allegra tossed it in the bin with a clatter and squared her shoulders. Only last week she'd written an article on the benefits of thinking positive and getting what you wanted. It was time to put all that useful research into practice.

Back in the sitting room, she batted at Max's knees until he shifted his legs and she could plonk herself down on the sofa next to him. 'Max,' she began carefully.

'No.' Max settled his legs back across her lap and crossed his ankles on the arm of the sofa, all without taking his eyes off the television.

'What do you mean, *no*?' Forgetting her determination to stay cool and focused, as per her own advice in the article, Allegra scowled at him. 'You don't know what I'm going to say yet!'

'I know that wheedling tone of old,' said Max. 'You only use it when you want me to do something I'm not going to want to do.'

'Like what?' she said, affronted.

'Like waste an entire hot bank holiday Monday sitting in traffic because you and Libby wanted to go to the sea.'

'That was Libby's idea, not mine.'

'Same wheedle,' said Max, still flicking channels. 'And it was definitely your idea to have a New Year's Eve party that time.'

'It was a great party.'

'And who had to help you clear up afterwards before my parents came home?'

'You did, because you're a really, really kind brother who likes to help his sister and his sister's best mate out when they get into trouble.'

Max lowered the remote and looked at Allegra in alarm.

'Uh-oh. You're being nice. That's a bad sign.'

'How can you say that? I'm often nice to you. Didn't I make you a delicious curry last weekend?'

'Only because you wanted some and didn't want to admit that you'd broken your diet.'

Sadly, too true.

'*And* I said I'd go to that dinner and pretend to be your fiancée,' she said. 'How much nicer can I get?'

Max pulled himself up to look at Allegra with suddenly narrowed eyes. 'You're not going to back out, are you? Is that what this is about? Now that Emma's not around, I really need you.'

'Aw, Max, that's sweet!'

'I'm serious, Legs. My career depends on this.'

'I do think the whole thing is mad.' Allegra wriggled into a more comfortable position, not entirely sorry to let the conversation drift while she worked out exactly how to persuade Max to agree to take part. 'I mean, who cares nowadays if you're married or not?'

'Bob Laskovski does,' said Max gloomily.

At first he had welcomed the news that the specialist firm of consulting engineers he worked for was to be taken over by a large American company. An injection of capital, jobs secured, a new CEO with fantastic contacts with the Sultan of Shofrar and some major projects being developed there and elsewhere in the Middle East: it was all good news.

The bad news was that the new CEO in question was

a nut. Bob Laskovski allegedly had a bee in his bonnet about the steadying influence of women, of all things. If ever there was going to be unsettling going on, there was bound to be a female involved, in Max's opinion. But Bob liked his project managers to be in settled relationships and, given the strict laws of Shofrar, that effectively meant that, male or female, they had to be married.

'God knows what he thinks we'll do if we don't have a wife to come home to every night,' Max had grumbled to Allegra. 'Run amok and seduce local girls and offend the local customs, I suppose.'

Allegra had just laughed. 'I'd love to see you running amok,' she'd said.

Max had ignored that and ploughed on with his explanation. 'If I don't turn up with a likely-looking fiancée, Bob's going to start humming and hawing about whether I'm suitable for the job or not.'

It was ridiculous, he grumbled whenever given the opportunity. He had the skills, he had the experience, and he was unencumbered by ties. He should be the perfect candidate.

There hadn't been a problem when Bob had first said that he was coming over to London and wanted to meet the prospective project managers. That was another of Bob's 'things', apparently: he liked to vet them personally over individual dinners. God knew how the man had had the time to build up a vast construction company.

Max hadn't thought about it too much when the invitation to dinner had arrived. He and Emma had been going to get married anyway, and she was bound to go down well with Bob. Max was all set for his big break.

And then Emma had changed her mind.

Max still couldn't quite believe it. He might have lost his fiancée, but he was damned if he was going to lose the

Shofrar job too. Still, at least Allegra had been quite will-ing to help when he broached the idea of her standing in for Emma. For all her silliness, she could be counted on when it mattered.

'But just for an evening,' she had warned. 'I'm not going to marry you and go out to Shofrar just so you can be a project manager!'

'Don't worry, it won't come to that,' said Max, shud-dering at the very thought of it.

'There are plenty of examples of relationships bust-ing up before and after engineers get out there, and once you're actually doing the job and behaving yourself it's not a problem. All I need to do is get Bob's seal of approval. Everyone says it's worth humouring him.

'It'll just be a dinner,' he assured her. 'All you need to do is smile and look pretty and pretend that you're going to be the perfect engineer's wife.'

Of course, *that* was going to be the problem. He'd eyed Allegra critically. She'd been dressed in a short stretchy skirt that showed off her long legs, made even longer by precarious heels. 'Maybe you'd better wear something a bit more…practical,' he'd said. 'You don't really look like an engineer's wife.'

Allegra, of course, had taken that as a compliment.

'I don't mind going along to the dinner with you,' she said now. 'I may not be much of an actress, but I expect I can pretend to love you for an evening.'

'Thanks, Legs,' said Max. 'It means a lot to me.'

'But…' she said, drawing out the word, and his eyes narrowed suspiciously; he never liked the sound of 'but'. '…there *is* just one tiny thing you could do for me in re-turn.'

She smiled innocently at him and his wary look deep-ened. 'What?'

'No, your line is, *Of course, Allegra, I'll do whatever you want.* Would you like to try it again?'

'What?' he repeated.

Allegra sighed and squirmed round until she was facing him. She tucked her hair behind her ears, the way she did when she was trying to look serious, and fixed him with her big green eyes.

'You know how hard it's been for me to make my mark at *Glitz*?'

Max did. He knew more than he wanted, in fact, about Allegra's precarious foothold on the very lowest rung of the glossy magazine, where as far as he could make out, emotions ran at fever-pitch every day and huge dramas erupted over shoes or handbags or misplaced emery boards. Or something equally pointless.

Allegra seemed to love it. She raced into the flat, all long legs and cheekbones and swingy, shiny hair, discarding scarves and shoes and earrings as she went, and whirled out again in an outfit that looked exactly the same, to Max's untutored eye.

She was always complaining, though, that no one at the magazine noticed her. Max thought that was extremely unlikely. Allegra might not be classically beautiful but she had a vivid face with dark hair, striking green eyes and a mobile expression. She wasn't the kind of girl people didn't notice.

He'd known her since Libby had first brought her home for the holidays. Max, callous like most boys his age, had dismissed her at first as neurotic, clumsy and overweight. For a long time she'd just been Libby's gawky friend, but she'd shed the weight one summer and, while it was too much to say that she'd emerged a butterfly from her chrysalis, she had certainly gained confidence. Now she was really quite attractive, Max thought, his gaze resting on her face and drifting, quite without him realising, to her mouth.

He jerked his eyes away. The last time he'd found himself looking at her mouth, it had nearly ended in disaster. It had been before he'd met Emma, a moment of madness one night when all at once things seemed to have changed. Max still didn't know what had happened. One moment he and Allegra had been talking, and the next he'd been staring into her eyes, feeling as if he were teetering on the edge of a chasm. Scrabbling back, he'd dropped his gaze to her mouth instead, and that had been even worse.

He'd nearly kissed Allegra.

How weird would *that* have been? Luckily they'd both managed to look away at last, and they'd never referred to what had happened—or not happened—ever again. Max put it out of his mind. It was just one of those inexplicable moments that were best not analysed, and it was only occasionally, like now, when the memory hurtled back and caught him unawares, a sly punch under his ribs that interfered oddly with his breathing.

Max forced his mind back to Allegra's question. 'So what's changed?' he asked her, and she drew a deep breath.

'I've got my big break! I've got my own assignment.'

'Well, great…good for you, Legs. What's it going to be? A hard-hitting exposé of corruption in the world of shoes? Earth-shattering revelations on where the hemline is going to be next year?'

'Like I'd need your help if it was either of those!' said Allegra tartly. 'The man who wouldn't know fashion if it tied him up and slapped him around the face with a wet fish.'

'So what do you need me for?'

'Promise you'll hear me out before you say anything?'

Max swung his legs down and sat up as he eyed Allegra

with foreboding. 'Uh-oh, I'm starting to get a bad feeling about this!'

'*Please*, Max! Just listen!'

'Oh, all right,' he grumbled, sitting back and folding his arms. 'But this had better be good.'

'Well…' Allegra moistened her lips. 'You know we have an editorial conference to plan features for the coming months?'

Max didn't, but he nodded anyway. The less he had to hear about the workings of *Glitz*, the better.

'So the other day we were talking about one of the girls whose relationship has just fallen apart.'

'This is *work*? Gossiping about relationships?' It didn't sound like any conference Max had ever been in.

'Our readers are *interested* in relationships.' Allegra's straight, shiny hair had swung forward again. She flicked it back over her shoulder and fixed him with a stern eye. 'You're supposed to be just listening,' she reminded him.

'So, yes, we were talking about that and how her problem was that she had totally unrealistic expectations,' she went on when Max subsided with a sigh. 'She wanted some kind of fairy tale prince.'

Princes. Fairy tales. Max shook his head. He thought about his own discussions at work: about environmental impact assessments and deliverables and bedrock depths. Sometimes it seemed to him that Allegra lived in a completely different world.

'We had a long discussion about what women really want,' she went on, ignoring him. 'And we came to the conclusion that actually we want everything. We want a man who can fix a washing machine and plan the perfect date. Who'll fight his way through a thicket if required but who can also dress well and talk intelligently at the theatre. Who can plan the perfect romantic date and sort out your tax and dance and communicate…'

Max had been listening with growing incredulity. 'Good luck finding a bloke who can do all that!'

'Exactly!' Allegra leant forward eagerly. '*Exactly*! That was what we all said. There isn't anyone like that out there. So I started thinking: what if we could *make* a man like that? What if we could create a boyfriend who was everything women wanted?'

'How on earth would you go about that?' asked Max, not sure whether to laugh or groan in disbelief.

'By teaching him what to do,' said Allegra. 'That's what I pitched to Stella: a piece on whether it's possible to take an ordinary bloke and transform him into the perfect man.'

There was a silence. Max's sense of foreboding was screaming a warning now.

'Please tell me this isn't the point where you say, *And this is where you come in*,' he said in a hollow voice.

'And this is where you come in, Max,' said Allegra.

He stared at her incredulously. She was smiling, and he hoped to God it was because she was winding him up. 'You're not serious?'

'Think about it: you're the ideal candidate. You haven't got a girlfriend at the moment…and frankly,' she added, unable to resist, 'unless you get rid of that polo shirt, you won't get another one.'

Max scowled. 'Stop going on about my shirt. Emma never minded it.'

'Maybe she never *said* she minded it, but I bet she did.' On a roll, Allegra pointed a finger at Max. 'The thing is, Max, that shirt is symptomatic of a man who can't be bothered to make an effort. I'm guessing Emma was just too nice to point that out.'

Max ground his teeth. 'For God's sake, Allegra! It's

*comfortable*. Since when has comfort been an indictable offence?'

'There are plenty of other new comfortable shirts out there that aren't striped or buttoned too high at the collar, but you won't buy them because that would mean changing, and changing is hard work,' said Allegra. 'And it's not just a question of clothes. You need to change how you communicate, how you *are*. How much effort you put into thinking about your girlfriend and what will make her happy.'

Closing his eyes briefly, Max drew a breath and let it out with exaggerated patience. 'Allegra, I have no idea what you're talking about,' he said.

'Why did Emma call off your engagement? I'll bet it was because you weren't prepared to make an effort, wasn't it?'

'No, it wasn't,' said Max, goaded at last. 'If you must know, she met someone else. It's not as if it's a big secret,' he went on, seeing Allegra's awkward expression. It was obviously just as much a surprise to her as it had been to him. 'I just don't particularly feel like talking about it all the time.'

'Emma seemed so nice,' said Allegra hesitantly after a moment. 'She didn't seem like someone who'd cheat on you.'

'She didn't.' Max blew out a breath, remembering how unprepared he had been for Emma's revelation. 'She was very honest. She said she'd met someone who works for one of our clients, and she didn't want to sleep with him until she'd told me how he made her feel. He made her realise that we didn't have any passion in our relationship any more.'

'Eeuww.'

That was exactly what Max had thought. 'I mean,

*passion!*' He practically spat out the word. 'What in God's name does *passion* mean?'

'Well, I suppose…sexual chemistry,' Allegra offered. She hesitated. 'So were things in the bedroom department…?' She trailed off delicately.

'They were fine! Or I thought they were fine,' Max amended bitterly. 'I loved Emma, and I thought she loved me. She was always talking about how compatible we were. We had the same interests. We were *friends*. It was her idea to get married in the first place, and I couldn't see any reason not to. We'd been together three years and it was the obvious next step.

'Then Emma meets this guy and suddenly it's all about magic and chemistry and getting swept off her feet!' Max's mouth twisted. 'I said to her, magic doesn't last. Having things in common is more important than sparks, but she wouldn't listen to reason.' He sighed, remembering. 'It was so unlike her. Emma used to be so sensible. It was one of the things I loved about her. She wasn't silly like—'

*Like you.*

Max managed to bite the words back in time, but he might as well not have bothered because they hung in the air anyway.

Allegra told herself she didn't mind. She had more important things to worry about, like getting her assignment off the ground.

'I don't think you should give up on Emma, Max,' she said persuasively. 'You two were good together. It sounds to me as if she was feeling taken for granted.'

'You being the great relationship expert,' said Max dourly.

'I know what I'm talking about when it comes to failed relationships,' Allegra pointed out, unfazed. 'It wouldn't surprise me at all if Emma is just looking for more attention from you. And that's where I can help you,' she added cunningly, gaining confidence from the fact that Max hadn't scoffed yet. 'If you really want her back, put yourself in my hands. It's a win for all of us, Max. I get my article written, you get Emma back, and Emma gets the perfect man!'

## CHAPTER TWO

THERE WAS A long silence. Max's eyes were narrowed. He was definitely thinking about it, Allegra realised jubilantly, and she forced herself not to say any more. If he felt she was pressurising him, he would back away. Softly, softly, catchee monkey.

'What *exactly* would be involved?' he asked cautiously at last, and Allegra kept her eyes downcast so that he wouldn't see the triumph in them. She didn't want to spook him now.

'The idea is for you to complete a series of tasks,' she began. 'Sort of like a knightly quest…' She stopped as his face changed. Oops, looked like she'd lost him already with the knightly quest. Hurriedly, Allegra switched tactics. Practical details, that would appeal to Max.

'So your first task would be to have cocktails—'

'I can't stand those poncy drinks,' he started grumbling immediately. 'I don't know how you women can sit there sucking through straws and fighting your way through umbrellas and cherries.'

'—with Darcy King,' Allegra finished talking over the top of him.

A pause. Max sat up straight. 'What, not…?'

'Yes, *the* Darcy King.'

Idiot. She should have mentioned Darcy right at the

start. Darcy was every red-blooded male's fantasy, a lingerie model with a sweet face and a sinful body. Allegra could practically see Max drooling already. If Darcy wouldn't win him round to the assignment, nothing would.

'You, Max Warriner, have the chance to go on a series of dates with Darcy King herself. Think about what your mates will say when they hear about *that!*'

'Darcy King wouldn't want to go out with me!'

'Not if you were wearing that shirt, she wouldn't, but that's the whole point,' said Allegra at her most persuasive. 'Can we take you—an engineer with no dress sense and rudimentary social skills but with some useful abilities like how to put a flat pack from Ikea together—and turn you into the sophisticated, well-dressed kind of man that Darcy would like to go out with?'

Max looked as if he wasn't sure how to take that. 'She must have a boyfriend already, looking like that.'

'Apparently she finds it hard to find men who can get past what she looks like and be interested in *her,*' said Allegra. 'Ianthe interviewed her a couple of months ago and it turns out she's just like the rest of us, kissing a lot of toads and still hoping to find her prince.'

On the other side of the sofa, Max didn't bother to disguise his incredulity. 'And you think *I* could be Darcy King's prince?'

'Actually, no.' Hmm, this was tricky. She didn't want to discourage him, but it wouldn't be fair to get his hopes up either. 'I mean, even if you were to fall madly in love, it's hard to imagine you having a future together. I don't see Darcy wanting to go off to Shofrar.'

'True. There's not a lot of work for lingerie models out there,' Max agreed. 'But if we were madly in love, would that matter?'

For one awful moment Allegra thought that he was

taking the whole matter seriously, but when she shot him a worried look he didn't quite have time to conceal the mocking gleam in his blue-grey eyes, and she grinned and shoved him.

'You know what I mean,' she said. 'It's just a fun assignment, but Darcy gets to have a good time, and you might learn something about dealing with women. If you want to get Emma back, Max, this could be just the chance you need. Are you really going to turn it down because you don't want to be seen sucking a cocktail through a straw?'

Max considered her. 'That would be it? Drinking a cocktail with Darcy King?'

'Well, obviously we'd need to make a few changes,' said Allegra airily. 'Get you a new wardrobe, a new haircut, that kind of thing, but the stylist would help you with that.'

'*Stylist?*'

'You're really lucky.' Allegra lowered her voice reverentially. 'Dickie said he'd style the shoot personally.'

'Shoot? What shoot? And who the hell is Dickie?'

He really didn't have a clue, did he? 'Dickie Roland is only the most famous stylist in London at the moment,' she said. 'He's a superstar! I think his name is actually Georges, but in the fashion world he's just known as Dickie after his trademark bow tie. He's worn it ever since he came to London from Paris, and it's hard to imagine him without one now.'

'I hope you're not planning to ask me to wear a bow tie!'

'No, no, that's Dickie's "thing". He'll just make you look fabulous.' Allegra sighed. Max clearly had no idea what an honour it was to be styled by Dickie. 'But you have to promise to be nice to him. Dickie's brilliant, but he can be a bit…temperamental.'

Max pinched the bridge of his nose. 'I can't believe I'm actually discussing being styled!' he muttered.

'You'd want to look nice for Darcy, wouldn't you?'

'I haven't said yes yet,' he warned quickly. 'What else is involved in this assignment of yours? It's got to be more than putting on a shirt and slurping a cocktail.'

'Once you've got through the cocktails, the next task is to cook Darcy dinner—and no ordering in a pizza. You have to cook it yourself.' Darcy was a vegetarian and the meal had to be a romantic one, but Allegra would break that to Max later. For now she just had to get him to agree in principle. There would be time enough to talk him through the pesky details once he'd agreed.

Max grunted. 'I could probably manage a meal, as long as she's not expecting anything fancy.'

'The whole point is to make an effort to cook something *Darcy* would like,' said Allegra, smoothing impatience from her voice. It wouldn't do to put his back up now, just when she had him nibbling at her hook! 'When you're having a drink, you'll have to talk to her and find out what sort of food she prefers, and if she likes fancy, then you're going to have to cook fancy. But I wouldn't be surprised if she likes things simple,' she added hastily as Max's brows drew together.

'Okay. So cocktail, cooking…what else?'

Best to take the next bit in a rush. 'You'd need to do something cultural without looking bored—we're thinking the theatre, perhaps, or the opening of an art exhibition—and that's it, really. Then it's just the ball,' Allegra finished breezily and put on a bright smile, hoping that Max might have missed the last task.

No such luck. 'Please tell me you're thinking about a round thing that you kick around a field!'

'Not *exactly*…'

'Come on, Legs, there's something you're not telling me, isn't there?'

'All right, it's a costume ball being held for charity. You'll have to dress up—and learn to waltz.'

There, it was out, but, as expected, Max had started shaking his head at 'costume'. 'No way,' he said firmly. 'I don't mind having a go at the other stuff, but dressing up? And *dancing*? I'd rather stick pins in my eyes!'

'Oh, Max, *please!* We have to have the ball. Darcy's really looking forward to it, and learning how to dance would be such a great gesture. It would be so...*romantic.*'

'What's romantic about making a tit of yourself on the dance floor?'

'I've always wanted to go to a ball like that. Not just a dinner dance bash but a real ball, with proper ball gowns and waltzing...' Allegra's eyes were dreamy at the mere thought of it, and she pressed a hand to the base of her throat as she sighed.

She had grown up in a house full of books, but Flick's shelves were lined with heavyweight biographies and award-winning literary novels. Flick was dismissive of commercial fiction, and as a child Allegra's books had been uniformly worthy. It had been a revelation to go and stay with Libby's family, where the house was full of dog-eared paperbacks with broken spines and yellowing pages.

Best of all, Max's mother had a collection of Regency romances and Allegra had devoured them every time she went. She loved the ordered world they portrayed with those rakish dukes and spirited governesses. She loved the dashing way the heroes drove their curricles, their curling lips, their codes of honour.

And their tight breeches, of course.

Best of all were the ball scenes, which were charged with sexual tension as the hero and heroine clasped hands and danced, oblivious to anyone but each other.

A wistful sigh leaked out of her. 'I'd love to waltz,' she

told Max, who was predictably unimpressed. 'It's my fantasy to be swept masterfully around a ballroom by a dashing hero, who knows just how to dance me unobtrusively out onto a terrace where it's dark and warm and the air is sweet with the scent of summer flowers and he's dancing with me along the terrace but he's overcome by passion and he presses me up against the balustrade and tells me he loves me madly and can't live without me and he's begging me to marry him—'

Running out of breath, she broke off to find Max watching her quizzically.

'I'm glad you stopped,' he said. 'I was wondering if I should throw a glass of water at you to stop you hyperventilating.'

'You've got to admit it would be romantic,' Allegra insisted.

Max showed no sign of admitting any such thing. He got back to the business in hand.

'Why not get that boyfriend of yours to take you if you want to go so much? What's his name? Jerry?'

'Jeremy.'

'That's right. Of course he's a Jeremy,' said Max dismissively. 'I bet he knows how to dance. I only met him once but he struck me as a guy who knows how to do everything.'

Jeremy had been very accomplished, that was for sure, but he was much too serious to go dancing. He was interested in politics and the economy. He could talk about the arts and international relations. He had been well-dressed and charming. Not the most practical guy in the world perhaps, but Allegra couldn't imagine him ever needing to assemble any flat packs in any case.

'In fact, why not get him to do your whole assignment?'

Max said and Allegra sighed and tucked her legs more comfortably beneath her.

'It wouldn't be much of a transformation story,' she said. 'Besides, I haven't seen him for a while. He wasn't really my boyfriend.'

She had tried to be upset when Jeremy stopped calling, but honestly, it had been a relief not to have to try quite so hard for a while. Jeremy's conversation might be impressive but it was light on humour and, in spite of growing up with Flick Fielding as a mother, the sad truth was that Allegra's interests veered more towards celebrity gossip and shoes than political intrigue. Flick would be appalled if she had guessed, and Allegra did her best not to disappoint her mother, but sometimes it was hard to keep up.

'We only went out a couple of times,' she said. 'Jeremy was just…someone Flick introduced me to.'

That would be right, thought Max. Allegra's mother liked to keep her daughter toeing the line and would soon veto any unsuitable boyfriends. Tricky Flicky, as she was known by those unfortunate enough to have been subjected to one of her gruelling interviews, was a media heavyweight, famous as much for her style as for her incisive questioning. Much as they might squirm under the lash of her tongue and steely-eyed gaze, politicians lobbied to be interviewed by Flick Fielding. Flick had gravitas, they all agreed that.

Whereas Allegra…Allegra was warm and funny and creative and kind, but gravitas? No.

Max had never understood why Flick, with all her brains, didn't just accept that rather than trying to force Allegra into her own mould.

'So, you're not heartbroken?' he asked Allegra cautiously. Because he had learnt that with women you never could tell.

'No.' Allegra blew out a long sigh and pushed her hair away from her face. 'Jeremy was just the latest in a long line of men who turned out not to be The One after all. I had such high hopes when I first met him too.'

'You know, you might get on better if you stopped letting your mother choose your boyfriends.' Max kept his voice carefully neutral but Allegra bridled anyway.

'She doesn't *choose* them!'

'Come on, when have you ever gone out with someone your mother wouldn't approve of?'

'I happen to like men who are attractive and intelligent and witty and successful,' Allegra said defensively. 'Of course she approves of them.'

'Maybe I should have said that you should try going out with someone because you like him, not because you think your mother will.'

'I *did* like Jeremy.' Clearly ruffled, Allegra wriggled her shoulders. 'Anyway, that's all beside the point. Jeremy's not around and you are, and Max, you're *perfect* for my assignment! There's so much scope for you to improve.'

'Thanks a lot!'

'You know what I mean. You could get so much out of it too. You should be leaping at the chance to learn how to give a woman what she really wants! You're going to Shofrar in a couple of months and the piece won't be out until after you leave, but if you play your cards right you could win Emma back and take her with you. That's what you want, isn't it?'

Was it? Max thought about Emma. She'd been so easy to be with. They'd been comfortable together, and it would be good to have that back again. Of course he wanted her back…but he wanted her the way she had been before she lost her head and started wanting more of everything: more excitement, more passion, more attention, more effort. Max thought the whole idea was to find someone you didn't *have* to make an effort for, but apparently he was wrong about that.

He missed Emma, though, and he missed the warm feeling of knowing that you'd found the woman you wanted to settle down with. He would never find anyone better than Emma. She was perfect for him.

'Yes,' he said. 'Of course I do.'

'Well, then,' said Allegra, satisfied. 'I bet if Emma gets wind of the fact that you're going out with Darcy she'll be jealous.'

'I wouldn't really be going out with her,' Max pointed out.

'Emma won't know that, will she? She'll be back in no time, you'll see.'

'I don't know.' Max pulled down his mouth. 'I wouldn't bet on it, and in the meantime I really don't want to dress up and learn to dance just on the off chance that she does. I can't imagine Emma caring about whether I can waltz or not.'

'You couldn't imagine her being carried away by passion either,' Allegra pointed out.

'No, but—'

It was at that point that Allegra gave up on arguments and threw pride to the winds. Grabbing his hand, she held it between her own.

'Oh, please, Max! Please, please, please, please, *please!* Please say you'll do it! This is my big chance to impress Stella. If I don't find someone to take part in this assignment, I won't get another one. I'll be a failure!' she said extravagantly. 'My career will be over before it's begun and how will I tell Flick?'

She leant beseechingly towards him and Max found himself snared in the big eyes. Funny how he had never noticed before how beautiful they were, or how green, the lovely dark mossy green of a secret wood...

Secret wood? Max gave himself a mental slap. God, he'd be spouting poetry next!

'I know you don't think much of *Glitz*,' Allegra was babbling on, 'but this is my career! What else am I going to do if I'm a failure as a journalist?'

'You could illustrate those children's books the way you always said you were going to.' He and his family shouldn't have been surprised when Allegra announced that she was going to follow Flick into journalism, but none of them had ever had her down as a writer. Max always thought of her drawing—quick, vivid sketches that brought a face or an animal to life in a few simple lines.

She drew back, thrown by his suggestion. 'I can't make a living as an illustrator.'

What she meant was: Flick wouldn't be pleased. Flick wanted a daughter who would follow in her footsteps, a daughter who would be a journalist on television or for some respected newspaper. Flick had no time for Allegra's 'little drawings'. Max thought it was a shame.

'It's just a few hours of your time, Max.' Allegra reverted to the problem in hand.

Would it cost him that much to help her? Max found himself thinking. She was so longing to be a success, and she deserved a break. She'd been a good friend to Libby— and to him, he acknowledged. Allegra tried so hard to be ruthless and driven like her formidable mother, but she just couldn't quite manage it. She liked to pretend that she was tough, but she was a sucker for every sob story that came along. Allegra would never admit it, but she was hampered by warmth and kindness and humour from ever pleasing Flick.

'And if I say no, I suppose you'll refuse to pretend to be my fiancée when I meet Bob Laskovski?'

Allegra looked momentarily disconcerted and Max had to stop himself rolling his eyes. It had obviously never crossed her mind that she could do more than beg him to help her. She had such a transparent expression. He could read the agonizing in her green eyes, practically hear her wondering how she could possibly threaten to go back on her promise when she'd given her word.

If he had any decency, he'd put her out of her misery and tell her that he'd do her stupid assignment, but it was fun to see how far she would go for a success she could lay at Flick Fielding's feet—and frankly, Max considered, if he was going to make an idiot of himself, he deserved some amusement in return.

'Er, yes…yes, that's right,' said Allegra after a moment and put up her chin in a futile attempt to look ruthless. 'A favour for a favour. If you don't help me with this, you can forget about me pretending to be your fiancée!'

'But you promised,' Max protested, scowling to disguise his amusement as Allegra squirmed. She was big on keeping her promises. 'If you don't come with me to that dinner, I won't get the job in Shofrar and you know how much that means to me.'

'This assignment means a lot to *me*,' Allegra pointed out, but she didn't look very comfortable about it. 'That's the deal: take it or leave it.'

'That's blackmail!' said Max.

'And your point is…?' she countered bravely.

It was all Max could do not to grin. He heaved a disgruntled sigh instead. 'Oh, all *right*. If you're going to be like that, I don't have much choice, do I? I'll take part in your precious assignment—but you'd better not have been joking about Darcy King!'

One moment he was pretending to glower at Allegra, the next his arms were full of her. Beaming, she launched herself at him, pushing him back down onto the sofa cushions as she hugged him. 'Oh, I love you, Max! Thank you, thank you, thank you!' she babbled, blizzarding kisses over his face. 'You won't regret it, I promise you. I'm going to change your life, and it's going to be perfect!'

Allegra ran from the lift as fast as she could on her polka dot slingbacks. The shoes were a fun twist to the rest of her look, a demure tweed two-piece with a short skirt and three-quarter length sleeves that channelled her inner executive-cum-fashion diva, and Allegra had been pleased when she left home. She projected confidence and style, as befitted a girl on the verge of her big break.

Until her tights laddered, that was.

If only she hadn't stopped to say hello to Mrs Gosling, but how could she run past when her elderly neighbour's face lit up at the prospect of someone to talk to? Mrs Gosling spent most of her days walking her dog, an excitable mutt called, for reasons Allegra had never understood, Derek, and that morning she had been all tangled up in the lead while Derek literally ran rings round her.

Late as she was, Allegra had had to stop and disentangle Mrs Gosling and hear about Derek's latest antics. Allegra had a friend whose small daughter Molly loved to be told how naughty Derek was, and Allegra had taken to writing out each story, exaggerating for effect, and illustrating them with little sketches of Derek's mischievous face. Molly adored them.

'You should put them into a book,' Libby had said. 'The Glorious Adventures of Derek the Dog. Mrs G would love it.'

But Allegra had shrugged the idea aside. 'They're just for Molly really.'

But that morning she had only listened with half an ear as she sorted out the lead and bent to greet Derek, who jumped at her in ecstasy.

That was the end of the tights.

Oh, God, she was so late! Red-faced and panting, Allegra practically fell through the doors into *Glitz*'s super hip offices. The editorial department sprawled over the top floor of a converted warehouse. Most days the buzz hit Allegra the moment she got out of the lift. She loved the gloss of the office, the smell of new clothes and expensive perfumes, the stark décor contrasting with the colourful scatter of accessories and shoes displayed like works of art. She loved the frantic thrum in the air, the way it was punctuated with dramatic cries and screams of excitement.

Except when Stella was present, of course, in which case everyone was very quiet unless asked to speak.

It was ominously silent when Allegra collapsed against the reception desk, a funkily curved piece of steel, and held her hand against her side.

'The editorial meeting's just started,' Lulu, the receptionist, lowered her voice and eyed Allegra with sympathy. 'You know Stella hates it when anyone is late. You'd better pretend you fell under a bus or something.'

'I might as well if I don't get in there and get my assignment,' groaned Allegra, forcing herself upright.

Smoothing down her hair, she took a deep breath and headed towards the conference room, only to be called back by Lulu's frantic whisper.

'You can't go in like that!' She pointed at Allegra's legs. 'Tights!'

Allegra clutched her head. She'd forgotten her tights

for a moment. She'd soon learnt to keep a spare pair in her bag, but changing them would take precious seconds.

'What's worse?' she asked Lulu desperately. 'Being late or laddered tights?' Lulu's astounded expression was answer enough. Clearly, Allegra shouldn't have needed to ask. 'You're right, I'd better change…'

It was Allegra's second mistake of the day. Dashing into the loos, she found Hermione, one of the marketing interns, sobbing her heart out in a cubicle, and by the time Allegra had coaxed her out and listened to her tale of woe, she was not only horribly late but had acquired two mascara smudges on the pale cashmere jumper tucked so stylishly into her skirt.

That was what you got for dispensing comforting hugs, thought Allegra bitterly as she stripped off her tights, but she was in such a hurry to get the new ones on that she managed to stick a finger through them.

'Oh, sod it!' At least this time the ladder was hidden under her skirt. Bundling the first pair into the bin, Allegra swiped at her hair. She looked completely manic, but there was nothing she could do about it now. If she didn't get into that editorial meeting, she'd lose out on the assignment. Ianthe Burrows was probably already putting forward an alternative.

'Sorry,' she mouthed generally, sliding into the conference room at last and every head swivelled to stare at her, with her flushed cheeks and tousled hair. There was a resounding silence. Stella didn't say anything but her gaze rested for a crushing few seconds on the smudges before dropping to Allegra's knees as she stood frozen just inside the room.

Against her will, Allegra found herself following her editor's gaze to where the ladder had snaked out from under her skirt. Horrified, she watched it unravel over her knee and head down her leg. She could practically hear the unzipping sound.

Why was there never a black hole around when you needed to jump into one?

'Editorial meetings start at ten,' said Stella, and Allegra cringed at the lack of inflexion in her voice.

'Yes, I know…I—' She broke off. She couldn't explain about Derek and Mrs Gosling and Hermione. Stella wouldn't care and Allegra would sound like an idiot. Even more of an idiot. 'I'm sorry,' she said instead.

A fractional incline of Stella's head served as her dismissal. The conversation returned to the latest couture debut, and Allegra slunk into a chair at the back. Pulling out notebook, pen, iPad and PDA, she willed the burning colour in her face to fade.

Fortunately, she didn't appear to have missed too much and as the discussion warmed up into articles about how to give a rock'n'roll twist to the latest looks, and the pros and cons of being friends-with-benefits, she kept her head down and let her racing pulse slow. Mindlessly doodling Derek winding Mrs Gosling up in his lead, she listened to the arguments for and against sleeping with a friend. It wasn't something she would do herself. She'd be afraid that it would spoil the friendship. Because how could it possibly be the same afterwards?

What would it have been like if Max had kissed her all those years ago? Allegra was aware of an odd jolt of heat at the thought. It had to be the thrill of the forbidden, because Max was practically her brother.

Eeuww, the very idea was disturbing at a whole load of levels! But there had been something hot and dangerous in the air that night, something that risked changing everything, and they'd both known it. Perhaps that was why they had pulled back before they did something they would both have regretted.

Because if they'd kissed, they wouldn't have stopped at a kiss, and then it really *would* have been awkward. It wasn't even as if Max was her type, Allegra thought, even as she began an absent sketch of how he had looked lying on the sofa the night before. And she certainly wasn't his. Emma was neat and dainty and blonde, a sweet little pixie, while Allegra was leggy and chaotic.

No, it was much better that they'd stayed just friends, without any jiggery-pokery, as Ianthe liked to refer to sex. They would never have been able to share the house, like now, if they'd slept together, and she wouldn't have felt comfortable asking him to take part in the assignment.

Thank God they hadn't actually kissed.

Or done anything else.

Pursing her lips, Allegra studied her drawing. It looked like Max, but the mouth wasn't *quite* right… She made a slight adjustment to his upper lip and his face sprang to life so abruptly that her heart jumped a little: steady eyes, stubborn jaw, a quiet, cool mouth. She hadn't realised how well she had memorised the angles of his cheek, the way his hair grew. She had made him look…quite attractive.

Her mouth dried and all at once she was remembering how she had hugged him in her excitement the night before. She hadn't thought about it. He was Max, and he'd just agreed to take part in something Allegra knew he was going to hate. Hugging him was the obvious thing to do.

But when her arms were around his neck and her lips pressed to his cheek, she had suddenly become aware of how solid he was, how *male*. How familiar and yet how abruptly strange. The prickle of stubble on his jaw had pressed into her cheek and she'd breathed in the clean

masculine smell of him and something had twisted hard
and hot in her belly.

Something that had felt alarmingly like lust. Which of
course it couldn't have been because, hey, this was *Max*.

Beside her, Georgie, one of the few journalists who was
as junior as Allegra, leant over and raised her eyebrows
appreciatively. 'Your guy?' she mouthed.

Allegra shook her head, unaccountably flustered. 'Just
a friend.'

'Right.' Georgie's smile was eloquent with disbelief.

Quickly Allegra sketched in Max's shirt, including
every stripe, and the collar that was buttoned too high,
and Georgie's smile faded.

'Oh.'

Quite, thought Allegra. She should do less thinking
about Max's mouth and more remembering his absolutely
appalling taste in shirts.

'Allegra!'

The deputy editor's voice made Allegra jerk her eyes to
the front, where Stella was looking sphinx-like and Marisa,
her deputy, harried. 'Could we have a moment of your attention?'

Allegra fought the impulse to say, *Yes, miss.* 'Yes, of
course.'

'*Making Mr Perfect*…did you get anywhere with that?'

Clearly expecting the answer to be no, their eyes were
already moving down the list, on to the next idea. This
was her moment.

'Actually, yes, I did,' Allegra said and a ripple of surprise ran round the room.

'You found someone to take part?' Stella's expression
was as inscrutable as ever but Allegra told herself that

the very slight life of her editor's immaculate brows was a good sign.

'Yes,' she said.

'Who is he?' That was Marisa.

'The brother of a friend of mine. Max.' Why did just saying his name suddenly make her feel warm?

'What does he look like?' asked Marisa practically. 'I suppose it's too much to hope that he's a hunk?'

Allegra glanced down at her sketch of Max on the sofa: solid, steady-eyed. Ordinary. Nothing special. Her eyes rested on his mouth for a moment and there it came again without warning, a quick, disturbing spike of her pulse. She looked away.

'I wouldn't say that he was a *hunk*, exactly,' she said cautiously, 'but I think he'll brush up well.'

'Sounds promising. What's he like?'

'He's a civil engineer,' said Allegra, as if that explained everything. 'He's pretty conventional, plays rugby and doesn't have a clue about style.' She lifted her shoulders, wondering how else to describe him. 'He's just a bloke, really.'

'No girlfriend in the wings? We don't want anyone making a fuss about him spending time with Darcy.'

Allegra shook her head. 'He's just been dumped by his fiancée and he's going to work abroad soon so he's not interested in meeting anyone else at the moment. He's perfect,' she said.

'And he knows exactly what's involved?' Marisa insisted. 'He's happy to go ahead?'

*Happy* might be stretching it, thought Allegra, remembering uneasily how she had had to blackmail Max, but this was no time for quibbling. Her big chance was *this* close, and she was ready to seize it.

'Absolutely,' she said.

Marisa glanced at Stella, who nodded. 'In that case, you'd better get on to Darcy King and set up the first date straight away.'

# CHAPTER THREE

'So this is where you work.' Max looked around him uneasily. The office was aflutter with gorgeous glossy women, all eyeing him as if they had never seen a man in a suit before and weren't sure whether to laugh or pity him.

It ought to have been gratifying to be the focus of so much undivided female attention, but Max was unnerved. He felt like a warthog who had blundered into a glasshouse full of butterflies.

Why the hell had he agreed to this stupid idea? He'd been lying there minding his own business and then Allegra had slid onto the sofa next to him and before he knew what was happening he'd been tangled up in her idea and lost in those mossy eyes and suddenly all he cared about was making her happy.

He'd even suggested his own blackmail. He must have been mad.

But the smile on Allegra's face had lit up the room and left him scrabbling for breath, and when she'd thrown herself into his arms the feel of her had left Max oddly light-headed. Her hair had trailed silkily over his face as she threw her arms round him and pressed her lips to his cheek, and the smell of her perfume had sent his mind spinning.

To Max's horror, his body had taken on a mind of its

own. Without him even being aware of what he was doing, his arms had clamped round her and for a moment he had held her against him and fought the crazy urge to slide his hands under that skimpy top and roll her beneath him.

Which would have been a very, very, very bad idea.

The next instant Allegra had pulled back, babbling excitedly about the assignment. As far as she was concerned, it had just been a sisterly hug.

That was all it *had* been, Max reminded himself sternly.

And now it seemed he was committed to the charade. 'The first thing is to smarten you up.' Allegra had gone all bossy and produced a clipboard and a list. 'Can you take an afternoon off? You're going to need a complete makeover.'

Max didn't like the sound of that. He didn't like the sound of *any* of it, come to that, but he'd given his word.

'I could take some flex leave,' he said grudgingly. He didn't want anyone at work to get wind of what was happening. That morning he'd told them that he was going to the dentist and, looking around *Glitz*'s glossy offices, he couldn't help thinking that root canal surgery might be preferable to what lay ahead.

He was going to be styled by the great Dickie himself. Allegra had impressed on Max what an honour this was. 'If he's bored or irritated, Dickie's likely to storm off, so please just be nice!' she said again as she led him between glass-walled offices and down to a studio, her sky-high heels clicking on the polished floor that she had told him was known as the runway. Apparently this was because everybody could see and comment on the outfits passing, something Max would rather not have known. He could feel all the eyes assessing his hair, his suit, his tie, his figure as he followed Allegra.

She was in businesslike mode today in skinny trousers, an animal-print top and those fearsome-looking boots, but he had to confess he preferred it when she wore a dress. She looked less…intimidating.

Plus, it showed off her legs, which were pretty spectacular.

'I'm always nice,' said Max.

Allegra cast him a look over her shoulder. 'You weren't nice about the outfit I wore last night.'

Max had been heating up a curry when she had appeared in the kitchen doorway, wearing the most extraordinary outfit. A riot of clashing colours and patterns, Max hadn't known how to describe what she was wearing, but when she'd twirled and asked what he thought, he'd made the big mistake of telling her. Words like fruit salad and dog's dinner had passed his lips.

He wouldn't be offering any more sartorial advice.

'Here we are.' Fretfully, Allegra pushed him into the studio. 'Just…nod and smile. And follow my lead,' she muttered under her breath, fixing a bright smile to her face and dragging Max towards a tiny, imperious figure with close-cropped grey hair, huge red spectacles and a red and white dotted bow tie.

'You didn't tell me I'd have to be careful not to step on him,' Max murmured and Allegra hissed at him to be quiet.

'Dickie, I'm so thrilled to be working with you,' she said, practically curtseying.

Dickie nodded regally, and they exchanged the obligatory air kiss before he turned his gaze to Max. 'And oo iz thees?' he said, his French accent so thick that Max thought he had to be putting it on.

'Max Warriner,' he said, stepping forward and shaking Dickie's hand firmly before Allegra could pretend that he was a deaf mute. He sure as hell wasn't going to kiss Dickie. 'Good to meet you,' he said briskly.

Dickie looked at his hand as if he had never had it wrung before, and then at Allegra, who smiled apologetically.

'Max is here for the *Making Mr Perfect* feature,' she said, lowering her voice. 'You know, the one with the complete makeover.'

'Ah, *oui*...' Dickie eyed Max's outfit, a perfectly serviceable suit and tie, and shuddered extravagantly. 'I see 'e needs one!'

'It's the first date tonight,' Allegra said. 'He's meeting Darcy King for cocktails at Xubu.'

Xubu, as Max had heard at length, was the latest hot ticket, the place to see and be seen, and Allegra had been desperate to go. Fortunately—for her, if not for Max— Darcy King's celebrity had opened the doors and Allegra was delighted.

'I don't see why you're so happy,' Max had said. 'You're not going.'

'Of course I have to be there,' Allegra said. 'I'm writing the article. And the photographer will be there too.'

'It doesn't sound like much of a date to me,' Max grumbled, but Allegra had brushed that aside.

'It'll be fun!'

*Fun.* Max shook his head, thinking about it.

'You can see how much work he needs,' Allegra was saying to Dickie, who was circling Max with much rolling of eyes and shrugging of shoulders. 'He'll need a whole new look if he's going to impress Darcy.'

'I will do what I can,' he said, plucking at Max's jacket with distaste. 'But zis, zis must go! And ze shirt—if you can call zat zing a shirt—and ze trousers...ze shoes too... Burn it all!'

'Now hold on—!' Max began, only to yelp as Allegra placed her heel firmly on his foot.

'Don't worry, Dickie. I'll take care of it. Take off your jacket,' she ordered Max out of the corner of her mouth.

'This is my work suit!' he muttered back as he took it off reluctantly. 'Don't you dare burn it.'

'Don't panic. I'll just take it home where it doesn't upset Dickie.'

'What about upsetting *me*?'

Allegra ignored him. 'What sort of look do you think for cocktails?' she asked Dickie. 'Funky? Or suave and sophisticated?'

Dickie stood back and studied Max critically, mentally stripping him of the offending clothes, and Max shifted self-consciously.

'I zink sophisticated, but with an edge,' Dickie proclaimed at last.

'Perfect,' said Allegra, the traitor. 'Not too obvious, but interesting. A look that shows Darcy he's confident enough to make his own fashion statement? A little quirky, perhaps?'

Fashion statement? Jeez…Max pinched the bridge of his nose as Allegra and Dickie talked over him. He should be checking the material testing results, or writing up the geological survey for the motorway-widening bid, not standing here like a dumb ox while they wittered on about fashion statements!

'Quirky?' Dickie considered. 'Per'aps you 'ave somezing zere…'

Max was convinced now that the French accent was put on. No one could really speak that ridiculously.

Although, for a man prepared to wear that bow tie, being ridiculous obviously wasn't a problem.

'What do you think?' Allegra asked anxiously. 'Can you do something with Max?'

For answer, Dickie spun on his heel and clapped his

hands at his minions, who had been waiting subserviently, talking to each other in hushed voices as they waited for the great man to pronounce.

'Bring out ze shirts,' he ordered.

'Behave,' Allegra whispered in Max's ear.

'I am behaving!'

'You're not. You're glaring at Dickie. Do you want me glaring at Bob Laskovski over that dinner?'

'No,' he admitted.

'Well, then.'

Allegra could see Max balking as racks of clothes surrounded him like wagons and Dickie started snapping his fingers at his assistants, who leapt forward and held up shirts side by side. Max's eyes were rolling nervously like a spooked horse and he practically had his ears flattened to his head, but Allegra stood behind Dickie and mouthed 'remember the dinner' at him until he sulkily complied and agreed to try on some shirts.

Unbuttoning his cuffs, he hooked his fingers into the back of his shirt and dragged it over his head and Allegra and Dickie both drew a sharp breath. Who would have guessed that Max had such a broad, smooth, *sexy* back beneath that dull shirt? Allegra felt quite...unsettled.

Dragging her eyes away, she made a big deal of making notes of Dickie's choices in her notebook, but her gaze kept snagging on the flex of Max's muscles as he shrugged in and out of shirts. Dickie kept turning him round—deliberately, Allegra was sure—so sometimes she saw his shoulders, sometimes his chest. And then they brought on the trousers, and there were his bare legs. Why had she never noticed before what great legs Max had?

'Allegra!' Dickie snapped his fingers in front of her face, startling her. 'What do you think?'

Allegra looked at Max. He wore a darkly flowered

button-down shirt with a striped tie that clashed and yet complemented the colours perfectly. Trousers and jacket were beautifully cut, shoes discreet. If it hadn't been for the mutinous expression, he would have looked super-cool.

'I love it,' she said. 'He's really rocking that flowered shirt.'

Max hunched a shoulder. 'I feel like a prat.'

'Well, you don't look like one for once,' she said.

'He needs an 'aircut of course,' said Dickie, eyeing Max critically.

Allegra checked her list. 'That's booked in next.'

'And a manicure.'

'Oh, no,' said Max, backing away. 'No, no, no, no, no!'

'Yes, indeed.' Allegra smiled blandly at him. 'Now don't make a fuss. It won't hurt at all.' She pretended to consult her list again. 'Although I'm not sure I can say the same for the back, sack and crack wax we've got you booked in for after the manicure…'

'Back, sack…?' Aghast, Max opened and closed his mouth before obviously spotting the dent in her cheek where she was desperately trying not to laugh. 'Why, you…' Grinning with relief, he playfully shoved at her arm.

Allegra was giggling, but tailed off when she realised everyone was standing around staring at them. How uncool of her.

She cleared her throat. 'Yes, well, take that outfit off for now. Let's do something about that hair.'

Max ran his finger around his collar. His *flowery* collar. He felt ridiculous. His hair had been washed and conditioned and cut and it was just as well it hadn't been any longer or that fool of a barber—excuse him, hairstylist—would have had it flopping all over his face. He had been shaved

too, swathed in hot towels. Actually that hadn't been too
bad—until they had slapped on some cologne without his
say-so. His eyes were still watering.

If any of his mates saw him now, or caught him stink-
ing like a tart's boudoir, he would never hear the end of
it. Thank God this was the last place he would meet anyone he knew. The dimly lit bar was crowded, but if anyone else in there was an engineer, they weren't like any
civil engineers Max had ever met. Everyone seemed to be
at least ten years younger than him and half of them were
outrageously dressed. Unbelievably, his own absurd shirt
didn't stand out at all compared to what everyone else was
wearing. He might have to forgive Allegra for it after all.
He'd been so certain that she'd deliberately manoeuvred
Dickie into choosing the flowery shirt as a joke.

'Isn't this place fab?' Across the table, Allegra was
bright-eyed as she surveyed the crowd. Dom, the photographer, was sitting next to her and together they were
keeping up a running commentary on celebrities they had
spotted and what everyone was wearing. Max had tuned
out after a while. He hoped Darcy King would turn up
soon and make this purgatory worthwhile.

'Don't look now…' Allegra leant forward with a little
squeal of excitement '…but that's Chris O'Donnell sitting
behind you!'

'No! Not Chris! Squeeeee!'

She looked at him. 'You don't know who Chris
O'Donnell is, do you?' Without waiting for his reply, she
turned to Dom. 'He doesn't know who Chris O'Donnell is.'

Dom stared at Max. 'You just jetted in from Mars or
something, man?'

'Chris O'Donnell is the ultimate bad boy rocker,' said
Allegra, apparently shocked to her core by the depths of
Max's ignorance. 'He just got voted sexiest man in the

country, and he'd certainly have had my vote...' She sighed wistfully.

Max raised his brows. 'I didn't know you had a taste for bad boy rockers, Legs. Not your usual type, surely? I don't see your mother approving.'

Allegra flushed. 'I wouldn't want him as a boyfriend or anything, but you've got to admit he's smokin' hot...'

'So have you told Flick about your major new assignment?' Max said, not wanting to get into a discussion about which men Allegra thought were hot. He was fairly sure the list wouldn't include a civil engineer, flowery shirt or not.

Not that he cared about that. It was just uncomfortable to talk about that kind of stuff with someone he'd known for so long. It would be like discussing sex with his sister.

'I rang her last night.' Allegra's brightness dimmed slightly.

'Was she pleased to hear about your big break?'

'Well, you know Flick.' Her smile was painful to watch and Max cursed himself for asking. He should have known Flick would disappoint her. 'She did say "Well done" when I explained that it might mean a promotion if the article was a success. But she's writing about the political implications of the economic crisis; you can't blame her for not being impressed by my piece on whether it's possible to create the perfect boyfriend. I suspect she thinks it's a bit silly.'

Max had thought precisely the same thing but now, perversely, he was outraged at Flick's dismissal of Allegra's assignment. 'Did you tell her all that stuff you told me, about how these were the kind of issues that really matter to a lot of young women?'

Allegra sighed. 'I don't think boyfriend trouble quite ranks with the global downturn in the economy in my mother's scheme of things.' She squared her shoulders, sat up straighter. 'And she's right, of course. I should take more interest in political issues.'

She was nothing if not loyal to her mother, Max thought, still irrationally annoyed by Flick's response. Would it have killed her to have encouraged her daughter for once? Poor Allegra tried so hard to get her mother's approval. She had to want it bad to feign an interest in politics, given that he'd never heard her or Libby utter a word on the subject.

And she was going to find it hard, as demonstrated by the fact that barely had her resolve to be more politically aware fallen from her lips than her attention was caught by a girl teetering past in ludicrously high shoes. 'Omigod, I am totally stealing that vampire chic look!'

Max was obscurely pleased to see her revert to her frivolous self. 'Vampire chic?' he echoed, knowing the disbelief in his voice would annoy her, and sure enough, she gave him the flat-eyed look she and Libby had perfected when they were twelve.

Back to normal. Good.

'You just don't get it, do you?' she said. 'Look at you! We bring you to the hottest place in town, and you sit there like you were wishing you were in some grotty pub!'

'There's no "like" about it. I *am* wishing I was in a pub.'

'Here, have a drink.' Allegra passed him the drinks list. 'Maybe that'll cheer you up—and no, you can't have a pint.'

Morosely, Max scanned the list and choked when he saw the prices. 'They want *how* much for a cocktail?'

'Don't panic, you're not paying for the drinks,' she said. 'But, in all other respects, this is a real date, so start looking as if you're looking forward to meeting Darcy, not as if you're waiting to have your eyes poked out with a sharp stick.'

She shook her head as Max tried to ease the tightness around his neck. Dickie had a throttling way with a tie. 'Relax!' she said, leaning across the table to slap his hand away from his throat, and the scent of her perfume momentarily clouded Max's brain.

'You're so repressed,' she told him as he blinked the disturbing awareness away. 'Now listen, you're going to meet Darcy any minute and you're going to have to make an effort. This is your first task. You need to make sure she likes you enough to accept your invitation to dinner cooked by you, which is your second task.'

'You've explained all this,' said Max grouchily.

'And, just in case you were thinking of falling at the first hurdle so that you don't have to carry on, I'll just remind you that we haven't had that dinner with your boss yet.'

Why had he ever put the idea of blackmail into her head? She had taken to it like a natural. He'd created a monster.

'Remember, you're interested in Darcy, not in a lingerie model,' Allegra carried on bossily. 'Ask her questions but don't interrogate her—and don't expect her to take all the burden of the conversation either.'

'I've been on dates before, you know.'

Allegra ignored that. 'She'll be hoping to meet someone interesting and interested, someone charming and witty who can make her laugh, but who's got some old-fashioned manners—don't forget to stand up when she arrives—and who can make her feel safe but sexy and desirable at the same time.'

'And I'm going to be doing all of this with you listening in and Dom here taking pictures?'

'You'll hardly notice us after a while,' she assured him, then straightened as Dom nudged her. 'And here she comes! Good luck,' she mouthed to Max as he adjusted his tie and slid out of the banquette to greet Darcy.

He couldn't help staring. Spectacular was the only word. Of course he'd seen photos before, blown up across billboards or plastered across magazines, but in the flesh Darcy was breathtaking. She glowed with sex appeal, from her artfully tumbled blonde hair to the bee-stung mouth and the voluptuous body.

'Your tongue's hanging out,' Allegra said in his ear, and Max shut his mouth with a snap.

'You must be Max,' said Darcy in the famously husky voice and Max unscrambled his mind.

'I am. It's good to meet you, Darcy,' he said and stuck out his hand, but she only laughed and brushed it aside as she moved forward to kiss him on the cheek, enveloping him in a haze of perfume and allure.

'Let's not be formal,' she said while every man in the room watched him enviously. 'I hear we're going to be great friends!'

Dry-mouthed, Max stood back to usher her into the banquette. 'It sounds like you know more than I do,' he said with an accusing glance at Allegra, who was greeting Darcy cheerfully. What else hadn't she told him?

'Don't worry, darling,' said Darcy, patting his hand. 'It's going to be fun.'

Darcy and Max were getting on like the proverbial fire in a match factory. Allegra told herself she should be pleased that it was going so well. She took a gulp of the sparkling water she'd ordered as she was supposed to be working.

Darcy was obviously enjoying herself. She threw her head back and laughed her glorious laugh. She propped her chin on her hands and leant forwards, as if the famous cleavage needed attention drawn to it. She flirted with those impossibly long lashes and ran her fingers up and down Max's arm. Max, unsurprisingly, wasn't complaining.

He was doing much better than she had expected, Allegra had to admit. After that stunned moment—and she couldn't honestly blame him for that—he had recovered quickly and, while he wasn't exactly *charming,* he had a certain assurance that came from not caring what anybody else thought of him, and a kind of dry humour that seemed to be going down well with Darcy anyway.

Which Allegra was delighted about, naturally.

No, really, she was. Personally, she didn't think it was necessary for Darcy to touch him *quite* so often, but Darcy was obviously the tactile type. Not her fault that Allegra's fingers were twitching with the longing to reach across the table and slap her hand from Max's arm.

Who would have thought Max would brush up so well too? She'd thought he would dig in his heels at the flowery shirt but, apart from a few fulminating glances sent her way he'd clearly decided to honour his part of the agreement. Unlikely as it was, the shirt suited him beautifully. Something about the fabrics and the exquisite cut of the garments gave him a style he had certainly never possessed before.

It would take more than a shirt to turn him into an über hunk, of course, but Allegra had to allow that he didn't look as ordinary as he usually did.

It was amazing what a difference a good haircut made, too. She found herself noticing all sorts of things about him that she had never noticed before: the line of his jaw, the crease in his cheek, the uncompromising brows.

Vaguely disturbed, Allegra bent her head over her notebook. She was listening to the conversation between Max and Darcy as unobtrusively as possible and scribbling notes for the article she would write up when the final task was completed.

The article that could change her career and put her in a position to apply for jobs on magazines with a little more gravitas. If she got it right.

So why was she letting herself be distracted by the way Max's smile had suddenly started catching at the corner of her eye, the way it had suddenly started making her pulse kick as if it had startled her?

He was only smiling, for God's sake. She *wanted* him to be smiling at Darcy. She was supposed to be pleased with the way it was going, not feeling cross.

Darcy was telling Max a long story about the house she was having built, and he was offering advice about foundations and geological surveys. He'd obviously forgotten her advice about being witty and charming, but Darcy was hanging on his every word.

Disgruntled, Allegra gave up listening after a while. She wasn't going to fill her article with engineering talk, however fascinating Darcy might find it. Dom had taken his pictures and left some time before, and she let her pen drift: Derek the Dog dancing on his hind legs, Mrs G tipsy on cocktails, Flick smiling proudly—Allegra had to imagine that one.

Then she sketched Darcy leaning forward, lips parted breathlessly, and Max himself. But somehow she found herself drawing the Max she knew, the Max who wore a crummy polo shirt buttoned too high at the neck and lay on the absurdly feminine sofa, king of the remote, and she felt a pang of something she chose not to identify.

'Hey, those are great!' Darcy leant across the table and plucked the notebook away before Allegra had a chance to react.

She studied the drawings, chuckling. 'Who's the cute

dog? Look, Max, that's you...' Her smile faltered as she took in the polo shirt. 'At least...?'

Max peered at the sketch. 'Yep, looks like me.'

Allegra was blushing furiously. 'They're just doodles...'

'No, really, they're very good,' said Darcy. 'You clever thing.' She tapped a finger on the picture of her. 'You've caught me exactly, hasn't she, Max?'

'It's unmistakably you, but a drawing can't really capture your charm,' he said and Darcy laughed her trademark husky laugh, delighted, while Allegra concentrated on not throwing up.

If she wasn't much mistaken, Max was *flirting*. He must really like Darcy. Perhaps it was time to leave them alone. Ignoring the sinking feeling in her stomach, she took her notebook back from Darcy. 'I should go.'

'Don't go yet.' To her surprise, rather than wanting to get rid of her, Max handed her the drinks list. 'If you've finished working, you might as well have a proper drink.'

'Absolutely,' said Darcy with a sunny smile. 'You deserve it for setting up this article. I just know we're going to have a good time.' Her fingers teased Max's shoulder and Allegra's fingers tightened around the menu. 'I can't believe Max here hasn't been snapped up already, can you?'

'It's beyond comprehension,' Allegra agreed, but then made the mistake of glancing at Max. A smile hovered around his mouth and, for no reason she could name, her mouth dried.

'Try something with a ridiculous name,' he said, deadpan, and nodded at the drinks list. 'I'm longing to make a fool of myself ordering for you.'

Allegra swallowed and wrenched her gaze away to concentrate fiercely on the drinks list. Could she be coming down with something? She felt feverish and twitchy, and a nerve was jumping under her eye.

The list kept swimming in front of her eyes and she frowned in an effort to focus, but whenever she did the only cocktails that jumped out at her were called things like Screaming Orgasm or Wet Kiss. This was supposed to be fun. She should take Max up on his challenge and make him order something silly.

Why couldn't she grin and say: *I'd like a Sloe Screw Against the Wall, please, Max? Could I have Sex on the Beach?*

But all at once her throat was thick and she was having trouble swallowing. She handed the list back without meeting his eyes. 'I'll...er...have a martini, please.'

'Chicken,' said Max, beckoning over a waitress.

Darcy started to tell Allegra about a shoot she'd been on the day before. She knew Dickie and Stella and a host of other people at *Glitz*, and she was so friendly that it was impossible to dislike her, in spite of the way she kept flirting with Max, little touches on his arm, his shoulder, his hair. Every now and then her hand would disappear under the table and Allegra didn't want to think about what she was touching down there.

Allegra kept her attention firmly focused on Darcy's face, which was easier than being stupidly conscious of Max sitting next to Darcy and not looking nearly as out of place as he should have done. More and more, Allegra was convinced that she was sickening for something. She didn't feel herself at all. She was glad when the drinks arrived, but she drank hers a little too quickly and, before she knew what had happened, Darcy was beckoning for another one.

'You're one behind us,' she said gaily.

# CHAPTER FOUR

So ALLEGRA HAD another and then she and Darcy agreed to have another. Why had she been so uptight earlier? She was having a great time now, exchanging disastrous date stories with Darcy while Max sat back, folded his arms and watched them indulgently.

'Like you've never had a disastrous date,' Allegra accused him, enunciating carefully so as not to slur her words.

'What about this one?' said Max.

'We're talking about *real* dates,' she said indignantly.

Darcy nodded along. 'When your heart sinks five minutes in and you spend the rest of the evening trying to think of an excuse to leave early.'

'Or, worse, when you really like someone and you realise they're just not that into *you*,' said Allegra glumly.

A funny look swept across Max's face. 'I've got no idea what you're talking about,' he said.

Darcy had already moved on. 'I blame my father,' she said. 'He's spoilt me for other men. None of my boyfriends has ever been able to live up to him.'

'You're lucky to have a father,' Allegra said wistfully.

Her birth certificate just showed her mother's name. Flick refused to talk about Allegra's father. 'He was a mistake,' was all she would ever say and turn the subject.

When she was a little girl, Allegra had dreamed that her father would turn up one day and claim his daughter. She could never decide if she'd rather he was a movie star or the prince of some obscure European principality. Usually she opted for the latter; she thought she would make a good princess.

But no father ever came for her.

Thinking about fathers always made Allegra feel unloved and unwanted. If she wasn't careful, she'd start blubbing, so she smiled instead and lifted her glass. 'Oh,' she said, peering owlishly into it when she discovered it was empty, 'let's have another round.'

'I think you've had enough,' said Max, signalling for the bill instead. 'It's time to go home.'

'I don't want to go home. I want another martini.'

Max ignored her and put a surprisingly strong hand under her elbow to lift her, still protesting, to her feet. 'Can I get you a taxi, Darcy?'

'You're sweet,' Darcy said, 'but I might stay for a while.' She waved at someone behind them, and Allegra turned to follow her gaze. 'I'm just going to say hello to Chris.'

'Omigod, you know *Chris O'Donnell*? Allegra squeaked, but Max had already said a brisk goodbye and was propelling her towards the exit while she gawked over her shoulder in a really uncool way.

'What are you *doing*?' she complained. 'I was *this* close to meeting Chris O'Donnell.'

'You're completely sozzled,' said Max, pushing her through the doors. 'You wouldn't even remember him tomorrow.'

'I so would,' she said sulkily, and then reeled when the cold hit her. It was September still but there was an unmistakable snap of autumn in the air. If it hadn't been for his firm grip on her arm, she might have keeled right over.

Max looked down at her shoes—they were adorable peep-toes in a dusty pink suede with vertiginous heels—but he didn't look impressed. 'We'd better get a taxi,' he sighed.

Allegra's head was spinning alarmingly and she blinked in a vain attempt to focus. 'You'll never get a taxi round here,' she said but Max just propped her against a wall while he put his fingers in his mouth and whistled for a taxi. Annoyingly, one screeched to a halt straight away.

Having taken up position by the wall, it was harder than Allegra had anticipated to get over to the taxi. In the end Max had to manoeuvre her inside, where she collapsed over the seat in an undignified sprawl. She managed to struggle upright in a brave attempt to recover her dignity, but then she couldn't find her seat belt.

Her fumbling was interrupted by Max, muttering under his breath, who reached across her to locate the belt and clip it into place. His head was bent as he fiddled with the clip, and Allegra's spinning head jarred to a halt with the horrifyingly clear urge to touch his hair.

Clenching her fists into her skirt to stop her hands lifting of their own accord, she sucked in a breath and pressed her spine away from him into the seat, desperate to put as much space between them as she could.

'I think it all went well tonight,' she said. The idea was to sound cool and formal, to show Max that she wasn't nearly as sloshed as he seemed to think, but perfectly capable of carrying on a rational conversation. Unfortunately her voice came out wheezy, as if she had missed out on her share of oxygen.

Allegra cleared her throat and tried again. 'Darcy's lovely, isn't she?'

Yes, she was. Max had to agree. Darcy was a fantasy come to life, in fact. She was gorgeous and sexy and friendly and sweet-natured. So why hadn't he been able to relax and enjoy himself?

Max scowled at the back of the taxi driver's head as he fastened his own seat belt. Beside him, Allegra was still burbling on about what a great evening it had been, and how nice Darcy was. She obviously hadn't spent the entire evening being distracted.

Darcy was very touchy-feely, that was for sure. Max had been aware of her fingers trailing up and down his arm and over his thigh, but how could he enjoy it when Allegra was sitting opposite, scribbling notes in her book as if he were some kind of experiment she was observing?

It was mad. He, Max Warriner, had Darcy King *right beside him*, Darcy King *flirting with him*, and he couldn't concentrate. He was too aware of Allegra, eyeing him critically, her mouth pursed consideringly while she watched Darcy paw him. It obviously didn't bother her in the least.

It wasn't even as if there was any comparison between the two women. Darcy was lush, flirty, sex personified, while Allegra was slender, too thin really. So why did he keep remembering how it had felt when she hugged him? She'd been so soft and so warm, and her fragrance had enveloped him, and every bit of blood had drained from his head.

'And you were brilliant too,' said Allegra indistinctly. Her head kept lolling forward and Max had a sudden and very weird compulsion to unclip her seat belt again and ease her down so that she could lie with her head in his lap and sleep all the way home.

The taxi turned a corner and Allegra leant right over towards him before the car straightened and he caught the tantalising scent of her hair before she was thrown upright again. 'I feel a bit strange,' she said in a small voice.

'You'll be fine when you've had something to eat,' said Max bracingly, and she made a face.

'Ugh…I couldn't face eating anything.'

'Of course you could. We'll pick up a pizza on the way home.'

'Pizza? Are you mad?' Allegra demanded, roused out of her dopey state. 'Do you know how many calories there are in every slice?'

'You've just been guzzling cocktails,' he pointed out. 'A bit of pizza isn't going to make much difference after that. Besides, you're skinny enough. You could do with putting on a bit of weight, if you ask me.'

Allegra just looked at him pityingly. 'You've never worked in women's fashion, have you?'

'And I dare say I never will,' said Max without the slightest regret.

'Oh, I don't know. Now you've worn a flowery shirt, who knows what will happen?'

'That's what I'm afraid of,' he said glumly.

There was a silence, not uncomfortable. Lost in thought, Allegra was looking out of the window at the imposing façades along Piccadilly. It was long past the rush hour, but the traffic was still inching through the lights. They could do with a decent traffic pattern analysis, Max thought, doing his best to keep his mind off the tempting line of Allegra's throat or the coltishly sprawled legs revealed by the short flirty skirt he had been trying not to notice all evening. It was a pale mint-green, made of some kind of floaty, gauzy stuff, and she wore it with a camisole and a pale cardigan that just begged to be stroked. Darcy had cooed over its softness when she reached over and ran her hand down Allegra's sleeve, exclaiming the way women did over each other's clothes. Max had watched, his throat dry, and he'd fought the weird compulsion to push Darcy aside and stroke Allegra himself.

It was all very unsettling. He'd never given any thought to what she was wearing before—other than to boggle at the shoes she wore sometimes—so why was he suddenly acutely aware of the way her skirt shifted over her thighs when she sat down, or how some silky fabric lay against her skin?

Her face was partly turned away, and what he could see of her cheek and jaw was soft in the muted orange glow from the street. It was just this stupid assignment of hers, throwing them together in a way they'd never been before, Max decided. The sooner they got back to normal the better.

Ignoring Allegra's protests, Max ordered a large pizza the moment they got in. Allegra collapsed onto the sofa, rubbing her poor toes and moaning about the calorie count, but her mouth watered when the pizza arrived.

'I suppose I could have a tiny slice,' she said.

They sat on the floor, leaning back against the sofa with the pizza box between them. Allegra lifted a slice and took a bite, pulling at the stringy cheese with her fingers as she chewed. She would regret it in the morning, but God, it tasted good! And Max was right; she was already feeling better.

Closing her eyes, she pushed the calorie count from her mind and savoured the taste and the contrasting textures: the smoothness of the tomato paste, the chunky onions, the rubbery cheese, the bite of chorizo.

'Mmm…' She pushed a stray piece of cheese into her mouth and opened her eyes only to find Max watching her with an odd expression. 'What?' she asked.

'Nothing,' he said, looking away. 'You ought to eat more often if you enjoy it that much.'

'Are you kidding? I'd be the size of a house!'

But in that brief moment when their eyes had met, something had shifted in the air between them. Something that reminded Allegra uneasily of the night when Max had *not* kissed her.

The last thing she ought to be remembering right now. She really shouldn't have had so many martinis. No wonder she was feeling so odd. Why did she suddenly feel as if she had to search around for something to say to break the silence? This was Max. She'd never needed to make conversation with him. Apart from that night, the one she wasn't thinking about. But now the silence between them thrummed with an unease that left her heart thumping inexplicably.

To distract herself, she picked up another piece of pizza. 'You'll have to do better than pizza when you invite Darcy over to supper.' There went her voice again, wobbling ridiculously up and down the register.

'I'm inviting Darcy to supper?'

'It's your second task,' she reminded him through a mouthful of pizza. 'The perfect boyfriend is not only sophisticated enough to enjoy cocktails, he's also a home-loving guy who can cook a delicious meal.'

'Well, I hope Darcy likes a roast, because that's all I can do.'

'Better make it a nut roast. She's a vegetarian.'

Max stared at her in consternation. 'A *vegetarian?* You didn't tell me that!'

'I didn't want to bamboozle you with too much information at once.'

'You mean you knew I'd back out,' he grumbled.

'Come on, Max, you make it sound like she eats babies!

They're only vegetables. I'm sure you can manage something. It doesn't have to be complicated, but you do need to cook it yourself. Libby's got a cookbook with some good recipes in it.'

Glad of an excuse to get away from the oddly strained atmosphere in the sitting room, Allegra pushed the last piece of pizza into her mouth and jumped up. Licking her fingers, she went into the kitchen and came back bearing the recipe book.

'Goat's cheese ravioli…that sounds nice,' she said as she flicked through the pages. 'Roasted vegetable tart… leek risotto…there's loads in here you could try.'

She handed the recipe book to Max, who looked through it without enthusiasm. 'Emma used to do all the cooking,' he said.

'Maybe she would have liked it if you'd done more,' said Allegra.

'Emma loves cooking,' he said defensively.

'I'm sure she does, but that doesn't mean that she wouldn't have appreciated it if you took a turn occasionally. You know, this is exactly the kind of thing you should get out of this exercise,' Allegra went on, warming to her theme. She was feeling more herself again, thank goodness. 'You've got a real chance here to learn how to please her. To show her that you've changed, that you're prepared to make an effort for her. I don't think you should give up.'

Max eyed her suspiciously. 'You seem very keen for me to get back together with Emma.'

'I'm keen for you to be happy,' she corrected him. 'And you seemed happy when you were with her.' It was true. Not to mention that *she* had been happier when he had been with Emma. There had been none of this uneasy awareness then. Max had just been someone to come across at the occasional family party—his family, not

hers, naturally; Flick wasn't big on jolly get-togethers—
to share a quick, spiky exchange for old times' sake and
forget about until the next time.

It wasn't that Max had been dull, but his life was so far
removed from Allegra's that she had never really *looked*
at him until that awkward evening when something had
clicked in the air, as surely as a bolt sliding into place.
She'd been able to convince herself that that had been an
aberration, especially when he'd met Emma, but now...
it was making her nervous. She shouldn't be feeling jit-
tery around Max. She shouldn't be noticing his mouth or
his hands or the fact that beneath that shirt he wore was a
lean, muscled body. It was all *wrong*.

The sooner he got back together with Emma the better.
Then everything could go back to normal.

And clearly Max thought the same.

'I *was* happy with her,' he remembered. 'We had so
much in common. We were friends! I still can't believe
she'd give up everything she had for some guy she'd only
known a few weeks.'

'It won't last,' Allegra said confidently.

'I didn't realise you were a great expert on passion!'

She forgave him the snide comment. Emma was still a
very sore point, that much was clear.

'I've done my share of falling passionately in love, only
to wake up one day and think: what am I doing?' she told
him. 'Trust me, Emma will do the same, and you need to
be there when she does. You need to show her that you've
listened to what she said and that you're prepared to do
whatever it takes to get her back.'

'Don't tell me: you're writing the *Glitz* agony column
this month?'

'You may mock,' said Allegra with dignity, 'but it's
good advice. If you really want Emma back, you should

start paying attention and, in the meantime, get in touch with her. Send a text or something, no pressure.'

'And say what?' asked Max, who was at least listening, if unwillingly.

'Just say you're thinking of her,' said Allegra. 'That'll be enough for now.'

'I can't believe you're making me do this.' Max was in a grouchy mood and Allegra had to practically push him along the street towards the dance studio.

She had booked a private lesson so that Max could learn how to waltz before the costume ball. Darcy was thrilled by the idea, a fact that Allegra had yet to pass on to Max. 'I can't wait,' she'd confided to Allegra. 'I've never been out with anyone who knew how to dance properly.'

It would be Max's hardest test, but Allegra was determined that he would succeed. It wouldn't be much of an article if she had to report that he could manage some chitchat over a drink but that when it came to really making an effort he had flunked out.

Besides, she was longing to learn how to waltz herself. Not that she had anyone to waltz with, but maybe her prince would be waiting at the ball. He'd be tall, dark and handsome, and unaccountably stood up by his date, and he would twirl her around the ballroom in his arms while Max was impressing Darcy with some nifty footwork.

Allegra's fantasy ground to a halt as Max balked at the sign on the door, an unfortunate pink decorated with fairies.

'We're not going in here?'

She could practically see him digging his heels into the concrete and she took his arm in a firm grip. 'There are no fairies inside, I promise. You just have to be brave and get past the door!'

Grumbling, Max let her manoeuvre him inside and up some stairs to the dance studio. Afraid that he would conveniently forget the arrangement, Allegra had gone to waylay him outside his office after work. She'd hung around on the pavement, feeling conspicuous in her pencil skirt, cropped jacket and funky boots, and deeply unimpressed by the style standards in civil engineering. Male or female, everyone who came out seemed to be safely dressed in sensible dark suits.

Allegra had twisted her ankle out to admire her studded suede boots. She would hate to work anywhere that dull. She hadn't seen a single outfit with any colour or flair. If this was the environment where Max spent his days, it was no wonder he had such appalling dress sense.

Hugging her arms together against the cool autumn breeze, she'd shifted from foot to foot as she kept an eye on the door. If Max didn't come out soon, she would have to go in and get him.

And suddenly there he was.

He'd pushed through the doors with two other men. They were identically dressed in suits and ties. Max wasn't the tallest or the best-looking, but for some reason Allegra's heart kicked when she caught sight of him. He was laughing at something one of the others said as he turned away, lifting a hand in farewell, and he ran lightly down the steps, scanning the street as he went.

He was looking for her. The realisation made her heart give another odd little jump and she was smiling foolishly when his gaze crossed hers, only to stop and swing back and meet her gaze. Their eyes locked with what Allegra could have sworn was an audible click and for a moment it was as if a question trembled in the air between them.

Then Max rolled his eyes and came towards her and

the moment was broken. He was just Max—staid, conventional Max. Libby's brother. Nothing more.

'I see you didn't trust me to make my own way to the dance studio,' he said as he came up.

Allegra felt as if she ought to kiss him on the cheek or something, but all at once she felt ridiculously shy. She wouldn't have hesitated at work, but she was on Max's ground now and it seemed too intimate to give him a casual hug.

So she kept her arms wrapped around herself and turned to walk beside him instead. 'You've got to admit that you didn't seem very keen when I reminded you about the dance lesson this morning,' she said. 'You'd rather stick pins in your eyes, you said.'

'I'm here, aren't I?'

'Only because I just happened to mention at the same time that I could still pull out of the dinner with your boss.'

'Yes, who would have guessed you'd turn into such a proficient blackmailer?'

Allegra spread her hands. 'We all have to use the talents we have,' she said modestly. 'I'm helping you with the dinner for Darcy too, don't forget. I believe in the carrot and stick approach.'

'I'm still waiting for some carrot,' said Max.

Now she put the flat of her hand against Max's back and pushed him into the studio. It was a large room with two mirrored walls and the faintly sweaty smell of packed exercise classes.

At least today they had the place to themselves. Allegra introduced Max to Cathy, the dance instructor she had hired at huge expense. A TV veteran, Cathy was famous for bringing unlikely celebrities up to scratch on the dancing front, but it was soon obvious that Max was going to be her biggest challenge.

'It's like trying to move a block of wood around the floor,' she complained. 'Allegra, you come and dance with him and see if he's more relaxed with you.'

It was exactly what Allegra had been hoping for. She leapt up and took her place in the middle of the empty floor with Max, but the moment she put one hand on his shoulder and the other in his palm, awkwardness gripped her. She hadn't anticipated how close Max would feel, how intimate it would seem to be standing together, holding each other.

'Right, Max, remember what I told you: you're stepping to the top of the box, and Allegra, you go back,' said Cathy, prowling around them. 'Off we go. One, two, three...top of the box, slide across, back...one, two, three...'

Allegra's mouth was dry, but she took a deep breath and tried to remember the instructions. She kept her eyes fixed on a spot behind Max's shoulder, which made it easier not to think about how warm and firm his fingers were, or the way his hand at her waist seemed to be sizzling through her top. Out of the corner of her eye, she could still see the edge of his jaw, rigid with concentration. It was very distracting and she kept forgetting where her feet were supposed to go.

'Stop! I can't stand it!' Cathy shrieked eventually, and Max and Allegra sprang apart with a mixture of relief and embarrassment.

Cathy heaved a dramatic sigh. 'I thought you told me you and Max were friends?' she said to Allegra.

Allegra and Max looked at each other. 'We are...sort of.'

'Sort of?'

'We've known each other a long time,' Max said after a moment.

Cathy arched an eyebrow. 'You surprise me. You were holding each other as if you'd never met before.' She sighed and regarded them both severely. 'Hug each other,' she ordered.

'What?'

'Hug each other,' Cathy repeated with exaggerated patience as Allegra and Max both did double takes.

'You mean…?' Allegra gestured vaguely, prompting another big sigh from Cathy.

'I mean put your arms around each other and squeeze. You know how to hug, don't you?'

'What's the object of the exercise?' asked Max, who clearly didn't want to get any closer than Allegra did.

'I want you to relax and feel comfortable with each other. A hug will help you get over any awkwardness. Well, go on,' she said when neither of them moved.

Clearing her throat, Allegra turned reluctantly to face Max. 'Sorry,' she mouthed at him and Max rolled his eyes in reply.

They had a couple of false starts where they stepped towards each other only to bang their heads together, or find their arms so awkwardly positioned that they had to pull apart and start again, but they were laughing by that stage and on the third try they got it right.

Allegra ended up with her arms around Max's waist, while he held her pressed against him. It felt as if they had slotted into place. Max was just the right height. Allegra fitted comfortably against him, her eyes level with his jaw, and if she turned her head, she could rest her face into his throat.

He had discarded his jacket but was still wearing a shirt and tie. The shirt was a very dull pale blue and the tie totally uninteresting, but Allegra had to admit that he smelt nice, of clean cotton and clean male. It was surprisingly reassuring being able to lean into his solid strength and feel that he wouldn't shift or topple over.

It had been another frenetic day at *Glitz* and Allegra had spent most of it galloping up and down the corridors and being screamed at. They were putting the next issue to bed and tension was running higher than usual, which made it stratospheric. It was as if the whole office was suffering from PMT.

But now she was being forced to rest against Max for a minute or two. In spite of herself, Allegra let out a little sigh and relaxed. It was weird, but being held by him like this felt...safe.

'Good,' said Cathy. 'Now squeeze each other tighter.'

Obediently, Allegra tightened her arms around Max's back as he pulled her closer, and suddenly it didn't feel safe at all.

Suddenly it felt dangerous, as if the floor had dropped away beneath her feet and left her teetering on the edge of a dizzying drop. The urge to turn into Max and cling to him was so strong that Allegra couldn't breathe with it. Her chest was tight, her pulse booming with an alarmed awareness of him. He held her rigidly and his body was hard—and when Allegra shifted uneasily against him she realised that—*oh?*—it wasn't just his chest that was hard.

Oh.

Before she had a chance to work out what she felt about that, Cathy was clapping her hands.

'Right, let's try again,' she said briskly and Max practically shoved Allegra away from him. His body might have been enjoying being pressed up against her, but his mind obviously hadn't. He scowled as Cathy ordered them back into position.

'Remember what I told you about the box step?' she said as Max and Allegra took hold of each other awkwardly, careful to keep a gap between them. 'Step to the top of the box, slide your feet together, step back, slide together… Off you go!'

It was easier without the distraction of being pressed right against him, Allegra told herself. That flood of heat had just been a physical reaction, exactly as Max's had been. It was what happened when you squashed a man and a woman together. It didn't *mean* anything.

'No, no!' Cathy threw up her hands. 'Max, you go *forward*, Allegra you're stepping *back*! Now, try again, and this time try and concentrate on what you're doing.'

Right, concentrate. Allegra stifled a nervous giggle as she fluffed it again, and Max muttered under his breath.

Cathy sighed.

They set off again, and managed two sides of the box before Max trod heavily on Allegra's foot, making her yelp, at which point they both started laughing. It was partly embarrassment, partly relief that the awful awareness had dissipated.

Cathy was less amused. 'You're both hopeless,' she said when their time was up. 'If you want Max to impress Darcy at the ball, you're going to have to practice. At least master the basic steps and we can try and add some turns next week.'

# CHAPTER FIVE

'TURNS?' MAX GRUMBLED as they slunk out. 'You mean we have to go round and round as well as backwards and forwards?'

'It's a lot harder than it looks,' Allegra agreed, winding her scarf around her throat. 'I've waltzed so often in my fantasies that I thought I'd be quite good at it. I can't believe I was so crap,' she said despondently.

'In your fantasy you don't dance with me, that's why,' said Max, feeling obscurely guilty about spoiling the waltz for her.

'True.' She perked up a little as they headed down the street. 'I'd be much better with my Regency duke.'

'Your what?'

'The duke who waltzes me out on the terrace, begs me to become his duchess and ravishes me,' said Allegra as if it was the most normal thing in the world. 'I told you about my fantasy.'

'You didn't mention any dukes.'

'I think he probably *is* a duke,' she said, having considered the matter. 'He's got a dreadful reputation as a rake, of course, but underneath he's deeply honourable.'

'He's not very honourable if he ravishes you right outside a crowded ballroom,' Max pointed out.

'You're such a nitpicker,' she said without heat.

Max shook his head. 'I can't figure you out, Legs. One minute you're obsessed with fashion or celebrity gossip, the next you're fantasising about dancing with dead aristocrats.'

And that was before you took into account the sweet and funny Allegra who drew cute cartoon animals, or the one who tried so hard and so unsuccessfully to be cool and high-minded so that she could please her demanding mother. The one who fretted constantly about her weight or the one who sat on the floor and ate pizza with relish.

It was only since moving into the house that Max had come to realise that there was more to Allegra than he had thought. If he'd been asked to describe her before then he would have said sweet, a bit scatty, a bit screwed up by her mother.

And now…now he was learning new things about her every day. Like the way she left the bathroom a tip, the way her face lit up when she smiled. Like the smell of her perfume. The way she tilted her chin.

The way she felt. Max's mouth dried at the memory of that ridiculous hug Cathy had insisted on. After a couple of false starts, Allegra had fitted into him as if she belonged there, and his senses had reeled alarmingly at the feel of her slenderness pressed against him.

And it wasn't just his senses that had reacted. Max shifted his shoulders uncomfortably in his jacket, remembering how aroused he had been. Hold her tighter, that fool Cathy had said. What was he supposed to do when a soft, warm woman was melting into him and her perfume filled his head and it was all he could do to stop his hands sliding under that silky top, rucking up that sexy skirt so that he could run them hungrily over her long thighs?

This was all Emma's fault. If they'd still been together, he wouldn't have been sex-starved, and he certainly wouldn't have been thinking about Allegra like some kind of pervert.

She was lucky that treading on her toes was all he had done.

At least it had been easier once they'd started laughing. It was a relief to know that Allegra couldn't dance for toffee either. When he wasn't wanting to rip her clothes off, he and Allegra got on much better than he had expected.

She'd been teaching him how to cook so that he could impress Darcy, and kept coming back from *Glitz* laden with ingredients and advice from the food editor. Max wasn't learning much, but he enjoyed leaning against the worktop and watching her face as she chopped enthusiastically, throwing weird ingredients together in ridiculously complicated meals. Emma was a great cook, Max remembered loyally. Meat and two veg, exactly what you wanted to eat, perfectly cooked. None of Allegra's nonsense.

Although there was something oddly endearing about the nonsense all the same. Even if it did taste rubbish.

'You say you want to be a serious journalist, but I've only ever seen you talk seriously about cosmetics or the latest soap,' he said, still puzzling over her.

A brisk wind was swirling dead leaves along the gutter and Allegra pulled her coat closer around her. 'People are more than one thing,' she said loftily. 'Talking of which, what did you do to Dickie?'

'I didn't do anything,' said Max in surprise.

'He was so fragile this morning that the entire office had to whisper! Stella's assistant told the intern who told me that when Stella asked him what was wrong, he said it was all your fault!'

'I just took him to the pub.'

Allegra had sent him off for another styling session with Dickie the night before. Max had grumbled, but he'd gone along and without Allegra there had been able to come to an understanding with Dickie. Make the whole process as quick and painless as possible, he had suggested, and they could go and have a decent drink.

'Can you believe it?' he went on. 'The guy's been in London for ten years and he's never had a decent pint.'

'You took *Dickie* to a *pub?*' Allegra had stopped dead and was looking at him in horror.

'You told me to be nice to him,' Max reminded her.

'Making him go to a pub and getting him drunk on beer isn't being nice!'

'He had a great time. I'm taking him to a rugby game next.'

Allegra opened and closed her mouth, unable to get out a coherent sentence. 'Dickie…rugby…?'

'I don't know why you're all so terrified of him. He's a perfectly nice guy once you get past all the affectation.'

'That's it. My career is over.'

'Don't be silly,' said Max, taking her arm and steering her across the road at the lights. 'Dickie likes me. Although if I'd thought about it, ending your career might have been a good move. I'd never have to waltz again.'

'Darcy's going to be here any minute. Are you almost ready?'

Allegra put her head around the door to the kitchen, where Max was putting the final garnish to the romantic vegetarian meal for two that they had planned together.

At least, she had planned it and Max had reluctantly agreed to cook it. 'I don't see why I can't just give her pasta with a tomato sauce,' he'd grumbled.

'Because this is a special occasion. You want Darcy to know that you've made a real effort to cook something that she'll really like.'

Eventually they had settled on a pear, walnut and gorgonzola salad to start, followed by mushroom strudels with a tarragon cream sauce, and then margarita ice cream with chocolate-dipped strawberries. Allegra had been pleased with it, but after several practice runs, she had strudel coming out of her ears and she couldn't face another chocolate-dipped strawberry, which wasn't something she ever thought she would say.

'I'm all set,' said Max. 'I just need to change.'

'I'll make the living room look nice,' Allegra volunteered. Max was supposed to be thinking about that as well, but when she had suggested it he had just looked blank.

At least everything was tidy, the way it always was when Max was around. Allegra set out candles and plumped up the cushions before putting on the playlist of romantic music she had compiled specially. Max didn't have a clue about music or romance, so she'd known better than to suggest that he did it.

She was lighting candles when he came back. 'It's a bit gloomy in here, isn't it?' he said, looking around. 'Darcy won't be able to see what she's eating.'

'It's not gloomy. It's *romantic*.'

Allegra straightened from the candles and studied Max, who had replaced his checked shirt with one in a dark mulberry colour that shrieked expensive and stylish. He was wearing new black jeans too, and all in all he was looking mighty fine. So fine, in fact, that she forgot about the match burning in her hand.

'Ouch!' Allegra shook the match from her hand and sucked her finger. 'Is that the shirt Dickie picked out for you?' she asked, covering her sudden confusion by bending to pick up the match.

'Of course.' Max plucked at it in distaste. 'You wouldn't catch me buying a red shirt, but Dickie insisted.'

'He was right. You look good,' said Allegra honestly. She tossed the blackened match into the bin and turned back to face him. She had herself back under control. 'If I could just make one teeny change…?'

Without waiting for Max to agree, she walked over and undid another button at his throat. Ignoring his protests, she turned her attention to his cuffs, unfastening them and rolling them up above his wrists.

But standing so close to him was making her feel a bit light-headed, and she was excruciatingly conscious of her fingertips grazing his forearms with their fine, flat hairs. The air had shortened, making her heart pound ridiculously. She wanted to say something light, something casual to break the atmosphere, but her mind was a blank and she didn't dare meet Max's eyes in case…

In case *what?*

In case he kissed her. In case *she* kissed *him*.

Allegra swallowed hard. This was silly. She'd just got over that mad period when she'd been so inexplicably conscious of him. The last few days had been fine, cooking, talking easily, sniping at each other, laughing with each other. They'd dutifully practised the basic waltz step and even seemed to be getting the hang of it. It had been just like the old days.

And now he'd put on a new shirt and that awful thump was back in her belly. Allegra didn't like it one little bit.

Clearing her throat, she patted the second sleeve into place and stepped back. 'There, that's better,' she said.

Max immediately started fidgeting with his cuffs. 'It looks so messy like this,' he complained until Allegra had to slap his hands away.

'Leave them! Those cuffs are the difference between looking like a nerd and looking like a hunk.'

'A *hunk?*' Max echoed, revolted.

'Okay, not a hunk,' she amended, 'but more normal, anyway. Like you might possibly have some social skills. And, talking of which,' she said as she struck another match to light the rest of the candles, 'remember this evening's about making Darcy feel really special. Ask her lots of questions about what she does and how she feels about things.'

'Yeah, yeah, we've been through this,' said Max, straightening the knives and forks on the table.

Allegra blew out the match and admired the way the flames danced above the candles. 'Are you sure it's all under control in the kitchen?'

'Positive. I wrote out a time plan, and I don't need to do anything until seventeen minutes after she arrives.'

'Right. Seventeen minutes. Because you wouldn't want to eat a minute later than scheduled, would you?' Allegra rolled her eyes, but Max was unfazed.

'You're the one who wants the meal to be a success,' he pointed out. He looked at his watch yet again. 'Shouldn't she be here by now?'

'I sent a car. I hope she's not going to be late. We can't really have a drink until she gets here, and I'm gasping for one.'

'We could practice our waltz steps,' Max suggested without any enthusiasm, but Allegra jumped up.

'That's a great idea. We need to be able to wow Cathy with our progress next week.'

They had practised several times now and it no longer felt uncomfortable to rest one hand on his shoulder, or to feel his arm around her waist. They set off briskly, moving their feet around an invisible box, the way Cathy had taught them, while Allegra hummed an approximation of a waltz.

'Hey, we're getting good at this,' Max said after a while. 'Shall we try a turn?'

Allegra was up for it but, the moment they tried to do something different, their feet got muddled up and they stumbled. Disentangling themselves, they tried again. This time they managed so well that Max got fancy. They were both elated at their success and, laughing, he spun her round and dipped her over his arm with a flourish.

And there it would have ended if they hadn't made the mistake of looking into each other's eyes. They could have straightened, still laughing, and it would have been fine.

But no! Their eyes had to lock so that the laughter evaporated without warning, leaving their smiles to fade. Allegra was still bent ridiculously over Max's arm but she couldn't tear her gaze from his. The air felt as if it was tightening around them, squeezing out all the oxygen, and her pulse was booming and thudding. She couldn't have moved if she had tried.

Later, she wondered if she had imagined the fact that Max's head had started to move down to hers. Certainly at the time she didn't know whether to be relieved or disappointed when the shrill of the doorbell jerked them both out of their daze.

'Darcy!' Flustered, Allegra pulled out of Max's hold and smoothed down her hair. What was she *doing*? She had forgotten all about the article for a few moments there.

Allegra had forgotten quite how beautiful Darcy was. Max greeted her at the door and when he showed her in she seemed to light up the room. Her blonde hair fell over one shoulder in a fishtail braid that looked casual but must have taken her hours to achieve, and her skin glowed. She was wearing an electric-blue dress that showed off her stupendous figure. If Allegra wasn't much mistaken, the dress was from a high street chain rather than a designer but Darcy made it look stunning. From her bee-stung lips to the tips of her Christian Louboutin shoes—no whiff of the high street *there*—she was perfect.

By rights, Allegra ought to hate her, but Darcy was so warm and friendly that it was impossible.

'This all looks wonderful,' she said, looking around the room. 'You've gone to so much trouble, Max!'

Max took it without a blink. 'Nothing's too much trouble for you, Darcy,' he said, but he avoided Allegra's eyes. 'Now, let's have some champagne…'

Everything was going swimmingly, Allegra thought later. Dom turned up a few minutes later and took a few pictures of Max in the kitchen, and then of Max and Darcy sitting at the table with the starter, but once he had gone they were able to enjoy the meal. The three of them chatted so easily that Allegra kept forgetting that she was supposed to be just an observer, and after a while she put her notebook aside.

She had imagined that taut moment of awareness just before Darcy rang the doorbell, she told herself. Look at them now, talking like old friends. There was no crackling in the air between them, no zing every time their eyes met. She had made the whole thing up.

The food wasn't too bad either. What it lacked in presentational flair, it made up for in efficiency, with Max putting each course on the table with military precision.

All in all, the second task was a huge success, Allegra congratulated herself.

'Coffee?' Max asked at last.

'Actually, I'd love a herbal tea if you've got one,' said Darcy, and Max rolled an agonized look at Allegra.

'In the cupboard above the kettle,' she said.

The moment Max went out to put the kettle on, Darcy leant towards Allegra. 'Can I ask you something?'

'Sure,' said Allegra in surprise.

'Are you guys…?'

'What?'

'You and Max,' said Darcy delicately. 'I asked Max if you were an item, but he said you were just friends.' She looked at Allegra. 'Is that right?'

Allegra felt unaccountably miffed at the way Max had disclaimed any interest in her, but she could hardly deny it. 'Of course,' she said, taking a casual sip of wine. 'Max is practically my brother.'

'Oh, that's good. So you won't mind if I asked Max to dinner at my place?'

Allegra choked on her wine. 'Dinner?' she spluttered.

'Yes. Not as part of the *Glitz* deal, but like a proper date.'

'You want to date *Max*?'

Darcy laughed a little self-consciously. 'I think he's cute.'

Max? *Cute*?

'He's not like the usual guys I date,' Darcy went on.

Allegra thought of the actors and rock stars who had been linked to Darcy, über hunks every one of them, and she blinked. 'You can say that again.'

'I kinda like him,' Darcy confessed. 'Do you think he'd say yes?'

A famous lingerie model inviting him to spend the evening alone with her at her house. Like Max would turn *that* invitation down.

'You should ask Max, not me,' said Allegra stiffly.

'You don't sound very keen on the idea,' said Darcy, who was a lot more perceptive than she looked. 'Are you sure you don't mind?'

'It's not that. It's just…well, Max puts on a good show, but his fiancée broke off their engagement not very long ago. I wouldn't want him to get hurt again. I mean…'

Allegra was floundering, wishing she had never started on this. '…It's just that you're so gorgeous and you must have so many men after you. I…I'd hate it if you were just amusing yourself with Max and he ended up taking you too seriously. And I can see why he would,' she said with honest envy. 'I can't imagine any guy not falling heavily for you.'

'You'd be surprised,' said Darcy with a touch of bitterness. 'I don't understand why I've got such a reputation as a man-eater. Nobody ever worries that I might be the one to get hurt, do they?'

'Max isn't your usual type,' Allegra pointed out and Darcy nodded.

'That's why I'd like to get to know him better. I'm sick of guys who are all moody and dramatic, or who just want to be with me so they can get their name in the papers.'

'Well, you certainly wouldn't need to worry about that with Max.'

'Great. Well, if you're sure you're okay with it, I'll ask him.'

Allegra wasn't at all sure that she *was* okay with it, but she couldn't think of a single reason why not. Max was a grown man. He didn't need her to look after him, and she could hardly veto his chance to fulfil every man's fantasy of going out with Darcy, could she? He deserved some fun after Emma's rejection.

So why did she have this leaden feeling in her stomach?

When Max came back with the coffee and the herbal tea, Allegra took her mug and excused herself. 'I'll leave you two together,' she said with a brilliant smile. 'I need to go and write up my notes. Have fun.'

* * *

'What do you mean, you're not coming?' Max stared at Allegra in consternation.

'I'm going to dinner at Flick's,' she pointed out. 'Plus, I'm not invited.'

'I thought you'd be going too. And Dom.'

'Max, Darcy's invited you to supper. It's nothing to do with the article.'

'Why?' he asked, puzzled.

'Crazy thought, but maybe she likes you.'

Thrown by this new information, Max dragged a hand through his hair. The truth was that he hadn't really listened when Darcy had invited him the evening he'd cooked her dinner. It was after Allegra had gone to her room, and he'd just assumed that another task was involved.

Darcy *liked* him?

'You mean, like on a date?' he asked cautiously and Allegra rolled her eyes. She was doing something complicated with her hair in front of the mirror over the mantelpiece.

'I'd have thought you'd have been over the moon,' she said, through a mouthful of hairclips.

'Darcy King wants to go out with *me*?'

'I know, I thought it was unlikely too,' said Allegra, fixing another clip into place.

Max sat on the sofa and tossed the remote from hand to hand. Darcy King. She was gorgeous, sexy, warm, *nice*. Why wasn't he ecstatic?

'I thought I was just signing up for this article of yours,' he said grouchily. 'I didn't realise I'd be getting involved in other stuff as well.'

'It's just dinner, Max. I don't suppose she's planning on a bout of eye-popping sex straight away.'

Apparently satisfied with her hair, Allegra turned from

the mirror. It never failed to amaze Max how she could spend so long achieving a range of hairstyles, each messier than the last. That evening she had twisted it up and fixed it into place with a clip, but bits stuck out wildly from the clip, and other strands fell around her face. Max's fingers itched to smooth them behind her ears, but the idea of sliding his fingers through that silky hair was so tantalising that for a moment he lost track of the conversation.

'You ought to be flattered,' she said.

'I am,' said Max, wrenching his mind back from a disturbingly vivid image of pulling that clip from her hair and letting it fall, soft and shiny, to her shoulders. 'It's just...I don't want to complicate things.'

'What's complicated about dinner? You had dinner with Darcy the other night and this time you won't even have to worry about the cooking.'

'It's not that.' How could he tell Allegra that, much as he liked Darcy, he found her a bit overwhelming? 'It's not long since I was engaged to Emma,' he said, grasping at the excuse. 'It feels too soon to be getting involved with anyone else.'

Allegra's face softened instantly and then she snarled every one of his senses by coming to sit on the sofa beside him and placing her hand on his knee.

'I'm sorry, I keep forgetting that you must still be gutted about Emma.'

Max didn't think gutted was quite the right word, in fact, but with Allegra sitting so close, her green eyes huge and warm with sympathy, it was all he could do to nod.

'Darcy knows you were engaged,' Allegra went on, with a comforting rub on his thigh. At least, Max assumed it was meant to be comforting, although in practice it was excruciatingly arousing. If she moved her hand any higher, he couldn't be responsible for his actions... As unobtrusively as he could, he shifted along the sofa.

Allegra was still talking, still looking at him with those big, earnest eyes, completely unaware of the effect she was having on him. 'She won't expect you to fall madly in love with her, Max. It'll just be dinner. Darcy's nice, and it'll be a boost for your ego, if nothing else. You should go and forget about Emma for an evening.'

It wasn't Emma he needed to forget, it was the feel of Allegra's hand on his leg, but Max heard himself agreeing just so that he could get up before he grabbed her and rolled her beneath him on the sofa. He had to give himself a few mental slaps before he had himself under control enough to change and go back down to the sitting room, where Allegra was perched on the armchair and bending over to ease on a pair of precipitously-heeled shoes. She was in a dark floral sleeveless dress with black lace over the shoulders and a skirt that showed off miles of leg in black stockings, and Max's throat promptly dried all over again.

Those loose strands of hair had slithered forward when she bent her head and she tucked them behind her ears as she glanced up to see Max standing in the doorway. There was an odd little jump in the air as their eyes met, and then both looked away.

'You look nice,' Max said gruffly.

'Thank you.' Her gaze skimmed his then skittered away. 'Is that one of the shirts Dickie picked out for you?'

'Yes.' Self-consciously, he held his arms out from his side. 'Why, is it too casual?'

'It's perfect—or it would be if you rolled up your cuffs, and...' Allegra pointed at her throat to indicate that his collar was too tightly buttoned.

She had a thing about his collar, but Max knew from experience that it wasn't worth the argument. With a long-suffering sigh, he unfastened another button before starting on his cuffs. She had a thing about those too. He could do them up again as soon as she'd gone.

'So, you're seeing your mother,' he said after a moment. 'What's it going to be? A cosy night in with just the two of you?'

Max knew as well as she did that Flick didn't do cosy, but Allegra couldn't help smiling a little wistfully. She adored her mother, and it made her feel disloyal to wish sometimes that Flick could be a little—just a little!—more like Libby and Max's mum, who was easygoing and gave wonderful hugs and would happily watch *I'm a Celebrity Get Me Out of Here!* instead of the news. The first time Allegra had been to stay with Libby they had had supper on their laps in front of the television, and it had felt deliciously subversive.

'I think there'll be a few people there,' she told Max as she wiggled her feet into a more comfortable position in her shoes. 'She says she's got someone she wants me to meet.'

Max started on his second cuff, his expression sardonic. 'Flick's setting you up with a new boyfriend?'

'Maybe.'

'You don't sound very keen.'

She hadn't, had she? She'd sounded like someone who would really rather be staying at home. That would never do.

Allegra stood up and tested her shoes. 'Of course I'm keen,' she said. 'The men my mother introduces me to are always intelligent, cultured, amusing, interesting… Why wouldn't I be keen?'

'No reason when you put it like that,' said Max. He had dealt with his cuffs and now he stood in the centre of the room with his hands in his pockets, looking sulky and surly and disconcertingly attractive. Allegra almost told him to button up his shirt again so he could go back to looking stuffy and repressed.

'I'm feeling positive,' she said airily. 'This guy could be The One. I could be on my way to meet true love!'

Max snorted. 'Well, don't make a date for Wednesday, that's all.'

He had finally heard from Bob Laskovski's office. Bob and his wife would be in London the following week and the dinner to meet Max and his 'fiancée' was arranged for the Wednesday night. Max was nervous about the whole business, Allegra knew. He wasn't comfortable with deception, but he was desperate for the Shofrar job. Perhaps that was why he was so grouchy at the moment?

Darcy was welcome to him, Allegra told herself as she flipped open her phone to call a cab. She couldn't care less that Max was having supper with a lingerie model. *She* was going out to have a great time and meet a fabulous new guy. And, who knew, maybe she'd find true love at last as well.

Flick still lived in the four-storey Georgian house in a much sought after part of Islington where Allegra had grown up but it never felt like going home. The house was immaculately decorated and most visitors gasped in envy when they stepped inside, but Allegra much preferred the Warriners' house with its scuffed skirting boards and faded chair covers.

Flick's dinner parties were famous, less for the food, which was always catered, than for the company. Politicians, media stars, business leaders, diplomats, writers, artists, musicians, journalists…anyone who was anyone in London jostled for a coveted invitation to sit at Flick's dining table. No celebrities, pop stars or soap opera actors need apply, though. Flick insisted on a certain intellectual rigour.

Thus Allegra found herself sitting between Dan, a fast-track civil servant, obviously destined for greatness, while William, on her right, was a political aide. They both worked in government circles and were both high-flyers, full of gossip and opinion.

Toying with her marinated scallops, Allegra felt boring and uninformed in comparison. She couldn't think of a single clever or witty thing to say.

Not that it mattered much. The conversation around the table was fast and furious as usual, but no one was interested in her opinion anyway, and it was enough for Allegra to keep a smile fixed to her face.

Beside her, Dan had launched into a scurrilous story about a politician everybody else seemed to know but who Allegra had never heard of. She laughed when everybody else laughed, but she was wondering how Max was getting on with Darcy. Would he sleep with her? Allegra realised that she had stopped smiling and hurriedly put her smile back in place.

Why did she care? Max would be leaving soon anyway, and it wasn't as if he was interested in her. True, there had been that moment when their eyes had met earlier, when she was putting on her shoes and had glanced up to find him watching her and something had leapt in the air between them.

It was just because they were spending so much time together for the article, Allegra told herself. It wasn't that she would really rather be sharing pizza with Max in front of the television than sitting here at this glamorous, glittering party. Of course she wouldn't.

Oh, God, she had missed Dan's punchline. At the other

end of the table, she caught Flick's eye and the tiny admonishing frown and sat up straighter.

Beside her, William was filling her glass, teasing her out of her abstraction. His eyes were warm, and she was picking up definite vibes. Allegra gazed at him, determined to find him attractive. She'd already established that he'd split up with his long-term girlfriend a year ago. A mutual thing, he'd said. They were still friends.

So no obvious emotional baggage. Unlike Max, who was still sore about Emma.

William was very good-looking. Charming. Assured. Also unlike Max.

He would be staying in London. Unlike Max.

He seemed to be finding her attractive. Unlike Max.

He was perfect boyfriend material. Unlike Max.

If William asked her out, she would say yes.

Definitely. She might even fall in love with him.

# CHAPTER SIX

'I HAVEN'T HAD a chance to talk to you yet, Allegra,' Flick said, coming back into the dining room, having said good-bye to the last of her guests, a cabinet minister who was tipped for a promotion in the next reshuffle. She frowned at Allegra, who was helping the caterers to clear the table. 'The caterers are paid to tidy up. Leave that and let's have a chat.'

No one looking at them together would guess that they were mother and daughter. Where Allegra was tall and dark and a little quirky-looking, Flick was petite and blonde with perfect features, steely blue eyes and a fero-cious intelligence. Allegra was super-proud of her famous mother, but sometimes she did wonder what it would be like to have a mother who would rush out to hug you when you arrived, like Libby and Max's mother did, or fuss over you if you were unhappy.

A chat with Flick didn't mean sitting over cocoa in the kitchen. It meant being interrogated in the study about your career and achievements. Which in Allegra's case were not very many.

Sure enough, Flick led the way to her book-lined study and sat behind her desk, gesturing Allegra to a chair as if for an interview.

'Another successful evening, I think,' she said complacently.

'The food was lovely,' Allegra said dutifully, stealing a surreptitious glance at her watch. One in the morning... Was Max still with Darcy? He'd seemed surprisingly reluctant to go, but surely, once faced with Darcy's glowing beauty, he wouldn't be able to resist?

'You seem very abstracted, Allegra.' Flick had her razor-sharp interviewing voice on. 'I noticed it during dinner too. Not very good manners. Would you rather go?'

'No, no, of course not...' Nobody could make her stammer like her mother and, because she knew it irritated Flick, Allegra pulled herself together. 'I'm sorry. I'm just a bit preoccupied with an assignment I've got for *Glitz*.'

Flick sat back in her chair and raised her brows. 'I hardly think an article on the latest fashion trend compares to the kind of issues that everyone else here has to deal with every day.' She unbent a little. 'But I read your little piece on shoes last week. It was very entertaining. The ending was a little weak but, otherwise, your writing has improved considerably. What's the latest assignment?'

Allegra started to explain about the idea behind the article, but it sounded stupid when her mother was listening with her impeccably groomed head on one side. 'I'm hoping that if I can make a success of it, Stella will give me more opportunities to write something different.' She stumbled to a halt at last.

Flick nodded her approval. She liked it when Allegra thought strategically. 'I suppose it's experience of a sort, but you'd be so much better off at a serious magazine. You remember Louise's son, Joe? He's at *The Economist* now.'

Allegra set her teeth. 'I'm not sure I'm ready to write about quantitative easing yet, Flick. *The Economist* would be a bit of a leap from *Glitz*.'

'Not for someone who's got what it takes—but you've never been ambitious,' said Flick regretfully. 'But you do look very nice tonight,' she conceded. 'Those dark florals are good for you. The earrings aren't quite right, but otherwise, yes, very nice. William seemed rather taken,' she added. 'Are you going to see him again?'

'Perhaps.' The truth was that when William had asked her out, Allegra had opened her mouth to say yes and then somehow heard herself say that she was rather busy at the moment.

'He's got a great future ahead of him. I'd like to see you spend more time with people like that instead of these silly little assignments for that magazine. I mean, who are you working with at the moment?'

'Max.' Funny how his name felt awkward in her mouth now. 'You remember, Libby's brother,' she said when Flick looked blank.

'Oh, yes…rather dull.'

'He isn't dull!' Allegra flushed angrily.

'I don't remember him striking me as very interesting,' said Flick, dismissive as only she could be.

Allegra had a clear memory of thinking much the same thing once. So why was she wishing that she could have spent the evening with him instead of flirting with William, who was everything Max would never be?

'I didn't realise he was a particular friend of yours.' Her mother's eyes had narrowed suspiciously at the colour burning in Allegra's cheeks.

'He wasn't. I mean, he isn't. He's just living in the house for a couple of months while Libby's in Paris.'

'I hope you're not getting involved with him?'

'Anyone would think he was some kind of troublemaker,' Allegra grumbled. 'He's a civil engineer. It doesn't get more respectable than that.'

'I'm sure he's very good at what he does,' said Flick gently. 'But he's not exactly a mover and shaker, is he? I've always worried about the way you seem happy to settle for the mediocre, rather than fulfilling your potential.' She shook her head. 'I blame myself for letting you spend so much time with that family—what are they called? Warren?'

'Warriner,' said Allegra, 'and they're wonderful.'

'Oh, I'm sure they're very kind but I've brought you up to aim for the exceptional.'

'They *are* exceptional!' Normally the thinning of Flick's lips would have been a warning to Allegra, but she was too angry to stop there. 'They're exceptionally generous and exceptionally fun. Max's mother might not win any style awards, but she's lovely, and his dad is one of the nicest, most decent, most honourable men I've ever met,' she swept on. 'I only wish I'd had a father like him!'

There was a moment of appalled silence, while her last words rang around the room. Flick had whitened. Allegra's lack of a father was a taboo subject and Allegra knew it.

'I'm sorry,' she said, letting out a long breath. 'But why won't you tell me about my father?'

'I don't wish to discuss it,' said Flick tightly. 'In your case, father is a biological term and nothing more. I'm sorry if I haven't been enough of a parent for you.'

'I didn't mean that,' Allegra tried to break in wretchedly, but Flick moved smoothly on.

'I can only assure you that all I've ever wanted is the best for you. You have so much potential if only you would realise it. I really think it would be a mistake for you to tie yourself down to somebody ordinary who'll just drag you down to his level.'

She should have known better than to try and press Flick about her father. 'You don't need to worry,' said

Allegra dully. 'There's no question of anything between Max and me and, even if there were, he's going abroad to work soon.'

'Just as well,' said Flick.

It *was* just as well, Allegra told herself in the taxi home. Flick had suggested that she stay the night in her old room, but she wanted to go back to the flat. She didn't want to admit to herself that she needed to know if Max had stayed with Darcy or not and it was like a sword being drawn out of her entrails when she opened the door and saw Max stretched out on the sofa.

'You're back early.' Funny, her voice sounded light and normal when her heart was behaving so oddly, racing and lurching, bouncing off her chest wall like a drunk.

'It's half past one. It's not that early.'

'I suppose not.' Allegra went to sit in the armchair. She picked at the piping. 'So, how was your evening?'

'Fine. Yours?'

'Oh, you know. Lots of clever, glamorous guests. Witty conversation. Delicious food. The usual.'

'Your average social nightmare.'

Allegra laughed and toed off her shoes so that she could curl her feet up beneath her. She was feeling better already.

'So, did you find your true love over the canapés?' Max asked.

'I don't know about that,' she said. 'I sat between two handsome, ambitious single men specially picked out for me by my mother.'

Max's gaze flickered to her face and then away. 'So who's the lucky guy?'

'Neither.' Reaching up, she pulled the clips from her hair and shook it loose, oblivious to the way Max's eyes darkened. 'I've decided I need a relationship detox. I might abstain from all men for a while.'

'That would be a shame.'

'I'm sick of feeling that they only ask me out because I'm Flick Fielding's daughter.' It was the first time Allegra had said it out loud and she winced as she heard the resentment reverberating around the room.

'That's not why they ask you out,' said Max roughly.

'Isn't it? Why else would they? I'm not clever the way they are. I can't contribute to the conversation. I've got nothing to offer.'

'You're beautiful,' said Max. 'Come on, Legs, you must know you are,' he said when she gaped at him. 'You're gorgeous. Any man would be glad to be seen with you. I don't know who you sat next to tonight, but if you think he was more interested in Flick's influence than in the way you looked, you're not thinking straight!'

He would have been the one not thinking straight if he'd been sitting next to Allegra while she was wearing that dress. He would have been mesmerised by her arms, bare and slender, by those expressive hands, by the glow of her skin and the way the straight shiny hair threatened to slip out of its clips. He would have spent his whole time imagining how it would look falling to her shoulders, the way it was now.

He wouldn't have been able to eat, Max knew. His mouth would have been too dry and he'd have been too busy watching the sweep of her lashes, the brightness of her eyes, the tempting hollow of her cleavage, the curve of her breasts… And thinking about her bare knees under the table, the long, sexy legs in those ridiculous shoes.

His head felt light and he realised it was because he'd stopped breathing. Max sucked in a steadying breath. Where had all that come from?

'I didn't know you thought I was beautiful,' said Allegra, sounding thrown.

'I thought so many other people would tell you there was no need for me to do the same. You're still deeply irritating, mind,' he said in an effort to drag the conversation back onto safe ground, 'but of course you're beautiful. I thought you knew.'

'No.' Allegra bent her head, pushing back the hair that slithered forward, but he still couldn't see her face properly.

It was probably just as well. Max was uneasily aware that something tenuous had insinuated itself into the air, like a memory hovering just out of reach, or a forgotten word trembling on the tip of a tongue. Something that seemed to be drawing the air tighter, squeezing out the oxygen so that his chest felt tight and his breathing oddly sticky.

Could Allegra feel it?

Apparently not. Even as he struggled to heave in another breath, she was lifting her head and focusing on him with those eyes that seemed to get more beautiful every time he looked into them.

'Tell me how you got on with Darcy,' she said, sounding so completely normal that Max squirmed inwardly with humiliation. *She* wasn't finding it hard to breathe. She wasn't aware of the tension in the air, or snarled in a knot of inconvenient and inappropriate lust.

'I wondered if you'd end up staying the night,' she went on, but not as if she cared one way or the other.

So he obviously couldn't admit that she was the reason he wasn't tucked up next to the world's favourite lingerie model right now.

Because Darcy had made it very clear that she was up for a lot more than just dinner, but it hadn't felt right, not when he'd spent most of the evening wondering what Allegra was doing and who her bloody mother had lined up to sit next to her. Flick might be keen on big brains, but

Max was prepared to bet that they were men too, and that they wouldn't be above a flirtatious touch every now and then: Allegra's shoulder, her hand, her knee…

It was only when Darcy had looked at him strangely that he'd realised he was grinding his teeth.

What was wrong with him? Max had wanted to tear out his hair. There he was, sitting across the table from *Darcy King*, with a clear invitation to get his hands on that luscious body. It was the opportunity of a lifetime, a fantasy come true for a million men like him, and all he could think about was his sister's scrawny friend! He had to be sickening for something. Or certifiable.

Or both.

He liked Darcy, he really did, but it had been awkward. He told Allegra what he'd told Darcy, which was the best excuse he could come up with at the time.

'I don't really want to get involved with Darcy,' he said. 'She's nice but…well, I don't see her fitting into my life, do you? I can't imagine someone like Darcy out in Shofrar, and I don't feel like being just a novelty plaything for her. I know most other men would give their eye teeth to be toyed with by her, but I'm not sure it would be worth it.'

It wasn't really an excuse. It was *true*. Not that Allegra seemed to be convinced.

She looked at him strangely. 'I doubt that Darcy's thinking about anything serious,' she said. 'It would only be a bit of fun. Where does Shofrar come into it?'

'That's where my life is going to be,' said Max stiffly, even as he winced inwardly at what a pompous jerk he sounded. But the words kept coming out of his mouth without taking the trouble of detouring through his brain. 'There's no point in getting involved with someone who can't hack it away from a city.'

Meaning *what* exactly? He wasn't surprised at the way Allegra's face clouded with disbelief.

'So, let me get this right. You're saying that you're not going to have sex unless you can get married to someone who won't mind being dragged out to some desert hell-hole so that she can play second fiddle to your career?'

'Yes…no!' What *was* he saying?

'Isn't that going to be a bit limiting?'

Max was beginning to sweat. He hadn't felt this out of control since Emma had blithely broken off their engagement.

Emma! He grabbed onto the thought of his fiancée. *Ex*-fiancée. 'Look, I'm not the sort of guy who goes out with models,' he said with a tinge of desperation. 'In a fantasy, maybe, but I really just want to be with someone like Emma. I think being with Darcy made me realise that I wasn't really over Emma yet.'

Which might even be true. Not the realisation, which in reality hadn't crossed his mind at the time, but that he was still missing Emma at some level.

Now that he thought about it, Max thought it probably was true. It would explain the muddle inside him, wouldn't it? Max *hated* feeling like this, as if he were churning around in some massive washing machine, not knowing which way was up. Not knowing what he thought or what he felt. He hadn't felt himself since Emma had wafted off in search of passion.

'I sent Emma a text, just like you suggested,' he told Allegra almost accusingly, and she sat up straighter.

'Did she reply?'

'While I was on my way to Darcy's. So I was thinking about her before I got there.'

That *was* true, although he hadn't really been thinking about Emma in a yearning way, more in a how-odd-I-don't-really-feel-anything-when-I-see-your-name-now kind of way. Until a week or so ago, Max would have said that all he wanted was to hear from Emma and try to get back to normal again, but when he'd read her text he hadn't felt the rush of relief and hope that he'd expected.

At least Allegra was looking sympathetic now. 'I can see that would throw you a bit,' she said fairly. 'What did Emma say?'

'Nothing really. Just that she was fine and how was I?'

'Oh, that's very encouraging!' Allegra beamed at him and he looked back suspiciously.

'It is?'

'Definitely. If Emma didn't want to stay in contact, she wouldn't have replied at all. As it is, she not only responded, she asked you a question back.'

'So?'

'So she's opening a dialogue,' Allegra said with heavy patience. 'She's asked how you are, which means you reply and tell her, and say something else, then she gets the chance to react to that... Before you know where you are, you're having a conversation, and then it's only a matter of time before you decide you should meet.'

She sat back, satisfied with her scenario. 'It's a really good sign, Max,' she assured him. 'I bet Emma's bored with her passionate guy already and was thrilled to hear from you.'

Max couldn't see it. *Thrilled*. There was an Allegra word for you. Emma wasn't the kind of woman who was *thrilled* about things. It was one of the things he had always liked about her. Emma didn't make a big fuss about anything. She was moderation, balance, calm—unlike some people he could mention.

He looked at Allegra, who was curled up in the armchair, bright-eyed and a little tousled at the end of the evening, apparently unaware that her dress was rucked up, exposing a mouth-watering length of leg. When he thought about Allegra, he didn't think moderation. He thought extravagance. Allegra dealt in extremes. She *adored* things or she *loathed* them. She was wildly excited at the prospect of something or dreading it. She was madly in love or broken-hearted. It was exhausting trying to keep up with the way her emotions swung around. Emma had never left his head reeling.

Of course, Emma was the one who had thrown up her nice, safe life for a passionate affair, so what did he know?

Max hunched his shoulders morosely. Women. Just when you thought you understood them, they turned around and kicked your legs out from beneath you, leaving you floundering.

Look at Allegra, who had just been Libby's mildly annoying friend. He'd known exactly where he was with her. True, there had been that odd little moment a few years ago but, apart from that, it had been an easy relationship. Nothing about her seemed easy now. He couldn't look at her without noticing her skin or the silkiness of her hair. Without thinking about her legs or her mouth or the tantalising hollow of her throat.

Without blurting out that she looked beautiful.

Max didn't know exactly what Allegra had done to change, but she had done *something*.

Now she was fiddling with her hair, smoothing it behind her ear, grooming herself like a cat. 'So have you replied to her?' she asked.

'What?' Mesmerised by her fingers, Max had forgotten what she was talking about.

Allegra looked at him. 'Have you replied to Emma?' she repeated slowly, and Max felt a dull colour burning along his cheekbones.

'Oh. No, not yet.'

'You're playing it cool?'

Max was damned if he knew.

What if Allegra was right? What if Emma really was waiting to hear from him? If they could miraculously make everything right, get married as planned, and go out to Shofrar? He ought to feel happy at the idea…oughtn't he? But all he really felt was confused.

He met Allegra's expectant gaze. Playing it cool sounded a lot better than not having a clue what was going on.

'Something like that,' he said.

'Allegra!' Max banged his fist on the bathroom door. 'What in God's name are you doing in there?'

'Nearly ready,' Allegra called back. Carefully, she smoothed her lipstick into place and blotted her mouth. She wouldn't for the world admit it to Max, but she was nervous about the evening ahead. This dinner with Bob Laskovski and his wife was so important to him. She didn't want to let him down.

Max had been in a funny mood for the last few days. Allegra had decided that hearing from Emma had thrown him more than he understood. He was in denial, but it was obvious that he really wanted Emma back. Why else would he resist Darcy?

It had been easier to go out and leave him to be morose on his own, and when William got in touch after dinner at Flick's she had agreed to meet him for a drink after all. The whole relationship detox thing would never have worked anyway, Allegra decided. She should at least give him a chance.

William was good company, good-looking, and she enjoyed herself, and she wouldn't let herself think that looking at William's patrician mouth didn't make her stomach hurt the way it did when she looked at Max's.

Because there was no point in thinking about Max that way.

Allegra couldn't even explain what kind of way that was, but it was something to do with a trembly sensation just below her skin, with a thudding in her veins that started whenever Max came into the room. It was something to do with the way every sense seemed on full alert when he was near.

Being so aware of him the whole time made her uncomfortable. It was crazy. It was inappropriate. It didn't make sense.

It was just the assignment, she tried to reassure herself. It was just spending so much time with him. It wasn't *real*. A temporary madness, that was all. Max would go to Shofrar and she would go back to normal.

She couldn't wait.

Max had been very clear. He wasn't interested in a quick fling. He was looking for someone who could be part of his life, someone who would share his interests and not mind being dragged around the world. It wasn't Darcy, and it sure as hell wasn't her either, Allegra knew. She was the last kind of girl Max would ever want to get involved with…and the feeling was mutual, she hurried to remind herself whenever that thought seemed too depressing. It wasn't as if she wanted to leave London. She had a career here.

She might not be changing the world or writing groundbreaking articles, but she was doing what she wanted to do…wasn't she? Allegra's mind flickered to illustration then away. Drawing cartoon animals wasn't a serious job. She could do better for herself, as Flick was constantly telling her.

Besides, the article about Max was going to be her big break. She had already written the first half and it was pretty good, even if she did say so herself. Perhaps she was spending rather too much time sketching Max while she thought, but it was inevitable that she should be thinking about him. Right now, that was her job, that was all.

'*Allegra*! We're going to be late!' Max had just raised his fist to rap the bathroom door again when Allegra pulled it open. She smiled brightly at him, gratified by the way his jaw slackened.

'What do you think?' She pirouetted in the doorway. She was in the most demure outfit she could find, a killer LBD with a sheer décolletage and sleeves. Even Max couldn't object to a black dress, Allegra had reasoned, but she'd been unable to resist pimping up the plainness with glittery earrings and bling-studded stilettos. There was only so much plain dressing a girl could do, and she was counting on the fact that Max and his boss were men and therefore unlikely to even look at her shoes.

'Do I look sufficiently sensible?' she asked, and Max, who had evidently forgotten that his fist was still raised, lowered it slowly.

'Sensible isn't quite the word I was thinking of,' he said, sounding strained.

Allegra was disappointed. 'I've put my hair up and everything,' she protested. Her hair was so slippery it had taken ages to do, too.

'You look very nice,' Max said gruffly. 'Now, come on. The taxi's waiting. We need to get a move on.' His gaze travelled down her legs and ended at her shoes. 'Can you make it to the taxi?'

'Of course I can,' said Allegra, unsure whether to be pleased or miffed that he had noticed her shoes after all.

Her hair was precariously fixed, to say the least, so

Allegra settled back into the seat and pulled her seat belt on with care. She loved London taxis, loved their bulbous shape and the yellow light on top. She loved the smell of the seats, the clicking of the engine, the straps that stopped you sliding around on your seat when they turned a corner. Sitting in a taxi as it drove past the iconic London sights made Allegra feel as if she was at the centre of things, part of a great vibrant city. It gave her a thrill every time.

Every time except that night.

That night, the streets were a blur. Allegra couldn't concentrate on London. She was too aware of Max sitting beside her. He was sensibly strapped in too, and he wasn't touching her. He wasn't even close, but that didn't stop her whole side tingling as if the seat belt had vanished and she had slid across the seat to land against him.

She swallowed hard. This was so *silly*. She shouldn't have to make an effort to sound normal with Max.

'So,' she said brightly, 'what's the plan?'

'Plan?'

'We ought to get our stories straight about how we met at least.'

Max frowned. 'Bob's not going to be interested in that kind of thing.'

'His wife might be.'

It was obvious Max hadn't thought of that. 'Better stick to the truth,' he decided, and Allegra's brows rose.

'Won't that rather defeat the object of the exercise?'

'I don't mean about the pretence,' he said irritably. 'Just that I know you through my sister, that kind of thing.'

It all sounded a bit thin to Allegra, but Max clearly didn't think his boss was going to interrogate them in any detail. She just hoped that he was right.

'I don't think you'll have to do much but smile and

look as if we might conceivably be planning to get married,' Max said.

'How besotted do you want me to be?' she asked provocatively. It was easier needling him than noticing how the street lights threw the planes of his face into relief, how the passing headlights kept catching the corner of his mouth. 'I could be madly in love or just sweetly adoring.'

'Just be normal,' he said repressively. 'If you can.'

They were to meet Bob and his wife at Arturo's, a quiet and classic restaurant no longer at the forefront of fashion but still famous for its food. When they got there, Max paid off the taxi and ran a finger under his collar. He'd wanted to wear a plain white shirt but Allegra had bullied him into putting on the mulberry-coloured shirt Dickie had picked out for him, with a plain tie in a darker hue.

'Bob's going to wonder what the hell I'm doing in a red shirt,' he grumbled as he eased the collar away from his throat.

'Stop fiddling, you look great,' said Allegra. She stepped up and made his senses reel by straightening his tie and patting it into place. 'Really,' she told him, 'you look good. You just need to relax.'

'Relax, right,' said Max, taking refuge in sarcasm. 'I'm just going for the most important interview of my career so far, which means lying through my teeth to my new boss. What's there to feel tense about?'

'We don't have to lie if you don't want to. Why not just tell Bob the truth about Emma?'

For a moment Max was tempted. Wouldn't chucking in the towel be easier than spending the evening trying to convince Bob Laskovski that it was remotely credible that a girl like Allegra would choose to be with him? She was so clearly out of his league.

When she had opened the bathroom door and smiled at

him, it had been like a punch to his heart. 'Do I look sufficiently sensible?' she had asked while he was still struggling for breath, while he was trying to wrench his eyes off the way her dress clung enticingly to her slender body.

True, her arms and shoulders were covered but that sheer black stuff was somehow even more tantalising than bare skin would have been. It seemed to beckon him forward to peer closer, hinting at the creamy skin half hidden beneath the gauzy film of black. Between the sheer arms and shoulders and the tight-fitting dress, Max felt as if there were great neon arrows angled at her throat, at her breasts, at the curve of her hips: *Look here! Look here!*

The dress stopped above her knees—*Look here!* — revealing those killer legs of hers—*And here!*—ending in absurd shoes that were studded with mock jewels. Her earrings swung and glittered in the light and her hair, twisted up and back more neatly than usual, gleamed.

Once the oxygen had rushed back to his head, Max had been able to think of lots of words to describe Allegra right then: sexy, erotic, dazzling, gorgeous... Had he already mentioned sexy? But *sensible? Suitable?* Max didn't think so.

Now she was adjusting his tie and standing so close her perfume was coiling into his mind, and lust fisted in his belly. For a wild moment the need to touch her was so strong all Max could think about was grabbing her, pushing her up against a wall and putting his hands on her, touching her, feeling her, taking her.

Horrified by the urge, he took a step back. What was happening to him? He didn't do wild. He was sensible, steady, an engineer, not some macho type acting out his caveman fantasies.

Max shook his head slightly to clear it. This whole article business was getting to him, that was all. The sooner he got to Shofrar, the better. *That* was what he wanted, not to rip his little sister's friend's clothes off. And for Shofrar he needed Bob Laskovski's approval. Was he really going to risk blowing the project manager role he'd coveted for so long just because he was distracted by Allegra's perfume?

'No,' he said. His voice was a little hoarse, but firm. 'I want to stick with what we agreed.'

'Okay.' Allegra smiled at him and tucked her hand through his arm. 'In that case, let's go and get you that job, tiger.'

# CHAPTER SEVEN

At work, Bob Laskovski was always referred to in hushed tones, and Max was expecting his boss to be an imposing figure. Headshots on the website showed a serious man with a shiny pate and a horseshoe of white hair but, in person, Bob was short and rotund with an easy smile and eyes that crinkled engagingly at the corners.

Max was relieved when Allegra let go of him so that he could shake hands with Bob, who turned to introduce his wife. No trophy wife for Bob: Karen Laskovski was silver-haired and very elegant. No doubt Allegra could have described what she was wearing in exhaustive detail, but Max just got an impression of warmth and charm and a light blue outfit.

And now it was his turn. Allegra smiled encouragingly when he glanced at her, and Max cleared his throat.

'This is my fiancée, Allegra.'

There, the lie was out. Max was sure he could hear it clanging around the restaurant and waited for the other diners to look up and shout *Liar! Liar!* but nobody seemed to notice anything unusual, least of all the Laskovskis. Couldn't they *see* what an ill-assorted couple he and Allegra were?

But no, apparently not.

'What a pretty name!' Karen exclaimed as Allegra beamed and shook hands.

'It means cheerful,' said Allegra.

'And you look like it's a good name for you,' said Bob, who had blinked a couple of times at Allegra's shoes.

Allegra smiled and, to Max's horror, she took hold of his arm once more and leant winsomely against his shoulder. 'I've got a lot to be cheerful about,' she said, fluttering her lashes at him. 'I'm just so excited to be marrying Max and going out to Shofrar with him. Hopefully,' she added, beaming a smile at Bob, who nodded approvingly.

'It's a great thing when you're both looking forward to a posting,' he said as he gestured for everyone to sit down. 'Especially a place like Shofrar, where there isn't much to occupy you if you're not working. Too often we see young engineers coming home early because their wife or partner isn't happy. But you're obviously going to be an ideal engineer's wife,' he said to Allegra.

Max covered his choke of disbelief with a cough. Hadn't Bob noticed Allegra's shoes? Couldn't he *see* that she was the last person who would be happy in the desert?

As for Allegra, she was well into her role. 'I don't mind where I am, as long as I'm with Max,' she said.

Forget journalism, she should have been an actress, thought Max, unaccountably ruffled. But Bob and Karen seemed to be lapping it up.

'It reminds me of when we were first married,' Karen said with a reminiscent smile at her husband. 'I didn't care as long as I could be with you.'

'Mind you, we were never really apart,' said Bob, covering her hand with his. 'We were high school sweethearts. I fell in love with Karen the moment I saw her, didn't I, honey?'

Max couldn't understand it. Bob was supposed to be

talking about contracts and deliverables, or quizzing Max on his project experience, not wittering on about love. Naturally, Allegra was encouraging him.

'Oh, that's so wonderful!' she cried, clapping her hands together. 'So you two believe in love at first sight?'

Max wanted to drop his head onto the table.

'We sure do,' said Bob with a fond glance at his wife, who gazed adoringly back at him. 'How about you two? You known each other a long time?'

'Years,' said Allegra, launching into an explanation of her friendship with Libby. 'For most of that time, Max and I ignored each other completely.'

'Aha!' Karen leaned forward. 'So what changed?'

For the first time, Allegra's cheery confidence faltered. 'I…well, I'm not sure…it just crept up on us, I guess.' And then she had the nerve to turn to *him*. 'What do you think, Max? When did you first realise that you were in love with me?'

It was as if the restaurant had jarred to a halt. The world went still and Max was frozen with it, pinned into place as Allegra's words rang in his head.

*When did you first realise that you were in love with me?*

He couldn't be in love with Allegra, Max thought in panic. There was some mistake. He'd put his hand up to momentary lust perhaps, but *love*? No, no, no, no. She was pretending, Max reminded himself with a touch of desperation. She didn't really believe he was in love with her.

So why had her words settled into place in his head as if they belonged there?

Allegra turned in her seat so that Bob and Karen couldn't see her give him a warning dead-eye look. 'Was it when I let you paint my toenails?' she asked.

Paint…? What? Max's brows snapped together until he

realised belatedly that she was trying to prod him into responding. God knew what his expression had looked like as he'd sat there, stunned at the realisation that he had, in fact, fallen in love with Allegra.

Fool that he was.

But not so foolish he would humiliate himself by letting anyone guess, Allegra least of all.

Max recovered himself with an effort. 'I think it was more when I realised how distraught you were at the idea of me going to Shofrar,' he said, pretending to consider the matter. He looked at Bob and Karen. 'It was only then I understood just what I meant to her.'

There was a whack on his arm. 'I was not distraught!' Allegra said indignantly.

'You were weeping and wailing and begging me not to go, remember?'

'You are such a big fibber!' she protested, but she was laughing too.

'*I'm* a fibber? What was that about me painting your toenails?'

'I never cry,' she insisted to Karen, who looked from one to the other in amusement.

'Well, however you fell in love, I can just tell that you two are perfect together!'

'We think so, don't we, sweetheart?' That was Allegra again, playing it for all it was worth. She leant confidingly towards Karen. 'Of course, Max can be a bit grumpy at times, but I know he adores me.'

The little minx.

Fortunately Bob chose that moment to ask Max about the project he was working on and Max seized on the chance to drag the conversation back to safe territory.

But Karen was asking about the wedding, and Max found it harder than he'd thought to concentrate on engineering while beside him Allegra had launched into a vivid description of an imaginary wedding ceremony, her dress, what the bridesmaids would be wearing, how the tables would be decorated, and a host of other details that Max had never even considered in connection with a wedding.

He listened incredulously with one ear. Where did Allegra *get* all this stuff from? Oh, God, now she was sketching outfits on the back of an envelope she'd dug out of her jewelled bag and Karen was oohing and aahing.

'Oh, that's darling!' she exclaimed, and in spite of himself Max craned his neck to see what Allegra had drawn. There she stood in a slender dress with a low wide neckline and that was unmistakably him next to her, dressed in a morning suit and a *flowery waistcoat*.

'Over my dead body,' he muttered in Allegra's ear, and she pressed her lips together but he could see her body shaking with suppressed giggles.

'Women and weddings, huh?' said Bob as Max caught his eye. 'Take my advice, just go along with whatever they want.'

'I guess your mom will want to be involved in the wedding plans too?' Karen said to Allegra, ignoring the men.

'Er, yes.' Max could see Allegra trying to imagine poring over table decorations with Flick. 'Yes, she will, of course, but really it's just between Max and me, isn't it?'

'Quite right,' said Bob, 'and the sooner you get on with it the better, am I right, Max? But I'm not sure you're going to have time to get married before you go out to Shofrar. You'll have to come back for the wedding.'

Max looked at Bob and then at Allegra, whose face lit with excitement. 'Does that mean…?' she asked Bob, and he nodded and smiled.

'Sure. Of course Max gets the job.'

Allegra squealed with excitement and flung her

arms around Max. 'Oh, Max, you got it! You're going to Shofrar!'

Her cheek was pressed against his, and unthinkingly his arms closed around her, pulling her tight. Bob and Karen were watching indulgently and when Allegra turned her head and smiled, it seemed the most natural thing in the world to kiss her.

Her mouth was soft and lusciously curved and so close it would have been rude not to, in fact. And it would look good, Max thought hazily, unable to wrench his gaze from her lips. The Laskovskis were expecting him to kiss Allegra. That was what engaged couples did when they got good news. It would seem odd if he *didn't* kiss her.

One hand slid up her spine to the nape of her neck. For one still moment he looked straight into the deep, mossy green of Allegra's eyes and all rational thought evaporated. There was nothing but her warmth, her scent, her mouth.

Her *mouth*.

He couldn't resist any longer. He'd forgotten why he needed to, forgotten everything but the need to seal the gap between them. He drew her head towards him—or perhaps she leant closer; Max never knew—and angled his lips against hers, and the taste and the touch of her blew his senses apart so that he could almost have sworn that the restaurant swung wildly around them.

She was warm and responsive, pliant against him, and their mouths fitted together as if they were meant for each other. The astonishing rightness of it rose in his chest and surged through him like a tide, blocking out doubts, blocking out reason, blocking out everything that wasn't Allegra: the scent of her, the feel of her, the sweetness of her.

Afterwards, Max calculated that the kiss couldn't have lasted more than a few seconds, but at the time it seemed to stretch to infinity and beyond. He never knew where he found the strength to pull away, but somehow he had drawn back and was staring into her eyes once more. The lovely green was dark and dazed, and her expression was as stunned as his must have been.

'Yep,' said Bob to Karen, 'the sooner those two get married the better, I'd say.'

Desperately, Max tried to pull himself together. His blood was pounding, which was crazy. It had just been a kiss, hardly more than a peck on the lips. There was no reason for his heart to be throbbing still like that, for his lungs to have forgotten how to function.

He had to get a grip, focus on the job. He had what he wanted. He was going to Shofrar to be a project manager, just like he had planned. He ought to be elated, not thinking about the way Allegra's words were ringing in his ears: *You're going to Shofrar*, she had exclaimed in delight. *You're going*, not *we're going*.

They were all picking up their glasses and Bob was toasting Max's promotion. Max stretched his mouth into a smile.

*You*, not *we*.

That was how it should be, Max told himself. In a few weeks, he would get on a plane and fly out to the desert and Allegra wouldn't be there. He would get on with his life and she would get on with hers. Their lives were on separate tracks, heading in different directions.

If Libby ever got married, they might meet at her wedding or the occasional christening but that was far in the future. They might have forgotten this evening by then, forgotten that kiss, or perhaps they would share a wry smile at the memory. It wouldn't matter then.

Max couldn't imagine it.

He stole a glance at Allegra. She looked as if she had forgotten it already, he thought with resentment. *She* wasn't flailing off balance. There was a faint flush along her cheekbones, but otherwise she seemed perfectly composed as she chatted to Karen.

'What are you going to do with yourself in Shofrar, Allegra?' Karen asked. 'If Max is anything like Bob, he'll be at work all day. You really need a career that can travel with you.'

Allegra opened her mouth but Max got in first. 'Allegra's an illustrator,' he said. 'She's going to write and illustrate children's books.'

'Really?' Karen was fascinated but Allegra was already shaking her head.

'Oh, well, I'm not sure I'm good enough,' she began.

'She's brilliant,' Max told Karen, ignoring Allegra's kick under the table. 'She just doesn't know it.'

It was true, he thought. She would be so much happier illustrating rather than running around meeting the crazy deadlines at *Glitz*, but she wouldn't change because for some reason Flick had a bee in her bonnet about Allegra's drawing. She was always putting it down, so of course Allegra thought it wasn't good enough, but Max was convinced her illustrations had something special about them.

Karen made Allegra tell her all about the book she was going to write and, in spite of the vengeful looks Allegra was sending his way, Max noticed that she had plenty of ideas. She might say that she was dedicated to journalism but she had obviously thought about the stories starring the infamous Derek the Dog. Max wished she would write the book and forget about Flick's opinion for once. Perhaps she never would in real life, but at least she could pretend to have the perfect career for this evening.

Because this evening was all they had. After tonight, the pretence was over. He had better not forget that.

Beside Max, Allegra was wishing Karen wouldn't ask quite so many interested questions about a book she had no intention of writing. They were just silly little stories she had made up, not even a real book, but Karen certainly seemed thrilled by the idea and claimed her grandchildren would love Derek the Dog. If she wasn't careful she would find herself writing the pesky thing, Allegra thought with an inner sigh. She could just imagine what Flick would think of *that*!

Perhaps she could use a pseudonym?

Aware of a flicker of excitement at the thought, Allegra pushed it firmly out of sight. She had enough going on in her head right now, what with thinking about a non-existent book and trying *not* to think about the way Max had kissed her.

And especially not about the way she had kissed him back.

There was a disquieting prickle still at the nape of her neck where his hand had rested. Her lips felt tender, as if his had seared hers, and she kept running the tip of her tongue over them, as surreptitiously as she could, checking that they hadn't swollen.

The jolt of sensation when their mouths met had shaken her. Kissing Max wasn't supposed to feel like that. It was supposed to be a meaningless peck of the lips, the kind of kiss she gave out every day to her colleagues at *Glitz*.

It was hard to tell what Max thought about it. For one breathless moment afterwards they had stared at each other, but then his eyes had shuttered and now he was immersed in a technical discussion with Bob. He was talking about *concrete*. It wasn't fair. He shouldn't be able to kiss her and then calmly carry on discussing road building!

Karen and Bob were entertaining company and the meal was delicious, but Allegra couldn't enjoy it. She was too aware of Max, who was his usual taciturn self, and who, having kissed her and dropped her in it with Karen, had proceeded to ignore her for the rest of the evening.

It wasn't good enough, Allegra thought crossly, tapping her Jimmy Choos under the table. She had done everything he'd asked of her. She'd been charming, but Max hadn't even *tried*. If it wasn't for her, he wouldn't even *have* his rotten job, Allegra decided, but now he'd got what he wanted he had obviously decided he didn't need to bother with her any more.

Her smile was brittle by the time they said goodbye to Bob and Karen outside the restaurant. The Laskovskis were walking back to their hotel and, after one glance at Allegra's shoes, Max didn't even bother to suggest the Tube. Instead he put his fingers in his mouth and whistled at a passing taxi. If it had been Allegra, the taxi would have sailed on past in the other direction and she didn't know whether to be relieved or put-out that it responded instantly to Max's whistle, turning across the traffic and drawing up exactly in front of them.

Her feet were definitely relieved.

Haughtily, she got in and made a big performance of putting on her seat belt. Max told the taxi driver the address and settled beside her, apparently unperturbed by the taut silence. Allegra folded her lips together. *She* wasn't going to break it. She had made enough small talk for one night, thank you very much! She turned her head away and looked pointedly out of the window, but she was so aware of him sitting just a matter of inches away across the seat that she might as well have turned and stared right at him.

It wasn't even as if he was doing anything. He was just sitting still, his face in shadow, his eyes fixed on the ticking taxi meter. He could at least jiggle his leg or do something annoying so that she had an excuse to snap at him

As it was, she was just getting crosser and crosser, and more and more frustrated.

Why, why, why had he had to kiss her like that? It had been all right up to then. The pretence had been fun and she had been able to dismiss her bizarre awareness of him as a temporary aberration, a passing symptom of sexual frustration. Nothing that meant anything, anyway. She'd been able to think of him as just Max.

He'd spoiled everything by kissing her. It had been so perfect, as if her whole life had just been about getting her to that place, that moment, where everything else had fallen away and there had just been her and Max and a longing for it never to end gusting through her.

How could she think of him as just Max now?

She wished he'd never kissed her.

She wished he'd kiss her again.

The realisation of just how much she wanted it made Allegra suck in her breath. This was mad. She was furious with Max. She couldn't want to kiss him at the same time. She couldn't want him to reach across and pull her towards him, couldn't want his hands on her, his mouth on her, not when he'd ignored her all night and clearly had no interest in kissing *her* again.

But she did.

The silence lengthened, stretched agonizingly. Just when Allegra opened her mouth to break it, unable to bear it any longer, Max let out a sigh.

'I'm sorry,' he said simply.

At least it gave her the excuse to turn and look at him. 'Sorry?' she echoed, unable to stop the pent-up frustration from tumbling out. 'I should think so! Do you have any idea how hard I worked all evening to suck up to the Laskovskis? I got you your bloody job all by myself!'

'I know,' Max began, but Allegra wasn't stopping now that she had started.

'You hardly said a word all evening—oh, except to embarrass me by telling Karen I was going to write a book! What did you do that for?'

'I think you should write one. I think it would be brilliant.'

Allegra wasn't going to be mollified. 'It would not be! It would be stupid! I had to sit there and pretend that I was all excited about it and now Karen's expecting me to send her a copy when it's published! It's not funny,' she added furiously, spotting the ghost of a smile hovering around Max's mouth. 'I felt an absolute fool. As if it wasn't bad enough pretending to be in love with you!'

'You did it really well,' said Max. 'You were brilliant at that too, and you're right, you got me the job. Thank you,' he said quietly. 'Really, Allegra: thank you.'

Perversely, his gratitude just made her feel worse. She hunched a shoulder. 'I only did it so that you'd do the article.' She sounded petulant, but that was how she felt.

'I know.'

'But you could have helped,' she grumbled. 'You were useless! I can't believe the Laskovskis were taken in. A real fiancé would have looked at me, maybe smiled occasionally, taken every opportunity to get close to me, but not you! It was like you couldn't bear to touch me.'

'That's not true,' said Max tautly. 'I kissed you.'

As if she could have forgotten!

'Only when I threw myself into your arms! *Pretending* to be a loving fiancée, thrilled for her future husband's promotion,' Allegra added quickly, just in case he had misinterpreted her instinctive reaction. She had been so pleased for him too, she remembered bitterly. 'Although I don't know why I bothered. You gave the impression you'd rather have been picking up slugs!'

'What?' Max sounded so staggered that Allegra wondered if she might have exaggerated a little, but she had gone too far to back down now. Besides, she had been bottling it up all evening and it was good to get it off her chest.

'I might as well have been a pillar of your precious concrete for all the notice you took of me all evening!'

Max uttered a strangled laugh and dragged a hand through his hair. 'It wasn't like that,' he began.

'Then why did you ignore me?'

'Because I didn't trust myself, all right?' he shouted, goaded at last. 'Because if I hadn't ignored you, I wouldn't have been able to keep my hands off you! I'd have kissed you again and again and I wouldn't have been able to stop. I'd have dragged you down under the table and ripped that bloody dress off you so I could kiss you all over your body and to hell with my boss sitting there with his wife and the rest of the restaurant...'

He broke off. His chest was heaving and he looked wild-eyed as he glared at Allegra. 'So now you know. There, are you satisfied now?'

'But...but...' It was Allegra's turn to gape.

'Of course I wanted to touch you!' Max said furiously. 'I've wanted it ever since you opened the bathroom door. I haven't been able to think about anything else all evening. I had to sit there, trying to talk to my boss, when all I could think about was how easy it would be to slide my hand under your dress, about how it would feel to unzip it, all the time knowing it would never happen! And you wanted me to do chit-chat as well?'

He was glowering at her as if he hated her, but a treacherous warmth was stealing along Allegra's veins, dissolving her own anger into something far more dangerous,

while the spikiness in the atmosphere evaporated into quite
a different kind of tension.

He wanted her.

Desire twisted sharp and sure in her belly. His hair was
standing on end where he had raked his hand through it
and he looked cross, rumpled, *gorgeous*. When had he become so…so…so *hot*? Why hadn't she noticed?

Allegra's heart thudded in her throat and her mouth
dried with a mixture of anticipation and apprehension. She
had been sent once to try bungee jumping for an article and
she had felt just like this when she'd stood on the edge of
the bridge: terrified, thrilled, longing to be brave enough
to jump but afraid that she would never have the courage.

She had done it, though. She could do this too, if she
really wanted to. Allegra moistened her lips.

Max wanted her.

She wanted him.

Allegra's mind was still busy calculating the risk when
her mouth opened and she heard herself say, 'How do you
know?'

Thrown, Max stared at her. 'How do I know what?'

'That it would never happen.' Allegra watched, appalled, as her body took over, shifting towards him, reaching out for his hand, setting it on her knee, all without a
single instruction from her brain.

What was she *doing*? she thought in panic, but her
hands seemed to have acquired a will of their own. *Stop
it*, she told herself frantically, but the message wasn't getting through, and now her legs were getting in on the act,
quaking with pleasure at the warm weight of his hand.

Max swallowed. 'I'm not sure this is a good idea, Legs,'
he said in a constricted voice, but he didn't seem to have
any better control over his hands than she did. His fingers
were curling over her knee, pressing through her sheer

tights into the soft skin of her inner thigh, and she couldn't prevent the shudder of response clenching at the base of her spine.

'I'm not sure either,' she admitted with difficulty. She willed her knees to press together and squeeze out his hand but they wouldn't cooperate.

'It could be that we're just getting carried away by the pretence,' Max said but he didn't lift his hand. Instead his knuckles nudged aside the hem of her dress so that he could stroke higher inside her thigh.

Allegra felt lust crawling deeper, digging in. It would take over completely if she didn't regain control, but his skimming fingers were searing such delicious patterns on her skin she couldn't think clearly.

'Bound to be that,' she agreed breathlessly. 'And the whole article thing. It's getting a bit out of hand. We're spending too much time together.'

'Yep,' said Max, as his fingers played on the inside of her thigh, higher, higher, higher, until Allegra squirmed in her seat. 'We should stop right now.'

'We should,' she managed.

'Unless…'

'Yes?' Her breathing was too choppy to get anything else out.

'Unless we get it out of our system,' Max suggested. Had his voice always been that deep, that darkly delicious? Just one night, and then we can forget all about it. What do you think?'

Think? How could she be expected to think when his fingers were stroking so exquisitely that she couldn't breathe properly and she was giddy with the dark pleasure of it? Oh, God, if his hand went any higher, she would come apart.

If it didn't, she would explode. Either way, they would end up with a horrible mess all over the taxi seat.

Struggling to stop herself pressing down into his hand, she scrabbled for some words to put together. 'I think… that's…a good idea…' she gasped and Max smiled, a wicked smile she hadn't known he possessed.

When he withdrew his hand, Allegra almost moaned in protest before she realised that the taxi had stopped in front of the house. Max paid the driver while she made it waveringly to the front door on legs that felt boneless.

She was still fumbling with the keys as Max came up behind her. Wordlessly, he took them from her and opened the door.

'After you,' he said, but there was a telltale hitch in his voice that made Allegra feel obscurely better. So it wasn't just her having trouble breathing.

She didn't want to put on the hall light, so she waited, trembling with anticipation, in the dark until Max had closed the door behind them. A muted orange glow from the street lights outside filtered through the glass pane above the door. It was enough to see him turn, see the gleam of his smile as he moved towards her, and then his hands were on her and at last—at last!—his mouth came down on hers, angling desperate and demanding.

This time there was none of the piercing sweetness she had felt in the restaurant. Instead his kiss was hot and fierce, and Allegra felt need explode inside her, vaporising the last lingering remnants of rational thought. Her mind went dark and she kissed him back, wild with hunger, wanting his hands on her harder, hotter, *harder*.

No, there was no sweetness now. It felt like more of a struggle as to who needed most, who could give most, who could take most. Allegra scrabbled for his tie, at the buttons on his shirt, while his hands pushed up her dress urgently and his mouth blazed a trail to her breast. The hunger rocketed through her, so powerful it thrilled and terrified her in equal measure, and when they broke apart the narrow hallway echoed with the rasp of their ragged breaths.

Chest heaving, Max pressed their palms together and lifted their arms slowly above her head so that he could pin her against the wall.

'We're going to regret this,' he said, even as he bent his head to kiss her throat, making every cell in her body jolt, turning her insides molten.

'I know.'

'It's crazy.' His lips drifted downward in a searing trail over her skin that left her breathing in tatters.

'You're right,' she managed, sucking in a gasp as he explored the sensitive curve of her neck and shoulder and arching into the wicked pleasure of his mouth.

When he released her wrists to jerk her closer, she whimpered with relief. Now she could tug his shirt free so that she could slide her palms over his firm, smooth back, letting herself notice how his muscles flexed beneath her touch. He was gloriously solid, wonderfully warm. She wanted to burrow into him, lose herself in him.

'It'll just spoil things,' she said unevenly, holding onto the track of the conversation with difficulty.

'It will. It'll never be the same again,' said Max, his voice low and ragged. 'I'm never going to be able to forget how you taste,' he warned her. 'I'll never forget how you feel, how soft you are.'

'So…we should stop,' she tried, even as she pressed him closer, revelling in the feel of how hard he was, how strong, how male. Her blood was thumping and thudding and throbbing with urgency and she wanted him so much that she couldn't think about anything else.

'We probably should,' said Max, his hands sliding

under her dress, his mouth hot on her skin. 'But there's a problem.'

Allegra shuddered under his touch. 'A...a problem?'

'Yes.' He lifted his head and brought his hands up to frame her face. 'The problem is, I don't want to stop, do you?'

She ought to say yes. She ought to put a stop to this right now. Max was right. They would regret this in the morning. But how could she say stop when her body was arching towards his and her skin yearned for his touch and her blood was running wild and wanting him blotted out everything else?

Her arms wrapped round his neck and she pulled him closer for a deep, wet kiss. 'No,' she murmured against his lips, 'I don't want to stop.'

# CHAPTER EIGHT

ALLEGRA SURFACED SLOWLY to an awareness of an unfamiliar weight lying across her waist. She blinked at a bedside table. Not hers. The arm thrown over her wasn't hers either. A warm male body was pressed against her back, a face buried in her hair. Steady breath stirred the air against her shoulder and she quivered as memory came whooshing back.

Max. Omigod, she had slept with Max!

*Now* what was she going to do?

Allegra lay very still. Max was sound asleep and she didn't want to wake him until she had worked out how she was going to react.

Could she pretend that she'd had too much to drink? But she had known exactly what she was doing, and Max knew it.

Okay, so she'd be casual. *Thank goodness we've got that out of our system, now we can move on*: that kind of thing.

Only being casual wasn't going to be easy when she'd just had the best sex of her life. Her body was still buzzing pleasantly in the aftermath, and she flushed at the memory of the careening excitement, the heart-shaking pleasure that had left her languid and replete at last.

It would be so much easier if the sex had been disappointing, or even average. If Max had been a pedestrian lover, as conventional and dull as his suits. Instead...Allegra's blood tingled, remembering the shattering sureness of his hands, of his mouth...oh, God, *his mouth*... In spite of herself, her lips curved. Who would have thought that the crisp and efficient engineer was capable of *that*?

How much more passion had Emma wanted?

Allegra wished she hadn't thought about Emma. She'd been on the verge of turning over and waking Max, but now she'd remembered reality. Last night hadn't changed anything. Max would be going to Shofrar soon, and if he took anyone with him it wouldn't be his sister's frivolous, fashionable friend.

And Libby! That was another complication. How would she feel if she knew Allegra had slept with her brother? But Allegra couldn't keep a secret from her best friend. Allegra gnawed her bottom lip. She wished she could rewind the hours and go back to the night, to the darkness where nothing had mattered but touch and feel and taste, the glorious slide of flesh against flesh, the spiralling excitement, the splintering joy.

What time was it anyway? Very cautiously, Allegra reached towards the phone on the bedside table. Sensing her movement in his sleep, Max mumbled a protest and tightened his arm about her, pulling her back against his hard body. It felt so good that Allegra's heart contracted, but she made herself wriggle free and grope once more for the phone.

Her fingers closed round it and she peered at the screen: 08:45. Holy smoke!

'Max!' She sat bolt upright in bed. 'Max, wake up! It's nearly nine o'clock!'

'Wha...?' Max struggled up, scowling at the abrupt awakening. His eyes were screwed up, his hair ruffled. Allegra wanted to take his face between her hands and kiss the grouchiness away. She wanted to push him down into the pillows and lose herself in his touch.

Instead she leapt out of bed, out of temptation. 'I'm going to be late!' she said, scrabbling frantically for her clothes. She found a bra, a pair of tights… What the hell had happened to her dress?

'Wait…' The sleep was clearing from Max's face and his expression changed as he watched Allegra pounce on the dress that lay in a puddle on the floor, where it had fallen last night. He had a vivid memory of unzipping it slowly, of listening to the enticing rustle as it slithered down over Allegra's hips, of catching his breath at the sight of her in a black push-up bra and lacy thong.

'Allegra, wait,' he said again as memory after memory of the night before flashed through his mind like an erotic slide show.

She turned, tousle-haired, wide-eyed, clutching her pile of clothes to her chest, forgetting that it was a little late for modesty. 'Didn't you hear what I said? It's nearly nine!'

'Nearly *nine*?' This time it got through. He scrambled out of bed, stark naked. 'Shit! I was supposed to be at work half an hour ago!'

'You can have the shower first,' she said. 'You're quicker than me.'

Max hesitated, dragged a hand through his hair. He was *never* late for work, but he couldn't leave it like that. He might not have thought ahead last night, but he knew the morning wasn't supposed to be like this, and he found himself saying the words he never thought he would hear coming out of his mouth: 'We need to talk.'

'I know,' said Allegra, not quite meeting his eyes, 'but later.'

Perhaps later was better, Max told himself as he showered and shaved as quickly as he could, which was pretty

damn quickly. By the evening he might have had a chance
to get a grip of himself. It would have been too hard to
talk with Allegra's scent still clogging his brain, with his
heart still thundering with the memory of her sweetness,
her warmth, her wicked, irresistible smile. She had turned
him upside down, inside out.

She had turned him wild.

Max shrugged on his shirt, knotted his tie, dressed
himself in his civilised suit, but underneath he still felt
stripped bare. He'd been unprepared for the wildness of
his need for her, for the way the feel of her set something
free inside him.

So free that he'd lost his mind, lost himself. Max set
his jaw, remembering the foolishness he'd spouted, the
incoherent words that had tumbled out of him as they'd
moved together, up and up through swirling darkness towards the shattering light. He hadn't known what he was
saying, but now the words were out, how the hell was he
going to put them back?

He was at the round table, filling out a visa form for Shofrar, when Allegra got home that night. The moment he
heard the key in the door, every cell in his body seemed to
leap in anticipation, but he had his expression well under
control by the time she appeared in the doorway.

There was a pause, then Allegra said, 'Hi.'

'You're back late.' Max hated the accusing note in his
own voice. Anyone would think that he was keeping track
of her, that he'd been sitting here, just waiting for her to
come home.

'I've been to the launch of a new jewellery collection.'
Allegra hesitated, then came into the room. She was wearing skinny leopard-print jeans, a tight T-shirt and a leather
jacket, with chunky earrings and shiny boots. Her hair was

pulled back in one of those messy twists that Max disliked. She looked funky, hip, a million miles from the elegant woman who'd taken his arm last night.

From the woman who'd short-circuited every single one of his fuses last night.

She unzipped her jacket and dropped her bag on the sofa. 'What are you doing?' she asked, perching on the arm so that she could take off her boots.

'A visa application for Shofrar,' said Max.

Allegra glanced up from her right boot. 'Already?'

'I saw Bob Laskovski again today. One of the project managers out there has been in a car accident. He's okay, I think, but they're bringing him back to hospital here. Bob wanted to know if I could go out earlier.'

She stilled. 'How much earlier?'

'The end of next week.'

'Oh.'

'Bob was asking about wedding dates,' said Max, relieved to hear that he sounded so normal. 'He was anxious to reassure me that I could come back in a month or so to sort stuff out, and that you could join me whenever you're ready.'

'I see,' said Allegra. She bent her head and went back to fiddling with her boot. 'Well…that's good. You must be pleased.'

'Yes,' said Max. He should be delighted. This was exactly what he had wanted, after all. So why didn't he *feel* pleased?

He wished Allegra would look up. He wished she didn't look so trendy. He wished they hadn't started on this awful stilted conversation when they should be talking about the night before. 'What about your article? Can we fit in the last tests by next week?'

She pursed her lips, considering, apparently unbothered

by the fact that he would be leaving so soon. 'I've arranged with Darcy that you'll go with her to the opening of the new Digby Fox exhibition on Tuesday evening,' she said.

'Who's Digby Fox?' he said, disgruntled.

'Only the hottest ticket in the art world at the moment. He's a really controversial artist but anyone who's anyone will be there to look at his new installations.'

'And Darcy wants to go to this?' Max couldn't hide his scepticism.

'She wants to change her image and be taken more seriously. And Digby Fox is really interesting,' she told him. 'But that would be your last challenge. The costume ball isn't for another month, you'll be gutted to hear, so you'll miss that.'

'What, no waltzing after all?'

'No.' Allegra's smile was a little painful.

'I'm sorry,' said Max.

'No you're not,' she said, sounding much more herself. 'You told me you'd rather stick pins in your eyes than waltz.'

'I'm sorry to let you down,' he clarified. 'I promised I'd do it.'

'It can't be helped. If you can make it to the Digby Fox preview I'll have enough material,' she said. 'It's a shame about the ball, but maybe I'll ask William if he'd go with Darcy. I'm sure he knows how to waltz.'

William? Max bristled at her careless assumption that he could be so easily replaced. The last thing he'd wanted to do was make a fool of himself at some stupid ball, but still…

Allegra was being exasperatingly reasonable. Why couldn't she go all dramatic and start weeping and wailing about the tragedy of her unfinished article? Max would feel so much better if she did. All this politeness was getting to him. They needed to stop this and talk about the night before.

'Look, Legs,' he began but, before he could finish, his phone started to ring. Max cursed.

'Aren't you going to get that?'

'It can go to voicemail.'

'It might be important.'

Muttering under his breath, he snatched up the phone and looked at the screen in disbelief.

'Who is it?' asked Allegra.

'It's Emma,' he said slowly.

Allegra got up, dropping her left boot on the floor. 'You should talk to her,' she said. 'I'm going to get changed anyway.'

She left her boots lying as they were, and Max watched, churning with frustration, as she walked out barefoot. The boots looked as abandoned and forlorn as he felt, and Max bent to put them neatly side by side as he pressed the answer button on his phone.

'Hello?' he said.

In her room, Allegra leant back against the door and drew a deep breath. That had gone better than she'd feared. She'd been calm, cool. She hadn't cried. She hadn't thrown herself into his arms and begged him not to go, although it had been a close run thing when he'd told her that he was going to Shofrar next week.

*Next week.*

It was all for the best, Allegra told herself. Let's face it, last night had been a one-off. It had been incredible, amazingly so, but they were still the same people as they'd been before, who had different lives and wanted different things. Of course it was tempting to imagine that they could recreate the previous night, but really, what would

be the point? It would just make it harder to say goodbye
in a week's time.

Emma had rung at just the right time. She was what
Max really needed. Allegra hoped that she was telling
Max that she had made a terrible mistake and wanted to
go back to him. She really did.

A nasty headache was jabbing right behind her eyes
and her throat felt tight. Allegra pulled the clip from her
hair and changed her tight jeans for a pair of pyjama bottoms patterned with faded puppies, sighing at the comfort.
Wrapping a soft grey cardigan around her, she padded back
down to the kitchen and poured herself a bowl of cereal.
She was tempted to eat it there but it felt like avoiding
Max, and that would make it seem as if last night was a
big deal, which it wasn't at all. Besides, she hadn't heard
his voice when she passed the sitting room door, so presumably he'd finished talking to Emma.

Sure enough, when she carried her bowl back to the living room Max was sitting at the table once more, but he
wasn't filling in his form. He was staring ahead, turning
his pen abstractedly between his fingers. He looked tired,
and a dangerous rush of emotion gusted through Allegra.

What would it be like if she could go over and massage
his shoulders? Would he jerk away in horror, or would he
let his head drop back against her breasts? Would he let
her slide her arms down to his chest so that she could press
her lips to his jaw and kiss his throat the way she had done
the night before?

Allegra's chest was so tight that for a moment she
couldn't move. She could just stand in the doorway in her
old pyjama bottoms and the sleeves of her cardigan falling
over her hands, and when Max glanced up and their eyes

met the jolt in the air was so unexpected that she jerked, slopping the milk in the bowl of cereal she held.

'Allegra…' After that one frozen moment, Max pushed back his chair abruptly and got to his feet, only to stop as if he had forgotten what he was going to say.

'How was Emma?' Allegra rushed to fill the silence. She slouched over to the sofa and stretched out on it to eat her cereal, deliberately casual.

Max hesitated. 'She wants to meet.'

'Hey, that's great news!'

'Is it?'

'Of course it is.' Allegra kept beaming, which was quite hard when you were trying to eat cereal at the same time. 'Come on, Max, you want her back. You know you do.'

'If I wanted her that much, I wouldn't have slept with you last night,' he said.

'That didn't mean anything. We both agreed that.' Deliberately she finished her cereal, scraping around the bowl, not looking at Max. Just another slobby evening, nothing on her mind.

'We knew what were doing,' she persevered when Max said nothing. 'It was meant to be a bit of fun, wasn't it?— and it *was*, but it's not as if either of us want a relationship. We know each other too well for that. We'd drive each other mad!'

Allegra had been practising this speech all day, but Max didn't seem impressed. He came over to the sofa, took the bowl from her unresisting hand and set it on the table. Then he nudged her legs so that she lifted them for him to sit down.

Just the way she had nudged his that night she had looked at him and decided that he was perfect for her article. Allegra almost winced at the jab of memory as she settled her legs across his lap. She had thought she had known Max then, but she hadn't had a clue. She'd known nothing about the clean male scent of his skin or the enticing scrape of his jaw. Nothing about the lean, lovely strength of his body or the dark, delicious pleasure of his hands. Nothing about how it felt when his mouth curved against her flesh.

Max studied the puppies on her pyjama bottoms a moment then lifted his eyes to hers. 'What if I *did* want a relationship, Legs?' he said, and the last of Allegra's breath leaked out of her lungs.

'You're...not serious?' she managed.

'Why not?'

'Because it's crazy. You said it yourself last night. Madness, you said. We'll regret it in the morning, you said.'

'I know I did,' he said evenly. 'But the thing is, I didn't regret it. I still don't.'

'Max...'

'Do you regret it?' he asked her and Allegra couldn't look away, couldn't lie.

'No. No, I don't.'

He stroked one of her bare feet thoughtfully, making her suck in a sharp breath. 'Then why don't we try it again? We might not regret that either.'

His hand was warm and firm and she could have sworn she felt his touch in every molecule. Unable to prevent a quiver of response, she made herself pull the foot away and draw up her legs.

'It was just sex,' she said, keeping her voice steady with an effort. 'It was great, don't get me wrong, but I don't think we should read more into it than that.'

'Okay,' said Max. 'So why don't we have great sex until I leave?'

'Because…' Couldn't he *see*? 'Because it's too hard to stop great sex becoming something else, and then where would we be?'

'In a relationship?'

'And what would be the point of that? You're going to Shofrar next week?'

'No, you're right,' Max said. 'What was I thinking?'

'I know what you were thinking *with*,' said Allegra in an effort to lighten the conversation, and a smile tugged at the corner of his mouth.

'Maybe,' he said.

'It *was* lovely,' she said, unable to keep the wistful note from creeping into her voice, 'but I can't see me in the desert, can you?'

'No,' he said slowly. 'No, I can't.'

'You need someone like Emma,' Allegra ploughed on, struggling to remember the script she had prepared. 'Someone who can really be part of your life.' Someone not like me, she added bleakly to herself. 'I'm sure that when you meet her again you'll remember just how important she was to you before. It's only a couple of months since you wanted to marry her,' she reminded him. 'You need to think about what really matters to you and let's go back to being friends.'

'And last night?'

No wonder she hadn't spent any time being sensible before. Being sensible hurt. But it didn't hurt as much as falling in love with him would hurt, or the inevitable moment when Max would realise that sex wasn't enough, that *she* wasn't enough.

Just like she hadn't been enough to keep her unknown father around.

Like she was never quite enough to please her mother.

Allegra drew a breath and summoned a smile. 'Last night wasn't real,' she said. 'It was lovely, but I think it would be easier if we pretended that it never happened.'

*Pretend it never happened.* Easy for *her* to say! Max yanked his tie savagely into place. Bloody Dickie had picked out another humdinger for him to wear to the preview of Digby Fox's exhibition: a fluorescent green shirt with a red tie, and a tweed jacket in hunter green.

'It's bold, it's assertive, it's *you*,' Dickie had assured him when Max had refused absolutely to consider any of it. 'Just try it,' he had coaxed and in the end, Max had given in for a quiet life. It was the last time he'd have to make a fool of himself, after all.

Dickie had been on the verge of tears when he'd heard that Max wouldn't be going to the costume ball after all.

'I had *such* a marvellous outfit in mind for you too,' he'd mourned.

Another reason to be grateful that he was going to Shofrar early, Max decided as he dressed grimly.

Allegra had cancelled their dancing lessons, which meant that he never needed to waltz again. And what a relief *that* was! He wasn't missing those lessons at all. If he had found himself remembering the times he and Allegra had practised twirling around the room, it was only because he felt bad at letting her down. He knew how much she had been looking forward to the ball.

Now she would be going with William.

Not that he cared that Allegra had been able to replace him so easily, Max reassured himself hastily. He was well out of it.

He regarded his reflection glumly. He looked a total prat. The neon-green shirt made him look as if he should be directing traffic. At least Dickie had had to accept his refusal to grow a designer stubble. Max rubbed a hand over his freshly shaven jaw. The truth was, he'd nearly given way on that too when he'd realised how disappointed Dickie was that Max wouldn't be able to take him to a rugby match the way he'd promised.

He seemed to be letting everyone down at the moment.

With a sigh, he picked up the jacket Dickie had assured him was the last word in style and headed for the door. He was to meet Allegra and Darcy at the gallery. Max couldn't say that he was looking forward to the evening ahead, but he'd done his homework. Allegra had pressed a book on modern art into his hands so that he would impress Darcy with his knowledge but, having ploughed through it, he was none the wiser. He would just have to wing it, he decided. He could look thoughtful and mumble something about challenging perceptions and that would have to do.

And, after tonight, his obligations would be over. He could concentrate on handing over his projects at work and pack up the few belongings he'd brought with him when he'd moved out of Emma's. Everything was already stored in the attic in his parents' house. Max had been home to say goodbye to his parents that weekend so that he didn't get in Allegra's way, but it hadn't been as restful as he'd hoped. His mother had an uncanny ability to home in on the things Max least wanted to talk about and she kept asking how Allegra was and how they were getting on sharing the house. Max tried an austere 'fine' in reply, but oh, no, that wasn't enough.

'What aren't you telling me?' she'd demanded.

She didn't seem to understand that there were some things you couldn't tell your mother.

He couldn't tell her about the way his breath clogged every time he looked at Allegra. He couldn't tell her about the memories that circled obsessively in his head, memories of the hot, sweet darkness, of the pleasure that had leapt like wildfire, consuming everything in its path. He couldn't tell her how the feel of Allegra had blotted everything else from his mind.

'Allegra is fine,' he'd insisted to his mother.

Allegra certainly seemed fine. She was doing a lot better than he was, anyway.

She'd been bright and brittle ever since she'd sat on the sofa looking soft and oh-so-touchable in those silly pyjamas. Max's hands had itched to slide beneath the faded material, to peel that baggy cardigan from her shoulders and lay her down beneath him once more, but the moment he'd succumbed to temptation and stroked her foot, she had pulled away.

*Last night wasn't real*, she'd said. *Let's pretend it never happened.*

Max hadn't tried to change her mind. Allegra had made it clear that she didn't want him to touch her again, and he wasn't about to start forcing himself on a woman. She might have dressed it all up as wanting him to be happy, but Max wasn't a fool. What she meant was that she wouldn't be happy with him.

And, anyway, she was right. It was all for the best. He *couldn't* imagine Allegra in Shofrar. She wanted to stay in London, in the gossipy, glamorous world that was *Glitz*. What could he offer compared to that? A prefabricated house on a compound in the desert. Big deal.

So Max was doing his best to behave normally. He wasn't going to follow her around making puppy dog eyes. A man had his pride, after all. He met Emma for lunch and thought about what Allegra had said about Emma being what he needed. It seemed hard to remember now, but Max was prepared to try and Emma herself was dropping hints about the possibility of getting back together. Max told

Allegra that he and Emma were 'talking' and she seemed delighted, he remembered sourly.

At least he'd made someone happy.

His mood was not improved when he made it to the gallery and found Allegra already there with Darcy and a smarmy-looking man who Allegra introduced as William.

Max disliked him on sight. William had the lean, well-bred air of a greyhound. He had floppy hair and tortoise-shell glasses, which Max privately decided were fake and designed purely to make him look intelligent. And God, the man could talk! Darcy hung on his every word as William pontificated. He had an opinion on everything, as far as Max could make out. Max would have liked him a lot better if he'd taken one look at the pile of pooh on display and admitted that he didn't have a clue what it was all about.

Every surface in the gallery was painted white which was disorientating. Max was glad he didn't suffer from seasickness or he'd have been desperate for a horizon. Not that anyone else seemed to notice how weird the décor was. The gallery was jam-packed with trendy types clutching glasses of champagne. They were all talking at the tops of their voices and vying for the accolade of most preten-tious comment of the evening. Clearly it was going to be a stiff competition.

Max himself was profoundly unimpressed by the so-called 'art' on display. As far as he could see, the 'artist' had run around gathering together as much junk as he could find, thrown it into piles and called it an installa-tion. There was more art in a beautifully designed bridge than this claptrap, in Max's humble opinion.

William disagreed. He appointed himself guide and in-sisted on explaining every exhibit. Phrases like 'implicit sexual innuendo', 'aesthetic encounter' and 'anthropomor-phic narratives' fell from his lips, while Darcy hung on every word. Allegra seemed distracted, though, and Max couldn't help wondering if she was jealous of the way William was so obviously basking in Darcy's attention.

That evening she was wearing a floaty skirt, clumpy boots and short tweedy jacket. Max wanted to think that she looked a mess, but somehow she looked as if she belonged there in a way he never would, neon shirt or no neon shirt. She had plenty of her old pizazz about her, but there was a tight look around her eyes and her smile wasn't as bright as usual.

'You okay?' he asked her as William steered Darcy on to the next exhibit.

'Yes. Why?'

'I don't know. You look a bit…tired.'

Great. Everyone knew that looking 'tired' meant you looked a wreck. The chatter bouncing off the white walls was making Allegra's head ache. She felt like a wreck too.

Usually she loved these gossipy, trendy affairs, but there were too many people crammed into the gallery and it felt claustrophobic in spite of the attempts to make the design feel airy and spacious. She had to squeeze her way through the throng. Digby Fox could pull in some A-list names. So far she had muttered 'sorry…excuse me…' to minor royalty, a prize-winning author and a celebrity chef. Ordinarily, Allegra would have been thrilled, but the only person she had eyes for was Max, who was looking resolutely out of place.

How on earth had Dickie persuaded him into that shirt? It was so loud it wasn't doing anything for her headache.

Allegra had had a tiring day listening to Dickie moaning about how much he was going to miss Max. Max had shown him how to order a pint in the pub; Max had introduced him to takeaway curry; Max had promised to take him to a rugby match. He seemed to hold her personally responsible for Max's promotion.

*Max made love to* me! Allegra had wanted to shout. *I'm going to miss him much, much more than you.*

She didn't, of course. Dickie was still Dickie and her career was all she had to hold onto at the moment.

'You should have said *non*,' Dickie had grumbled in the accent Max swore was put on. 'Non, ze article isn't finished, you cannot go yet.'

If only it had been that easy.

She had tried to convince him that she had enough for an article, but Dickie had been counting on dressing Max for the costume ball. ''e would 'ave looked *magnifique*,' he said forlornly.

Allegra secretly thought that was unlikely. Max would never be handsome. He would never be magnificent. He was quietly austere and understated and ordinary and she wanted him more than anything she had ever wanted in her life.

And, oh, she would have loved to have waltzed with him at the ball!

The last few days had been awful. It was exhausting trying to pretend that everything was fine, reminding herself again and again that she'd done the right thing in turning down the chance to spend this last week with him. She had told Max that she wanted him to be happy, and she *did*. She'd just been unprepared for how much it would hurt when he took her advice and contacted Emma. Max was being a bit cagey about things and Allegra supposed it was none of her business, but she knew that he and Emma had met and that they were 'talking'. If she were Emma she would be moving heaven and earth to get back together with Max.

If she were Emma, she would never have left him in the first place.

Allegra had tried hard. She had thrown herself into work and been to every party she could blag herself into. She'd called William and invited him tonight, hoping that Max would somehow be less appealing in contrast, but instead the contrast had worked in Max's favour, and William was dazzled by Darcy. For all his intellect and ambition, he was clearly just as susceptible to Darcy's gorgeous face and even more gorgeous body as the next man, and Allegra herself might just as well have been invisible for all the notice he took of her.

It was lucky that she wasn't in love with William, Allegra reflected glumly. Nobody wanted her at the moment.

Max had wanted her. For a moment Allegra let herself remember the heat that had burned like wildfire along her veins, the taste of his skin and the wicked, wonderful torment of his mouth. The way the world had swung giddily around, the shattering pleasure. She could have had that again, but she had said no, and now it seemed that he was getting back together with Emma.

Allegra sighed. It made it so much worse when the only person you could blame for your misery was yourself.

# CHAPTER NINE

THINK ABOUT YOUR *career*, Allegra told herself fiercely.
*Think about this amazing article you're going to write
that's going to impress the notoriously unimpressable
Stella and open doors for a career in serious journalism. Think about how pleased Flick is going to be with
you when your analysis of the latest political crisis hits
the headlines.*

But before she could tackle politics and the global economy she had to make a success of *Making Mr Perfect*.

Rousing herself, Allegra poked Max in the ribs as
William headed into the next room of the gallery, Darcy
breathlessly in tow. Caught up in the crowd, Allegra and
Max were trailing behind them.

'You're supposed to be impressing Darcy with your
knowledge of modern art,' she muttered.

'I would if there was any art here,' said Max. 'How does
this guy get away with it?' He studied a plate, encrusted
with dried baked beans, that was set carefully on a table
next to a rusty oil can. Craning his neck, he read the price
on the label and shook his head. 'He's having a laugh!'

'Digby Fox likes to challenge conventional expectations
about art,' Allegra said dutifully, but her heart wasn't in it.

'You can't tell me you actually like this stuff?'

'Not really,' she admitted, lowering her voice as if confessing to something shameful. 'I prefer paintings.'

Ahead of them, William had stopped in front of a collection of torn bin bags that were piled up against the stark gallery wall. 'A searing commentary on modern consumption,' he was saying as Max and Allegra came up.

Allegra was sure she heard Max mutter, 'Tosser.'

'One can't fail to be struck by the nihilistic quality of Digby's representation of quotidian urban life,' William went on while Darcy looked at him with stars in her eyes.

'It's powerful stuff,' she said, her expression solemn. 'It makes you feel *small*, doesn't it?'

William nodded thoughtfully, as if she had said something profound, and turned to Max, evidently deciding it was time to include him in the conversation. 'What do you think, Max?'

Max pretended to contemplate the installation. 'I think it's a load of old rubbish,' he pronounced at last.

William looked disapproving and Darcy disappointed, but a giggle escaped Allegra. Oh dear, sniggering at childish jokes didn't bode well for her future as a journalist with gravitas.

'Yes, well, shall we move on?' said William, taking Darcy's arm to steer her on to the next exhibit.

Max caught Allegra's eye. 'Let's get out of here,' he said. 'This is all such bollocks and we can't even get a decent drink.'

She opened her mouth to insist that they stayed, to point out that she had a job to do, but somehow the words wouldn't come. 'I don't suppose it would matter if we slipped out,' she said instead, looking longingly at the exit. Max was right. What was the point of staying? 'I'd better go and tell Darcy and William, though.'

'You really think they're going to notice that we've gone?'

'Probably not—' she sighed '—but allegedly Darcy's here for the article, and I invited William. I can't just abandon them without a word. I'll go and tell them I've got a headache and see you outside.'

It was amazing how her spirits lightened at the prospect of escaping with Max. By the time Allegra had pushed her way through the crush to William and Darcy, who were at the very back of the gallery by then, and then to the front again, she was hot and bothered and practically fell out of the door to find Max waiting for her.

Outside, a fine London mizzle was falling and Max's hair was already damp, but it was blessedly cool and Allegra fanned herself with the exhibition catalogue. 'That's better,' she said in relief, heading away from the noise of the gallery.

'I was beginning to think you'd changed your mind,' said Max, falling into step beside her.

'No way. I had to fight my way out, though. I can't believe how many people there were in there.'

Max snorted. 'Talk about the emperor's new clothes!'

'It was a bit rubbish,' Allegra allowed.

'Literally,' he said sardonically. 'So, do I gather Darcy wasn't devastated about me leaving her with William?'

'I'm afraid she was delighted. She might have thought you were pretty cute once, but she's forgotten all about you now that she's met William.'

'She wasn't really interested in me anyway,' said Max. 'She was just bored and looking for someone different.'

'Well, William's certainly that. Political aide and lingerie model…it's not an obvious combination, is it? But Darcy thinks William's really clever, and she loves the way he talks to her as if she'll understand what he says.'

A grunt. 'He was showing off, if you ask me.'

'Yes, but can you blame him? Darcy's so beautiful.'

'I can blame him for ignoring *you*,' said Max, scowling. 'I thought you two were going out?'

'Not really. We'd just had a drink a couple of times. It's not as if we'd ever—' Allegra stopped.

*Slept together. Like she and Max had done.*

There was a tiny pause while her unspoken words jangled in the silence. Allegra developed a sudden fascination with the shop window they were passing.

Max cleared his throat. 'Do you mind?' he asked. 'About William?'

'No, not really,' she said with a sigh. 'He's nice, but I don't think he's my kind of guy.'

'Who is?'

*You are.* The words rang so loudly in Allegra's head that for one horrified moment she thought that she had spoken them aloud.

'Oh, you know, the usual: tall, dark, handsome, filthy-rich…' She hoped he realised that she was joking. 'The truth is, I'm still trying to find a man who can match up to my Regency duke.'

'The terrace ravisher?'

'That's the one. I don't know anyone with a fraction of his romance,' she told Max.

'You don't think holding out for an aristocrat who's been dead for a couple of hundred years is going to limit your options a bit?'

'I'm hoping they'll invent a time travel machine soon,' said Allegra. 'In the meantime, I've got my fantasy to keep me warm.'

Max raised his brows. 'Whatever turns you on,' he said and they promptly plunged into another pool of silence.

*He* had turned her on. Allegra's pulse kicked as she remembered that night: the way they had grabbed each other, the frenzy of lust and heat and throbbing need. It hadn't been tender and beautiful. It had been wild and frantic and deliciously dirty. A flush warmed her cheeks, thinking about the things Max had done, the things she had done to him. She had turned him on too.

They had turned each other on.

Desperately trying to shove the memories away, Allegra was glad of Max's silence as they walked. At that time of the evening the back streets of Knightsbridge were quiet, apart from an occasional taxi passing, engine ticking and tyres shushing on the wet tarmac. Allegra was glad she had worn her boots rather than the more glamorous stilettos she'd dithered over. At least her boots were comfortable—well, relatively. She had to be careful not to twist her ankle falling off their substantial platform soles but otherwise they were almost as good as the trainers Max had once suggested she wear to work.

Max. Why did everything come back to him now?

She was agonizingly conscious of him walking beside her. His shoulders were slightly hunched and he had jammed his hands into his trouser pockets. Damp spangled his hair whenever he passed under a street lamp. He seemed distracted and she wondered if he was thinking about Shofrar. This time next week he'd be gone.

Something like panic skittered through Allegra at the thought, and she shivered involuntarily.

'You cold?' Max glanced at her.

'No, not really.'

His brows drew together as he studied her skimpy jacket. 'That's not enough to keep you warm. Didn't you bring a coat?'

'No, I—' But Max was already pulling off his jacket

and dropping it over her shoulders. It was warm from his body and the weight was incredibly reassuring.

'I'm not cold,' he said, 'and, besides, it doesn't matter if this shirt gets ruined. I am never, ever going to wear it again!'

'To be honest, I wouldn't have said it was really you,' said Allegra as she settled the jacket more comfortably around her, and Max smiled faintly.

'Don't tell Dickie that. It'll break his heart.'

She longed to take his arm and lean into his side, but she couldn't do that. Allegra kept her eyes on the pavement instead and clutched the two sides of the jacket together. She needed to show Max that she was fine about him leaving, that she had put that night they had shared behind her, just as she had said she would.

He had been in touch with Emma and it was too late now to tell him that she had changed her mind. It would make things even more awkward if he knew that she thought about him constantly, and that a dull ache throbbed in her chest whenever she thought about saying goodbye.

So she lifted her chin and summoned a bright smile. 'I don't suppose you'll have much need of a fancy wardrobe in Shofrar,' she said, determinedly cheerful.

'Nope. White short-sleeved shirt, shorts, long trousers for business meetings, and that's about it,' said Max. 'I won't ever need to dither over my wardrobe again.'

Allegra's smile twisted painfully. 'A life away from fashion. That'll make you happy.'

'Yes,' said Max, but he didn't sound as sure as he should have done. Of course he would be happy when he was there, he reassured himself. He couldn't wait. No styling sessions. No dancing lessons. No being told to roll up his cuffs, no need to consider what to wear. No messy house.

No Allegra.

The thought was a cold poker, jabbing into his lungs and stopping his breath. It was all for the best, of course it was, Max reminded himself with a shade of desperation. Going out to Shofrar was the next step in his career. It was what he had worked for, what he wanted. He would love it when he was there.

But he was going to miss her, there was no use denying it.

They were making their way slowly towards Sloane Street, along a side street clustered with antique shops and art galleries. Many were open still to cater for the after work crowd, and they had passed more than one gallery having a preview party much like the one they had just come from.

Allegra was absorbed in thought, her gaze on the window displays, which meant Max could watch her profile. Knowing that he could only look at her when she wasn't looking at him now made his chest tighten. When had she become so beautiful to him? Max's eyes rested hungrily on the curve of her cheek, on the clean line of her jaw and the lovely sweep of her throat. With her face averted he couldn't see her mouth, but he knew exactly how luscious it was, how her lips tipped upright at the corners and curved into a smile that lit her entire face.

God, he was going to miss her.

'Oh…' Unaware of his gaze, Allegra had stopped short, her attention caught by a single painting displayed in a gallery window.

The painting was quite small and very simple. It showed a woman holding a bowl, that was all, but something about the colours and the shapes made the picture leap into life. Compared to this, Digby Fox's installations seemed even more tawdry. This quiet painting was clearly special even though Max didn't have the words to explain how or why that should be so.

Holding the jacket together, Allegra was leaning forward to read the label. 'I thought so,' she said. 'It's a Jago Forrest. I've always loved his paintings.'

Max came closer to read the label over her shoulder. At least, he meant to read it, but he was too distracted by Allegra's perfume to focus. 'I've never heard of Jago Forrest,' he said.

'I don't think many people have. My art teacher at school was a fan, or I wouldn't have known about him either. He's famously reclusive, apparently… Oh, it looks like he died last year,' she went on, reading the label. Cupping her hands around her face, she peered through the window into the gallery. 'It says this is a retrospective exhibition of his works.'

'Why don't we go in and have a look?' said Max on an impulse. If you'd asked him a day earlier if he'd voluntarily go into an art gallery, he'd have scoffed, but the little picture in the window seemed to be beckoning him inside. 'At least we can look at some real art this evening as opposed to piles of rubbish.'

Inside, it was quiet and calm with none of the aggressive trendiness of the earlier gallery. A strikingly beautiful woman with cascading red curls welcomed them in and told them they were welcome to wander around, but she looked at Allegra so intently that Allegra clearly began to feel uncomfortable.

'If you're about to close…'

'No, it's all right. I'm sorry, I was staring at you,' said the woman. She had a faint accent that Max couldn't place. Eastern European, perhaps. 'We haven't met before, have we?'

'I'm sure I'd remember,' said Allegra. 'You've got such gorgeous hair.'

'Thank you.' The woman touched it a little self-consciously. 'I think perhaps I'm too old for such long hair now but Jago would never let me cut it.'

Her name, it turned out, was Bronya, and she had been Jago Forrest's muse for nearly twenty years, living with him in secluded splendour in an isolated part of Spain. She told Allegra that Jago had refused to see anyone, but that after he'd died she had decided to make his work accessible once more.

'But his portraits are so tender,' said Allegra. 'It's hard to believe that he disliked people that much.'

Bronya smiled faintly. 'He was a complicated man,' she said. 'Not always easy to live with, but a genius.' She looked sad for a moment. 'But I mustn't hold you up. Take your time looking round,' she said, gesturing them into the gallery. 'This is his most recent work down here, but some of his earlier paintings are upstairs if you'd be interested to see those too. Are you *sure* we've never met?' she said again to Allegra. 'You seem so familiar…'

Max found Jago Forrest's paintings oddly moving. Many were of Bronya, but he'd also painted countrywomen with seamed faces and gnarled fingers, and there were several young models he'd painted in the nude, portraying their bodies with such sensuousness that Max shifted uneasily.

'Let's go and look upstairs,' said Allegra eventually, and Max followed her up the spiral staircase. At the top she stopped so abruptly that he ran into her.

'Careful—' he began, but then he saw what had brought her up short. A huge portrait dominated the wall facing the staircase. It showed a young woman in a languorous pose, her arm thrown above her head and a satiated smile on her face. But it wasn't the overtly sexual feel to the painting that made Max's face burn. It was the woman's face, and the expression that was carnal and tender at the same time.

'She's beautiful, isn't she?' Bronya had followed them upstairs and stood beside them, misinterpreting their silence. She glanced at Max and Allegra. 'She and Jago had a passionate affair, oh, it must be twenty-five years ago now.' She laughed lightly. 'I was jealous of her for a long time. I was so afraid that Jago would go back to her, but their affair must have ended very bitterly, I think. She was his passion, and I was his love, that's what he always told me. It's sad it didn't work out. You can see how much she loved him in her face, can't you?'

'Yes,' said Allegra in a strange wooden voice. She was very white about the mouth, and Max moved closer to put a steadying hand on her shoulder.

'Perhaps you recognise her?' Bronya paused delicately, looking curiously at Allegra.

'Oh, yes,' Allegra said, and turned to look straight at her. 'That's my mother.'

'Oh my God...' Bronya's hand crept to her mouth. 'Your eyes! That's why you seemed familiar...you've got Jago's eyes!' She stared at Allegra. 'You're his daughter!'

Max was worried about Allegra. She looked cold and lost as she stood on the pavement outside the gallery. He'd tried to put his arms round her, but she side-stepped his hug, holding herself together with an effort that left her rigid.

'I'll take you home,' he said, but she shook her head.

'I need to talk to my mother,' she said, and Max flagged down a taxi without arguing.

She hadn't said anything in the taxi, and now the taxi was pulling up outside Flick's house. 'Would you like me to come in with you?' he asked, not liking the frozen expression on her face.

'I'll be fine,' she said. 'I think this is a conversation Flick and I have to have on our own.'

'I'll wait then,' said Max.

'Don't be silly.' At least he'd brought a flicker of animation to her face and she even managed a smile of sorts. 'I could be hours. You go on home.'

Max didn't like it, but he could hardly insist on barging in with her so he waited until Allegra was inside before giving the taxi driver directions back to the house.

He couldn't settle. He threw himself on the sofa, then got up to go to the kitchen. He switched on the television, turned it off. He kept thinking of Allegra, and how she must have felt learning who her father was after all those years of not knowing. Why hadn't Flick told her? Max knew how much Allegra had yearned for a father. He'd seen how wistfully she had watched his father with Libby and, although his father treated her as an honorary daughter, it wasn't the same as having a father of her own.

The sound of her key in the lock had him leaping to his feet and he made it into the narrow hallway in time to see Allegra closing the front door. She was still wearing his jacket and when she turned her face wore an expression that made Max's heart turn over.

He didn't think. He just opened his arms and she walked right into them without a word.

Max folded her against him and rested his cheek on her hair as she clung to him, trembling. She was cold and tired and distressed, but holding her gave him the first peace he'd had in days.

'Come on,' he said gently at last. 'I'll get you a drink. You look like you need it.'

He made her sit on the sofa while he poured her a shot of whisky. Allegra eyed the glass he handed her dubiously. 'I don't really like whisky,' she said.

'Drink it anyway,' said Max.

Reluctantly she took a sip and choked but, after patting her chest and grimacing hugely, the colour started to come back to her cheeks and she tried again.

Max sat on the sofa beside her, but not too close. 'Better?'

'Funnily enough, yes.' She swirled the whisky around in the glass and her smile faded. 'I just made my mother cry,' she told Max. 'I don't feel very good about it.'

The indomitable Flick Fielding had *cried*? Max couldn't imagine it at all.

'What did she say when you told her about the portrait?'

'She was furious at first,' said Allegra. 'The portrait was supposed to have been destroyed, Bronya had no right to bring it to London, she would slap an injunction on her to make her remove it... She was pacing around her study, absolutely wild, but when I said it was a beautiful picture she just stopped and covered her face with her hands. It was like she just collapsed.' Allegra took another slug of whisky. 'I've never seen Flick cry before. It was awful.'

'Is it true? Was Jago Forrest your father?'

She nodded. 'Everything Bronya told us was true. They did have this incredibly passionate affair. Flick said that she was too young to know better but it's obvious even now that she loved him. Maybe she still does. She said that it almost destroyed her when he left her.'

Absently, Allegra sipped her whisky. 'It's funny to think of her being young and desperately in love, but it also makes a kind of sense now. She's hidden behind a mask of cool intelligence so that no one guesses that she was ever that vulnerable. I suppose keeping everyone at arm's length means that nobody has a chance to hurt you.' Allegra's expression was sad. 'Poor Flick.'

'Poor you,' said Max, unable to resist reaching over to tuck a stray hair back behind her ear. 'What happened?'

'Flick got pregnant but Jago didn't want a child.' Max could tell Allegra was struggling to keep her voice level, and he moved closer to put a comforting arm around her shoulders. She leaned into him gratefully, still cradling the glass between her hands.

'He gave her the money for a termination, but at the last moment, Flick decided she didn't want to go through with it and Jago was furious. He told her it was him or the baby, and she chose to have the baby.' Allegra swallowed. 'She was convinced that he loved her too much to really let her go, and she thought if she could just show him his child he'd change his mind.'

'And he didn't?'

Allegra shook her head. 'Flick said she took me round to his studio after I was born. She said she couldn't believe he would be able to resist me. She said I was perfect.' Her voice wobbled a little and she took another slug of whisky to steady it.

'She said, "You were absolutely perfect, and he looked at you as if you were a slug", and then he told her she would have to choose once and for all. He wanted her to get rid of me, apparently, and when she refused, that was it. He said that as far as he was concerned he'd washed his hands of the problem when he gave her money for the abortion, so she could forget asking him for any support.'

Max tightened his arm around Allegra. She was doing pretty well telling the story, but he'd seen her face when she repeated what Flick had told her about Jago's reaction. Doubtless it had been hard for Flick, but couldn't she have spared Allegra knowing that her father had looked at her as if she were a slug?

'And was that it?' he asked.

'She never saw him again and she was too angry and bitter to pursue him for support. She wouldn't discuss him at all.'

'I can see it was hard for her,' said Max, 'but why didn't she tell you? You had a right to know who your father was.'

Allegra let out a long sigh. 'She said she knew that if she told me I'd want to get in touch with Jago, and she was afraid that he'd reject me the way he'd rejected her. And I think, from what Bronya told us, he probably would have done. He was a genius, but he doesn't sound a very kind person. Flick said she couldn't bear the thought of him hurting me.' She swallowed hard. 'She said she was sorry—I don't think she's ever said that to me before. I hated seeing her so upset. It was like the world turning upside down.'

'You're upset too,' Max pointed out. 'It's been just as hard for you.'

'Well, at least I know who my father was now,' said Allegra bravely. 'And I understand Flick better. I used to think that she didn't really want me,' she confided, 'but she gave up her great passion for me, and she tried to protect me, so that feels good to know.'

'It was a lot for you to learn in one day,' said Max, a faint frown in his eyes. Allegra's composure was brittle and he could feel the tension in her body. 'How do you feel?'

'I'm fine,' she said brightly. 'I just…well, it's not every day you find out your father is a famous artist.'

'Would you rather not have known?' Max asked gently.

'No, it's better to know,' said Allegra. 'At least I can stop dreaming.' She smiled as if it hurt. 'I used to think that the only reason I didn't have a father was because Flick hadn't told him about me. I dreamt that he'd find out about me somehow and come and find me, and I'd be so precious to him. He'd look at me the way your dad looks at Libby.'

Her mouth started to wobble and she took her bottom lip between her teeth to keep it steady. 'So I suppose…I always, always wanted a father, but now it turns out that I had a father but he didn't want me.'

Her face crumpled and Max, who was normally terrified of tears, gathered her on to his lap as she let go of the storm of emotion at last. His throat tight, he held her softly and let her cry it all out until the wrenching sobs subsided to juddering sighs.

'Jago might have been a genius, but he was a fool,' he murmured, touching his lips to her hair without thinking. 'He missed out on knowing just what an amazing daughter he had.'

'I'm not amazing,' she said, muffled in his collar. 'My father was a genius, and Flick's got drive and intelligence, and I'm just…me. I'm not particularly good at anything.' Her voice clogged with tears again. 'And now I know what Flick gave up for me, I can understand just what a disappointment I am to her. I can't be what she wants me to be.'

'Then be what *you* want to be,' said Max. He put her away from him and held her at arm's length so that he could smooth her tangled hair back from her face and look straight into her eyes. 'You've spent your whole life trying to please your mother, Legs, and now it's time to please yourself. Decide what you want to do, and do it.'

*Decide what you want.* What Allegra really wanted was for Max not to go to Shofrar, but how could she beg him to stay when she knew how much the job meant to him? He'd let her cry over him, and she knew how much he must have hated that. Telling him how much she dreaded him going would have been little more than emotional blackmail.

So she'd knuckled the mascara from under her eyes and put on a smile and pretended that she was fine.

And now he was leaving. His bags were packed and sitting neatly in the hallway. The taxi to take him to Heathrow was due any minute.

The last few days had been a blur. Max's colleagues had thrown a leaving party for him. Allegra hadn't asked, but she was sure that Emma would have been there. The following night Dickie had insisted on farewell drinks in the pub Max had introduced him to. Darcy had come with William. She'd hugged Max and wished him well but it was obvious that she only had eyes for William now. Libby rang from Paris, Max's parents from Northumberland.

But now everybody had gone, the phone was silent and it was just the two of them waiting for the taxi in the sitting room. Allegra's heart was knocking painfully against her ribs. She didn't know whether she was dreading the moment of saying goodbye or longed for it to come so that at least this awful waiting would be over. It was early, not yet seven, and Allegra would normally have been in bed, but she couldn't let him leave without saying goodbye.

Without saying thank you.

She had come downstairs in her old pyjama bottoms and a camisole top, pulling on a cardigan against the crispness of the autumn morning. Her face was bare, her hair tousled.

There was too much to say, and not enough. Allegra's throat ached with the longing to tell Max that she loved him, but what would be the point? She didn't want to embarrass him, and besides, Emma would be waiting for him at the airport.

'Can you let me have Max's flight details?' Emma had rung the night before. Allegra had forgotten how friendly and downright *nice* Emma was. It was obvious that Max hadn't told her about the night he and Allegra had spent together, and it had certainly never crossed Emma's mind that Allegra might be any kind of rival.

Because she wasn't. She was the one who had told Max that they should pretend that night had never happened, Allegra reminded herself. She could hardly blame him when that was exactly what he did. It wasn't his fault that she had fallen in love with him.

Allegra was doing her best to convince herself that her feelings for him were just a temporary infatuation. Falling properly in love with him would be such a totally stupid thing to do. Again and again, Allegra ticked her way through a mental list of reasons why loving Max was a bad idea, and Emma was right there at the top.

Emma would be waiting for him when he got to the airport, and Allegra was fairly certain that she was going to tell Max that she loved him. If Allegra told him the same thing, it would put Max in an impossible situation.

Or maybe not. If you were Max, going out to work in the desert, and you had to choose between a ditzy fashionista and a genuinely nice, attractive fellow engineer who would be able to share your life completely, how hard a choice would it be?

Not very hard at all.

So Allegra stuck with agonising small talk when all she wanted to say was *I love you, I love you, I love you*.

Max was no more at ease and their conversation kept coming out in sticky dollops, only to dry up just when they thought they'd got going.

He hadn't learnt a thing about style. He was wearing one of his old suits, and if he hadn't deliberately chosen his dreariest shirt and tie it had been a lucky accident that he'd succeeded in putting on both. He looked dull and conventional.

He looked wonderful.

Allegra had to hug her arms together to stop herself reaching for him.

For the umpteenth time, Max pulled up his cuff to check his watch, but when his phone rang they both jumped.

'Taxi's here,' he said unnecessarily.

'Yes.' Allegra's throat had closed so tight it was all she could force out.

'So…it looks like this is it.'

'Yes.'

'I'd better go.'

Allegra was gripped by panic. She hadn't said anything that she wanted to! Why had she wasted these last precious minutes? Now all she could do was follow him out to the narrow hallway. She opened the door while Max picked up his briefcase and suitcase. He stepped out and looked at the taxi which was double-parked in the street before turning back to Allegra. He put down his cases again.

'Come out to the airport with me,' he said impulsively, and Allegra's heart contracted. She would have given anything to have an extra half hour with him in the taxi but she thought about Emma, waiting there to surprise him. It would spoil everything if she turned up too.

Emma was perfect for Max. He would realise that when he was in Shofrar, and he so deserved to be happy.

'I can't.' Allegra swallowed painfully. 'I need to get to work, but have a good flight,' she said with a wobbly smile, and stepped forward to give him what was meant to be a quick hug. 'I'll miss you,' she whispered.

Max's arms closed around her and he held her to him, so tightly that Allegra could hardly breathe, but she didn't care. She wanted to stay like that for ever, pressed against him, smelling him, loving him.

'I'll miss you too,' he whispered back.

They stood there, holding each other, neither wanting to be the first to let go, but eventually the taxi driver wound down his window. 'You planning on catching that plane, mate?' he called.

Reluctantly, Max released Allegra. 'I need to go.'

She nodded, tears shimmering in her eyes, and wrapped her arms around herself as she stood on the doorstep, careless of the cold on her bare feet, and watched as Max threw his cases into the back of the taxi. With his hand on the open door, he hesitated and looked back at Allegra as if he would say something else. For one glorious moment she thought that he was going to change his mind and stay after all, but in the end he just lifted his hand, got into the back of the taxi and shut the door.

The driver said something over his shoulder and put the taxi into gear. He put the indicator on and waited for a car that was coming up the street to pass. The car paused and flashed its lights politely to let him out. *No!* Allegra wanted to scream at it. *No, don't let him go!*

But it was too late. One last glimpse of Max through the window, and then the taxi was drawing away. Her heart tore, a slow, cruel rip as she watched it down the street, watched it turn left and out of sight.

And then he was gone.

# CHAPTER TEN

'WHAT'S THE LATEST on the *Making Mr Perfect* piece?' Stella's steely gaze swept round the editorial conference before homing in on Allegra, who was doing her best to hide in the corner.

'Er, it's almost done,' said Allegra. The truth was that she couldn't bring herself to reread what she'd written about Max. It was all too raw.

She missed him terribly. In the past, when a relationship had ended, she'd been miserable for a day or two, but all it had taken was a new pair of shoes or a funny tweet to perk her up again. Now, it felt as if there was a jagged rip right through her heart, a bloody wound clawed open afresh every time she thought about Max. Missing him wasn't the vague sense of disappointment she'd felt before. It was the leadenness that had settled like a boulder in the pit of her stomach. It was the ache in her bones and the awful emptiness inside her.

Allegra was wretched. She hated going back to the house, hated going into the sitting room and seeing the empty sofa. She ached for the sight of him stretched out on it, rolling his eyes at her shoes. She missed the way he tsked at her untidy ways, the way that smile lurked at the corner of his mouth.

Without realising it, she had memorised every angle of

his face, every crease at the edges of his eyes. She could sketch him perfectly, but you couldn't hold a drawing, you couldn't touch it and feel it. You couldn't lean into it and make the world go away.

She hadn't been able to face finishing the article and had spent her time reading obsessively instead, escaping into the ordered world of her favourite Regency romances. A world where there were no exasperated civil engineers, no stupid jobs that took the hero overseas, no heartbreak that couldn't be resolved and sealed with a waltz around a glittering ballroom.

Now, with Stella's beady eye on her, Allegra struggled to remember that she had a job to do. 'I just need to tidy it up.'

'Done?' Stella snapped. 'How can it be done? You haven't been to the costume ball yet.'

Allegra cleared her throat. 'Unfortunately, we're going to have to miss out the ball. Max can't take part any longer. He's gone overseas.'

'What do you mean, *he's gone*?' Stella demanded. 'What about the article?'

'I thought I could end it at the Digby Fox preview.'

That didn't go down well. Stella's eyes bored into her. 'The whole point was to end with the ball,' she said icily. 'The fairy tale/knightly quest angle only makes sense if you follow it through to the ball. Get whatever-his-name-is to come back.'

Her immaculately polished fingernails drummed on the table while the rest of the editorial staff studiously avoided looking at either her or Allegra. Stella's displeasure could be a terrible thing to behold and nobody wanted to be associated with Allegra if she was in the firing line.

'I can't do that,' Allegra protested. 'He's got a job to do.'

Around the table there was a collective sucking in of breath. When Stella told you to do something, you did it. You didn't tell her that you couldn't. Not if you wanted to keep your job, anyway.

Incredibly, Stella didn't erupt. Her nails continued to click on the table, but her eyes narrowed thoughtfully. 'Then I suggest you find some way of including the ball anyway. Get Darcy to go with this new man of hers. She's always tweeting about how perfect he is. You could compare and contrast,' said Stella, warming to the idea. 'Show how what's-his-name was a failure and the new guy isn't.'

'His name's Max,' said Allegra clearly, ignoring the winces around her. 'And he isn't a failure!'

'He is as far as *Glitz* is concerned,' said Stella. 'Set up the ball and take a photographer. At least this way you can salvage something from the mess this article seems to have become.' Her eyes rested on Allegra's outfit. 'And sharpen yourself up if you want to stay at *Glitz*,' she added. 'You've let yourself go lately, Allegra. Those accessories are all wrong with that dress, and your shoes are so last season. It gives a bad impression.'

Allegra didn't like it, but she knew Stella was right. She *had* let herself go. She'd been too miserable to care about what she wore, but misery wasn't getting her anywhere. Every day when she checked her email she let the mouse hover over the 'new message' icon and thought about sending Max a message. She could keep it light, just ask how he was getting on. Just to hear from him.

But what would be the point? She didn't want to hear that he was enjoying Shofrar or that he was perfectly happy without her. She didn't want to hear that he had taken her advice and made it up with Emma. And what else could he tell her? That he loved her and missed her as much as she loved and missed him? Allegra couldn't see Max sitting at his computer and writing anything like that, even if he felt it. It just wasn't his style.

Once or twice, she poured out her feelings in an email, but she always came to her senses before she clicked 'send' and deleted it all instead. Max would be appalled, and it wasn't fair to embarrass him like that.

No, it was time to accept that Max had gone and that he wasn't coming back, time to stop reading and start deciding what to do with her life.

*Be what* you *want to be.* Max's words ran round and round in her head. Somewhere between finding out who her father was and Max leaving, Allegra had lost her certainty. What if Max had been right all along and she didn't really want to be a journalist at all?

The assignments Stella gave her now seemed increasingly silly. Allegra wrote a piece comparing the staying power of various lipglosses, and another on whether your hairdresser knew more about you than your beauty therapist. One day she did nothing but follow celebrity tweets and write a round up of all the banal things they'd said.

When Stella told her to invent some reader 'confessions' about their kinkiest sex exploits, Allegra couldn't even enjoy herself. She even got to work at home so that she didn't have to worry about anyone looking over her shoulder and raising their eyebrows. Once she would have found it fun, and let her imagination run wild, but now all she could think of was that night with Max, when they hadn't needed handcuffs or beads or uniforms. They hadn't needed a chandelier to swing from. They'd just needed each other.

Her blood thumped and her bones melted at the mere memory of it.

Allegra dropped her head into her hand and rubbed her forehead. Max was right about this too. She couldn't persuade herself any longer that working for *Glitz* was a stepping-stone to a glittering career in serious journalism. The *Financial Times* seemed further off than ever.

And who was she trying to fool? She didn't have what it took to be a serious journalist. She didn't even *want* to be a serious journalist.

Now all she had to do was decide what she *did* want to be. Allegra pushed her laptop away and picked up a pencil. She always thought better when she drew.

Except when she drew Max, when she just missed him.

With an effort, Allegra pushed him from her mind and sketched a quick picture of Derek the Dog instead. She drew him with his head cocked, his expression alert. He looked ready and eager to go. Allegra wished she felt like that.

Smiling, she let her pen take Derek on an adventure involving a double-decker bus, a steam engine, a jumbo jet and an old tugboat, and so absorbed was she that she missed the couture debut of the funkiest new designer in town. Everyone at *Glitz* had been buzzing about it, and Allegra too had one of the hottest tickets in fashion history.

She looked at her watch. If she rushed, she might still be able to squeeze in at the back, but then she'd have to get changed out of her vegging wear and she just couldn't be bothered.

Allegra sat back, startled by what she had just thought. Couldn't be bothered for *the* collection of the year? She examined herself curiously. Could it be true? Had she really changed that much?

Yep, she decided, she really had. Now all she had to do was think up a convincing excuse for her absence when everyone asked the next day. It would need to be a *really* good reason. Being struck down by a deadly virus wouldn't cut it. Any fashionista worth her salt would drag herself out of hospital if she had a ticket.

Allegra scratched her head with her pencil. She would just have to tell them she had been abducted by aliens— Struck by a thought, she ripped off a clean sheet from her drawing pad. Maybe it was time Derek went into space...

'You look amazing, like a fairy tale princess,' Allegra told Darcy. It was the night of the ball and they were squeezed in at the mirror in the Ladies', along with all the other women who were checking their lipstick and adjusting the necklines of their ball gowns. None of them looked as stunning as Darcy, though.

'I *feel* like a princess!' Pleased, Darcy swung her full skirt. The eighteenth-century-style dress was silver, with a embroidered bodice and sleeves that ended in a froth of lace at her elbows, and the skirt was decorated with bows and ruffles. On anyone else it would have seemed ridiculous, but Darcy looked magical. 'I always wanted to wear a dress like this when I was a kid,' she confided.

What little girl hadn't? Allegra had to admit to some dress envy, even though she knew she would never have been able to wear anything that fussy. She herself was in a slinky off-the-shoulder number that Dickie had found in one of the closets at *Glitz* that morning. It was a gorgeous red and it flattered her slender figure, but Allegra was feeling too dismal to carry it off.

'Ah, bah!' Dickie had said when she tried to tell him that. 'Eez *parfaite* for you.'

Allegra protested that she was only there as an observer to watch Darcy and William so she didn't need a ball gown, but Dickie had thrown such a hissy fit about her ingratitude that in the end she had just taken it.

Not that it mattered *what* she was wearing. Next to

Darcy, nobody was going to notice her. At least she wouldn't have to watch Max dancing with her. Remembering how they had learnt to waltz together brought such a stab of longing that Allegra had to bite her lip until it passed. She had left her hair loose, the way Max liked it. Oh, God, she *had* to stop thinking about him…

'Hey, I hear you wrote a book, you clever thing,' said Darcy, leaning into the mirror and touching the tip of her ring finger to her flawless cheekbones, just to check that her make up was perfect. It was.

Allegra was startled out of her wretchedness. 'Who told you that?'

'William.' Darcy practically licked her lips every time she said his name. The two of them had been inseparable ever since the preview. It was an unlikely combination, the political aide and the lingerie model, but they were clearly mad about each other. 'Your mum told him. He says she's boasting about you to everyone.'

'*Really?*' Allegra was surprised. Flick had been delighted to hear that her daughter was planning to resign from *Glitz* as soon as the *Making Mr Perfect* article was finished, but she was much less impressed by Allegra's idea of working freelance until she could find a publisher for her Derek the Dog stories.

'An illustrator?' she had echoed in dismay, and then her mouth tightened. 'This is because of Jago, isn't it?'

'No,' said Allegra evenly, 'I'm never going to be an artist like him, just like I'm never going to be a journalist like you.' She thought about her old dreams. 'I'm not a princess in disguise or a governess in a Regency romance. I'm just ordinary, and I'm going to stop trying to be anything but myself. I draw silly little pictures of animals. It's not much, but it's what I can do.'

Flick had been taken aback at first. 'Well, I *suppose* I

could introduce you to some agents,' she had offered reluctantly at last.

'Thanks,' said Allegra, 'but I've already approached one. She likes my illustrations, but she's less keen on the story. She's talking about teaming me up with a writer she knows.'

'Oh.'

Allegra suspected Flick was rather miffed by the fact that she hadn't traded on her famous mother's connections, but if Flick had talked about her to William she must have come round. As far as Allegra knew, Flick had never once told anyone that she was working for *Glitz*. The fact that she might have done something to please her mother at last gave Allegra a warm feeling around her heart for the first time since Max had left.

William was waiting for them in the lobby of the hotel, carrying off his Prince Charming costume with aplomb. Remembering how seriously he had talked the first time she had met him, Allegra smiled to herself. He really must be smitten by Darcy if he was prepared to dress up. 'I'd rather stick pins in my eyes,' Max had said.

In contrast, Dom, the photographer, stood out from the crowd in his jeans and leather jacket. He took some photos of William and Darcy together and then they all moved into the ballroom, where the ball was already in full swing.

Allegra found a place on the edge of the room. It was a classic ballroom, with glittering chandeliers and a high, elaborately decorated ceiling. One wall was punctuated with elegant long windows, open in spite of the dreary November weather to let some much needed air into the crowded ballroom. An orchestra at one end was playing a vigorous waltz, and couples in gorgeous costumes whirled around the floor.

Everything was just as Allegra had always dreamed

a ball would be. It was perfect—or it would have been if only Max had been there with her. The thought of him triggered a wave of loneliness that hit her with such force that she actually staggered. Her knees went weak and all the colour and gaiety and movement of the scene blurred before her eyes.

She couldn't bear it without Max.

Blindly, she started for the doors. It was noisy and crowded and empty without him. She would wait for Dom outside. It was too painful to be here, with the music and the laughter and the memories of how she and Max had waltzed around the sitting room, of how useless they had both been, how they had laughed together.

'Excuse me…sorry…sorry…' Allegra squeezed her way through the throng, too intent on escaping to enjoy the fantastic costumes. She kept her head down so that no one would see the tears pooling in her eyes and it was perhaps inevitable that she ended up bumping into a solid male body.

'Sorry…I'm so sorry…' Desperate to get away, she barely took in more than an elaborate waistcoat. Another Prince Charming in full eighteenth-century dress, she had time to think before she side-stepped to pass him, only to be stopped by a hand on her arm.

'Would you do me the honour of this dance?'

Allegra had already started to shake her head when something familiar about the voice filtered through the music and the chatter and her heart clenched. How cruel that her longing should make it sound so like Max's.

Blinking back her tears, she summoned a polite smile and lifted her eyes from the waistcoat and past the extravagant cravat to Prince Charming's face underneath his powdered wig.

'I'm afraid I'm just lea—' Her voice faded as her gaze

reached his eyes and she blinked, certain that she must be imagining things, but when she opened her eyes again he was still there.

'Max?' she quavered, still not sure that her longing hadn't conjured him up out of thin air.

'I know, I look a prat,' said Max.

Astonishment, joy, incredulity, shock: all jostled together in such a fierce rush that Allegra couldn't catch her breath. For a stunned moment all she could do was stare in disbelief. Max was out in the desert, in shorts and sunglasses, not dressed up as a fairy tale prince in a crowded ballroom.

*'Max?'*

'Yes, it's me.' Incredibly, he looked nervous.

'Wh…what are you doing here?' Still unable to believe that it could really be true, she had to raise her voice above the noise in the ballroom, and Max leant closer to make sure that she could hear.

'I've been doing some thinking, and I decided it would be a shame if we wasted all those waltzing lessons,' he told her, and he held out his hand. 'Shall we dance?'

In a blur, Allegra let him lead her onto the floor, finding a place on the edge of the other couples who were whirling around the floor in an intimidatingly professional fashion. She didn't understand anything, but if this was a dream, she didn't want to wake up.

Max swung her round into position. He held one of her hands in his, and set the other on his shoulder so that he could take hold of her waist. 'Okay,' he yelled, looking down at their feet. 'Remember the box? Let's go…*one*, two, three, *one*, two, three…'

They made a mess of it at first, of course. They stumbled and trod on each other's toes, but all at once, magically, they clicked and found the rhythm. True, they could

only go round and round the 'box' but they were on the
floor and they were moving together in time to the music—
sort of. Allegra's heart was so full, she was crying and
floating in delirious joy at the same time.

Laughing through her tears, she lifted her face to Max's.
'We're *waltzing!*' she shouted.

'Ready to try a new manoeuvre?' he shouted back and,
without waiting for her answer, he lunged with her further
into the crowd. This was a whole new step outside their
safe box, as they had never really mastered turning, but
Max had a determined look on his face and Allegra followed as best she could.

'Where are you going?' she yelled in his ear.

'Terrace,' he said briefly, face set as he concentrated on
steering her through the throng of dancers.

The *terrace?* Allegra thought about the chill drizzle
that was falling outside, but it was too noisy to have a
conversation and, anyway, Max seemed set on the idea.
He danced her grimly across the floor. They'd lost their
rhythm again and kept bumping into other couples, but
somehow they made it to the other side. Max took a deep
breath and somehow manoeuvred them through one of
the windows and out onto the terrace that overlooked the
hotel's garden.

'That was harder than I thought,' he said, and let Allegra go.

Outside, the air was damp and cold, but it was bliss-
fully quiet after the noise in the ballroom. Still gripped
by a sense of unreality, Allegra shook her head slightly.

'Max, what are you doing here? I thought you were in
Shofrar.'

'I was, but I told Bob that I needed to come back to
London.'

She looked concerned. 'Aren't you enjoying the job?'

'The job's great.' It was. 'It's everything I ever wanted to do, and the desert is beautiful. I wish you could see it, Legs. The light is extraordinary.'

'Then why come back to London?' she asked, puzzled.

Max took a deep breath. 'Because you weren't there,' he said. 'The thing is…' He'd rehearsed this speech in his head but now that the moment had come, his mind had gone blank. 'The thing is, I missed you,' he finished simply.

'But…what about Emma?' Allegra's eyes were huge. She looked as if she was unsure whether she was dreaming or not, and Max couldn't blame her. One minute she had been heading out of the ballroom and the next she was faced with an idiot in full eighteenth-century dress.

'She told me she wanted to say goodbye to you at the airport,' Allegra went on. 'I thought she was going to suggest that you got back together.'

'She did,' said Max, remembering how long it had taken him to understand what Emma was saying. Her timing hadn't been good, to say the least. His mind had been too full of Allegra, standing on the doorstep, watching as he drove away. 'She said she wanted to try again, that she'd realised that friendship was a better foundation for marriage than passion.'

'Which was what you'd said all along.'

'I did say that and I believed it, but I've changed my mind,' Max said. 'Friendship isn't enough on its own, nor is passion. You need both. I told Emma that I'd like to be friends, but I knew that I'd never be happy unless I could be with you.'

'With me…' she echoed incredulously, but a smile lit her eyes, and he took hold of her hands.

'I love being with you, Legs. I don't care what we're doing. Even when you were making me dress up and make a fool of myself, it was fun. I missed being able to talk to you and hear you laugh, I missed you nagging about my clothes. God, I even found myself rolling my cuffs up!' he said, and Allegra laughed unsteadily.

Tears were trembling on the end of her lashes and Max tightened his grasp on her fingers, desperate to tell her how he felt before she cried. 'I missed you as more than a friend, though. I wanted to be able to touch you and feel you…I haven't been able to stop thinking about that night. It's never been like that for me before,' he said honestly. 'It was as if everything else had been a practice and suddenly with you it was the real thing. Like I'd never understood before that was how it was supposed to be. I can't explain it. With you, it just felt right…' He trailed off, seeing the tears spilling down her cheeks. 'Don't cry, Legs, please. I just wanted to tell you how I felt.'

'I'm crying because I'm happy,' she said, trying in vain to blink back the tears. 'Oh, Max, that was how it was for me too.'

The tight band around Max's chest unlocked and he released her hands to take her face between his palms.

'Allegra,' he said unevenly, 'I know I'm stuffy and I can't dance and I've got no dress sense but I love you. That's why I came back. I had to tell you.'

Incredibly, she was smiling still. 'I love you too,' she said, sliding her arms around his waist. 'I've missed you so much.'

A smile dawned in Max's eyes as his heart swelled. Tenderly, he grazed her jaw with his thumbs. 'You love me?' he repeated, dazed at the wonder of it.

'I do,' she said and her voice broke. 'Oh, Max, I do.' And she clung to him as he kissed her at last, the way he had dreamt of kissing her for so many long and lonely nights, so many bleak days.

She kissed him back, a long, sweet kiss edged with the same giddy relief at having been pulled back from an abyss at the last moment. They ran their hands hungrily over each other, a remembered inventory of pleasure. Heedless of the drizzle that was rapidly turning to rain, they forgot the ball, forgot the cold, forgot everything but the dazzling joy of being able to touch each other again, feel each other again.

Max was rucking up Allegra's skirt with an urgent hand before a splatter of rain right down his neck brought him reluctantly back to reality. Grumbling at the weather, he pulled Allegra into the shelter of an overhanging balcony and rested his forehead against hers.

'I wish you'd said something before you left,' she said, softening her criticism by clinging closer. 'I've been so wretched without you.'

'I couldn't. You made it pretty clear that night was just a one-off as far as you were concerned,' he pointed out. 'We've got different lives, you said, and you were right. I could see that. God, Legs, I only had to look at you. You were having so much fun in London. You've got a great life, doing what you want to do. You're so bright and warm and funny and gorgeous. How could I possibly imagine you wanting to be with a boring civil engineer?'

Allegra couldn't help laughing. 'Nobody looking at you dressed up as Prince Charming could possibly describe you as boring, Max!' For the first time she took in the full glory of his costume. His jacket was made of plum-coloured velvet, and he wore tight breeches and silk socks held up with garters. The satin waistcoat was the same colour as the jacket, and an intricately arranged necktie frothed at his throat. 'Where on earth did you find your outfit?'

'Dickie got it for me.'

'Dickie!' She gaped at him. 'He didn't tell me that you'd been in touch!'

'I asked him not to and, anyway,' said Max, drawing her back into him and putting on a superior air, 'I'm not Prince Charming, I'm a duke.'

'*Are* you?' Allegra tucked in the corners of her mouth to stop herself laughing.

He pretended to be hurt. 'I thought you'd have recognised a Regency duke when you saw one!'

'Hmm, I think you and Dickie might have slipped a century,' said Allegra. 'My Regency duke didn't wear a powdered wig.'

'Thank God for that!' Max snatched off his wig and cast it aside, before taking Allegra back in his arms. 'I couldn't find a time travel machine, so this was the closest I could get to your fantasy,' he confessed. 'I had this great plan. I was going to recreate it for you exactly,' he told her as her eyes widened. 'I was going to waltz you out onto the terrace, just the way you told me about, and then I was going to tell you how passionately I loved you and beg you to marry me, and bowl you over with the romance of it all. I wanted you to have the perfect proposal.

'But I made a mess of it,' he said. 'The fact is, I'm not a duke, I can't dance, I look like an idiot and it's raining. Where's the romance in that?'

'It's the most romantic thing I could imagine,' said Allegra, her voice tight with emotion. 'The duke's just a fantasy, but you're *real*.' She kissed him softly. 'Maybe you can't dance, and no, you're not the sharpest dresser, but you're perfect for me and I love you just as you are.'

'What, even buttoned up to my collar?'

'Even then.'

Max grinned, pleased. 'Hey, you really must love me,' he said and she laughed.

'I really do,' she said, and he kissed her again, pressing her against the wall until they were both breathless and shaky with desire.

'We've wasted so much time,' Max grumbled against her throat. 'I wish I'd known how you felt before I left.'

'I couldn't tell you,' Allegra protested, snuggling closer. 'You told me yourself you needed someone sensible like Emma.'

'I thought that too,' he said, as his hands slid possessively over her curves. 'But it turns out that I need fun and frivolity instead. I've asked Bob if I can transfer back to the London office. I thought even if my Regency duke impersonation didn't work, it would be easier to be in the same city. At least then I'd get to see you.'

Allegra pressed closer, loving the hard demand of his hands. 'Ask him if you can stay in Shofrar after all,' she said. 'It turns out that I don't have any fun if I'm not with you, so why don't I come with you?'

'But what about your job at *Glitz*?'

'Well, I've made some decisions since you left.' She told him what the agent had said about her drawings. 'It's a long shot but who knows? It might come off and I can always try my hand at other illustrations. I'm sure I'll be able to keep myself busy during the day, anyway,' she said. 'And you can keep me busy at night,' she added with a wicked smile.

'I'll do my best.' Max kissed her again, and that was the last they spoke for some time. Careless of the rain puddling on the terrace around them, oblivious to the music spilling out from the ballroom, they lost themselves in the heady wonder of touch and taste.

'You know we'll have to get married?' said Max eventually, resting his cheek against her hair.

Allegra tipped back her head to smile at him. 'I'm counting on it,' she said.

Max felt his heart swell until it was jammed almost painfully against his ribs. 'Allegra…' he said, shaken by the rush of emotion. 'I don't want to be apart from you again. How soon do you think we can arrange a wedding?'

'As soon as possible.' Allegra looked demure. 'I'm sure Dickie will be happy to find a flowery waistcoat for you to wear.'

'I don't mind what I wear as long as you're standing there saying "I do",' he said.

'You might regret saying that!'

'The only thing I'll regret is not telling you I loved you earlier,' he said seriously, and her lips curved under his as he kissed her once more.

Inside, the orchestra struck up another waltz, and they smiled at each other as they moved into the dance. Max's arm was around her, his fingers warm and firm around hers as they danced through the puddles, heedless of the rain.

Allegra's heart was floating. 'This is perfect,' she said, as Max twirled her around. 'Waltzing on the terrace, a proposal of marriage… What more could I want?'

'I seem to remember something about being ravished against a balustrade,' said Max, and his eyes gleamed in the dim light as he danced her over to it. Turning so that she was pressed against the balustrade, he smiled lovingly down into her face. 'You, my darling, are about to have your dream come true.'

Allegra heaved a contented sigh and wound her arms around his neck to pull him closer. 'It already has,' she said.

*MAKING MR PERFECT by* Allegra Fielding
Can you create the perfect boyfriend? We set one guy a modern-day quest, a series of challenges he

had to complete successfully in order to win the love of today's demanding damsels who want their man to be everything: socially skilled, emotionally intelligent, well-dressed, practical, artistic; a cook, a dancer, a handyman…

We took an uptight, conventionally dressed bloke with zero interest in the arts and a horror of the dance floor, and we asked him if he could change. Could he learn to dress stylishly and navigate a cocktail menu without cringing? Was he prepared to throw away the takeaway menu and go to the effort of cooking a meal from scratch? Could he talk knowledgeably about modern art? Could he learn how to waltz?

If you've been following Max's progress over the past few weeks, you'll know that he sailed through some of the 'tests' but crashed and burned on others, notably the exhibition of contemporary art installations. In spite of his grumbling, Max claims to have learnt something from the process. 'I learnt to make an effort,' he says. 'I learnt to think about what women really want and—more importantly, I gather—not to button my collar quite so tightly.'

But the truth is that Max didn't learn nearly as much as I did. Whether he succeeded or failed, he remained resolutely himself. Yes, he made an effort, but he didn't change. He's never going to be a snappy dresser. He's always going to prefer a beer to a fancy drink, and he's still going to have to be dragged kicking and screaming to anything remotely smacking of the arts. The tests were pointless: anyone can pretend, but what's the point of pretending? Nobody wants to fall in love with a fake.

There's no formula for a perfect man, unless it's for a man who doesn't need to pretend, a man who's happy to be himself. A man who might not be able to dance, but who makes you laugh and holds you when you cry, who makes you feel safe and gives you the strength to be the best you can be. Who will stay by your side, through good times and bad. A man who makes you feel the most beautiful and desirable woman in the world when he kisses you.

A man who sees you for what you really are, and who loves you anyway.

So let's not ask our men to be everything. Let's love them with all their imperfections, because those are what make them who they are. Max doesn't have a single one of the qualities I once thought necessary in my perfect man, and yet somehow that's exactly what he is: my very own Mr Perfect.

* * * * *

# THE PLUS-ONE
# AGREEMENT

## CHARLOTTE PHILLIPS

*For Gemma, who makes my day every day.*
*With all my love always.*

**Charlotte Phillips** has been reading romantic fiction since her teens, and she adores upbeat stories with happy endings. Writing them for Mills & Boon is her dream job.

She combines writing with looking after her fabulous husband, two teenagers, a four-year-old and a dachshund. When something has to give, it's usually housework.

She lives in Wiltshire.

# CHAPTER ONE

*Q: How do you tell your fake boyfriend that you've
met a real one and you don't need him any more?*

*A: However you like. If he's not a real boyfriend, it's
not a real break-up. Hardly likely that he'll start de-
claring undying love for you, is it?*

CHANCE WOULD HAVE been a fine thing.

This Aston Martin might fly before arm candy ad-
dict Dan Morgan developed anything more than a fake
attraction for someone as sensible and boring as Emma
Burney, and it wasn't as if she hadn't given it time. Getting on for a year in his company, watching an endless
string of short-term flings pout their way through his
private life, had convinced her she was never going to
be blonde enough, curvy enough or vacuous enough
to qualify. In fact she was pretty much the opposite of
all his conquests, even dressed up to the nines for her
brother's art exhibition.

She glanced down at herself in the plain black boat-
neck frock and nude heels she'd chosen, teamed as usual
with her minimal make-up and straight-up-and-down
figure. Romance need not apply.

She did, however, possess all the qualities Dan wanted in a supportive friend and social ally. As he did for her. Hence the fake part of their agreement.

An agreement which she reminded herself she no longer needed.

Not if she wanted to move forward from the suspended animation that had been her life this last year. Any residual hope that what was counterfeit between them might somehow turn genuine if she just gave it enough time had been squashed in these last few amazing weeks as she'd been swept off her feet by a whirlwind of intimate, luxurious dinners, expensive gifts and exciting plans. What was between her and Dan was now nothing more than a rut that needed climbing out of.

She watched him quietly for a moment from the passenger seat of his car, looking like an aftershave model in his dark suit and white shirt. His dark hair was so thick there was always a hint of spike about it, a light shadow of stubble lined his jaw, and his ice-blue eyes and slow smile had the ability to charm the entire female species. It had certainly worked on her mother, whose ongoing mission in life was to get Emma and Dan married off and raising a tribe of kids like some Fifties cupcake couple.

Perpetuating her gene pool was the last thing Emma wanted—a lifetime in the midst of her insane family had seen to that. Having Dan as her pretend boyfriend at family events had proved to be the perfect fob-off.

But now she had the real thing and the pretending was holding her back. All that remained was to explain that fact to Dan. She gathered herself together and took a deep breath.

'This has to stop,' she said.

\* \* \*

'You're dumping me?'

Dan shifted his eyes briefly from the road to glance across at her, a mock grin on his face. Because of course this was some kind of joke, right? She simply looked back at him, her brown eyes serious.

'Well, technically, no,' she said. 'Because we'd have to be in a *proper* relationship for me to do that, and ours is a fake one.' She put her head on one side. 'If it's actually one at all. To be honest, it's more of an agreement, isn't it? A plus-one agreement.'

He'd never seen fit to give it a name before. It had simply been an extension of their work dealings into a mutually beneficial social arrangement. There had been no conscious decision or drawing up of terms. It had just grown organically from one simple work success.

Twelve months ago Emma, in her capacity as his lawyer, had attended a meeting with Dan and a potential client for his management consultancy. A potentially huge client. The meeting had overrun into dinner, she had proved a formidable ally and his winning of the contract had been smoothed along perfectly by their double act. She had seemed to bounce off him effortlessly, predicting where he was taking the conversation, backing him up where he needed it. He'd ended the evening with a new client, a new respect for Emma and the beginnings of a connection.

After that she'd become his go-to ally for social engagements—a purely platonic date that he could count on for intelligent conversation and professional behaviour. She'd become a trusted contact. And in return he'd accompanied her to family dinners and events like this one today, sympathising with her exasperation at her slightly crazy family while not really understanding it.

Surely better to have a slightly crazy family than no family at all?

He'd never been dumped before. It was an odd novelty. And certainly not by a real girlfriend. It seemed being dumped by a fake one was no less of a shock to the system.

'It's been good while it lasted,' she was saying. 'Mutually beneficial for both of us. You got a professional plus-one for your work engagements and I got my parents off my back. But the fact is—'

'It's not you, it's me?' he joked, still not convinced she wasn't messing around.

'I've met someone,' she said, not smiling.

'Someone?' he said, shaking his head lightly and reaching for the air-conditioning controls. For some reason it was suddenly boiling in the car. 'A work someone?'

'No, not a work someone!' Her tone was exasperated. 'Despite what you might think, I do have a life, you know—outside work.'

'I never said you didn't.'

He glanced across at her indignant expression just as it melted into a smile of triumph.

'Dan, I've *met* someone.'

She held his gaze for a second before he looked back at the road, her eyebrows slightly raised, waiting for him to catch on. He tried to keep a grin in place when for some reason his face wanted to fold in on itself. In the months he'd known her she'd been on maybe two or three dates, to his knowledge, and none of the men involved had ever been important enough to her to earn the description 'someone'.

He sat back in his seat and concentrated hard on driving the car through the London evening traffic. He supposed she was waiting for some kind of congratulatory comment and he groped for one.

'Good for you,' he said eventually. 'Who is he?'

'He was involved in some legal work I was doing.'

So she *had* met him through her job as a lawyer, then. Of course she had. When did she ever do anything that wasn't somehow linked to work? Even their own friendship was based in work. It had started with work and had grown with their mutual ambition.

'We've been on a few dates and it's going really well.' She took a breath. 'And that's why I need to end things with you.'

*Things?* For some reason he disliked the vagueness of the term, as if it meant nothing.

'You don't date,' he pointed out.

'Exactly,' she said, jabbing a finger at him. 'And do you know *why* I don't date?'

'Because no man could possibly match up to me?'

'Despite what you might think is appealing to women, I don't relish the prospect of a couple of nights sharing your bed only to be kicked out of it the moment you get bored.'

'No need to make it sound so brutal. They all go into it with their eyes open, you know. I don't make any false promises that it will ever be more than a bit of fun.'

'None of them ever believe that. They all think they'll be the one to change you. But you'll never change because you don't need to. You've got me for the times when you need to be serious, so you can keep the rest of your girlies just for fun.'

She looked down at her hands, folded in her lap.

'The thing is, Dan, passing you off as my boyfriend

might keep my family off my back, and it stops the swipes about me being single and the comments about my biological clock, but it doesn't actually solve anything. I didn't realise until now that I'm in a rut. I haven't dated for months. All I do is work. It's so easy to rely on you if I have to go anywhere I need a date that I've quit looking for anyone else.'

'What are you saying?'

She sighed.

'Just that meeting Alistair has opened my eyes to what I've been missing. And I really think our agreement is holding us both back.'

'Alistair?'

'His name is Alistair Woods.'

He easily dismissed the image that zipped into his brain of the blond ex-international cycling star, because it had to be a coincidence. Emma didn't know anyone like *that*. He would know if she did. Except she was waiting, lips slightly parted, eyebrows slightly raised. Everything about her expression told him she was waiting for him to catch on.

'Not *the* Alistair Woods?' he said, because she so obviously wanted him to.

He stole a glance across at her and the smile that lit up her face caused a sorry twist somewhere deep in his stomach. It was a smile he couldn't remember seeing for the longest time—not since they'd first met.

The glance turned into a look for as long as safe driving would allow, during which he saw her with an unusually objective eye, noticing details that had passed him by before. The hint of colour touching the smooth high cheekbones, the soft fullness of her lower lip, the way tendrils of her dark hair curled softly against the creamy skin of her shoulders in the boat-neck dress. She looked absolutely radiant and his stomach gave a slow and unmistakable flip, adding to his sense of unreality.

'Exactly,' she said with a touch of triumph. 'The cyclist. Well, ex-cyclist. He's in TV now—he does presenting and commentating.'

Of course he did. His face had been a permanent media fixture during the last big sports event in the UK. Dan felt a sudden irrational aversion to the man, whom he'd never met.

'*You're* dating Alistair Woods?'

He failed to keep the incredulity out of his voice and it earned him a flash of anger that replaced her bubbling excitement like a flood of cold water.

'No need to make it sound so unbelievable,' she snapped. 'You might only see me as some power suit, great for taking on the difficult dates when one of your five-minute conquests won't make the right impression, but I do actually have a dual existence. As a woman.'

'How long have you been seeing him?' he said.

'What are you? My father?' she said. 'We've been out a few times.'

'How many is a few?'

'Half a dozen, maybe.'

'You're ending our agreement on the strength of half a dozen dates?'

'Yes, well, they weren't dates in the way you think of them. He hasn't just invited me out for an impressive dinner as a preamble to taking me to bed. You can actually get to know someone really well in half a dozen dates if you approach them in a more...*serious* way.'

The thinly veiled dig didn't escape him and indignation sharpened his voice.

'OK, then, if he's so bloody marvellous, and you're so bloody smitten, why the hell isn't *he* on his way to look at your brother's wacky paintings and meet the parents? Couldn't you have dumped me on the phone and saved me a load of time and hassle?'

He pulled the car to a standstill outside the gallery steps and turned off the engine.

'I'm not dumping you! How many times? It's a *fake* relationship!'

A uniformed attendant opened Emma's car door and she got out. Dan threw his keys to the parking valet and joined her on the steps.

'So you keep saying,' he said, keeping his voice low. 'I could have spent this evening working.'

'Like you don't spend enough of your life doing that.' She led the way through the high arched doorway·into the gallery. 'You can easily afford an evening. Alistair's out of the country until next week, and I need this opportunity to draw a thick, black and irreversible line under the two of us for my parents' eyes and undo the tissue of fibs I've told them.'

They walked slowly down the red-carpeted hallway, his hand pressed softly at the small of her back—the perfect escort as always.

'I really don't see why I need to be there for you to do that,' he said, smiling politely at other guests as they passed, maintaining the perfect impression. 'Especially since it's only a *fake* relationship.'

Even as he piled heavy sarcasm on the word *fake* he wondered why the hell he was turning this into such a big deal. Why should he care? It had simply been a handy arrangement, nothing more.

'Because the problem with it being a fake relationship

is that it was a pretty damn perfect one,' she snapped. 'And so now I need a fake break-up.'

She outlined her suggestion as they walked down the hall and it sounded so insane that his mind had trouble processing it.

'You can't possibly be serious. You want to fake an argument in front of your family so you can make some kind of a righteous point by dumping me?'

'Exactly! Shouldn't be too hard. I'll choose a moment, start picking on you, and then you just play along.'

'Why can't you just tell them we broke up? That things didn't work out?' He ran an exasperated hand through his hair. 'Why do I need to be here at all?'

'Because I've spent the last year building you up as Mr Perfect, bigging you up at every opportunity. You've no idea what it was like before we started helping each other out. The constant questions about why I was still single, the hassle about my body clock careering towards a standstill, the negativity about my career. Introducing you as my boyfriend stopped all that like magic. They think you're the son-in-law of their dreams—a rich businessman who adores me, good-looking, charming, not remotely fazed by my mother. They'll never just take my word for it that we broke up amicably. I'd spend the rest of my days being questioned about what I did to drive you away. You'd be forever name-dropped as the one that got away. No man I bring home would ever live up to your perfect memory.'

'You don't think you're going a bit overboard?'

'Are you really asking me that? You've met my mother. You know what she's like.'

He had to concede that Emma's mother was without a doubt the most interfering person he'd ever come across, with an opinion about everything that was never wrong. Her relationship with Emma seemed to bring out the critic in both of them. Mutual exasperated affection was probably the nearest he could get to describing it.

'This way your fabulous reputation will be ruined, by the time Alistair and I finish our trip to the States you'll be a distant memory, and they'll be ready to accept him as my new man.' She shrugged. 'Once I've…you know… *briefed* him on what they can be like.'

Trip to the States? His hands felt clammy. He stopped outside the main gallery and pulled her to one side before they could get swept into the room by the crowd.

'You're going on holiday?'

She looked at him impatiently.

'In a few weeks' time, yes. I'm going to meet some of his friends and family. And then after that I'm going to travel with him in Europe while he covers an international cycling race for American TV. I'm taking a sabbatical from work. I might not even come back.'

'What?' His mind reeled. 'You're giving up your life as you know it on the strength of a few dates? Are you mad?'

'That's exactly it! When do I *ever* do anything impetuous? It isn't as if sensible planning has worked out so well for me, is it? I work all hours and I have no social life to speak of beyond filling in for you. What exactly have I got to lose?'

'What about your family?'

'I'm hardly going to be missed, am I? My parents are so busy following Adam's ascent to celebrity status with his art that they're not going to start showing an interest in my life.'

She leaned in towards him and lowered her voice, treating him to the dizzying scent of her vanilla perfume.

'One of his pictures went for five figures last month, you know. Some anonymous buyer, apparently. But two words about *my* work and they start to glaze over.'

She leaned back again and took a small mirror from her clutch bag.

'And you'll be fine, of course,' she went on, opening the mirror and checking her face in it, oblivious to his floundering brain. 'You must have a whole little black book of girls who'd fall over themselves to step into my shoes. You're hardly going to be stuck for a date.'

True enough. He might, however, be stuck for a date who made the right kind of impression. Wasn't that how this whole agreement of theirs had started? He didn't go in for dating with a serious slant—not any more. Not since Maggie and...

He clenched his fists. Even after all these years thoughts of her and their failed plans occasionally filtered into his mind, despite the effort he put into forgetting them. There was no place for those memories in his life. These days for him it was all about keeping full control. Easy fun, then moving on. Unfortunately the girls who fitted that kind of mould didn't have the right fit in work circles. Emma had filled that void neatly, meaning he could bed whoever the hell he liked because he had her for the serious stuff—the stuff where impressions counted.

It occurred to him for the first time that she wouldn't just be across London if he needed her. He felt oddly unsettled as she tugged at his arm and walked towards the main door.

'You've had some mad ideas in your time, but this...' he said.

\* \* \*

As they entered the main gallery Emma paused to take in the enormity of what her brother had achieved. The vast room had a spectacular landing running above it, from which the buzzing exhibition could be viewed. It had been divided into groupings by display screens, on which Adam's paintings—some of them taller than her—were picked out in pools of perfect clear lighting. A crowd of murmuring spectators surrounded the nearest one, which depicted an enormous eyeball with tiny cavorting people in the centre of it. His work might not be her cup of tea, but it certainly commanded attention and evoked strong opinions. Just the way he always had done.

She took two crystal flutes of champagne from the silver tray of a pretty blonde attendant, who looked straight through her to smile warmly at Dan. For heaven's sake, was no woman immune? Emma handed him one of the flutes and he immediately raised it to the blonde girl.

'Thanks very much…' He leaned in close so he could read the name tag conveniently pinned next to a cleavage Emma could only ever dream of owning. 'Hannah…'

He returned the girl's smile. Emma dragged him away. Why was she even surprised? Didn't she know him well enough by now? No woman was safe.

Correction: no curvy blonde arm candy was safe.

'For Pete's sake, pay attention,' she said in a stage whisper. 'You're meant to be here with me, not eyeing up the staff.'

She linked her arm through his so she could propel him through the crowd to find her parents. It wasn't difficult. Her mother had for some insane reason chosen to wear a wide flowing scarf wrapped around her head and tied to one side. Emma headed through the crowd, aiming for it—aqua silk with a feather pin stuck in it on one side. As her parents fell into possible earshot she pasted on a smile and talked through her beaming teeth.

'They'll never just take my word for it that we've just gone our separate ways. Not without a massive inquest. And I can't be doing with that. Trust me, it'll work better this way. It's cleaner. Just go with everything I say.'

She speeded up the end of the sentence as her mother approached.

'And you don't need to worry,' she added from the corner of her mouth. 'I'll pay for the dry-cleaning.'

'You'll what? What the hell is *that* supposed to mean?'

He turned his face towards her, a puzzled frown lightly creasing his forehead, and his eyes followed her hand as she raised her flute of champagne, ready to tip the contents over his head. She saw his blue eyes widen in sudden understanding and realised far too late that she'd totally underestimated his reflexes.

Dan's hand shot out instantly to divert hers, knocking it to one side in a single lightning movement. And instead of providing the explosive beginning to her staged *we're finished* argument, the glass jerked sharply sideways and emptied itself in a huge splash down the front of her mother's aquamarine jumpsuit. She stared in horror as champagne soaked into the fabric, lending it a translucent quality that revealed an undergarment not unlike a parachute harness.

She'd inadvertently turned her mother into Miss Wet T-Shirt, London. And if she'd been a disappointing daughter before, this bumped things up to a whole new level.

# CHAPTER TWO

'Aaaaargh!'

The ensuing squawk from Emma's mother easily out-did the gallery's classy background music, and Dan was dimly aware of the room falling silent around them as people turned from the paintings to watch.

'An accident—it was an accident...' Emma gabbled, fumbling with a pack of tissues from her tiny clutch bag and making a futile attempt at mopping up the mess.

As her father shook a handkerchief from his pocket and joined in, her mother slapped his hand away in exasperation.

'It'll take more than a few tissues,' she snarled furiously at him, and then turned on Emma. 'Do you know how much this outfit *cost?* How am I meant to stand next to your brother in the publicity photos now? I've never known anyone so *clumsy.*'

Emma's face was the colour of beetroot, but any sympathy Dan might have felt was rather undermined by the revelation that she'd intended, without so much as a word of warning, to make a fool of him in front of the cream of London's social scene. *That* was her plan? *That?* Dumping him publicly by humiliating him? If he hadn't caught on in time it would have been him standing there dripping Veuve Clicquot while she no doubt laid into him with a ludicrous fake argument.

No one dumped him. *Ever.*

'An accident?' he said pointedly.

She glanced towards him, her red face one enormous fluster. He raised furious eyebrows and mouthed the word *dry-cleaning* at her. She widened her eyes back at him in an apologetic please-stick-to-the-plan gesture.

Emma's brother, Adam, pushed his way through the crowd, turning perfectly coiffed heads as he went, dandyish as ever in a plum velvet jacket with a frothy lace shirt underneath. There was concern in his eyes behind his statement glasses.

'What's going on, people?' he said, staring in surprise at his mother as she shrugged her way into her husband's jacket and fastened the buttons grimly to hide the stain.

'Your sister has just flung champagne *all over me,*' she snapped dramatically, then raised both hands as Adam opened his mouth to speak. 'No, no, don't you go worrying about it, I'm not going anywhere. I wouldn't *hear* of it. This is your night. I'm not going to let the fact that my outfit is *decimated* ruin that. I'll soldier on, just like I always do.'

'I've said I'm sorry. I'll pay for the dry-cleaning,' Emma said desperately.

Dan's anger slipped a notch as he picked up on her discomfort. Only a notch, mind you. OK, so maybe he wouldn't have it out with her in public, but he would most certainly be dealing with her later.

Emma closed her eyes briefly. When did it end? Would everything she ever did in life, good or bad, be somehow referenced by Adam's success? Then again, since her mother was already furious with her, she might as well press ahead with the planned mock break-up. Maybe then at least the evening wouldn't be a total write-off.

She drew Dan aside by the elbow as Adam drifted away again, back to his adoring public.

'We can still do it,' she said. 'We can still stage the break-up.'

He stared at her incredulously.

'Are you having some kind of a laugh?' he snapped. 'When you said you needed a fake break-up I wasn't expecting it to involve my public humiliation. You were going to lob that drink over *me,* for heaven's sake, and now you think I'll just agree to a rerun?'

She opened her mouth to respond and he cut her off.

'There are people I *know* in here,' he said in a furious stage whisper, nodding around them at the crowd. 'What kind of impression do you think that would have given them?'

'I didn't expect things to get so out of hand,' she said. 'I just thought we'd have a quick mock row in front of my parents and that would be it.'

'You didn't even warn me!'

'I didn't want to lose the element of surprise. I wanted to make it look, you know, *authentic.*'

He stared at her in disbelief.

There was the squeal of whiny microphone feedback and Adam appeared on the landing above the gallery. Emma looked up towards her brother, picked out in a pool of light in front of a billboard with his own name on it in six-foot-tall violet letters. She felt overshadowed, as always, by his brilliance. Just as she had done at school. But now it was on a much more glamorous level. No wonder her legal career seemed drab in comparison.

No wonder her parents were expecting her to give it all up at any moment to get married and give them grand-children. Adam was far too good for such normal, bor-ing life plans.

His voice began to boom over the audio system, thanking everyone for coming and crediting a list of people she'd never heard of with his success.

'I can't believe you'd make a scene like that without considering what effect it might have on me,' Dan said, anger still lacing his voice.

The blonde champagne waitress chose that moment to walk past them. Emma watched as Dan's gaze flickered away from her to follow the woman's progress and the grovelling apology she'd been about to give screeched to a halt on the tip of her tongue. Just who the hell did he think he was, moaning about being dumped, when *his* relationship principles were pretty much in the gutter? OK, so they might not have actually *been* a couple, but she'd seen the trail of broken hearts he left in his wake. He had no relationship scruples whatsoever. One girl fol-lowed another. And as soon as he'd got what he wanted he lost interest and dumped them. As far as she knew he'd never suffered a moment's comeback as a result.

Maybe this new improved Emma, with her stupid un-requited girlie crush on Dan well and truly in the past, had a duty to press that point on behalf of womankind.

'Oh, get over yourself,' she said, before she could change her mind. 'I'd say a public dumping was prob-ably long overdue. It's just that none of your conquests have had the nous or the self-respect to do it before. There's probably a harem of curvy blonde waitresses and models who've thought about lobbing a drink over you when you've chucked them just because you're bored.

And I didn't actually spill a drop on you, so let's just move on, shall we?'

Adam smiled and laughed his way back through the crowd towards them, and she seized the opportunity as he neared her proudly beaming parents.

'Same plan as before, minus the champagne. I'll start picking on you and…'

The words trailed away in her mouth as Adam clamped one arm around Dan's shoulders and one around her own.

'Got some news for you all—gather round, gather round,' he said.

As her parents moved in closer, questioning expressions on their faces, he raised both hands in a gesture of triumph above his head.

'Be happy for me, people!'

He performed a jokey pirouette and finished with a manic grin and jazz hands.

'Ernie and I are getting married!'

Beaming at them, he slid his velvet-sleeved arm around his boyfriend and pulled him into a hot kiss.

Her mother's gasp of shock was audible above the cheers. And any plans Emma might have had of staging a limelight-stealing break-up went straight back to the drawing board.

Emma watched the buzzing crowd of people now surrounding Adam and Ernie, showering them with congratulations, vaguely relieved that she hadn't managed to dispense with Dan after all. From the tense look on her parents' faces, as they stood well away from the throng, dealing with the fallout from Adam's announcement wasn't going to be easy. And despite the fact that it was a setback in her plans to introduce Alistair, there was no doubt that her mother was much easier to handle when she had Dan in her corner.

Dealing with her parents without him was something she hadn't had to do in so long that she hadn't realised how she'd come to rely on his calming presence. They might have only been helping each other out, but Dan had had her back where her family were concerned. And he'd never been remotely fazed by her overbearing mother and downtrodden father.

She wondered for the first time with a spike of doubt whether Alistair would be as supportive as that. Or would he let her family cloud his judgement of her? What was that saying? *Look at the mother if you want to see your future wife.* If that theory held up she might as well join a nunnery. Alistair would be out of her life before she could blink.

She couldn't let herself think like that.

Calling a halt with Dan was clearly the right thing to do if she was so ridiculously dependent on him that she could no longer handle her family on her own. But she couldn't ruin Adam's excitement. Not tonight. She'd simply have to reschedule things.

And in the meantime at least she wasn't handling her mother's shock by herself. She took a new flute of champagne gratefully from Dan and braced herself with a big sip.

'I'm sure it must just be a publicity stunt,' her mother was saying.

Denial. Her mother's stock reaction to news she didn't want to hear.

'It's not a publicity stunt,' Adam said. 'We're getting married.'

He beamed at Ernie, standing beside him in a slim-cut electric blue suit. He certainly *looked* the perfect match for Adam.

Her mother's jaw didn't even really drop. Disbelief was so ingrained in her.

'Don't be ridiculous, darling,' she said, flicking an invisible speck of dirt from Adam's lapel. 'Of course you're not.'

Adam's face took on the stoic expression of one who knew he would need to press the point more than once in order to be heard. Possibly a few hundred times.

'It's the next logical step,' he said.

'In what?' Her mother flapped a dismissive hand. 'It's just a phase. You'll soon snap out of it once the right girl comes along. Bit like Emma with her vegetarian thing back in the day.' She nodded at Emma. 'Soon went back to normal after a couple of weeks when she fancied a bacon sandwich.'

'Mum,' Adam said patiently, 'Emma was thirteen. I'm twenty-nine. Ernie and I have been together for nearly a year.'

'I know. Sharing a flat. Couple of lads. No need to turn it into more than it is.'

Emma stared as Adam finally raised his voice enough to make her mother stop talking.

'Mum, you're in denial!'

As she stopped her protests and looked at him he took a deep breath and lowered his voice, speaking with the tired patience of someone who'd covered the same ground many times, only to end up where he'd started.

'I've been out since I was eighteen. I know you've never wanted to accept it, but the right girl for me *doesn't exist*. We're having a civil partnership ceremony in six weeks' time and I want you all to be there and be happy for me.'

'I'm happy for you,' Emma said, smiling tentatively.

Happiness she could do. Unfortunately being at the wedding might be a bit trickier. Her plans with Alistair lurked at the edge of her mind. She'd been so excited about going away with him. He'd showered her with gifts and attention, and for the first time in her life she was being blown away by being the sole focus of another person. And not just any person. Alistair Woods had to be one of the most eligible bachelors in the universe, with an army of female fans, and he had chosen to be with *her*. She still couldn't quite believe her luck. Their trip was planned to the hilt. She would have to make Adam understand somehow.

He leaned in and gave her a hug. 'Thanks, Em.'

She had grown up feeling overshadowed by Adam's achievements. Just the look of him was attention-grabbing, with his perfectly chiselled features and foppish dress sense. And that was just now. She couldn't forget the school years, where for every one of Emma's hard-earned A grades there had been a matching two or three showered effortlessly on Adam. His flamboyant, outgoing personality charmed everyone he came into contact with, and her mother never ceased championing his successes to anyone who would listen.

It hadn't been easy being her parents' Plan B. Competing for their interest with someone as dazzling as Adam was an impossible, cold task.

'I blame you for this, Donald,' her mother snapped at her father. 'Indulging his ridiculous obsession with musical theatre when he was in his teens.'

Sometimes Emma forgot that being her parents' Plan A was probably no picnic either.

Adam held up his hands.

'Please, Mum. It's not up for discussion. It's happening with or without your approval. Can't you just be pleased for us?'

There was an extremely long pause and then her mother gave an enormous grudging sigh.

'Well, I can kiss goodbye to grandchildren, I suppose,' she grumbled. 'We'll have to count on you for that now, Emma. *If* you can ever manage to find a man who'll commit.'

She glared pointedly at Dan, who totally ignored the jibe. Emma had been wondering how long it would be before her biological clock got a mention. Terrific. So now Adam could carve out the life he wanted without bearing the brunt of her parents' wrath because they had Emma lined up as their biological backup plan to carry on their insane gene pool.

Going away with Alistair was beginning to feel like a lucky escape. She just needed to get her plans back on track.

Dan scanned an e-mail for the third time and realised he still hadn't properly taken it in. His mind had been all over the place this last day or two.

Since the night of Adam's exhibition, to be exact.

There was a gnawing feeling deep in his gut that work didn't seem to be suppressing, and he finally threw in the towel on distracting himself, took his mind off work and applied it to the problem instead.

He was piqued because Emma had ended things with him. OK, so her plans to dump him publicly hadn't come off, thankfully, but the end result was the same. She'd drawn a line under their relationship without so much as a moment's pause and he hadn't heard from her since. No discussion, no input from him.

He was even more piqued because now it was over with he really shouldn't give a damn. They were friends, work colleagues, and that was all there was to it. Their romantic attachment existed only in the impression they'd given to the outside world, to work contacts and her family. It had always been a front.

His pique had absolutely nothing to do with any sudden realisation that Emma was attractive. He'd always *known* she was attractive. Dan Morgan wouldn't be seen dating a moose, even for business reasons. That didn't mean she was his type, though—not with her dark hair and minimal make-up, and her conservative taste in clothes. And that in turn had made it easy to pigeonhole her as friend. A proper relationship with someone like Emma would be complex, would need commitment, compromise, emotional investment. All things he wasn't prepared to give another woman. Tried, tested and failed. Dan Morgan learned from his mistakes and never repeated his failures.

It had quickly become clear that Emma was far more useful to him in the role of friend than love interest, and all thoughts of attraction had been relegated from that moment onwards. It had been so long now that not noticing the way she looked was second nature.

But the gnawing feeling in his gut was there nonetheless. Their romantic relationship might have been counterfeit, but some element of it had obviously been real enough to make the dumping feel extremely uncomfortable.

He'd never been dumped before. *He* was the one who did the backing off. That was the way he played it. A couple of dinner dates somewhere nice, the second one generally ending up in his bed, a couple more dates and then, when the girl started to show signs of getting comfortable—maybe she'd start leaving belongings in his flat, or perhaps she'd suggest he meet her family—he'd simply go into backing-off mode. It wasn't as if he lied to them about his intentions. He was careful always to make it clear from the outset that he wasn't in the market for anything serious. He was in absolute control at all times—just as he was in every aspect of his life. That was the way he wanted it. The way he *needed* it.

He was amazed at how affronted he felt by the apparent ease with which Emma had dispensed with him. Not an ounce of concern for how *he* might feel as she'd planned to trounce him spectacularly in front of all those people. His irritation at her unbelievable fake break-up plan was surpassed only by his anger with himself for actually giving a damn.

Feeling low at being dumped meant you had feelings for the person dumping you. Didn't it?

Unease flared in his gut at that needling thought, because Dan Morgan didn't *do* deep feelings. That slippery slope led to dark places he had no intention of revisiting. He did fun, easy, no-strings flings. Feelings need not apply. Surely hurt feelings should only apply where a relationship was bona fide. Fake relationships should mean fake feelings, and fake feelings couldn't be hurt.

That sensation of spinning back in time made him feel faintly nauseous. Here it was again—like an irritating old acquaintance you think you've cut out of your life who then pops back up unexpectedly for a visit.

That reeling loss of control he'd felt in the hideous few months after Maggie had left, walking away with apparent ease from the ruins of their relationship. He'd made sure he retained the upper hand in all dealings with women since. These days every situation worked for *him*. No emotion involved. No risk. His relationships were orchestrated by *him,* no one else. That way he could be sure of every outcome.

But not this time. Their agreement had lasted—what?—a year? And in that time she'd never once refused a date with him. Even when he'd needed an escort at the last minute she'd changed her schedule to accommodate him. He'd relied on her because he'd learned that he *could* rely on her.

And so he hadn't seen it coming. That was why it gnawed at him like this.

*You don't like losing her. You thought you had her on your own terms. You took her for granted and now you don't like the feeling that she's calling the shots.*

He gritted his teeth. This smacked a bit too much of the past for comfort. It resurrected old feelings that he had absolutely no desire to recall, and he apparently couldn't let it slide. What he needed to do now was get this thing back under his own control.

Well, she hadn't gone yet. And he didn't have to just *take* her decision. If this agreement was going to end it would be when *he* chose—not on some whim of hers. He could talk her round if he wanted to. It wouldn't be hard. And then *he* would decide where their partnership went.

If it went anywhere at all.

He pulled his chair back close to the desk and pressed a few buttons, bringing up his calendar for the next couple of weeks with a stab of exasperation. Had she no idea of the inconvenience she'd thrust upon him?

Not only had Emma dumped him, she'd really picked a great moment to do it. *Not.* The black tie charity dinner a week away hadn't crossed his mind the other evening when she had dropped her bombshell. It hadn't needed to. Since he'd met Emma planning for events like that had been a thing of the past. He simply called her up, sometimes at no more than a moment's notice, and he could count on the perfect companion on his arm— perfect respect for the dress code, perfect intelligent conversation, an all-round perfect professional impression. There was some serious networking to be had at such an event, the tickets had cost a fortune, and now he was dateless.

He reached for the phone.

It rang for so long that he was on the brink of hanging up when she answered.

'Hello?' Her slightly husky voice sounded breathless, as if she'd just finished laughing at something, and he could hear music and buzzing talk in the background, as if she were in a crowded bar or restaurant.

From nowhere three unheard-of things flashed through his mind in quick succession. Emma never socialised on a work night unless she was with him; she never let her phone ring for long when he called her, as if she was eager to talk to him; and in the time that he'd known her she had never sounded this bubblingly happy.

'What are you doing a week from Friday?' he said, cutting to the chase.

'Hang on.'

A brief pause on the end of the phone and the blaring music was muted a little. He imagined her leaving the bar or the restaurant she was in for a quiet spot, perhaps in the lobby. He sensed triumph already, knowing that she was leaving whoever she was with to make time to speak with *him*.

'Tying up loose ends at work, probably. And packing.'

So she was storming ahead with her plans, then. The need for control spiked again in his gut. He went in with the big guns.

'I've got a charity ball in Mayfair. Black tie. Major league. Tickets like hen's teeth. It promises to be a fabulous night.'

He actually heard her sigh. With impatience, or with longing at the thought of attending the ball with him? He decided it was definitely the latter. She'd made no secret of the fact she enjoyed the wonderful opulence of nights like that, and he knew she'd networked a good few new clients for herself in the past while she was accompanying him—another perk of their plus-one agreement.

For Pete's sake, she had him giving it that ludicrous name now.

Their usual dates consisted of restaurant dinners with his clients. Pleasant, but hardly exciting. Except for Dan's own company, of course. Luxury events like this only came up occasionally. He waited for her to tear his arm off in her eagerness to accept.

'What part of "it's over" did you not understand, Dan?' she said. 'Did you not hear any of what I said the other night?'

It took a moment to process what she'd said because he had been so convinced of her acceptance.

'What I heard was some insane plan to desert your whole life as you know it for some guy you've known five minutes,' he heard himself say. 'You're talking about leaving your friends and family, walking out of a job you've worked your arse off for, all to follow some celebrity.'

'It would be a sabbatical from work,' she said. 'I'm not burning my bridges there. Not yet. And you make me sound like some crazy stalker. We're in a relationship. A proper grown-up one, not a five-minute fling.'

He didn't miss the obvious dig at his own love life, and it made his response more cutting than he intended.

'On the strength of—what was it?—*half a dozen dates?*' he said. 'I always thought you were one of the most grounded people I know. You're the last person in the world I'd have expected to be star-struck.'

He knew from the freezing silence on the end of the phone that he'd sunk his foot into his own mouth up to the ankle.

'How dare you?' she said, and a light tremble laced her voice, which was pure frost. 'It was obviously too much to hope that you might actually be *pleased* for me. Yes, Alistair is in the public eye, but that has *nothing* to do with why I've agreed to go away with him. Has it occurred to you that I might actually like him because he's interested in *me* for a change? As opposed to the grandchildren I might bear him or the fact I might be his carer when he's old and decrepit. Or…' she added pointedly '…the fact that I might boost his profile at some damned work dinner so he can extend his client list a bit further because he never quite feels he's rich or successful enough.'

She paused.

'You're saying no, then?' he said. 'To the all-expenses-paid top-notch Mayfair ball?'

He heard her draw in a huge breath and then she let

it out in a rude, exasperated noise. He held the phone briefly away from his ear. When he put it back her voice was Arctic.

'Dan,' she was saying slowly, as if he had a problem understanding plain English, 'I'm saying no to the Mayfair ball. I'm through with posing as your professional romantic interest so you can impress your damned client list while you date airhead models for a week at a time.'

Had he really thought this would be easy? It occurred to him that in reality she couldn't be further from one of his usual conquests, of which currently there were two or three, any of whom would drop everything else at a moment's notice if he deigned to call them up and suggest getting together.

You didn't get as far up the legal career ladder as she had by being a 'yes' girl. But her easy refusal bothered the hell out of him. He'd expected her to agree to resurrect their agreement without even needing persuasion. Had expected her to thank him, in fact.

The need to win back control rose another notch with her unexpected refusal of his offer, and also her apparent indifference to it. It put his teeth on edge and gnawed at him deep inside.

'How about helping me out with this one last time, then?' he pressed, confident that in an evening he could quickly turn the situation around. Reinstate their agreement and then decide what he wanted to do with it. End it, change the terms—whatever happened it would be up to him to decide, *not* her.

'Dan, you don't need my help,' she said patiently. 'I'm in the middle of dinner and I haven't got time to discuss this now. It's not as if you're short of dates. Grab your little black book and pick one of your girlies from there. I'm sure any one of them would love to go with you.'

There was a soft click on the end of the phone as she hung up.

That went well. *Not.*

# CHAPTER THREE

'LET ME JUST recap. You're in a relationship with Alistair Woods—*the* Alistair Woods, the man who looks a dream in Lycra—and you're not planning on mentioning it to Mum and Dad?'

Adam's eyebrows practically disappeared into his sleek quiff hairstyle and Emma took a defensive sip of coffee. The fantasy she'd had of disappearing around the world on Alistair's arm and calling up her parents from Cannes/LA/somewhere else that screamed kudos, to tell them she would be featuring in next month's celebrity magazine, had turned out to be just that. A fantasy.

Because Adam was getting married.

Her big brother, Adam—who never failed to make her laugh, and who was so bright and sharp and funny that she'd never for a moment questioned her role in family life as the forgettable backing act to his flamboyant scene-stealer. Of *course* she had paled into insignificance in her family's eyes next to Adam—not to mention in the eyes of schoolteachers, friends, neighbours... But only in the way that everyone else had faded into the background next to him in her own eyes. He was simply someone who commanded success and attention without needing to put in any effort.

She couldn't exit her life without telling Adam, and she'd asked him to meet her for coffee to do exactly that. She'd even tried to sweeten the news by buying him an enormous cream bun, which now sat between them untouched. If she'd thought he'd simply scoff the bun and wave her off without so much as a question, she'd been deluded.

'You're not going yet, though, right? You're at least waiting until after the wedding?'

'Erm...'

He threw his arms up theatrically.

'Em! You can't be serious! How the hell am I going to keep Mum under control without you? I can't get married without my wingman!'

'Woman,' she corrected.

He flapped both hands at her madly.

'Whatever. You saw what Mum was like the other night. The wedding is in Ernie's home village. He's got a massive family, they're all fabulously supportive, and if you don't come along our family's big impression on them will be Mum telling everyone I'll get over it when I get bored with musical theatre and meet the right girl.'

'Dad will be there,' she ventured. 'Maybe you could talk to him beforehand, get him to keep Mum on a short leash.'

'He'd be as much use as a chocolate teapot. We both know he's been beaten into submission over the years. Since when has Mum ever listened to him? She just talks over him. I *need* you there.'

His voice had taken on a pleading tone.

'It's not as simple as that. Alistair's covering another cycling race in a few weeks' time. We're meant to be having a break before it starts because it's pretty full-on. I'm flying out to the States, meeting some of his friends and family, relaxing for a couple of weeks. It's all been arranged.'

She looked down at her coffee cup because she couldn't bear the disappointment on Adam's face.

*Adam* had never made her feel insignificant. Any inability to measure up was her failing, not his. And she was the one who let it bother her.

'Then there's no problem! Bring Alistair to the wedding,' Adam said, clapping his hands together excitedly. 'You've already said he's got time off from work. The guy's probably got a private jet. You could zoom in and zoom out on the same day if you had to.' He made a soaring aeroplane motion in the air with his hand.

She suppressed a mirthless laugh.

'You mean introduce him to Mum and Dad? A whole new person for Mum to drive insane?' She narrowed suspicious eyes at him. 'It would certainly take the heat off you and Ernie.'

He held his hands up.

'You'll have to introduce him at some point anyway. OK, so you might travel with him for a while, maybe even settle in the States with him, but you'll have to come home to visit, won't you?'

She didn't answer. Visiting wasn't something she'd thought about much in her excitement about getting away. It hadn't crossed her mind that she'd be missed that much.

'Bloody hell, Em.'

She sighed. She couldn't say no to Adam any more than the rest of the world could. He just had that gift.

'It'll be a nightmare if I bring Alistair,' she said. 'Mum will be all over him like a rash, demanding marriage and grandchildren and mentioning my biological clock. He's a free spirit. He'll run a bloody mile.'

Adam was on the comment like a shot.

'Then you definitely *should* bring him. You're talking about leaving your whole life behind to be with him— don't you think he ought to prove himself a bit before you take that kind of plunge? If he's really the guy you think he is—if he's really going to put you first above everything else in his life—then he'll love you no matter what crazy relative you introduce him to, right?'

She couldn't help latching on to that thought—that desire for a level of regard where she would come absolutely first with someone for a change. Was that what this was really about? Was she afraid to bring Alistair to the wedding because of some stupid subconscious conviction that he might see through her? Might see that she really was a plain and inferior mousy girl, despite all the years she'd put in on breaking away from that persona?

'He does love me,' she insisted, mainly to bat away the prickle of unease that had begun in her stomach. It was all Adam's fault for questioning her perfectly laid plans.

'Great. Then put your man where your mouth is. Introduce him to Mum and watch him prove it.'

Dan clicked his phone off with ill-suppressed irritation.

Cancelling a working lunch at a moment's notice was extremely bad form. Focused to a pinpoint on work performance himself, he found it difficult to tolerate lateness or bad planning in others. Especially when it meant he'd interrupted his day to turn up at a restaurant when he could have eaten lunch on the run or at his desk.

He gave the menu an uninterested glance and was on

the point of calling for the bill for the two drinks he'd ordered while waiting for the no-show client when he saw Emma cross the restaurant. A waiter showed her to a table by the window and she sat down alone, so engrossed in scrolling through her phone that she didn't even notice he was in the room.

The news that she was leaving seemed to have given him a new heightened perspective, and he picked up on tiny details about her that had simply passed him by before. He saw her objectively for once, as someone else might. Alistair Woods, for example. This time his gaze skimmed over her usual business dress when previously it would have stopped at observing the sharply cut grey suit. Instead he now noticed how slender she was. How had he never picked up before on the striking contrast of her double cream skin with her dark hair? The ripe fullness of her lower lip? When you had reason to look past the sensible work image she was unexpectedly cute. He'd been so busy taking her presence for granted he'd failed to notice any of those things.

Maybe this lunchtime wouldn't be a total waste of time after all. Dealing with her on the phone had been a bad choice. A face-to-face meeting might be a better approach to talking sense into her.

He picked up his drink and crossed the room towards her. His stomach gave a sudden flutter that made him pause briefly en route to the table—then he remembered that it was lunchtime. He was obviously just hungry, and since he was here maybe he should take the chance to grab a sandwich as well as a drink and a smoothing-over session with her. Not that his appetite had been up to much this last week or so.

'Dan!'

Her eyes widened in surprise as he slid into the seat opposite her and put his drink down on the table. She glanced quickly around the restaurant, presumably for a waiter.

'Really glad I bumped into you,' he said. 'Just wanted to say no hard feelings about the other night.'

A smile touched the corner of her lips, drawing his eyes there. She was wearing a light pink lipstick that gave them a delectable soft sheen.

'The other night?' she said.

'The charity ball.'

'I hadn't realised there *could* be hard feelings,' she said, toying with her water glass. 'It was just a work arrangement we had after all, right? Not like I broke off a date, is it?'

She held his gaze steadily and for the first time it occurred to him that it might take a bit more than sweet-talking for him to regain the advantage between them. His own fault, of course. He was judging her by the standards of his usual dates, who seemed to fall over themselves to hang on his every word. Emma was a different ball game altogether. Taking her for granted had been a mistake.

He gestured to the waiter for a menu.

'How did it go, then?' she said.

'How did what go?' he evaded.

'The charity ball?' she said. 'No-expenses-spared Mayfair hotel, wasn't it? Who did you take?'

'Eloise,' he said shortly.

She had to bring it up, didn't she? When what he'd really like would be to erase the entire evening from history.

'Which one's that?'

She cranked her hand in a come-on gesture and looked at him expectantly until he elaborated.

'She's a leg model,' he said. 'You know—tights, stockings, that kind of thing.'

The woman had the best legs in the business. Unfortunately she was entirely defined by that one physical feature. Tact, sense and reliability didn't come into it.

'Did you make any new contacts?' Emma said. 'Normally charity bashes are great for networking, aren't they? Perfect opportunity for a shared goal, loads of rich businessmen?'

'Normally they are,' he said. 'But normally I have you with me, oozing tact and diplomacy and class.'

It had been kind of hard to hold a professional conversation with Eloise's arms wound constantly around his neck like a long-legged monkey. The one time he had begun to make headway with a potential client she'd returned from the bar with two flutes of pink champagne and positioned herself between them by sitting on his lap.

He watched Emma carefully, to see if his compliment had hit its mark, and was rewarded with the lightest of rosy blushes touching her high cheekbones. Hah! Not so easily dismissed after all. A proper in-depth talk about her whirlwind plans and he was confident he could sow a few seeds of doubt. From there it would be a short step to convincing her to stay put, reinstating their working agreement, getting things back to normal.

He was giving her a quick follow-up smile when he realised her eyes were actually focused somewhere over his shoulder and the blush had nothing to do with him. A wide smile lit up her face and suddenly she was on her feet, being drawn into a kiss by a tall blond man with a deep golden tan and perfect white teeth. No matter that he was wearing a sharply cut designer suit and an open-necked silk shirt instead of clinging Lycra cycling shorts and a helmet. He was instantly recognisable—by Dan and by the room at large.

Alistair Woods was on the premises.

The surrounding tables suddenly appeared to be filled with rubberneckers. Clearly basking in the attention, he offered a wave and a nod of greeting to the tables either side of them before sitting down—as if he was a film star instead of a has-been athlete. Dan felt an irrational lurch of dislike for the guy, whom he'd never met before but who clearly made Emma brim with happiness.

*Jealous?* his mind whispered.

He dismissed the thought out of hand. This wasn't about jealousy. Emma was clearly star-struck and on the brink of making a rash decision that could ruin her working life and her personal life before you could say *yellow jersey.* If anything, he would be doing her a favour by bringing her back down to earth.

'Alistair, this is Dan,' Emma said, taking her seat again, her hand entwined in Alistair's. 'Dan, this is Alistair Woods.'

She glanced pointedly at Dan.

'Dan happened to be here meeting someone,' she said. 'He just came over to say hello.'

She didn't want him to join them. It couldn't be clearer.

'Heard a lot about you, friend,' Alistair said in a strong American accent, stretching in his seat. 'You're the platonic plus-one, right?'

Of all the qualities he possessed that Emma could choose to reference him by she'd chosen that. Just *great.*

'Did you get my phone message?' Emma asked Alistair eagerly. 'I know it means rejigging our plans a little, but I just can't let my brother down. It's his wedding day. And it'll be a good chance for you to meet my family.'

She was taking Alistair to Adam's civil partnership ceremony?

Dan felt a deep and lurching stab of misplaced envy at the thought of this guy slotting neatly into his recently vacated place—fake though it might have been—in regard to Emma's family. OK, so they were opinionated and mouthy, and in her mother's case that translated as being downright bigoted at times, but he'd never felt anything but welcomed by them, and their simple mad chaos had been something he'd enjoyed.

An unhappy flash of his own childhood rose in his mind. His mother, hardly more than a child herself. No father—at least not in any way that mattered to a kid. Plenty of 'uncles', though. He hadn't been short of those. And plenty of random babysitters—friends of his mother's, neighbours, hardly the same person twice. What he wouldn't have given for an interfering nosy mother at the age of thirteen, when babysitters had no longer been required and he'd been considered old enough to be left home alone.

He dismissed the thought. Things were different now. He'd learned to rely only on himself, without influence from anyone else. Maggie had been the one time he'd deviated from that course, and it had turned out to be an agonising mistake that he had no intention of repeating. He had no need for family. Past or future.

'Got your message, baby, but there's no way we're going to be able to make the gay wedding,' Alistair said.

Dan watched Emma's smile falter and suppressed an unexpected urge to grab Woods by the scruff of the neck.

'Why not?' she said. 'I can't miss Adam's wedding. I promised him.'

Dan recognised her tone as carefully neutral. She was upset and trying to cover it up. Did this Alistair know her well enough to pick up that little nuance? *Hardly.*

Emma took a sip of her coffee in an effort to hide her disappointment. Had she really thought it would be that simple? That he would just agree to her every whim?

'We're spending that weekend in the Hamptons,' Alistair was saying. 'I've been in talks to land a movie role and one of the producers is having a garden party. Can't miss it. Lots riding on it. I'm sure Arnold will understand. Career first, right?' He leaned in towards her with a winning expression and squeezed her hand. 'We agreed.'

*His* career first.

'Adam,' Emma corrected. She could hear the disappointment, cold and heavy, in her own voice. 'His name is Adam. And I really *can't* miss his wedding.'

Alistair sat back and released her hand, leaving it lying abandoned in the middle of the white tablecloth. His irritation was instant and palpable, and all the more of a shock because he'd never been anything but sweetness and light so far. But then, she hadn't demanded anything from him so far, had she? She'd been only too eager to go along for the ride. *His* ride.

'You do whatever you have to do, baby,' he said dismissively. 'You can fly out and join me afterwards.'

'But I really wanted you to be there, to meet my family.'

'Sorry, honey, no can do.'

Alistair turned to the waiter to order a drink. She noticed that Dan was looking at her with sympathy and she looked away. Everything was unravelling and it was a million times worse because he was here to witness it. She tried to muster up an attitude that might smother the churning disappointment in her stomach as her high hopes plummeted.

From the moment she'd met Alistair he had made her feel special, as if nothing was too much trouble for him. But it occurred to her that it had only related to peripheral things, like flowers and restaurants and which hotel they might stay in. Now it had come down to something that was truly important to her he hadn't delivered the goods. It wasn't even up for discussion. Because it clashed with his own plans.

Disappointment mingled hideously with exasperated disbelief. She felt like crashing her head down despairingly on the table. Would she ever, at any point in her life, meet someone who might actually put her first on their agenda? Or was this her lot? To make her way through life as some lower down priority?

'Look, I don't want to interfere,' Dan said suddenly, leaning forward. 'But how about I step in?'

'What do you mean, step in?' she asked, eyes narrowed.

*Suspicion. Not a good sign,* Dan thought. On the other hand Alistair was looking more than open to the suggestion.

Dispensing with Alistair to some swanky party on a different continent was far too good an opportunity to pass up. All he needed to do was step into Alistair's shoes as Emma's date and he'd have a whole weekend to make her rethink her actions and to get the situation working for him again.

'I got my invitation to the wedding this morning,' he said, thinking of the gaudy card that had arrived in the post, with *'Groom & Groom!'* plastered across the front in bright yellow, very much in keeping with Adam's usual in-your-face style.

*'You've* been invited?' she asked with obvious surprise, as if their interaction had been so fake that all the connections he'd made with her family were counterfeit, too. But he genuinely liked Adam—they'd always had a laugh.

'Yes,' he said. 'So if Alistair is away working I can fill in if you like—escort you. It's not as if I haven't done it before. What do you think?'

She stared at him.

'For old times' sake?' he pressed. 'I'm sure Alistair won't mind.'

He glanced at the ex-cyclist, who held his hands up.

'Great idea!' he said. 'Problem solved.'

Emma's face was inscrutable.

'That won't be necessary,' she snapped. 'And actually, Dan, if you don't mind, we could do with a bit of time to talk this over.'

She looked at him expectantly and when he didn't move raised impatient eyebrows and nodded her head imperceptibly towards the door.

All was no longer peachy with her and Mr Perfect and that meant opportunity. He should be ecstatic. All he needed to do was leave them be and let the idiot drive a wedge between them, because one thing he knew about Emma was that her parents might drive her up the pole but Adam meant the world to her. Yet his triumph was somehow diluted by a surge of protectiveness towards Emma at Alistair's easy dismissal of her. He had to force himself not to give the smug idiot a piece of his mind.

He made himself stand up and excused himself from the table.

Give the guy enough leeway and he would alienate Emma all by himself. Dan could call her up later in the role of concerned friend and reinstate their agreement on his own terms.

Bumped to make room for Alistair's career?

Her mind insisted on recycling Adam's comments from the day before. *'Don't you think he ought to prove himself before you take that kind of plunge?'* Was it really so much to ask?

The insistent 'case closed' way Alistair had refused her suggestion told her far more about him than just his words alone, and it occurred to her in a crushing blow of clarity. How had she ever thought she would come first with someone who had an ego the size of Alistair's? An ego which was still growing, by the sound of it, if he was trying to break into the movies.

The waiter brought their food and she watched as Alistair tucked in with gusto to an enormous steak and side salad, oblivious to the fact that there was anything wrong between them. He'd got his own way. For him it was business as usual. His whole attitude now irked her. It was as if she should be somehow grateful for being invited along for the ride. She'd been too busy being swept away by the excitement of someone like him actually taking an interest in her to comprehend that being with him would mean giving up her life in favour of his. Where the hell did she come first in all of that?

It dawned on her that he'd have a lot of contractual issues coming his way with his broadening career. Was that what made her attractive to him? The way she dealt so efficiently with legal red tape on his behalf? Had he earmarked her as his own live-in source of legal advice?

This wasn't a relationship; it was an *agreement*. All she'd done was swap one for another. She could be Dan's platonic plus-one or Alistair's live-in lawyer. Where the hell was the place for what *she* wanted in any of that?

'It's all off, Alistair,' she said dully. It felt as if her voice was coming from somewhere else.

He peered at her hardly touched plate of food.

'What is, honey? The fish?'

He looked around for a waiter while she marvelled at his self-assurance that her sentence couldn't possibly relate to their relationship. Not in *his* universe. Alistair probably had a queue of women desperate to date him, all of them a zillion times more attractive than Emma. He had international travel, a beach home in Malibu, a little getaway in the Balearics, his own restaurant and a glittering media career in his corner. What the hell did she have that could compete with that? Interfering parents and a tiny flat in Putney? Why the hell would he think she might want to back out?

'Us,' she said. 'You and me. It's not going to work out.'

He gaped at her.

'Is this because I won't come to your gay brother's wedding? Honey, have you any idea how much is riding on this new contract? This is the next stage of my career we're talking about.' He shook his head at her in a gesture of amazement. 'The effort that's gone into lining up this meeting. I'm not cancelling that so you can show me off to your relatives at some small-town pink wedding. And it's not as if I'm stopping you going. That Neanderthal platonic pal of yours has said he'll step up to the plate.'

She was vaguely aware of people staring with interest from the surrounding tables. His slight about Dan irked her. Neanderthal? Hardly. He looked like an Adonis, and he was smart, sharp and funny. She clenched her teeth defensively on his behalf.

'I want *you* to come with me. I want you to meet my family.'

'And I will, honey. When the time's right.'

'It's a family wedding. Everyone who knows me will be in one place for the first time in years. When could the time possibly be more right than that?'

His face changed. Subtly but instantly. Like the turning of a switch. The easy, open look that had really taken her in when she'd first met him, the way he'd listened to her as if she mattered and showed her real, genuine interest, was gone. That look was now replaced by a sulky, petulant frown.

'Because it's all about *you,* of course,' he said. 'No regard for *my* career. You have to make these opportunities, Emma, and then follow them up. You don't mess people like this about, because there are no second chances. I can't believe you're being so selfish.'

For a moment the Emma she'd grown up to be actually questioned her own judgement on the strength of that last comment of his. The insecure Emma, whom she'd begun to push out of her life when she'd at last moved away from home and gone to university—a place where she had finally been accepted without reference to Adam or anyone else. With her own successes not watered down but recognised. After university she'd moved to London instead of going home to the West Country, in case that old, pessimistic Emma was somehow still there, lurking, ready to take over.

No way was she going back to *that* mindset now.

She pushed her plate to one side and leaned down to pick up her bag and take out her purse. She took enough money to cover her own meal and put it down on the table. She didn't throw it down. She wasn't going to resort to stupid tantrum gestures—she was a professional.

'I'm sorry, Alistair.' She shook her head at him. 'I don't know what I was thinking. I thought there would be more to us than being driven by your career. You want me to travel with you so I can iron out your legal issues, don't you? Maybe draw up the odd contract, or just hand out advice where you need it?'

He didn't say anything.

'Come on—be honest with me. Is that what this has really been about?'

A long pause.

'Well, you can't deny it's an advantage,' he said eventually. 'But only in the same way as if you were a hairdresser or a stylist.'

'I thought we were having a relationship. I didn't realise I was joining your entourage,' she snapped. 'I should never have let myself get swept away by this. Have a nice trip back to the States.'

She left the table and aimed her shaky feet at the exit, determined not to look back. When she did, inevitably, she saw that he was signing autographs for the people at an adjacent table. No attempt to follow her or talk her round. But why would he? He undoubtedly had a queue of people waiting to take her place.

She pressed her teeth hard together and concentrated on them to take her mind off the ache in her heart and the even worse heat of stupidity in her face.

She'd bigged up her relationship with him beyond all reason. How could she have been such a fool?

Now she had to face the climb down.

# CHAPTER FOUR

EMMA GLANCED AROUND the half-empty office, grateful that her colleagues had finally drifted out for lunch. She'd informed HR first thing that her new, glamorous life as the jet-set girlfriend of Alistair 'White Lightning' Woods was no longer happening and the news had quickly filtered through the staff. At least she hadn't jacked her job in completely. That would have made things a whole lot worse. And it was best to get the humiliation over with, right?

Except that she wasn't sure how many more sympathetic stares she could take.

Her phone blared into life and she looked down at the display screen.

Dan. Again.

She pressed her hot forehead with the heel of one hand, as if it might help her think clearly. There'd been rather a lack of clear thinking around her lately.

What the hell had possessed her to let Alistair Woods sweep her off her feet? She was a sensible professional. She knew her own mind and she never took risks. Was she so bogged down in a stupid teen inferiority complex, in a lifetime of failed one-upmanship with Adam, that she'd momentarily lost all common sense? She'd built a life here in London, where she blended in. She'd excelled at not being noticeable and her professional life had flourished. And now, the one time she'd ventured out of that safe box, the same old outcome had happened. Her judgement had been rubbish, she hadn't measured up and it had all come crashing down around her ears. Why had she ever thought things would be different with Alistair?

Defensive heat rose in her cheeks even as she picked up the phone. By extreme bad luck Dan had been there in the restaurant to see that her romance with Alistair wasn't such a bed of roses after all. The thought of filling him in on all the details made a wave of nausea rise in her throat and her eyes water.

'Hello.' She shaped her voice into the most neutral tone she could muster.

'Hey.'

His voice was warm, deep and full of concern, and her heart gave a little flutter because as a rule Dan Morgan didn't do concern. He did sharply professional business demands, he did high expectations, he did arm's length.

'Just checking that you're OK.'

*I blabbed to everyone who knows me in London that I was on the point of eloping with the most desirable man in sport. I've made the biggest fool of myself and now I have to tell everyone that, actually, he's an arse and it's not going ahead. So, yes, thanks, I'm just peachy.*

Climbing down in front of Dan was somehow worst of all. And not just because she was embarrassed at her own poor judgement when she should have known better. There was a tiny part of her mind that was busy pointing out that for the first time ever Dan was showing interest and support for her beyond what she could do for him and his work. Had he suddenly realised he valued her as more than just a handy plus-one? How many missed calls from him had she had since lunchtime? Five? Wasn't that a bit excessive?

'Why wouldn't I be?' she said.

'Things just seemed a little tense at lunch yesterday.'

*As if you could cut the atmosphere with a chainsaw.*

'Did you get everything sorted with Alistair?'

A rush of bitterness pelted through her as she answered. 'Oh, yes. I *definitely* got everything sorted with him.'

'He's changed his plans, then? He's coming to the civil partnership?'

*Oh, bloody hell, the civil partnership.*

An unsettling wave of trepidation turned her stomach over. The biggest Burney family get-together in years and she no longer had a date. Could her crushed and battered ego survive a whole weekend of jibes from her mother about the race for grandchildren being hampered by her inability to keep a man?

'Not exactly,' she said.

'How do you mean?'

There was a sharp over-interested edge to his voice that she recognised from the many work dinners she'd accompanied him to. This was how he sounded when he was on the brink of nailing a new client—as if nothing could distract him from his goal. *Five missed calls and now he was hanging on her every word.*

*Oh, hell.*

She leaned forward over the desk in exasperation and pressed her hot forehead against its cold wooden surface.

'Alistair and I are off,' she blurted out. 'He's a total *arse*. He wouldn't even talk about making it to the wedding.'

'You broke up because he won't come to your brother's wedding?'

'Pretty much, yes,' she said.

She couldn't bring herself to tell him the truth—that Alistair had only treated her like a princess because he'd wanted a live-in lawyer. Her cheeks burned just at the thought of it.

'I couldn't let Adam down and he just couldn't see that. It made me realise that work will always come first for him.'

'Sorry to hear that.'

Was there a twist of cool I-told-you-so about his voice? She pulled her head from the desk and narrowed her eyes, trying to decide. He was probably glad it was all off. Wasn't that exactly what he'd wanted? For things to get back to normal? Then again, at least he wasn't saying it out loud.

She tightened her grip on the phone.

Wallowing in self-pity was one thing, but it didn't change the fact that in a week's time she had to keep her parents in check while surrounded by Ernie's family. Knowing Adam, it would be the most stuffed-with-people event of the year. She'd become so used to relying on Dan at family get-togethers that the prospect of coping with that by herself filled her with dread.

With her dreams in tatters there was a warm tug of temptation just to scuttle back to the way things had been. And wasn't that exactly what Dan had been angling for all along? Why not resurrect the old plus-one agreement? That nice, safe social buffer that had stood between her and humiliation until she'd stupidly given it up. Her reason for ending it was on its way back to the States right now. She'd dipped a toe in the murky waters of proper dating and it had turned into a train wreck.

She thought it through quickly. Dan was brilliant with her mother, never remotely fazed and the epitome of calm. Exactly what she needed to get her through that scary event. And maybe then she could begin to look forward, put Alistair behind her, make a fresh start.

'Actually, about the wedding…' she said.

'You want to reinstate the plus-one agreement?' He might as well give it its proper ludicrous name.

'Yes. I know it's a bit of a turnaround.'

*Just a bit.*

He couldn't quite believe his ears. So *now* she wanted him to step back in as her handy fake boyfriend, as if the last couple of weeks had never happened? What about her insane plan to dump him in public? And she hadn't done him the one-off favour of going with him to his Mayfair charity ball—oh, no. He'd had to spend the evening peeling Eloise off him. But *now* she needed *him* things were different.

And he wasn't about to make it easy for her.

'I thought having each other as a social backup was *holding us back?*' he said. 'Your words.'

A pause on the end of the phone, during which a hint of triumph coursed through him as he reclaimed the upper hand. He was back in control. How they proceeded from here would be *his* decision, not hers.

'I may have been a bit hasty.'

He didn't answer.

'Please, Dan. Ernie has a massive family and his father's a High Court Judge. Our family is me and my parents plus a few distant relatives that my mother's alienated over the years. I've promised Adam I'll keep my mum in check, and the thought of doing it on my own fills me with horror. *Please.* You're so good with them.'

She paused again, and when he didn't immediately leap in to agree, deployed the big guns of guilt.

'I thought this was what you wanted—everything back the way it was? I know I screwed up, and I'm sorry. But how many times have I helped *you* out at the last minute? What about that race meet where you landed your biggest client? You called me two hours before and I stepped in. Won't you even consider doing this one tiny event for me?'

He hesitated. She had a point about the race meet.

'Please, Dan. I want to make sure everything runs smoothly for Adam. You know how hard it is to please my mother.'

She'd lowered her voice now and a pang of sympathy twisted in his gut because he *did* know.

He could tell from her defeated tone that she thought he was going to refuse. This was his opportunity to bring things right back to where he wanted them. Their agreement had paid dividends—there was no denying that—but he'd let it run on far too long. He'd become complacent and let her become too important to drop easily. He couldn't have someone like that in his life, even if it *was* supposed to be under the heading of 'work'. She wanted a fake boyfriend for the wedding? He'd be the best fake boyfriend in the world. For old times' sake. And then he'd dump their agreement without looking back for a second.

'OK,' he said.

Emma took a deep breath as sweet relief flooded her. It had absolutely nothing to do with the prospect of Dan's company of course. She was way past that. It was just the thought of having an ally in what was bound to be a social minefield.

'Really?' she said. 'I wasn't sure you'd agree after I said no to your charity thing. Thank you *so* much. And you know I'm happy to step in next time you need someone—'

'Please let me finish,' he cut in. 'I'll do it. But this is the last time. I'll stand in for you in acknowledgement of all the times you've stepped in for me at the last minute. But when we head back to London after the wedding, that's it. Our agreement is over. I'll manage my own socialising going forward, and you can carry on as before.'

Emma took a sharp breath, because for some reason that hurt in a way that the Alistair debacle hadn't. He didn't sound inclined even to retain a friendship between them. They would revert to being Mr Morgan and Ms Burney, businessman and lawyer, nothing more. Had she really meant so little to him?

It was a stupid, stupid pang of disappointment because she'd already *dealt* with the idea that nothing would ever happen between her and Dan. Her ridiculous crush on him was a thing of the past. She'd been planning to travel the world with Alistair, for Pete's sake, never looking back.

It had somehow been much easier to deal with when *she'd* been the one making that choice.

Emma glanced around the lobby of the Cotswolds hotel that Adam and Ernie had chosen as their wedding venue, surprised at the stunning old-world charm of the place.

Huge vases of spring flowers softened the dark wood panelling of the walls. Beautifully upholstered chairs and sofas stood in cosy groupings around the fireplace, which was taller than she was.

She would have expected Adam to want to make his vows somewhere screamingly modern in the midst of the buzz of London. Apparently Ernie's family were a lot more old-school than that. They'd lived here in this honey-coloured stone village for generations. She felt a stab of envy at the give and take in her brother's relationship. It seemed *Adam* didn't have a problem putting his partner's family first.

On the other hand it might have been less nerve-racking if the wedding *was* taking place on home ground. Here they would be surrounded by Ernie's nearest and dearest, all eagerly awaiting the impression the Burney family would make. Her stomach gave a churn of unease at the thought.

'What name is it?'

The blonde receptionist ran a manicured fingernail down her computer screen.

'Burney,' Emma said. 'I'm part of the Burney-Harford wedding party.'

Adam had made a block reservation.

Dan strode through the door, fresh from parking the car. He rested one hand on the desk and ran the other through his dark hair, spiking it more than ever. His blue eyes crinkled as he smiled his gorgeous lopsided smile—the one that had melted half the female hearts in London.

The manicured fingernail came to an instant standstill and the receptionist's jaw practically fell open as she gazed at him.

'Mr and Mrs Burney?' she asked.

Emma sighed.

'No, that would be my parents.' Mercifully they weren't here yet. 'It will be under Miss.'

The girl handed over keys—proper old-fashioned ones—and a wad of check-in paperwork.

Emma gave Dan an expectant look.

He smiled at her.

'Great venue.'

'What about you?' she said.

'What *about* me?'

'Your booking,' she whispered.

In her peripheral vision she picked up the interested change in the receptionist's posture. She'd seen it a hundred times before. She took in her appearance. Blonde hair—*check*. Sleekly made-up face—*check*. Eager smile—*check*. She knew exactly what would come next.

She waited for Dan to confirm loudly that he had a separate booking—ergo, he was free and single, and in possession of a hotel room and a shedload of charm. Instead he held her own gaze steadily, as if his radar no longer picked up pretty blondes. Not a hint of a flirt or smoulder. Not so much as a glance in the girl's direction.

'Didn't make one,' he said cheerfully.

Emma stared at him incredulously for a moment, before realising that the receptionist was watching them with an interest that was way beyond polite. She walked away into the corner and when he didn't immediately follow gave him an impatient come-on beckoning gesture. He sauntered over. The receptionist made a poor attempt not to watch the laconic grace of his movements.

'What do you mean, you didn't make a booking? You had your invitation—where did you think you were going to sleep? On the lawn?'

He shrugged. 'I never got round to booking a room and then, when you asked me to step in as your date, I didn't need to. I'll be staying in your room, won't I?' He put an arm around her shoulders and gave her a squeeze. 'All part of the façade, right?'

She was rendered momentarily speechless by a wave of spicy aftershave and the sudden closeness of him, and then his assumption about their sleeping arrangements slammed into her brain.

'You can't stay in *my* room,' she squeaked.

'The whole weekend takes place at this hotel. It's hardly going to give a loved-up impression if we sneak off to separate rooms at the end of the night, is it?'

'In the Burney family we'd fit right in,' she said, thinking of her parents, who'd had separate bedrooms since she was in her late teens.

He ignored her and turned his head sideways to read the number on the key fob in her hand.

'Eighteen,' he said, heading for the stairs. 'First floor.'

She stumbled after him, her mind reeling. The thought of their sleeping arrangements hadn't entered her head. This was the first time they'd faked their relationship for longer than a couple of hours. She'd simply *assumed* he would have a separate booking.

An image of her vanity case full of embarrassing toiletries danced through her mind, swiftly followed by the fact that her hair looked like a fright wig when she woke up. She gave herself a fast mental slap, because she absolutely did *not* care whether she looked attractive or not, and any attempt to make herself look good was *not* for the benefit of Dan Morgan.

She made a grab for his arm and he turned round on

the landing and looked at her, an expression of amusement on his face.

'I don't see what the problem is,' he said. 'This is a professional arrangement, right? We'll treat it as such. Or were you thinking that I might take advantage of the situation and jump your bones?'

His ice-blue eyes crinkled at the corners as he grinned at her and a flare of heat crept upwards from her neck.

'What am I supposed to think?' she snapped defensively. 'I know what you're like with your five-minute flings. So don't be getting the wrong idea. I am most definitely *not* interested in any shallow no-strings fling. If I'd wanted that I would have stuck with Alistair.'

'I wouldn't *dream* of suggesting one,' he said, holding his hands up. 'The thought never even occurred to me. You're perfectly safe with me.'

Her face burned hotter than ever, because if that wasn't a knock-back she didn't know what was. He was basically telling her she was arrogant for assuming he would *want* to hit on her. Of course he wouldn't. He'd had a year's worth of chances and he'd passed them all up. Her toes curled and she turned away, because her face undoubtedly looked like a tomato right now.

'Look, it's no big deal,' he said. 'We can just shelve the idea. I'll head back to London and you can go it alone.'

A sudden bolt of dread made her stomach lurch as a familiar bugling voice drifted through from Reception.

'Booking for Burney. It'll be one of the higher-end suites—parents of the groom.' A pause. 'The *real* groom, that is…'

Her parents were on the premises and her mother

was obviously on her usual form. Poor Adam. He was relying on her.

She glanced back at Dan. He spread his hands questioningly.

'Your call. Do you need a plus-one or not?'

'This is gorgeous, isn't it?' She sighed as she turned the huge key in the lock and walked ahead of him through the door.

Their cases and bags stood waiting for them at one side of the room, efficiently delivered by the porter. It was everything that a country house hotel bedroom should be. The floorboards were suitably creaky, the dark wood panelling of the walls gleamed, the bed had four posts draped with a soft voile fabric, and there was a pile of squashy pillows and a floral bedspread that matched the silk curtains. Behind a door to one side was a luxurious *en-suite* bathroom.

Dan had to bend slightly to avoid smacking his forehead on the doorjamb. He followed her into the room. She hovered awkwardly by the window, clearly still on edge at the whole room-sharing thing.

'Very nice,' he said and, unable to resist the tease, added, 'Nice, large bed.'

He found his gaze drawn to her face as she dropped her eyes and saw faint colour touch her pale cheekbones. Her obvious awkwardness was seriously cute. His usual dates were pretty full-on—a fast track to the physical. Shyness didn't come into it. It was an odd novelty to be sharing a bedroom with someone without bed actually being on the agenda.

He took pity on her and held his hands up.

'You don't need to worry. I'll take the couch.'

There was a squashy sofa to one side of the window, upholstered in a lavender floral fabric. It would be too short for him, but for a couple of nights it would do.

'We can take it in turns,' she said. 'You take the couch tonight. I'll take it tomorrow.'

Momentarily surprised at the counter-offer, he nodded. Not that he would let her.

'Deal.'

She clapped her hands together and took a business-like breath, as if she were about to start a work meeting.

'Right, then, let's get organised, shall we? This can be my space...' she moved one of the smaller pieces of her vast luggage collection onto a dark wood bureau with an ornate mirror '...and this can be yours.' She waved a hand at the antique desk. 'You get the desk and complimentary Wi-Fi. Should be right up your street. I can't imagine you needing much else.'

'You make me sound like some workaholic.'

'I hate to break it to you...' she said, nodding at his minimal luggage, which included a laptop bag. 'It's hardly a get-away-from-it-all minibreak, is it? You've brought your office with you!'

'Only out of habit,' he protested. 'I take the laptop everywhere. Doesn't mean I'm going to use it.'

She turned back to him and pulled a sceptical face. He held his hands up.

'And somewhere in here...' she shuffled through the wad of check-in bumph '...is the itinerary for the weekend. Might as well know what we're up against. Blimey, we'll hardly have time to draw breath.'

He took it from her—a piece of stiff white card decorated in eye-watering yellow. He was suddenly very aware as he looked at the packed agenda that he would be joined at the hip with her pretty much twenty-four-seven for the next couple of days—a situation he hadn't really considered properly when he'd made light of the room-sharing thing.

It all seemed a bit less amusing now they were actually in the room and she was talking him through their shared personal space and unpacking what seemed like endless belongings. He avoided guests at his flat as much as possible. One night was his limit, with sex the sole item on the agenda. Conversation and space-sharing didn't come into it. He simply didn't *do* the give and take required to cohabit. Not any more. He'd done it once and he had no inclination to be reminded of the lash-up he'd made of it.

*Just a weekend.* He latched on to that thought.

'Certainly not doing a small quickie wedding, are they?' he commented, speed-reading the itinerary.

Emma leaned in close to look at the card with him and he picked up a soft, sweet wave of the scent she always wore as she tucked a stray lock of hair behind her ear. His pulse stepped up a notch in response.

He wasn't used to her looking dressed down like this. That was all it was. Their usual encounters involved smart, polished business dress or the occasional evening gown for gala dinners and the like. Even then her outfits were always reserved, and he couldn't remember a time when he'd seen her in jeans or when she'd worn her hair down. Now it fell softly to her shoulders in waves, framing her heart-shaped face. When you took the time to look behind her uptight attitude, she was actually very pretty.

'When has Adam ever done anything on a small scale?' she said. 'It just wouldn't be him, would it?'

He refocused his attention on the itinerary.

'So, this evening there's welcome drinks on the terrace. Then tomorrow the wedding is here in the grounds, followed by a night of celebration. And then a slap-up cooked breakfast the morning after. That marquee must be for the wedding.' He nodded out of the window.

She followed his gaze, then moved away and sat down on the edge of the bed.

'Adam must be mad,' she said. She bounced up and down on the mattress approvingly.

Dan leaned against one of the posts at the foot of the bed, watching her. Diaphanous fabric softly draped over it—white with a tiny pale yellow flower print.

'Why? Because his wedding's the size of an elephant or just because there *is* a wedding?' he said.

She looked up at him, a tiny smile touching the corner of her lush mouth, and he had a sudden image of himself leaning her slowly back onto the floral quilt and finding out what she tasted like.

He stood up straight and gave himself a mental shake. What the hell was he thinking? This was a last-ditch platonic date—not one of his conquests. The fact that the venue involved a bedroom instead of a boardroom didn't change the fact that their relationship was work-based. It also didn't seem to stop the slow burn that had kicked in low in his abdomen.

'Both,' she said, and shrugged.

'Is that because of Alistair? I mean, you've got to admit he was a bit of a curveball. You *never* date. Not in all the time I've known you. And then suddenly in the space of a few weeks you're packing up and leaving.'

She didn't answer for a moment. There was a distant expression on her face, as if she was thinking it over.

'Partly because of Alistair,' she said at last. 'But really what happened with him was probably inevitable. Meeting the right person isn't something I've excelled at so far. He was so attentive and considerate that I thought for once I'd really cracked it. I really believed it was something special. But it was the same old story.'

She smiled at him, an I-don't-care smile that was just a bit too small to be convincing, and he felt a sudden spike of dislike for Alistair.

'Same old story?'

She sighed. 'Maybe you had a point when you said I was a bit star-struck—I don't know,' she said, picking at a loose thread on the floral quilt.

There was an air of defeat about her that made him want to kick Alistair's butt.

'I got a bit swept up in all the excitement of it. It wasn't so much him as the idea of *life* with him. It was exciting. It was glamorous. It was everything that I'm not.'

'It was two-dimensional Hollywood claptrap. Who wants to live in a shallow world like that? You can't be the first person to get sucked in, but you're the most grounded person I know. You'll soon get over that cardboard idiot.'

That made her smile, lighting her face. He liked her looking happy like that. He liked that he'd *caused* her to look like that.

'I won't be making the same mistake again,' she said. 'I'm going to put *myself* first from now on. But even if one day I do find the right person I won't be getting married with my parents in tow. *No way.* Nice plane trip to a beach somewhere with a couple of random witnesses.'

He grinned.

'What about you?' she said, wiping the smile right off his face.

'What *about* me?'

'Come on—surprise me. What kind of wedding would you have if you could choose?' She leaned back on her palms and narrowed her eyes at him. 'Some beach thing in the Maldives?' She flapped a hand. 'No, no, let me guess… It would be something small. You could probably do it in a lunch hour if you wanted to—take an hour or so out and nip to the registry office. Quick glass of champagne, handful of confetti, and then you could get back to work.'

'Very funny.'

*Terrific.* He should have seen that coming. The last thing he needed right now was a chat about marriage aspirations. He just wanted to get through this weekend and get on with his life. And he didn't even have his own hotel room to retreat to.

He moved away from the bed to look out of the window, his back to her.

'Of course you'd have to stick at a relationship for longer than a month, then, wouldn't you?' she teased.

He didn't look round. 'It has nothing to do with sticking at a relationship. I have to prioritise. The business is growing at a massive rate. I need to put all my energy into that.'

'Nobody needs to work twenty-four-seven,' she said. 'Not even you. Maybe you should think about slowing down, or at least taking a breather. I just don't get why you're so crazy for work. I've never known anyone so obsessed. And it's not like you've got anyone to share the rewards with. None of your girls last five minutes.'

He stared across the hotel lawn at the dense woodland right in the distance on the skyline. Stared at it but didn't see it.

Another image flashed through his mind in its place. *Sticking at relationships. Sharing the rewards. Maggie.* Dark-haired Maggie with her gentle smile and her kindness.

Maggie and—

He stamped hard and fast on that thought before it could multiply. What the hell was his stupid brain doing, dragging that old stuff up?

At the faint sound of voices and car doors slamming he glanced down onto the gravel drive as Adam emerged, beaming, from a yellow Rolls-Royce, quiff cemented in place, wearing dark glasses like a celebrity. Ernie was right by his side. A gang of porters staggered under a stack of luggage. Obviously overpacking ran in the family.

'Your brother's here,' he said, to distract her, because he couldn't imagine a time when he'd be keen to discuss his future wedding plans.

Emma scrambled off the bed and joined Dan at the window.

'We'd better get ready for the drinks party,' she said, turning to her heap of luggage and proceeding to unzip.

He checked his watch.

'But it's *hours* away.'

As if that mattered…

'I need to make a good impression,' she said. 'I hate being late. And you have to help me keep my parents in check.'

She looked up at him, suddenly feeling awkward,

with a bottle of pink shower gel in one hand and a loofah in the other.

'Do you want to use the bathroom first? I mean, perhaps we should work out some kind of rota.'

'For Pete's sake, we don't need a rota,' he said, his tone exasperated. 'It's two days. You take the bathroom first. You're bound to take longer.'

'What's that supposed to mean?' She made an indignant face. 'That you look great just the way you are but I'm some hag who needs work?'

He laughed out loud.

'No. It means I've never met a woman who takes less than half an hour to get ready.'

She turned towards the bathroom, her arms now full of toiletries.

'And you don't look like a hag,' he called after her. 'You never have.'

It was the nearest thing to a compliment he'd ever given her.

# CHAPTER FIVE

DAN GAZED OUT of the open hotel room window and listened to the soft sound of falling water from the shower in the *en-suite* bathroom. It had kicked in five minutes after Emma had shut the door firmly and twisted the lock, as if she thought he might burst in on her.

The marquee was now bathed in early-evening golden sunshine. The sweeping lawns were perfectly manicured, and a lily pond lay on the far right of his view. If he leaned forward far enough he could see an ornate wrought-iron bench set to one side of it. He wondered how many brides' backsides had been plonked there over the years. It really was the perfect photo opportunity.

He was at the cream of wedding venues in the south of England and it was only natural that it might whip up a few passing thoughts of his one and only brush with marriage, right? Just fleeting thoughts... That was all.

*Maggie and Blob.*

The name filtered back into his mind before he could stop it.

Blob, he had called him—or her—after the fuzzy early scan which had been completely unintelligible to both of them except for the blob with the strong and speedy heartbeat. It had made Maggie laugh. An interim holding name while they bandied about proper full-on names. Andy or Emily. Sam or Molly. To delete as appropriate once they knew the gender, at a later date that had never arrived.

Four months hadn't been later enough.

*Maggie and Blob.*

An unexpected twist of long-suppressed dull pain flared in his chest—the blunt ache of an old injury. He wrenched his mind away forcibly. For Pete's sake, what was he *doing?* He did *not* need a pointless trip down memory lane right now.

He rationalised madly. He hadn't been near a wedding in donkey's years. Without a family to speak of, things like weddings didn't crop up all that often, and this place was Wedding Central. It was bound to stir things up. But that was all this was—just a momentary blip. He had dealt with Maggie and Blob. They were part of the past and he'd left them there with admirable efficiency. He'd dealt with it all and moved on.

Perhaps that was part of the problem. His life was drifting into predictability, leaving his mind free to wander where it shouldn't be going. He needed to up the stakes at work—perhaps a new business venture. Work had always been the solution before.

The shower splashed on and on, and judging by the enormous bag of toiletries Emma had heaved in there with her she wasn't going to be emerging any time soon. There was no time like the present when it came to refocusing your mind. He unzipped his laptop bag and sat down at the antique desk.

Emma gave her reflection one last glance in the steamy-edged mirror and paused to let her heart reconsider its decision to take a sprint. She knew she'd spent far too long rubbing in scented body lotion and blitzing body hair, telling herself it was because she wanted to make a good impression on Ernie's family. For Adam. It had absolutely nothing to do with the fact that Dan was on the other side of that door. He was fully rationalised. Whatever there was between them, it would always have terms. It would always be about work.

But he could easily have refused to accompany her here. I mean, really, what was in it for him? She knew she'd annoyed him with the public break-up thing, but he had no real understanding of how things were with her parents—how the pursuit of an easy life had become the norm for her. It was her defence mechanism against the endless nagging, and that was what Dan had been. Her route to an easy life. Shame it had all been fictional.

But still he was here.

And now there was that tiny nagging voice, whispering that he might just have come to his senses since she'd broken the news that she was leaving. He might have suddenly realised she meant more to him than a handy work date. Could that be why he now *wanted* the arrangement to end, despite his reluctance to let it go at first? Perhaps this weekend could lead to something more than a platonic agreement between them.

It was a *stupid* nagging voice. To listen to it, or even worse to act on it, would be to set herself up for humiliation. Was the Alistair debacle not enough evidence that she had warped judgement when it came to decoding male behaviour?

The twisty lurch of disappointment in her stomach when she opened the bathroom door told her she'd been stupid to read anything into his presence here.

He was still wearing the same jeans and T-shirt, he'd clearly made zero effort to unpack his minimal luggage, and worst of all he was leaning into his laptop where it stood open on the desk, surrounded by the usual scattering of work papers.

Had she actually thought for a moment that his presence here might have anything to do with an increased regard for her? What a fool she was. Nothing had changed between them at all. She was imagining the whole damn thing just because he'd shown her some support. Clearly she was desperate for attention now Alistair had humiliated her.

At best, Dan wanted to part on good terms—*that* was why he'd decided to accompany her to the wedding and help her out this last time. There was nothing more to it than that.

Undoubtedly the fact that the hotel had complimentary Wi-Fi had made the decision a whole lot easier for him.

Dan stared at her as she stood in the doorway, the deliciously sensual scent of her body lotion mingling with steam, epically failing to register the look of resigned disapproval on her face because of her transformation from office starch.

Her dark hair fell in damp tendrils, framing her heart-shaped face, and there was a pink hue to her usually pale skin. She was totally swamped by one of the enormous white his 'n' hers hotel bathrobes, and his mind immediately insisted on debating what she might or might not be wearing underneath.

He stared hard at the e-mail on his computer screen until his eyes watered, in the hope that his stupid body would realise that they might be sharing a bedroom and a bathroom but their interaction was limited to the professional—just the way it always was. For the third time he read it without taking a single word in.

'You're working,' she said with ill-hidden disappointment. 'Don't you ever take a break?'

He felt a surge of exasperation.

'What else was I meant to do? Take a stroll round the grounds? Sit and watch the bathroom door? It's just a couple of e-mails while I waited for you to be finished.'

'Well, there's no need to snap,' she said, crossing the room to the bureau and squeezing a handful of her hair with the corner of a towel. 'You could have gone first if you'd wanted to.'

Oh, for Pete's sake! He hadn't counted on the inconvenient need to be constantly polite that their space-sharing had caused. Without the shared goal of sleeping together it boiled down to a *you-go-first-no-you-I-insist* awkwardness about using the facilities.

With a monumental effort he curbed his irritation.

'I'm sorry,' he said. 'I'm just not really used to sharing my personal space, that's all. I'm used to doing what I like whenever I want to.'

She glanced at him and smiled.

'That's OK.'

She began combing her long hair out, looking at her reflection in the mirror.

'You have a different girlfriend every week,' she said. 'I'd have thought bedroom etiquette was your speciality.'

He watched as she sprayed perfume on her neck and pulse points. The intense scent of it made his senses reel.

'That's different.'

'I don't see how.'

He shrugged.

'There's no give and take needed. They stay over and the next morning they leave. There's no personal belongings cluttering up every surface.' He glanced at the bed, currently festooned with her clothes. 'There's no pussy-footing around each other over who's hogging the bathroom. It's done and dusted, with minimal disruption.'

And minimal emotional input. Which was exactly how he liked it.

'You make it sound *so* romantic,' she said sarcastically, dipping her finger in a pot of pink make-up and dabbing it gently over her mouth.

His eyes seemed to be glued to the tiny movements and to the delicious pink sheen it gave her luscious lower lip. She didn't notice, focusing on what she was doing in the mirror.

'It isn't *meant* to be romantic,' he said. 'It is what it is.'

A temporary and very enjoyable diversion, with no lasting repercussions.

'So it's fine for them to stay over until you get what you want, and then they're ejected from the premises at breakfast time? Is that it?'

'You make it sound callous,' he said, snapping his laptop shut and gathering up his work papers. 'When actually it's fun.' She threw him a sceptical glance and he couldn't resist adding, 'Hot, steamy, no-holds-barred fun,' just to see if he could make her blush again.

'You have no scruples,' she complained.

He saw the flush of pink creep softly along her cheekbones, highlighting them prettily. Sparring with her was actually turning out to be enjoyable.

'I don't need scruples,' he said. 'We're all adults. I never make any promises that I don't keep. I'm honest with them about not wanting anything serious and they appreciate that.'

'No, they don't,' she said. 'They might say they're fine with it, but in reality they're hoping it will turn into more. It's not the same for women. Sleeping with someone isn't some throwaway thing. It's a big deal—an emotional investment. And, anyway, if you always put those limits in place when you meet someone you're cutting out the chance of ever having a proper relationship. You could meet the perfect person for you and she'd just slip through your fingers unnoticed.' She fluttered her fingers in the air to press her point. 'You'd never even know. You'll be perpetually single.'

'And that,' he said, grabbing his bag and making for the bathroom, 'is exactly the point.'

He smiled at the roll of her eyes as he closed the door.

Emma didn't usually go in for a second coat of mascara. Or a second squirt of perfume just to make sure it lasted the distance. But then she didn't usually go in for room-sharing. She wished someone would tell her stupid pulse rate that it was supposed to be platonic.

He had the speediest bathroom habits she'd ever come across, and as a result she was still balancing on one leg, one foot in her knickers and the other out, when the lock clicked and the bathroom door opened. Heart thundering, she thanked her lucky stars that she'd decided to keep the bathrobe on while dressing, and covered her fluster by whipping her panties on at breakneck speed, clamping the robe around her and then giving him a manic grin that probably bordered on cheesy.

Her entire consciousness immediately zeroed in on the fact that he had a fluffy white towel wrapped around his muscular hips and absolutely nothing else. The faint hint of a tan highlighted his broad chest and the most defined set of abs she'd ever seen outside a magazine. He rubbed a second towel over his hair, spiking it even beyond the usual.

She forced her eyes away, snatched the bathrobe more tightly around her and crossed to the bed.

'I think we should have a quick round-up of the ground rules for tonight,' she said, flipping through some of the clothes laid out on the bed, not really seeing them, just aiming to look busy.

'Did you just say "ground rules"?'

She glanced up and had to consciously drag her eyes upwards from his drum-tight torso. His amused grin told her that unfortunately he'd clocked her doing it, so she pressed the platonic angle hard to show him that they might be sharing a hotel room but she had no romantic interest in him whatsoever. None. Zilch.

'I did. We need to pull off being the perfect couple.'

He let out an amused breath. 'I think you can count on *me* to know how to do that,' he said.

She silently marvelled. He obviously thought a few posh dinners and hot sex was all it took.

'This is a whole different ball game. When you've been my date before it's mostly been an hour or two alone with my family in a restaurant. A trained chimp could probably pull that off. This is going to be a lot more full-on. The place is going to be stuffed with Ernie's family. We need to make a good impression for Adam. We have to look totally together but in an *über*-normal way, so we can counteract my parents' dysfunctional relationship.'

He looked briefly skyward. One hand rested on the

desk; the other was caught in his hair. By sheer will she didn't look at the towel, held up only by a single fold. Instead she fixed her eyes on his face.

'You're over-analysing,' he said. 'Trust me on this.'

He pulled a few items from his bag and headed back to the bathroom with them slung over his arm.

'I know how to pull off loved-up,' he called over his shoulder, with not a hint of trepidation at the evening ahead when *she* was a bag of nerves. 'Just like you know how to pull off professional couple. Just leave it to me.'

A couple of hours' work had certainly done the trick in terms of refocusing him. He'd fired off a ton of important e-mails, had a look through some figures, and if he needed any more of a distraction to stop his mind dredging up the past, looking at Emma as he emerged from the bathroom again was it.

Fully dressed now, she was wearing her hair long again, this time brushed to one side, so it lay gleaming over one shoulder of the soft green maxi-dress she wore. Her newly applied perfume made his pulse jump and she wore more make-up than usual, highlighting her wide brown eyes and the delectable softness of her lips.

Playing the part of boyfriend to *that* for the evening was hardly going to be a chore.

He could tell she was nervous just by the way she was behaving. Give her a room full of professionals and she could network her way around it with the best of them, holding her own no matter who he introduced her to. But with the prospect of a weekend with her own family she was reduced to a quivering shadow of her work self.

That very jumpiness seemed to heighten his aware- ness of her on some level, and it felt perfectly natural for him to lean in close to her on the way down the passage towards the stairs. He rested his hand lightly around her waist, conscious of her slenderness beneath the light flowing drape of her dress.

Emma was hotly aware of him next to her as he escorted her along the landing. As his arm curled around her waist she picked up the spicy scent of his aftershave on warm skin and her stomach gave a slow and far too delicious flip. Everything about him seemed to be overstepping the lines of her personal space in a way it never had before. The way he stood just a fraction closer to her than strictly necessary... The way he'd held her gaze a beat too long when he'd teased her about wanting ground rules.

'Er...there's no one actually here to see us,' she pointed out, glancing down at his hand, now resting softly on her hip. She looked up at him questioningly.

'Just getting into character,' he said easily, not moving his hand.

'I'm determined to inject a bit of tradition if it kills me, Donald,' she heard suddenly.

Her mother's distinctive tones drifted down the corridor from behind them and she froze next to Dan. And then they were getting louder.

'I think I'll have a word with Ernie's parents about top tables and speeches. It's a family occasion. They'll be expecting us to have some input.'

Emma's heart began to sink at the thought of her mother instigating a cosy chat about traditional wedding roles with Ernie's clearly far more liberal parents and she stopped at the top of the stairs, intending to intercept her and suggest a new approach of just enjoying the celebrations without actually *criticising* any of them.

The coherence of that thought dissolved into nothing as Dan suddenly curled his hand tighter around her waist and propelled her back against the nearest wall. Before she could so much as let out a squeak, he kissed her.

## CHAPTER SIX

NIGH ON EIGHT months of conditioning herself that her attraction to him was just a stupid crush, and all it took to get every nerve-ending of attraction right back in action was one kiss. One kiss that made her toes curl and her stomach feel as if it might have turned into warm marshmallow.

He caught her lower lip perfectly between his own lips and sucked gently on it, his hand sliding lower to cup the curve of her bottom. The smooth wood panelling of the wall pressed against her back. She could feel every hard, muscular contour of his body against hers, and sparks danced down her spine and pooled deliciously between her legs.

Her eyes fluttered dreamily shut—and when she opened them she was staring right into the disapproving gaze of her mother, a vision in purple sequins, a few feet away over Dan's shoulder.

Reality clattered over her like a bucket of ice cubes and she wriggled away from him, the flat of her hand against the hardness of his chest, her heart racing. He made no effort to disengage whatsoever, so she added an extra pace's worth of space between them herself.

He was watching her steadily, the petrol-blue shirt he

was wearing making his eyes seem darker than usual, a grin playing about his lips. Her heart raced as if she'd just sprinted up and down the creaky stairs a few dozen times.

She tore her gaze away from his.

'Mum!' she gabbled.

'Hello, darling.' Her father leaned in to give her a kiss and shook Dan's hand.

Her mother glanced at him disapprovingly.

'Really, Emma,' she remarked. 'A little class would be good. *Anyone* could walk along this corridor and how do you think it would look to find you two in a clinch?' She radiated criticism, despite the fact that she was intending to steam in and openly re-evaluate the wedding plans. When it came to social etiquette she could be remarkably selective. 'You're not sixteen, you know. A little decorum would be good. Thank goodness Adam can rely on your father and me to make a good impression.'

She swept past them down the stairs.

Emma stared after her incredulously and then rounded on Dan.

'What the hell was that about?' she snapped. 'What did you think you were *doing?*'

'We've got an image to keep up,' he said, shrugging as if he'd done nothing wrong.

So he'd just been playing a part, while her knees had turned to jelly. There had been a moment back there when she'd thought she might simply fold into a hot puddle on the floor.

But he didn't need to know that, did he?

'I don't think we need to take things quite *that* far,' she said, trying to breathe normally.

'Are you complaining that my kisses are somehow

substandard?' he said, his gaze penetrating, a grin touching the edge of his mouth and crinkling his eyes.

Her blush felt as if it spread all the way from the roots of her hair to her toes, because as kisses went it had been utterly off-the-scale sublime.

'Of course I'm not saying that,' she snapped. 'It's just that when I said we were aiming for perfect couple I obviously should have specified that I didn't mean perfect couple at honeymoon stage.'

'What *were* you aiming for, then?' he said, blue eyes amused. He rubbed his lips thoughtfully with his fingers, as if he was savouring the taste of her.

She ran a hand self-consciously over her hair. Perhaps if she could smooth the muss out of it she could smooth the fluster out of the rest of her.

'I was thinking more comfortable in each other's company. You know the kind of thing. More the on-the-brink-of-settling-down stage.' She shrugged, her pulse returning to normal now. 'Then again, you're clearly drawing on your own experiences. When did you last have a relationship that made it past loved-up? You go from meet straight to dump. You miss out everything in between.'

He laughed, clearly amused by the whole affair.

'You gave it one hundred and ten per cent when you were staging our "break-up",' he pointed out, making sarcastic speech marks in the air with his fingers. 'Right the way down to the spectacular drink-throwing. What's the matter with that approach now?'

She could hardly say it made her knees unreliable, could she?

'Because the whole point of this is to stop my parents showing Adam up,' she said. 'And they've actually as good as just told *us* to get a room. I think we might have taken it a *teensy* bit too far.'

She led the way down the stairs

'Spoilsport,' he called after her, kick-starting her blush all over again.

As they walked out through wide-open double doors onto a stone-flagged terrace she was more aware than ever of his hand pressed softly in the hollow of her back. It seemed to generate sparks of heat that climbed tantalisingly up her spine. Her mind insisted on re-playing his kiss on a loop, making her feel completely flustered.

Fortunately she had the reality check of Adam's flam-boyant styling to smack her between the eyes. The ter-race was softly lit by hurricane lamps on tables and pin-lights strung along the stone balustrade. A band were set up to one side, playing jaunty music to which none of the guests were dancing because they were all crowded around the centrepiece in the middle of the terrace.

For a moment she had to lean back and narrow her eyes while her brain processed exactly what it was.

Adam and Ernie had apparently commissioned a life-size ice sculpture of themselves. It gleamed in the floor-level spotlighting. It depicted Adam with one fin-ger pressed against his temple in a thoughtful pose while Ernie looked on.

Her parents were standing to one side, and her moth-er's face was a stunned picture. On the bright side, at least it appeared to have rendered her speechless. As soon as she saw Emma and Dan she crossed to them, the beads on her purple evening dress shimmering as she walked. She wouldn't have looked out of place in a ballroom dance show.

The real Adam and Ernie joined them, wearing complementary head-to-toe designer suits, with a group of Ernie's relatives flanking them.

'Aren't they *fabulous?*' Adam was gushing, clasping his hands together in delight. 'And the best thing about having yourself carved is that you can tweak the way you look. So I made myself taller and we had a bit shaved off Ernie's nose.'

'Well, I've got to be honest, I'm not that impressed,' her mother sniffed, deploying her usual tactic: if it was outside her comfort zone then she was suspicious of it. She leaned backwards appraisingly. 'They've made your ears stick out,' she remarked to Adam. 'How much did you pay for them?'

'Mum, you can't ask things like that,' Emma said, smiling nervously at the group.

Her mother drew herself up to her full height and pursed her lips. 'Of course I can. Adam's my son. We're parents of the groom. I'm entitled to my opinion.'

'They were a gift,' Adam said, pink-cheeked. 'From Ernie's aunt. She's a sculptress. She spent *hours* working on them. In a freezer.'

There was an ensuing pin-drop silence, during which Emma's father took a canapé from a passing waiter and attempted to lever it into his mouth.

'No more of those tartlets, Donald,' her mother said, leaning in as if with a sixth sense. She expertly took the canapé out of his hand and his teeth closed over thin air. 'Cholesterol!' she snapped.

Ernie dragged a blushing Adam away to circulate, and Emma did her best to stand in as sounding board for her

mother's stream-of-consciousness opinions on every mi-
nuscule aspect of the proceedings. She was vaguely and
gratefully aware of Dan's calming presence at her side.

How would she manage at things like this in future,
without him watching her back? The thought of losing
that comfort gave her a needling sense of dread.

A couple of hours later she was worn out with smiling and small talk and her mother seemed to have re-
connected with a kindred spirit in the shape of Emma's
spinster aunt Mabel, last seen at a childhood Christmas
before moving up north. Emma watched them across the
terrace, their arms folded in matching poses, matching
critical expressions on their faces. Although her voice
was drowned out by the music, she saw her mother's
lips form the word *grandchildren* as the pair of them
looked her way.

She turned to see her father surreptitiously sliding
food from the buffet table onto an already heaped plate
while her mother was preoccupied.

'Your mother's got me on a diet,' he said when he saw
her disbelieving stare.

'Doesn't sound like much fun,' Dan said.

He shrugged.

'It's not so bad. I have a second lunch down at the golf
club most days. They do a fantastic pie and crinkle-cut
chips. What she doesn't know, and all that.'

Oh, for Pete's sake, she'd had just about enough of
this.

'I need a walk,' she said, heading for the steps down
from the terrace and onto the lawns.

'I'll come with you.'

Dan followed her away from the party, grabbing a
couple of champagne flutes from a passing waiter.

* * *

It was a beautiful clear summer night, the velvety cropped lawn silver in the moonlight. Strings of pearly pin-lights lent the trees a fairy-tale quality.

Emma walked on her toes at first, to stop her three-inch heels sinking into the grass, then gave up and took them off, walking barefoot, with the hem of her dress sweeping the grass. Dan was acutely aware of the change in their height difference. Now she seemed small and fragile as she walked next to him.

The faint sound of music and laughter drifted after them on the night air as the party carried on up on the terrace. The lawn swept gently downwards towards a small lake, molten metal in the moonlight. The fresh, sweet scent of dewy grass hung on the cool night air.

'And you wonder why marriage doesn't appeal to me,' she said as he fell into step beside her. 'If I ever found the right man why the hell would I marry him, if that's what it does to you? They lead separate lives. Separate rooms, separate friends. He spends his life trying to exist below her radar and she's got zero excitement in her own life so she makes up for it with gossip and by meddling in Adam's life and in mine. And yet they think they're presenting the image of joint marital solidarity.'

She warmed to her subject, flinging up an exasperated hand.

'Is that how I'll end up if I have kids? With them arguing over who *isn't* going to have the annoying old cow over at Christmas?'

He couldn't keep in a grin. She was so indignant.

'It's not all bad,' he said. 'At least they *are* interested in you.'

She sighed.

'On an interfering kind of a level, maybe.'

He shook his head.

'Maybe it comes across like that. OK, OK—it *does* come across like that,' he said as she gave him an incredulous look. 'But still you're lucky to be part of a family. I couldn't believe it when you said you were thinking about throwing it all away for some guy you'd known five minutes.'

Emma hid her fluster at his unexpected mention of Alistair by zeroing in on his other point. *Family* and *Dan* weren't really two words she thought of in the same sentence.

'That was part of the attraction,' she said. 'The idea of having some fun, for a change, with someone who put me first without criticising, without comparing me— who put me ahead of everything else. And with Alistair there was no prospect of settling into anything like my parents' take on domesticity. It would have been loads of travel and excitement, minimal chance of ending up in separate bedrooms living my life through my kids.'

'So the whole thing with Alistair was about you proving a point to your family? Why does it bother you so much what they think?'

Dan's comment made her feel as if she was being sloshed with cold water—especially as it was so astute. She *had* been blinded to Alistair by the desire to impress her parents.

'It had nothing to do with proving a point,' she lied. 'I'm a grown-up. What bothered me when I was a kid is just an exasperation now.'

She stopped to sit down on the bench he'd seen earlier from the bedroom window. He sat down next to her, the hard wrought-iron pressing cold through his shirt. He handed her one of the champagne flutes.

'Then what is it?' he said. 'You handle yourself brilliantly back in London. You're a real slick professional. You don't need to let anyone's criticism bother you.'

She stared across the silvery lawn. Faint laughter drifted across from the terrace.

'Ah, but that's exactly the point,' she said. 'When we see each other it's usually for some work reason or other. When it comes to work I know I can hold my own. I know what I'm talking about. I make sure I won't get caught out or make a slip-up.' She paused. 'It hasn't always been like that for me.'

'So what *was* it like, then?'

Emma looked at him, trying to gauge whether his interest was real or counterfeit. He'd never shown an interest in finding out more about her before—not unless it was related to work, of course. His blue eyes held hers steadily. She took a sip of her drink and smiled a little, remembering, letting the years fall away.

'Growing up, I was the clumsiest kid you can imagine,' she said. 'If anyone was going to make a fool of herself it was me. And it was even more difficult because Adam's always been such an overachiever. I started out at school trying to work hard, but it never seemed to matter how much effort I put in. I was never quite good enough to earn Adam's level of interest or praise. He was picking up A grades, winning competitions, excelling at everything. After a while I learned not to put myself in a position where people could notice I was falling short.'

A memory returned to her in all its cringeworthy glory.

'I had a part in the school musical once.' She looked

up at him. 'When I was thirteen. Can you imagine me doing that?'

He shrugged, a small smile on his face. A polite response.

'They used to do a musical every year. It was so popular. Everyone would come and watch—parents, locals. And that year they were doing *Grease*. Loads of singing and dancing. I was so excited by the whole idea. I just wanted to be part of it. It didn't occur to me that there could be a negative side, that things could go wrong. I was so naïve.'

'What happened?'

She put her head in her hands and pulled a cringing face.

'I forgot my lines. I stood on that stage and looked out at the hall, knowing it was packed, and I couldn't remember a word. And I don't mean I stumbled over my lines. I didn't just have a bit of a blip and then pick things up. My mind went completely blank. I froze. The lights were bright in my face, but I could still see the shadows of all the people. The music was so loud I could hardly think.'

'What did you do?'

'I ran off the stage and refused to go back on. They put the understudy on instead. My parents were in the audience and my mother gave me hell. She still brings it up now and then. I think in some part of her mind I'm still that nervy thirteen-year-old who had a public meltdown onstage and showed her up.'

She took a sip of her champagne, thinking back. The bright lights in her eyes. The cold horror rushing through her as she tried and failed to make her panicked brain work. The slick of sweat on her palms.

She looked across at Dan, easily pasting a smile on

her face. She'd had years of practice at doing it. She was an adult now, with her own life, and she didn't need to be defined by that awful feeling of failure—not any more. Yet on some level maybe it could never be erased.

'That's awful.'

She shrugged, smiling a little.

'It was at the time. I was mortified. And it never happened again—not to that extent. I never put myself out there again after that—not in any situation where I couldn't trust myself to get it right. I concentrated on academic stuff instead of the arts. Left all that to Adam. And, well, you can see how good *he* was at it. That's partly why I decided to study law. A lot of it is about bulk learning. If you know the rules you can apply them. If you put the work in you can build a career. It isn't left to the whim of anyone else liking what you do in order to secure your success.'

He watched her, looking down at her hands, her skin silvery pale in the moonlight, contrasting with her gleaming dark hair. The air of vulnerability about her made his heart turn over softly. He had an unexpected urge to sweep her into his arms and erase all that self-doubt, make her feel special.

'You care far too much what people think of you,' he said.

She frowned.

'Isn't that what everyone wants, though? Validation from everyone else? Or at least from the people you care about.'

'Maybe. But sometimes love doesn't show up as hugs and presents,' he said. 'Not everything is that in-your-face in life. Your mum, for example, shows she cares by—'

'By being the most interfering woman on the planet?

Maybe. But just a little…' she searched for the right word '…*positivity* might be nice now and then.'

She leaned back a little, surveying him with interest.

'I didn't think you had such strong feelings about family,' she said. 'It's not like I see you jumping through any hoops to see yours. You never seem to visit them—you never even mention them. They can't be any more of a nightmare than mine are, and even I do my duty and see them every few months.'

'Why?'

'What do you mean, *why?*'

'Why do you do your duty and see them? It's perfectly clear you don't relish spending time with them. Why don't you just cut them out of your life if they're that much of a chore?'

He made a slicing motion with his hand while she stared at him, momentarily speechless.

'I couldn't do that,' she said at last. 'They're my family.'

'You mean you care about them?'

'Of course I do. I've kind of got used to the criticism in a way. It's who they are. They might be a nightmare, but at least they're mine.'

'And there's your answer.'

She shook her head faintly at him.

'To what?'

'You were wondering why I never mention or see my family. There's your answer. That's the difference between you and me. I don't really have a family—not as such. And what I did have of one was never remotely interested in me, even in a critical way.'

She dropped her eyes from his.

'Look, I'm sorry…' she began.

He smiled at her.

'Don't be. I'm fine with it. It's always been that way. I don't *need* a family, Emma. What you don't have you don't miss. When I was a kid we didn't do overbearing parents or criticism or sibling rivalry.' He paused. 'We didn't actually *do* family.'

His mind waved the memory of Maggie before him again with a flourish and he clenched his teeth hard. Talking about family with Emma wasn't so difficult when it related to his mother. His feelings for her had progressed over the years to end up somewhere near contempt. But family as related to Maggie meant something completely different. That had been his hope. That had been their plan. Losing that planned future had somehow been so much worse than losing any excuse for a family he might have had in the past.

She was staring at him. He could feel it. He stood up, began walking back to the terrace, deliberately not looking at her.

'What do you mean, you didn't do family?' she said, catching him up, her long skirt caught in one hand.

He thought fleetingly about simply closing the conversation down, but found that on some level he didn't want to. When had he last talked his childhood over with anyone? His usual conquests were happy to go along with however much he told them about himself—or, more to the point, however little. There had never been any need to give much away. Dinner and a cocktail or two seemed to be all that was needed to get to first base, quickly followed by second and third.

'Exactly that,' he said. 'My upbringing wasn't in a nice suburban house with a mum and dad, siblings, pets. Out of all those things some of the time I had a mum.'

'What about your dad?'

'I've never known him.'

The look of sympathy on her face was immediate and he instantly brushed it away with a wave of his hand.

'I've never needed to know him. It's no big deal.'

It was a billion times easier to talk about the family he'd actually had than the one he'd wanted and lost. The two things were worlds apart in his mind.

'Yes, it is. That's awful.'

He shrugged.

'What about your mum, then? You must have been close if it was just the two of you.'

He could feel his lip trying to give a cynical curl.

'Not especially. She wasn't exactly Mother of the Year.' He caught sight of her wide-eyed look and qualified resignedly, 'Oh, hell, she was very young. It can't have been easy, raising a kid by herself. It just was what it was.'

Maggie flashed through his mind again. They'd been young, too, and totally unprepared for parenthood. But walking away had never been an option for him. He'd known that from the very first moment she'd told him about her pregnancy.

'She worked on and off,' he said. 'Bar work, mostly. When I was smaller I used to stay with a neighbour, or one or other of her friends. There was never any consistency to it. Then when I got older it was just me.'

He paused for a second, because that couple of sentences didn't really sum up what it had felt like in that house by himself. It had been cold, with a musty smell of damp that had never gone away, even in the summer. Never tidy. Ready meals and late-night movies because no one cared if he stayed up late or if he was getting enough sleep for school. Sometimes his mother had stayed out all night until he'd wondered if she'd return at all. What would happen to him then? Where would he go? The uncertainty of it all had made him constantly on edge.

'I'd never have known,' she said. 'You've done so well to get out from under all that.'

Emma felt a sudden stab of shame at her fussing about her own childhood. She must sound like some dreadful attention-seeker to him, with her comfortable middle-class upbringing, moaning that she'd never seemed able to please her family when he'd barely had one.

'Not especially. I think it did me a favour. I was so determined to find a way out of there, and when I went to college I found it. Not long after that I had the idea for my first business. It was a coffee kiosk. The cafeteria on campus really sucked. It was poorly run, and there was no facility for grabbing a coffee on the go. So I plugged the gap. It wasn't much more than a trolley at first, but I could see what worked and what didn't. I developed the business, ran it during my free periods, and pretty soon I was making good money. And that was when I *really* knew.'

'Knew what?'

He glanced across at her then, and the look in his eyes was intense in the moonlight, making her pulse flutter.

'That work can be your ticket out of anything,' he said. 'Anything at all.' He smiled at her, a half smile that was steely and determined. 'I just grabbed the coffee kiosk success and ran with it. Built it up, sold it, invested and started over. You can be in control of your own destiny through work. And that's why work will always come first with me.'

So that was why his relationships never amounted to anything. She saw now why their agreement had been of such use to him. She'd furthered his work. She'd provided a date so he didn't need to be distracted.

There had never been any prospect of him wanting more, then. She swallowed as she took that in.

'You'll meet someone one day who'll make you want to put work second,' she said. 'You won't know what you're missing until then.'

He shook his head.

'The moment someone becomes that important you start to lose focus. And things start to go wrong. I just don't need that kind of complication.'

She had the oddest feeling he wasn't just talking about overcoming his childhood.

'I think I'm going to turn in,' she said as they neared to the hotel. 'It's getting late now.'

The music continued on the terrace, more mellow now, and the crowd had dispersed a little. Adam stood to one side, mobile phone clamped to his ear, a stressed expression on his face.

That didn't come as any surprise to Dan. He could think of few things less stressful than getting married. Emma's parents were nowhere to be seen, but obviously just their presence on the premises was enough. In the centre of the terrace the ice sculpture continued its slow melt.

'I'll come with you,' he said.

The memory of kissing her danced slowly through his mind as they made their way inside. He'd known it might put her on edge—that had rather been the point…proof that he was calling the shots now. He hadn't thought it through any further than that. He hadn't counted on the way she would feel in his arms, all long limbs and fragile bone structure, such a contrast to the voluptuous curves that had always been his short-term fling diet. Or the way that satiny full lower lip would feel tugged between his own. There was a hotly curious part of him wondering how it might feel to take things further. He crushed that thought—hard.

His perception of her had changed. And not just because of the kiss but because of tonight. When had they ever discussed anything before that didn't have the ultimate goal of helping them in their jobs? It had been all insider tips from her. Who might be tendering for this contract, what their bid might be, who in her work circles might be looking for troubleshooting services. From him it had been handy introductions—name-dropping Emma to contacts who might want or need legal advice. All of it professional on one level or another.

This weekend was meant to be all about him taking charge, making the point that *he* was the one doing *her* the favour and then breaking off their arrangement the moment the wedding was over. The plan had seemed so easy in the wake of her insulting dumping of him—the perfect way to redress control and get rid of the gnawing feeling that he'd let her become indispensable in his life.

But the connection between them now felt more complex instead of more detached. The idea of walking away from it felt suddenly less gratifying. He'd been so busy taking what he could get from their agreement, manipulating it to suit his own ends so he could avoid close relationships, that he hadn't considered what might be in it for *her* beyond the shallow work reasons they both had.

For Emma it had been a way of making life easier.

Because to be 'good enough' she believed she had to fit a certain stereotype. He wasn't sure which was worse—using their agreement to escape past failures or using it to avoid any remote likelihood of ever having any.

As they walked up the stairs to their room Emma realised suddenly that he still had his arm loosely draped around her. There was no one around them to see it. No family members, no staff. Just what did that mean? Or did it mean anything at all?

She wondered if it felt as natural to him as it felt to her and gave herself a mental slap for even *thinking* about reading something into it. Really? This was Dan—Mr Two-Week Relationship himself. Even if that arm resting on her shoulders right now meant something—which it didn't—it would only ever be that.

Nothing meant anything to Dan Morgan except his work. He'd made that crystal clear this evening. And she wasn't in the market for anything that could be described as a fling. What would be the point? She'd had that with Alistair. What she wanted was not to be some throwaway bit of arm candy but to feel special, to come first, and she wasn't going to get that from Dan.

A hot kiss followed by a night sharing a room with him… The stuff of her dreams a few months ago. And now she had it, it was all for show. How par for the course of her life. They'd been alone together *loads* of times and he'd never had any intention of making a move. Pretend Emma got the hot kiss and the envious glances from female wedding guests over her gorgeous male companion. Real Emma got the awkwardness of bunking in with a work colleague.

She wriggled away from his arm and fumbled in her bag for the room key.

It had taken *months* to get over her stupid crush on him and to reinstate it now would be madness. She was just flustered, that was all, over a stupid fake kiss and a bit of a personal conversation. It didn't mean *anything*.

# CHAPTER SEVEN

WHEN HAD HE last shared a bedroom with someone for a reason that had nothing to do with sex? Dan couldn't actually remember. It must have been Maggie. Way back when he was still at college and anything had seemed possible.

Had he now become so accustomed to room-sharing being about sex that his body simply expected it as part of the deal? Was that why he felt so damned on edge as he waited for Emma to change in the bathroom? Every nerve in his body was wound into a tense knot.

The air of awkwardness from earlier was back. But now there seemed a new, deeper edge to it. It was more than just the logistics of sharing a small space with someone you only knew on a work basis. His growing attraction to her was heightened by his new understanding of her. A few feet away from him in the velvet-soft darkness she would be there, lying in that bed, with her long, slender limbs and her silky dark hair.

His body matched his racing mind with a rigid, hot tension the like of which was going to make sleep an impossibility.

His pulse jolted as the bathroom door clattered open and she crossed the room to the bed, not looking at him.

Her dress was now lying over one arm, her hair loose and gleaming in the soft glow of the table lamp next to the bed. She was wearing a sleep vest and shorts which showed off the most impossibly perfect pair of long, slender legs.

He made an enormous effort not to stare at them as his mind insisted on wondering what other glorious secrets she might be hiding under her sensible work dresses and wide-leg trousers. He stared hard out of the window. His preoccupation became slightly less fake as he noticed movement in the grounds.

'Is that your brother down there?'

He immediately regretted mentioning it because she tossed the dress over the back of a chair and crossed the room to join him at the window, padding across the deep carpet in bare feet. What he *really* needed right now, with his entire body wound up like a coiled spring, was her standing next to him in her flimsy shorts and vest combo. Without her heels she just about reached his shoulder...

'Where?'

He pointed and she craned closer to him to see the lily pond bench. A figure was sitting and staring at the ground contemplatively, a bottle of champagne in one hand and a glass in the other. Her sudden nearness let Dan pick up the faint trace of vanilla perfume still clinging to her hair and his stomach gave a slow and delicious flip in response.

'It's Adam, all right,' she said. 'Even in silhouette that quiff is unmistakable. He's probably taking a break from negotiating family. Can't say I blame him.'

The soft breeze drifting in through the open window

ruffled her hair lightly. She turned away from the view and smiled up at Dan.

'Don't snore,' she said, her eyes teasing.

'I *don't* snore.'

She was close enough that in one swift tug she could be in his arms. He swallowed hard, his throat paper-dry.

Oblivious, she narrowed her eyes at him, considering.

'How do you know?'

'I've never had any complaints,' he said. Her lips, scrubbed of lip gloss, were a soft pale pink in the muted light. His eyes were drawn to them.

'That doesn't mean you don't snore,' she said. 'It just means no one's wanted to put you off them by telling you.'

'Whereas you…?'

'Will have no compunction whatsoever about lobbing a pillow at you.' She pressed an emphatic finger against his chest that made a wave of heat pulse through his veins. 'I'm not afraid to tell you what I think.'

'I know.'

For some reason the novelty of that was alluring. It occurred to him that the willingness to please of his usual girlfriends was something else besides easy and no-fuss. It was also very bland. When had he last felt on his toes with a woman?

He'd become slowly more aware of her looks this evening: the fragility of her skinny frame, her dark-hair-pale-skin combo—such a contrast to his usual choice—and now there was her liveliness, her cheek, sucking him in all the more.

For the first time he picked up on her physical similarities to Maggie. She was taller and slimmer, but the smooth dark hair was the same. Was that what this was about? Was that why she seemed to have slipped through his careful filter? Was that why it had been so easy to keep her at a distance and categorise her as a work colleague? Because his knee-jerk avoidance of any thought of attraction to a girl who might remind him of Maggie had gone on so long it had become automatic?

But he hadn't had the complication of being at such close quarters with her back then. Nuances and habits were laid bare now. The fun-loving, cheeky side of her was so much more obvious outside the work environment, where everything needed to be serious and professional. This weekend he'd begun to see what lay beneath. And it drew him in as no woman had. Not since Maggie had walked away.

She was smiling cheekily up at him, her brown eyes wide, and he marvelled again at how softly pretty she was when you took the time to look past her stiff outer layer. Her face was tilted up to his, at the perfect angle for him to kiss her. The warm, sweet scent of her hair filled his senses, and without taking time to think he lifted a hand to touch her cheek—just to see if it felt as satiny as it looked.

That one tiny connection with her gave his pulse an immediate leap and hot desire rushed through him. And in that fleeting moment he knew he had no chance.

Knowing he was acting off-plan now—and not just off-plan for this weekend but for his whole damned philosophy on life—was suddenly not enough to stop him. His mental filters weren't working. She'd already got past them. This was physical now, and there was nothing he could do about it.

Her eyes widened as he let his fingers trace further, around to the soft skin at the nape of her neck, beneath the fall of her hair. All thought of consequences gone, he lowered his mouth towards the silk of that tantalisingly full lower lip. He pulled her closer, melded her body hard against his, felt the contours of her long, slender limbs through the thin cotton of the shorts and vest she wore.

Sparks of hot longing fizzed in his abdomen as he let his hand slide lower, to find the soft cream of those long, slender thighs. Desire flooded through him, deeper than he was used to, steeped in the familiarity of her, the laughs they'd had together, their newfound closeness. This was not his usual throwaway date. He'd stepped outside the norm. The very novelty of that seemed to hike up his want for her to a new level.

A squeak of shock caught in Emma's throat as his thumb stroked along her jawline, his fingers tangling in her hair.

She hadn't imagined the shift in balance between them after all. She hadn't been seeing things that weren't there.

Despite all the flirting and the signs, the new feeling of intimacy as they started to get to know each other beyond the barriers of their previous life, she now realised that she'd never truly believed he could ever be interested in her. Not in *that* way. She'd quit any delusions about that months ago as she'd observed his repetitive dating habits, certain that unless she happened to morph overnight into a pouting curvy blonde, boring old plain Emma Burney simply wouldn't do it for him.

Her pulse had upped its pace so acutely that she felt light-headed. As his lips met hers she could taste a faint twist of champagne on them, warming her mouth as his tongue slipped softly against hers. Hot sparks began to tingle their way through her limbs to simmer hotly between her legs.

How many times had she dreamed of this moment in the dim and distant past when they'd first met? Every nerve-ending was tinglingly aware of him. She was drowning, every sense in her body filled with him. The lingering spicy notes of his aftershave made her senses reel. She let her fingers sink into his hair, its thick, soft texture exactly as she'd imagined it so many times.

The desire that had bubbled beneath the surface of her consciousness until she had abandoned all hope of it ever being reciprocated made a heady comeback, and she grabbed at the last thread of sense before it slipped away.

It was utterly, sublimely delicious, but none of it really counted because he was ending their agreement.

She latched on to that thought. Was that what all this had been about? The warmth of his newfound support and interest in her had delighted her, but she'd assumed it was simply down to friendship. His kiss was something she'd dreamed of, but if he'd wanted to snog her because of *her* he'd had *months* to do it.

All those months waiting for him to notice her, taking extra care with her hair and make-up when she knew she was going to see him, dropping everything to fit in his last-minute work dates. Months when he'd barely noticed she was alive. Months of opportunity, time alone together, work dinners out. None of it had been enough because he'd needed her for work then.

It had taken *this* for him to make a move on her. The fact that he was ending their agreement and had no need for her any more. Dan only slept with dispensable women. And now she was dispensable.

None of this had anything to do with real feelings for her.

With a monumental effort she stopped her arms from entwining around his neck and groped for his hands, grabbing them at the wrists and disentangling herself from his embrace. The sensation of loss as she took a step back made her suck in a sharp breath and she steeled herself against it. She was *not* going to be sucked into another bad decision because of some stupid age-old crush. She was in full control here.

'Why now?' she panted at him.

His eyes seemed a darker blue than ever, a light frown of confusion touching his forehead. She could hear that his breath had deepened.

He reached for her.

'What do you mean, why now?'

She took another step back, away from his hands, because if she found herself in those arms again she wasn't sure her resolve would stand up.

'We've known each other for months,' she said. 'And in all that time you've never looked twice my way. No matter what I did. No matter how many times I swung business deals for you or put myself out on your behalf. No matter how I tried. And then you decide we're going to go our separate ways, and out of the blue suddenly I'm fair game? Well, I'm not interested.'

She took a slow step back, shaking her head, avoiding his eyes, looking everywhere except at his face. Everything about her told him a very different story. Her shortness of breath, the flushed cheeks, the hard points of her nipples beneath the thin fabric of her vest.

His mind zeroed in on her words. *'No matter what I did.'* The meaning of that slammed into his brain and turned it to mush. Their agreement had always been about more than platonic convenience for her and he'd never even noticed. His stupid work tunnel vision had neglected to pick up on that point. The surge of excitement it now evoked shocked him to the core, telling him his belief that he was in control here was seriously misplaced.

'I'm not going to be your alternative choice because there's no handy blonde available and you're stuck sharing a room with me,' she said.

Clearly, to her, he was the same old work-obsessed confirmed bachelor.

'This has nothing to do with that.'

She gazed up at him, wariness in her wide brown eyes, and then they both jumped at a sudden flurry of knocks on the bedroom door.

She took a couple of fast paces away from him, her fingers rubbing slowly over her lips as if echoing his kiss. Another surge of desire flooded through him at the sight. She cut her eyes away from his.

Another mad cacophony of knocks sliced through the tension.

She made an exasperated noise and turned away from him towards the door, one hand pushing her hair back from her face in a gesture of fluster.

'Who the hell is that?'

'Emma, ignore it,' he said. 'We need to sort this out. You've got it wrong.'

The knocking graduated to a muffled banging of the kind a fist might make, and she shook her head lightly at him and moved towards the door again.

He glanced down at himself. In a sudden flash of clarity it occurred to him that the visitor might feasibly be Emma's mother, and his arousal would be obvious to her in the space of one look. He glanced at the door to the *en-suite* bathroom, thinking vaguely that he might take refuge in there for a couple of minutes while Emma got rid of whoever it was and then they could pick up where they'd left off.

He was on his way across the room when she opened the door and Adam, who had clearly been leaning on it, stumbled into the room, performed a twisty lurching pirouette and threw up into the nearest pot plant.

Oh, just bloody *perfect!*

'For Pete's sake, help me get him to the bathroom!'

Emma had managed to pull Adam to his extremely unsteady feet and struggled to hold him upright as he lurched about. Dan rushed in and took over, throwing one of her brother's arms around his neck and heaving him into the bathroom before he could collapse again. She followed them in.

'The wedding's off!' Adam groaned, slumping over the sink. His always-perfect hair hung in a dishevelled mess and his face was a sickly shade of green.

'What the hell's happened?' she said.

He lifted his head and pointed an emphatic jabbing finger at her as he swayed drunkenly.

'I'm a has-been, darling,' he drawled. 'It's all over. It's all gone.'

His knees gave way unexpectedly and Dan made a lunge to catch him before he hit the white-tiled floor.

'He's absolutely wasted,' Emma said, staring down at him. 'What the hell do I do?'

'Call down to Room Service,' Dan said. 'Black coffee. He needs to sober up.'

She left the pair of them in the bathroom and went to use the phone, her mind reeling. She'd never seen Adam lose his cool before. He had no worries that she knew of. His life was only ever full of things to celebrate. As she replaced the receiver there was the sound of gushing water from the bathroom and a piercing shriek of shock. Dan had obviously stuck him in the shower. She grinned in spite of her worry. Whatever she had to cope with now, at least Adam might be more lucid.

Adam emerged from the bathroom, still hideously pale, but his shocked eyes were now wide and staring. Water dripped from his face and his hair and he was clutching a towel and madly rubbing it at his front.

Dan followed him, his hands spread apologetically. 'Look, I'm sorry,' he said. 'I know cold water's a bit of a shock to the system, but it's great for sobering you up and I couldn't think what else to do.'

'Cold?' Adam wailed. 'It's not the bloody *cold!*' He cast horrified hands downwards at his sopping wet purple suit. 'What the hell have you done? This jacket's *designer!*'

# CHAPTER EIGHT

DAN TURNED OVER for the fiftieth time on the sofa, knees bunched up because the damn thing was too short for him. Unfortunately that wasn't the only reason why sleep was totally elusive. The way Emma had felt in his arms had been far too delicious, far too enticing, for him to simply brush it out of his mind. Add in to that the way she'd put an end to it without having time to give a proper explanation and every nerve in his body was on full-scale alert, his arousal refusing to stand down even in her absence.

And, as interruptions went, needy family crises just about ticked his worst possible box. His stomach lurched between desire for her and the more rational desire to run a mile. It was bad enough to be in the middle of a huge family event when the last thing you wanted to be reminded of was the fact that you couldn't actually *do* family. He'd thought he was holding his own on that front pretty well, but now family complications were seeping in at every turn and he couldn't think of anything worse…

Somewhere in the small hours, after he'd finally given up on her returning to the room—not that it had made any change to his sleepless state—there was a soft click as the door opened. The benefit of his eyes being used to the velvet darkness meant he could watch the silhouette of her every move, while she had to feel her stumbling way from one piece of furniture to the next. Had he ever been more wide awake?

She muffled a yelp as she tripped over a chair and he took pity on her and reached to turn on the table lamp. She blinked at him in the muted golden light. She wore a sweater over her sleep shorts and vest that wasn't long enough to hide her gorgeous legs. His pulse immediately picked up where it had left off a couple of hours ago.

He heard her sigh as she clocked that he was still awake. He watched her run a hand through her already dishevelled hair as she sat down hard on the bed. Her face was a pale oval and there were dark shadows of tiredness beneath her eyes.

'You're still up,' she said.

He sat up on the sofa, the sheet bunched around his waist.

'I wasn't sure you were coming back tonight,' he said.

'Neither was I,' she said. 'I think Adam's drained the hotel's supply of black coffee.'

'He's sobered up, then?'

She nodded.

'He's sobered up. I thought that stuff about calling off the wedding was just cold feet—the usual night-before thing, down to him having drunk too much champagne. But there's more to it than that.'

She held his gaze for a moment.

'He's in financial trouble, Dan,' she said.

Worry etched her face and tugged at his heart.

'He's going under unless he can come up with a plan pretty damn quick.'

'For Pete's sake, what's he gone and done now? Spent a huge wad on a purple Bentley?'

She didn't smile.

He sat up straighter.

'Didn't you tell me his pictures sell for five figures?' he said, scratching his head and trying to think clearly. Tiredness was kicking in now. He had absolutely no desire to discuss Adam's spending habits at two in the morning.

'One of his pictures was supposed to. A month or so ago. Adam borrowed a wodge of cash on the back of it and then the sale fell through. He's been so in vogue recently that even *he* believed the hype. Instead of being productive he's been spending money he doesn't have like water. A new swanky flat here, a shedload of designer furniture there... And now things have reached breaking point. He only found out this afternoon.'

'Can't Ernie bail him out? I thought his family were swimming in cash.'

She frowned at him.

'That's exactly why he doesn't want to *tell* Ernie. He doesn't want him to think he's marrying him for a bail-out. And, more than that, he doesn't want Ernie to think he's a failure. You can't imagine what that means to Adam—he never fails at anything. *Ever.* He's refusing to change his mind about calling off the wedding. It was all I could do to make him promise not to do anything until the morning. I need to think of a way to persuade him by then.'

Dan looked at the worry darkening her face and saw a flash of hope in her eyes as she fixed them on his.

'What he really needs is some sound business advice,' she said, with a pointed tone to her voice that really wasn't necessary. 'From someone who knows what they're doing.'

She wanted him to step in. The unspoken request hung in the air as clearly as if she'd shouted it.

Cold clarity immediately took over his brain with the automatic response that had been honed and conditioned in him over the course of the last ten years.

*Not his problem.*

He didn't *do* family problems. That was actually the one big advantage of not having a family—not getting sucked into other people's dramas, not having anyone rely on him for help. He'd thought he'd done a pretty good job of distancing himself from the blasts from the past that the whole family wedding ambience kept lobbing his way this weekend, but this was a step too far.

'You want *me* to talk to him?' He could hear the note of frosty defensiveness in his own voice. 'I'm not convinced that would be a good idea. It's his private business—nothing to do with me. He needs to discuss it with Ernie. Isn't that the whole point of marriage—shared problems and all that?'

He dropped his eyes from hers so he wouldn't see the disappointment seeping into them. He ran a hand awkwardly through his hair.

'There isn't going to *be* a marriage unless someone gets him back on track,' she hissed.

'What makes you think that someone should be *me*? I don't think Adam would thank you for involving a stranger in his personal problems. This isn't down to me,' he said.

'A stranger?'

He glanced up and caught her gaze again. Bitter disappointment lurked there. Deep in his stomach a spike of regret kicked in unexpectedly at the idea of letting her down. He steeled himself against it. He shouldn't care about this.

She paused a beat too long, during which he held his position and didn't give in, and then she exploded.

'Fine. Absolutely fine,' she snapped, leaping to her feet.

Had she really thought he would step up to the plate? Why the *hell* had she assumed that? Because he'd kissed her? After months of zero romantic interest he'd kissed her. OK, so she'd thought there had been something more than their usual work relationship growing between them this last day or so, but clearly she'd imagined that. Her first instincts had been spot on and she'd been totally right to stop him in his tracks.

Her mistake had been in hoping that what was between them was in any way about more than the kiss and what he'd obviously intended to follow that kiss up with if Adam hadn't interrupted them spectacularly.

'You didn't even ask me what was wrong with Adam,' she said dully. Her head ached tiredly and she rested her hand against her scalp, lacing her fingers through her hair to pull the roots back from her face, trying to clear her thoughts. 'I thought you were waiting up for me all this time to make sure I was OK, to be supportive, but you weren't actually wondering for one second what the problem was. If I hadn't just told you, you would never have asked me about Adam, would you?'

She glanced down at her fingers.

'That's not what you were waiting up for at all, is it? You just wanted to pick up where we left off earlier. You thought I'd sort Adam out, get him over his hissy fit, and then we'd have the rest of the night to make it into that bed.'

She nodded across the room at the four-poster.

For a moment she got no response and she raised her eyebrows at him expectantly. See if he could talk his way out of this. Or if he would even be bothered to try.

'This has nothing to do with what happened earlier,' he said, not meeting her eyes. 'I just think Adam is big enough to sort out his own problems. I don't get why you need to get sucked into this. His overspending isn't down to you.'

She stared at him, incredulous at his lack of concern.

'Because that's what families do,' she said. 'You know, I always thought nothing could ever touch Adam. He's led a charmed life. As if everything he ever touches is sprinkled with happy dust. When I was a kid I sometimes used to wish for just one time when he would stuff up, show everyone that he wasn't perfect.'

She paused briefly, thinking of how upset Adam was now. There was no joy in that for her. She wasn't a stupid kid any more.

'For once I'm not the one who's screwed up, but I have no good feeling about that. What good would it do if my parents knew what had happened? I just want him to go back to his usual crazy self.'

She made a conscious effort to curb her voice. It was so late now the hotel was pin-drop quiet. Every word she spoke felt amplified in the silence.

'Of course you do,' he said. 'You're comfortable in his shadow, so you're hardly about to want that shadow to get smaller, are you?'

She stared at him.

'Just what the hell is *that* supposed to mean?' She

wanted to shout it. Her voice felt shaky on her tongue. She kept her tone measured with great difficulty.

He shrugged.

'It's safer, isn't it? Believing that you're always going to be inferior? Means you don't have to put yourself out there. You rely on Adam being the star that he is in every possible way because it's an excuse for you to take the safe option.'

'That's not true.'

'Isn't it? Look at our plus-one agreement. I know what *I* was getting out of it—easy networking, work contacts. But what about you? Your dates were all about presenting a front to your family, because that way you didn't have to put yourself there in reality. With me you couldn't fail.'

For a moment she had trouble comprehending what he meant because it came as such a shock. A sharp, hot lurch hit her in the stomach. She shoved away the thought that this was what it felt like to have someone touch a nerve. Refusing to engage in one-upmanship with Adam was a way of avoiding grief from her over-interested parents, *not* a way to embrace the safe option because she was afraid of failure.

Dan saw the dark, defensive anger flush her face and wondered for a moment if he'd gone too far. She'd made him feel such a lightweight for not pitching in instantly to help Adam—who, frankly, was responsible for his own cock-up. Discomfort at the situation had stopped him holding back, and second thoughts seeped in a moment too late.

Her hands flew to her hips, her eyes flashed in anger

and her previous attempts to speak in a low voice went totally out of the window.

'You're twisting things!' she yelled. 'I don't know where the hell you get off, preaching to me about family bloody values. Your concern gene is mutated. All this has been about—all anything has *ever* been about for you—is getting someone into bed. In this case, in the absence of any willing curvy blondes, that happens to be me. Well, I'm not interested in being one of your dispensable little-black-book girlies. I don't need you as a boyfriend—not even as a fake one. If this wedding goes ahead—which, the way it looks right now, is unlikely—I'll go it alone. I don't need you. So first thing in the morning you can get back to your sad workaholic singleton life in London.'

He'd never seen her lose her temper. Her voice shook with the force of it and she stood at her full height, her eyes wide and her cheeks flushed. Even in his amazement at her overreaction—which told him he'd not only touched a nerve but had held on to it and twisted it hard—the most visceral part of him zeroed in on how utterly beautiful she looked in that animated moment.

Then admiration fell flat as she turned her back on him, stalked into the bathroom and slammed the door so hard he was surprised the hotel didn't collapse into rubble around them.

Not the delicious uninhibited night of passion he'd expected when he'd kissed her a few hours earlier. Admittedly at the time his mind hadn't been working ahead by more than a few minutes. He certainly hadn't thought about the consequences—it had been very easy to discount those. Any possible repercussions had seemed very far away when the silk of her skin had been beneath his fingers.

If he'd been lying in a regular bed he would have been ramrod-straight. Instead he was cramped into a hunch with his knees up. His body was one big throb of pent-up sexual energy. Every muscle was tightly coiled up with it. And did he really think he could pass the whole night like this?

She'd spent an hour in the bathroom before she'd re-emerged into the darkened room and stalked past him into bed. No attempt to make conversation. Now a silver shaft of moonlight filtered through a chink in the curtains and fell on her bare shoulder as she lay with her back to him. The long legs were drawn up; she was curled beneath the sheet.

For an endless length of time he had felt sure, despite her silence, that she was awake. Her angry vibe had been palpable. Tension still filled the room. He shifted again, in a vain attempt to get comfortable, and wondered what exactly he was bothering with all this for.

He should be looking on Adam's rubbish timing as a very fortuitous wake-up call, shouldn't he? He'd been completely focused on the overwhelming physical pull of her. If he'd stopped for a second to analyse it he would have assumed it would be a one-night stand. After all, he'd made it clear that their agreement had run its course, and that had removed any benefit of keeping things platonic between them. He'd been thinking quick weekend fling.

*Hadn't he?*

If his interest in her was purely physical, dispensable, then why did her furious criticism of him gnaw at his insides like this? He had no obligation to her or her family, and yet somehow she'd managed to instil guilt because he didn't want to get involved in Adam's undoubtedly crazy problems.

He didn't *do* guilt. That was one of the main benefits of keeping his relationships shallow. He and Emma didn't even *have* a relationship and he couldn't bloody sleep. He had no idea how she'd managed to do this to him.

There was a part of him that was halfway back to London in his head already, keen to do exactly as she had suggested.

She shifted gently in her sleep and he sat up on the sofa, throwing back the crumpled sheet. He could see the smooth pool of her dark hair on the pillow. The quality of the light in the room had changed almost imperceptibly and he glanced at the luminous face of his watch. Dawn would be kicking in before he knew it. He could be back in his Docklands flat in an easy couple of hours if he left now. No need to battle London traffic if he left this early. Why the hell was he even still here?

*You want to help. You want this involvement with her and her family.*

He absolutely *did not*.

Every sensible instinct told him to get some serious distance from this situation but he rationalised furiously. A brief chat with Adam—and a brief chat was all it *would* be, too—might be the perfect way to take control of this situation. He wasn't about to quietly slink back to London on her say-so, leaving her with the upper hand.

He ignored the inner voice whispering that he didn't like being labelled as selfish, because labels were to him completely irrelevant. Results mattered. Successes.

Not good or bad opinions. Even if they happened to be *her* opinions.

Help Adam out and Emma would be in his debt. The fact that after that kiss she felt very much like unfinished business was beside the point. He was not about to fall for her. He was in total control here. When they got back to London he would end their agreement, as planned, in full possession of the moral high ground. It wasn't as if she wasn't expecting him to. He'd made it clear this was their last outing together. There would be no need to see her again after that. It would be over.

There was a chink in the curtains that let the sunlight in.

It took a moment for her brain to process the fact that the bedroom window of her flat in Putney looked out onto a tiny enclosed yard which the sun penetrated for roughly ten minutes somewhere around noon. Additional details seeped into her consciousness. This bed was hard, where hers was soft, and was that *birdsong* she could hear? Where was the roar of rush-hour traffic?

This was *not* her flat in Putney.

Reality rushed in. Luxury country house hotel. Adam's mad-as-a-box-of-frogs wedding. Disastrous room-share with her crush of the year.

She sat bolt upright and stars swam in front of her eyes at the unexpected movement. She turned instantly to look at the sofa. Every bone in her body ached with tension and her eyes felt gritty when she blinked. She could have sworn she'd been awake all night. Yet that couldn't be so. Last seen lying on the sofa as she climbed back into bed at two-thirty and turned her back on him in fury, at some point Dan had managed to get up and exit the room without her noticing.

She checked the time and that was enough to get her out of bed in a split second. How the hell had she managed to sleep in? Her stomach kicked into churning with a sudden sense of urgency. She needed to get up, check on Adam and find out if the wedding was going ahead or not.

The thought of dealing with the fallout if his world imploded filled her with dread. Adam would be in the doghouse and the spotlight would be right back on her life—her failure to keep a man, her failure to produce grandchildren. Her mind stuttered on that thought with a sharp stab of shame. Surely her only concern should be for Adam, for how she could best help him sort out the mess that was his life, how she could support him through the stress. The thought of the effect it might have on *her* shouldn't even be entering her mind.

Dan's accusation from the previous night rose darkly in her mind. Could he have a point about her living in Adam's shadow because it was safer there?

She crossed the room swiftly to the *en-suite* bathroom, knowing from the silence that Dan wasn't there but sticking her head around the door anyway to check.

Nothing.

She glanced at the hotel information brochure on top of the bureau. Breakfast had been running for at least an hour already—maybe he'd gone down to the dining room. The possibility that he'd upped and left lurked at the very edge of her consciousness but she delayed any consideration of it. And then, as she turned, her eyes took in the antique desk and her heart gave a miserable lurch that she refused to acknowledge.

His holdall wasn't in the room. And, worse, nor were

his laptop and all the associated office stuff which basically provided his identity. All of it was gone.

She threw on jeans and a T-shirt and speed-walked down the deep-carpeted hall to the honeymoon suite. Ernie had spent the previous night at his parents' home and had planned to get ready there, so Adam should still be alone.

He opened the door on her first knock and stood aside to let her in before crossing the room back to the full-length mirror. He was wearing an ivory crushed velvet slim-cut suit with gold piping and super pointy shoes that even *she* would think twice about squashing her toes into. He looked her up and down, an eyebrow cocked.

'I do hope you're not wearing that,' he said, waving a hand at her jeans-and-old-T-shirt combo. 'This is a classy event.'

'Of course I'm not wearing this,' she snapped.

There was something incredibly exasperating about the way he was acting, as if the events of the previous night had never happened when they'd caused her a stress-fest of monumental proportions.

'I didn't see the point in putting on a swanky wedding outfit and doing my hair when the likelihood of it going ahead was somewhere around fifty-fifty. At least it was when I left you in the small hours.'

She sat down on the enormous bed. Everything in the honeymoon suite was supersized, albeit in a country hotel kind of a way. The four posts were taller, the swags of fabric bedecking them were bigger and sweepier, and through the door of the *en suite* she could see an enormous sunken bath.

'Oh, that!'

Adam flapped a dismissive hand at her and turned

back to his reflection in the mirror. He looked a little tired and drawn but otherwise remarkably like his usual upbeat self. She caught sight of her own reflection behind him. She looked an exhausted wreck. How bloody unfair.

'That's all sorted now.'

She stared at him in disbelief.

'What about last night's meltdown?' His lack of reaction combined with her tiredness made her temper strain to breaking point. 'You puked in my plant, for Pete's sake! You had a total emotional meltdown. Your life was *over*.'

'Oh, that,' he said again, glancing back at her.

At least he had the good grace to look sheepish now.

'Sorry about that, sweetie. Glass of champagne too many. Still, there were compensations. In fact some might say it had elements of stag night perfection.'

He grinned at her mystified expression.

'Sharing a shower room with the gorgeous Dan, for example,' he said mischievously, spraying a toothbrush with hairspray and smoothing his already perfect quiff into place. 'Even if he did ruin my suit.' He tapped the side of his nose with one finger in a your-secret's-safe-with-me gesture. 'Lucky old you. I know you thought you hit the jackpot with Alistair Woods, but I've always thought Dan was in a league of his own. Nice work.' He winked at her and turned back to the top of the bureau, which was groaning under the weight of male grooming products. 'I never did think Lycra cycle wear was a good look—didn't like to mention it.'

He lavishly sprayed a five-foot-high cloud of oriental spiced aftershave into the room beside him and stepped into it.

Emma pinched her nose to stifle a sneeze. She shook her head in automatic denial.

'It's not like that. We're just work friends.'

He cackled mad laughter.

'Sure you are! That's why he's just given me an *enormous* business loan with zero interest and his personal phone number so I can tap him for strategic advice whenever I need it.' He winked. 'Either that or maybe he's got the hots for *me*. Maybe you've got competition, sweetie.'

She stared at him in disbelief and he obviously mistook incredulity for angry possessiveness.

'I'm joking!' He held his hands up and laughed. 'For Pete's sake, where's your sense of humour?'

*'When?'* she said, as if in a dream. 'When did he do all this? His stuff's gone from the room. I can't find him anywhere.' She paused. 'We had a bit of a disagreement.'

Adam shook his head.

'He'll be back. He turned up here around dawn, woke me up, ordered a gallon of black coffee and forced me to come clean about my debts.' He coloured a little. 'It wasn't pretty. Then he talked me through a business plan for the next three years and touted unbelievable terms for a loan. I thought he'd want a cut of everything I make for life at the very least, and I would have agreed to it, too. Frankly, I would have put up my *granny* as security to dig me out of this hole. But no.' He shook his head wonderingly. 'He is *so* into you.' He pointed the toothbrush at her.

Her brain was spinning, trying to process what all this meant.

'Where is he now, then? He didn't come back to the room.'

Adam shrugged. 'Around, I think. He was going to make a few calls, draw up some papers and get the ball rolling. I'm sure he'll show up once it's all organised, sweetie. He's probably in the lobby soaking up the free Wi-Fi.'

Or en route back to the city and deliberately avoiding her. Her heart gave a half plummet at the thought and she gritted her teeth. She tugged her fingers through her hair, as if she could somehow smooth some sense into her muddled brain.

She'd told him to go back to London and instead he'd stayed to put together a bail-out package for Adam. Her heart turned over meltingly and she desperately tried to rein it in, to come up with an alternative explanation to the one that was slamming into her brain.

*He'd done this for her.*

He'd done it to prove her wrong about him.

She cringed inwardly as she remembered the awful things she'd said to him in the throes of her enormous meltdown tantrum. What possible other explanation could there be? It was way above and beyond Dan's normal remit. Dan didn't step in to fix other people's crises. Ever. Since he kept the world at arm's length it was usually impossible to get close enough to his shoulder to cry on it.

He'd stepped outside the box. And what the hell was she meant to make of that?

# CHAPTER NINE

DAN RAN A hand through his hair distractedly as his phone kicked in for the third time in the last ten minutes. Each of the calls had been from Emma. For the third time he pressed 'call reject' on the dashboard and fixed his expression on the road. The motorway would still be pretty clear this time of the morning, but he'd hit traffic when he reached London. It was a Saturday so would be marginally better.

Dealing with Adam had taken a good deal longer than he'd thought it would. Still, it was done now. Loan organised, cash transfer organised, soul sold. Point made. The wedding would go ahead without a hitch and he would return to his work in London. The ridiculous plus-one agreement would be discharged exactly as he'd planned. They would move forward separately, but Emma would go with the knowledge that she'd been wrong about him.

*Sad workaholic singleton.*

Was that really what he boiled down to? His mind gnawed at it relentlessly and, try as he might, he couldn't shake the feeling that the reason it bothered him so much was because *she'd* said it. He, who didn't give a toss about how he came across to people so long as the job got done, *cared* what she thought of him.

A miserable, dark churning was kicking into his stomach with every mile he drove further away.

Emma pelted back up the stairs for the third time, having performed a whirlwind circuit of all the public rooms and lounges in the hotel, her heart sinking lower by the second. The marquee was teeming with hotel staff transforming it from plain tent into what was, by the look of it, to be some kind of yellow-themed fairy grotto, all under the supervision of a pristinely dressed wedding coordinator with a clipboard and a voice like a sergeant major.

There wasn't another guest in sight, she hadn't showered, washed her hair or applied a dab of make-up, and she only had an hour or so left to get ready before pre-wedding cocktails and nibbles were served. Her mother was probably already wearing her mother-of-the-bride outfit and preparing herself for an afternoon of wedding critique. Wherever Dan had disappeared to, catching up with him and sorting things out would have to go maddeningly on hold now that the wedding was going ahead as planned.

Maybe he'd come back while she was getting dressed...

She showered and changed with minutes to spare and there was still no sign of him.

Maybe he had no intention of coming back at all while she was there. She had told him he was selfish for not helping out a friend, that he cared about no one but himself. Without him here there was only one conclusion. This wasn't about any regard for *her*—it was about making a point, showing her she was wrong about him and then exiting her life with the moral high ground.

The finished marquee turned out to be a yellow flower explosion. Huge floral arrangements stood on plinths in every spare space. Yellow silk bunting decked the roof, and the chairs were wrapped in huge yellow bows, standing in twin rows separated by a wide aisle covered with a thick-pile yellow carpet. At the very front a perfectly dressed white table was decked in yellow flowers.

She was one of the last people to take her seat, earning a glare from her mother, who was perched in the front row rubbernecking at the other guests. Her furious face was topped by an enormous salmon-pink feather hat which clashed eye-wateringly with the mad overuse of yellow.

In a sudden burst of exasperated defiance Emma stood straight up again. She could just nip outside and try his phone again. And maybe while she was there check the car park. At least that would be conclusive.

She sidestepped out of her row and turned back down the aisle to the door. She had to get hold of him. She wasn't about to let this go now—wedding or no wedding. She was stopped in her tracks by a deafening funked-up version of the 'Bridal March' as Adam and Ernie blocked the door in front of her. They were both wearing dark glasses, probably in defence against the major overuse of yellow. Ernie's small niece walked at their feet, lobbing yellow rose petals. The eyes of everyone in the room bored into her back and she had no choice but to slink back to her seat.

What was she thinking? She might as well face facts.

The wedding was under way. And he was clearly not coming.

The wave of sadness that realisation evoked took her breath away and made her throat constrict. The assumption that he'd helped Adam for her, because he *cared* about her, seemed unlikely now that he hadn't hung around to soak up her gratitude. The surge of excitement she'd felt when Adam had told her what had happened took a nosedive into stomach-churning disappointment. She would have to resign herself to coping with the ceremony and its aftermath by herself.

It was an odd novelty to be stressed about something else for a change, instead of the usual prospect of mad parental behaviour. The thought of being without him beat all her other problems into submission. Nothing seemed to bother her now. Her parents could do their worst, and probably would.

And then, just as she mentally gave up on Dan and tried to steel herself to get through the day without losing her sanity, her stomach gave an unexpected and disorientating flip as he walked into the marquee.

He strode casually down the aisle behind Adam and Ernie, crushing the trail of yellow rose petals under his feet, and slid into the seat next to her as if he was just a couple of minutes late instead of having gone AWOL for the last twelve hours. Any possible annoyance with him was immediately sidelined by her heart, which went into full thundering mode. To hide it, she immediately faked irritation.

She spoke from the corner of her mouth as Adam launched into his personally written over-emotional vows. Ernie was gazing at him adoringly.

'You're late,' she whispered.

He stared straight ahead. In his dark suit and crisp white shirt he looked ready for cocktails at some trendy London wine bar. A yellow carnation had been pinned to his lapel by one of the super-efficient attendants. There was a hint of stubble lining his jaw and one tiny sign that he'd cut it fine—the spikes of his hair were still slightly damp from the shower.

'I'm not. I'm bang on time.'

'I thought you'd gone back to London.'

This time he looked her way and gave her a half smile that made her stomach go soft.

'Just because you told me to? You don't get rid of me that easily.'

Her stomach gave a slow and delicious flip. What the hell did *that* mean? That he wanted to stay or that he was making a point?

The service progressed at the front of the room and she barely heard a word of it. Her mind continued to whirl while cheers rang out around them and a shower of yellow confetti fluttered over Adam and Ernie as they raised triumphant hands above their heads. She hardly took in any of it. All she wanted was to drag Dan somewhere quiet to talk.

Nerves twisted inside her as she followed the rest of the guests back up the yellow-ribbon-lined aisle and into the hotel's conservatory for drinks while the marquee was reset for dinner. A string quartet kicked into action at one side of the room as waiting staff with trays of canapés began to mingle with the guests. Dan nodded around, smiling and winking at people, working the fake plus-one wedding guest image to a tee, and suddenly she could stand it no longer.

She grabbed him by the elbow and tugged him to a quiet corner of the room.

'Where *were* you all morning, then?' she said. 'You don't get off that easily.'

She waited for him to regale her with how he'd single-handedly solved Adam's problems and then sit back to watch her eat her words.

Instead he shrugged easily and took a sip of his champagne.

'Around. I'm an early riser. You were dead to the world, snoring away.'

He grinned broadly as she aimed an exasperated slap at his shoulder.

'I do *not* snore.'

So he was clearly not immediately going to volunteer what he'd done. What was the point of actually *doing* it, then, if it hadn't been to impress her?

She ran her hand through her hair, trying to think straight. She was so confused.

Dan watched her over the rim of his glass, trying to maintain a relaxed air of mingling wedding guest when all he wanted to do was stare at her. She looked prettier than ever in a silver-grey silk dress that set off her creamy complexion. Her hair was lying in soft waves, one side held back from her face by a sparkly clip. His desire for her was as strong as it had been the previous night. Nothing had changed. Had he really thought it would?

She held his gaze boldly and he heard her take a deep breath.

'You helped Adam,' she said. 'I know about the loan. I thought you didn't want to get sucked into family stuff.'

He deliberately didn't meet her eyes and kept his tone light.

'Yeah, well, I wasn't thinking straight when you first suggested it,' he said. 'Maybe I just wasn't crazy on Adam's timing.'

He watched the blush rise on her cheeks at his reference to the previous night and heat began to pool deep in his abdomen.

'Well, if you think I'll just hop into bed with you now, because you stepped up to the plate with Adam, you're wrong,' she said.

If only that were the limit of his need for her.

'If I'd wanted to go to bed with someone I wouldn't have wasted half the night counselling Adam. I would have been down in the lobby chatting up the receptionist.'

If he needed any reminder that he was in over his head here, there it was. This was *not* just about getting her into bed.

He'd actually done far more than he'd intended when he'd left her sleeping in the small hours. The plan to just give Adam some kind of rousing pep talk had gone out of the window when he'd realised the monumental size of the mess he was in. Within five minutes it had become clear that a couple of websites and the number of a debt helpline were simply not going to cut the mustard, and the temptation had never been stronger to simply bow out of the situation and leave all of them to it while he went right back to his safe and organised life in London.

But all he'd been able to think about was Emma floundering the next morning, trying to pick up the pieces, and he simply hadn't been able to do it to her.

And what that decision meant filled him with far

more trepidation than practically writing out a blank check to her lunatic brother.

*He had feelings for her.* Beyond anything he'd felt since Maggie. And even she now seemed to be taking on a vagueness in his mind that she hadn't had before—as if the edges of her memory were being softened by the reality of the present.

'To prove a point, then,' she said, narrowing her eyes. 'You can't stand being wrong and I touched a nerve.'

He cocked an eyebrow.

'With your "sad workaholic singleton" comment, you mean? I think I've had a few worse insults than that over the years.'

'Then what? Why would you do that about-face if it wasn't so you could have the last word?'

The cynical tilt of her chin finally tipped him into irritation.

'I notice you haven't asked me if I just did it out of the goodness of my heart. It hasn't occurred to you that I might just want to *help*.'

'Of course it hasn't. Because there's always an ulterior motive with you. Normally it's to do with work. Or possibly sex.'

'Emma, are you so used to being second best that you have to find some negative reason when the truth is staring you in the face? Why is it that you can't possibly contemplate that I might have just done the whole bloody thing for *you?*' he blurted in exasperation. 'You're maddening, your family are insane, you snore and your luggage habits are scary. But for some reason I'd rather commit myself financially to your mad brother and stay here with you instead of going back to London and my nice, peaceful, "sad workaholic singleton" life. Do you think I don't want to run for the hills? Truth is, I can't. I've realised there's nowhere I'd rather be than here.' He paused for breath. 'With you.'

She was staring at him.

His pulse vaulted into action as he met her wide brown eyes. He could see the light flush on her cheekbones. All the unrequited tension of the night before seeped back through his body. All around them the socialising carried on, and the urge raced through him to ignore the lot of them, grab her by the hand and tug her upstairs—let this crazy charade go on without them.

He closed the gap between them and lifted a hand to her cheek. The softness of her skin was tantalising beneath his fingers.

'Dinner is served.'

The Master of Ceremonies' curt tones cut through the background buzz of chatter and snapped him out of it.

'Do stop dawdling, darling,' Emma's mother called as she swept past them in her ghastly coral ensemble, undoubtedly en route to the top table.

Oh, for Pete's sake...

By the time the meal was over the presence of Adam's entire social circle was beginning to seriously annoy Emma. It was extremely difficult to have an in-depth personal conversation while seated at a table of eight overenthusiastic art groupies.

Dinner finished with, the marquee was cleared of the tables in the centre to reveal a glossy dance floor. Strings of fairy lights and candelabra supplied a twinkly, magical ambience. You couldn't move without tripping over a champagne waiter. And this after the most sumptuous four-course meal she'd ever been too strung-out to eat. Clearly there had been no expense spared. She wondered just how big Dan's loan to Adam was. If this was the level of his spending habits he'd still be paying it off when he was drawing his pension.

'I mean, really—no speeches? No best man. No bridesmaids. No tradition whatsoever! I just want to *know*—and I'm sure I'm not alone in this—' her mother glanced around for confirmation '—what happens about the name-change? Who takes whose name?'

She looked expectantly at Adam, standing nearby, who shifted from foot to foot.

'Mum, it's no different to any other wedding. You can take or not take whatever name you please,' Emma said, pasting on a smile to counteract any offence that might be caused. 'You're living in the past.'

'I don't agree. I don't see why Adam should change his name.'

'I'm not,' Adam said. 'And neither is Ernie.'

Her mother rounded on Ernie, who took an automatic defensive step backwards.

'Why not?' she demanded. 'Is our family name not good enough?'

'Mum, please…' Emma said.

Ernie held his hands up.

'It's perfectly fine, Emma. It's nothing to do with family names.' He looked kindly at her mother. 'I'd walk over hot coals for him, darling, but I cannot possibly be known as Ernie Burney.'

Adam took his arm and they moved away. Her mother gaped for a moment, and then took refuge in her usual critical safe bet in order to save face.

'Of course if *you* could only find a man who would commit there wouldn't be any of this lunacy,' she snapped at Emma. 'We could have a proper wedding with all the trimmings.'

The band chose that moment to launch into full-on swing music, mercifully making it impossible to hear any further argument, and the compère took to the glossy parquet floor.

'Ladies and gentlemen, I give you…the groom and groom.'

Her mother's mouth puckered and then disappeared as a pool of light flicked on in the centre to reveal Adam and Ernie striking a pose. A kitsch disco track kicked into action and they threw themselves into a clearly pre-rehearsed dance routine.

Dan stared in amazement as Adam danced past them, finger stabbing the air above his head, back to his full quota of sweeping flamboyant enthusiasm. Ernie skidded across the parquet on his knees, snapping his fingers above his head. A circle of guests began to form at the edges of the dance floor, clapping along. The room worked itself into a crescendo of rhythmic toe-tapping. It was bedlam.

'And…the parents of the happy couple…'

Ernie's father, completely unaware of what he was letting himself in for, held out a hand to Emma's mother and began propelling her around the floor. Emma watched her mother's stiff and obvious fluster with a grin.

'She can't complain. She did want a bit more tradition after all,' she said.

'And…family and friends…please take the floor…'

Dan held his hand out, a smile crinkling his eyes. She stared at him, her heart skipping into action.

'I don't dance,' she said, shaking her head.

He totally ignored her. Before she could wriggle free

he'd caught her fingers in his own and tugged her against him, curling his free hand around her waist.

'Just hang on, then,' he said.

The jaunty music demanded a lot more balance and rhythm than a swaying slow dance, and Emma silently cursed Adam for his disco obsession.

Dan turned out to be an excellent dancer. He propelled her smoothly around the floor in perfect time to the music and she somehow managed to hold on to him instead of falling over. Then at last the music mercifully slowed and embarrassment slowly gave way to consciousness of him. She could feel the hard muscle of his thighs moving against her own. Sparks jumped from her fingers as he laced them through his. His heartbeat pressed against hers.

'Why now, then?' she said, looking up at him, a light frown shadowing her face. 'You haven't answered that question. You had *months* to make a move on me if you were interested. Months of work dates back in London. Why now? Why here? Because you'd made it clear our agreement was over? Is that it? You were pretty keen to draw a line under our relationship when this weekend finished, so did that make me fair game?'

'If I'd known you were interested maybe I would have made a move before,' he said, knowing perfectly well he'd never have allowed himself to do so.

She made an exasperated sound.

'That's crap. I'm *so* not your type.'

'In actual fact you're *exactly* my type. And that's why I never made a move. I met you in your work role and you were so bloody good at it I wasn't about to ruin that by sleeping with you. I needed you too much.'

She pulled away from him a little as she processed what that might mean.

'And now you don't need me any more, sleeping with me is suddenly back on the agenda? Is that it?'

'That's not it at all. This weekend is the first I've spent with anyone at such close quarters without sex being the only thing on the agenda. And it isn't a piece of cake, I'll be honest with you. Nothing about you is easy. You're a pain to share a room with, and your family are more bonkers than I realised, but for the first time in I don't know how long work isn't the first thing I'm thinking about.'

She looked up at him and met his eyes, his expression clear and genuine.

'When I talked to Adam I realised there would be a massive fallout if the wedding didn't go ahead. I could imagine the embarrassment, the fuss, having to send the guests away. It wasn't about Adam. He's got himself into trouble and he should dig himself out of it. It might even be character-building. When I couldn't walk away I realised that the person I was really doing it for was you. And that's when I knew that, whatever I felt about you, platonic work colleague didn't really cover it any more.'

He carried on talking, thinking vaguely that they seemed to have lost time with the jaunty beat of the music. Other guests began to whirl past them.

She stopped dancing. He attempted a couple more steps before giving up and joining her. The thing about dancing was that you needed your partner at least to *attempt* to engage—otherwise it was akin to dragging a sack of potatoes around the floor at speed. Trepidation spiked in his stomach at the look of disbelief on her face, telling him that his feelings for her had climbed way further than he'd thought. He'd been kind of banking on a smile at the very least.

'Say that again.'

'Emma, we're in the middle of the bloody dance floor. Let's go and sit down, get a drink.'

'I don't want a drink. Say that again.'

'I couldn't give a toss about Adam getting into trouble?'

She punched his shoulder.

'Not that bit.'

He saw the mock-exasperated smile on her lips, saw it climb to her eyes.

'Platonic work colleague didn't cover it any more?'

The smile melted away. She was looking up at him, brown eyes wide, soft lips lightly parted, and the madly circling dance floor around them disappeared from his consciousness.

'Yes. That bit.'

He tightened his grip around her waist and slid his fingers into her hair, stroking his thumb along her jawline as he tilted her lips to meet his.

Emma's heart was thundering as if they'd done another disco turn instead of swaying languorously around the dance floor.

The Dan she'd known for a year and long given up on would never have helped Adam out for nothing in return—would never have taken the time to explain his feelings to her. And he would never have turned back having driven halfway to London—not when he'd made his point before he left. She'd bucked his little-black-book no-strings trend. He'd put her first.

Sweet excitement began to swirl in her stomach as

her mind focused on the feel of his body hard against hers and she breathed in the scent of spicy aftershave and warm skin as he kissed and kissed and kissed her.

At last she opened her eyes to see the *déjà-vu* disapproving stare of her mother across the room. Necking on the dance floor, this time, instead of in corridors—how common. Except that this time she found she really couldn't give a *damn*.

She laced her hand through his and tugged at his arm. 'Let's go upstairs.'

# CHAPTER TEN

SHE FOLLOWED HIM into the hotel room, buying a bit more time and space for her skittering nerves by leaning gently back against the door until it clicked shut. The party carried on in the marquee below them and music and faint laughter drifted in through the window, open a crack. The closed curtains fluttered lightly in the night breeze.

Delicious anticipation fluttered in her stomach as he turned back to her in the soft amber glow of the table lamp and tugged her into his arms, his mouth groping for hers, finding it, sucking gently on her lower lip and caressing it softly with his tongue.

His fingers slipped beneath the fall of her hair to find the zip of her dress and he pulled it slowly down in one smooth motion, sliding the fluttering sleeves from her shoulders, his mouth tracing the blade of her collarbone with tiny kisses. He smoothed her dress lower, until it fell from her body into a gleaming puddle of silk on the floor. And then her mind followed his hands as they explored her body, as he unhooked her bra, cast it aside and cupped her breasts softly in his palms. Her nipples were pinched lightly between his fingers, sending dizzying flutters down her spine where they intensified hotly between her legs.

Then came brief unsteadiness as he slid his hands firmly beneath her thighs and lifted her against him. She could feel his rigid arousal press against her as she curled her legs around his waist and he carried her the few paces across the room to the antique desk. He held her tightly against him and she leaned sideways as he swept her belongings carelessly onto the floor. Body lotion and hairbrush fell with meaningless thuds onto the deep-pile carpet, and then there was cool, smooth wood against her skin as he put her down on the desk in just her panties.

She'd had a few boyfriends, yes. In the dim and distant past she'd done the rounds, albeit in a minor way, at university. None of it had felt like this. And if during the last year she'd let herself imagine what it might feel like to be with him it had never touched this reality. His every touch made her heart leap and her stomach flutter. His touch was expert, but there was nothing by rote about this. He seemed in tune with her every need and desire, as if he could read her mind.

His hands found her thighs again, parting them softly, and then he was tracing kisses down her neck, his mouth sliding lower until he closed his lips over her nipple, teasing it softly with his tongue. Heat simmered in her stomach and pooled meltingly between her thighs as he sank to his knees and traced his mouth lightly over the flat of her stomach. She sucked in a sharp breath as his lips sank lower still and the heat of his breath warmed her through the lace of her panties. She gasped as his fingers teased the thin fabric aside and his tongue slipped against the very core of her.

Her hands found his hair and clutched at it as he stroked and teased until she ached for him to go further, and then delicious pleasure flooded her veins as he slid two fingers inside her in one slow and smooth movement. She moaned softly as he found his rhythm, moving his fingers steadily as his tongue lazily circled the nub of her, moving with her, until she cried her ecstasy at the ceiling and he moved both hands beneath her, holding her against his mouth, wringing every last second of satisfaction out of her.

Anonymity was gone. That inconsequential, easy gratification wasn't there. Because for once this wasn't about quick fun, satisfaction. Dispensable satisfaction.

This was about her. Wanting to please *her*. And that was a real novelty that knocked his senses sprawling.

The light change in her breath as he ran his fingertips over the softness of her thighs, the way she gasped and clutched at his hair as he moved them higher—all those little gestures delighted him and turned him on all the more.

Dan got to his feet in the hollow between her parted legs and pulled her close. She curled her arms around him, tugging him against her, her fast, short breaths warm against his lips. Her evident excitement, such a foil to her usual carefully controlled attitude, thrilled him to the core, and in the all-encompassing heat of his arousal he marvelled at the surge of excitement pleasing her elicited.

He had been going through the motions all this time. His dates, his easy flings... Plenty of them, but all a simple good time means to an end. The cost of that had been the detached quality about them that meant pleasure had failed to touch him below the physical surface. The combination of his visceral hot need for Emma, his delight at her eagerness to please him and his own desire to please her took him way beyond that level. There was nothing run of the mill about this.

The thought crept through his mind, tinged with fear at the deeper meaning of it, but he moved on regardless, powerless to stop.

He lifted her, his hands sliding across the cool satiny skin of her lower back, the sweet vanilla scent of her hair dizzying his senses, and crushed his mouth hard against hers. His desire for her was rising inside him like a cresting wave, driving him forward. Her legs wrapped around his waist as he carried her the few paces from desk to four-poster and eased her down gently onto the softness of the quilted bedspread.

And now he moved with intimate slowness, the better to savour every second, to explore. She slid gentle hands over his back and sparks of arousal jumped and flickered in his abdomen as her fingers found his hard length and stroked with deliciously maddening softness. A guttural moan escaped his lips as he tangled a hand in the silk of her hair and crushed his mouth against hers, easing her lips apart with his tongue.

Before he could be consumed by the deliciousness of it he caught her hand and moved away briefly to find a condom. And then control was his again as he moved against her, and her gasp thrilled him as he eased slowly into her. As she raised her hips with a soft moan, urging him on, sliding her hands around him to push him deeper into her, greedy for more, his spirits soared. And only as she clutched at his back and cried her pleasure against his neck did he finally let himself follow her over that delicious edge.

Bewildering *déjà vu* kicked in as Emma woke to bird-song and sunshine for the second time in a weekend. And then all thoughts of her surroundings disappeared as she came fully awake in one crushing instant of con-sciousness. She turned her head slowly on the pillow.

Not a hallucination brought on by wedding stress and too much champagne.

*Dan was in the bed next to her.* And they'd spent the night exploring every inch of one another. Hell, her cheeks fired just at the thought of what they'd done and she pressed her face against the cool top sheet. Had that *really* been her? Super-cool, professional Emma? Bra-zen—that was what she was.

His dark hair was dishevelled even beyond its usual spikes by action and sleep, and there was a light shadow of stubble now defining his jaw. She lifted a hand to her dry mouth as her gaze ranged down the defined muscles of his torso to the sheet that lay haphazardly over his hips. He was the stuff of dreams.

But the cold light of day was streaming in right through that window. She'd joined the ranks of Dan's little-black-book girls. How long did he usually leave it before he did his backing off? A day? Two?

She held her breath and without sitting up began wrig-gling inch by slow inch towards the edge of the bed, not really thinking much further at this point than getting some clothes on. They might have spent half the night screwing, but that didn't mean he'd have the chance to ogle her cellulite in daylight.

She was right on the edge of the bed and just thinking

about how to manoeuvre her feet onto the floor when he took a deep, relaxed breath and opened his eyes.

She froze like a rabbit in headlights.

'You look surprised,' he said, stretching easily.

He gave her that slow, laconic grin that never failed to make her stomach do flip-flops. Clearly she had the *look* of a rabbit in headlights, too.

'Is it such a disappointment to wake up next to me?'

She clutched the top of the sheet a modest few inches above nipple height and tried to move her bum cheeks back fully onto the bed so he wouldn't realise she'd been trying to make an exit.

'I wasn't sure I would,' she said. 'I half expected you to make a swift exit under cover of darkness. Didn't you tell me that was your usual modus operandi? Not to make it through to breakfast?'

He pulled himself up onto one elbow and smiled down at her. The benefit of having hair that naturally spiked was that he actually looked *better* first thing in the morning. How typical. She could just imagine the fright wig on her own head after the active night they'd spent.

'Emma, nothing about this is my usual modus operandi.'

His blue eyes held her own and her stomach gave a slow and toe-curling flip as the delectable things he'd done to her last night danced through her mind. He reached a hand out to stroke her cheek softly and a surge of happiness began to bubble through her. He was right. None of this fitted with him acting to type. Yet still it was hard to let herself trust him.

'I know you too well,' she said. 'That's the thing. None of your usual lines will work on me.'

'I wasn't aware I'd used any,' he said.

He had a point. He'd bailed her brother out, he hadn't washed his hands of her and disappeared to London after she'd called him selfish, he'd carried himself brilliantly through her brother's crazy wedding and he was still here at breakfast time. She let her guard slip.

Self-doubt. Any other reaction from her would be a surprise, wouldn't it?

Just looking at her lying next to him, all long limbs and messy hair and uncertainty, made heat begin to simmer again deep inside him. The night they'd spent replayed in his mind on a loop—the way she'd slowly put her trust in him, shedding her inhibitions, giving as much as taking. He wanted to smooth every kink of doubt out of her, convince her that this was far more than the throwaway night she clearly thought it might be.

He reached across and pulled her into his arms, fitting her long, slender body against his own, breathing in the faint sweet vanilla scent that still clung to her hair. His mouth found hers and he parted her lips hungrily with his tongue and kissed her deeply.

Desire rippled through her, peaking at her nipples and pooling between her legs as he gently turned her over, his mouth at her shoulder.

In her dreams of all those months ago he had been skilled. In reality he was melt-to-the-floor perfect. How did he know how to make her feel that sublime? Where to touch her? How hard to stroke? How softly to caress?

He lay behind her now, her pleasure his sole focus. One hand was circling her waist, his fingers easing slowly between her thighs, softly parting them to expose the core of her. She felt his moan of satisfaction against her neck as he discovered how wet she was. His thumb found her most sensitive spot and circled it with tantalising slowness. His fingers slid lower, teasing until she ached with emptiness and desire.

And then he was turning her expertly, one hand pressed flat beneath her stomach, the other cradling her breasts as he moved behind her. A moment of delicious anticipation as he paused to grab a condom, then she felt him press against her. And then he was thrusting smoothly deep inside her, filling her deliciously, his free hand teasing her nipples to rock-hard points, his mouth at her neck. As she cried out in uncontrolled pleasure he moaned his own ecstasy against the smooth contours of her back, not slowing or changing pace until he knew she was satisfied.

Afterwards, she lay in his arms, the warm length of his torso against her back, his soft breath against her hair. His hand circled her body, lightly cupping her breast, caressing it. They fitted together perfectly, as if they were meant to be together. For the first time she let herself tentatively believe that they might be. He'd made love to her again instead of making a sharp exit. He was still here with her. Yet still there were things that needed to be said.

'I didn't say thank you, did I?' she said softly. When he didn't answer she turned her head slightly, to catch his expression at her shoulder. 'For restoring Adam's shadow for me.'

She felt him tense briefly, then he tugged gently at her shoulder until she turned over in his arms and lay facing him. His mouth was inches from her own and his gaze was holding hers steadily.

He looked at her resigned expression and mentally kicked himself.

'I didn't mean that,' he said. 'It was a crappy thing to say. I know how difficult your family can be.' He paused as if groping for the right words. 'It wasn't a personal dig at you. It was more about reacting to your telling me where to get off.'

'You always have to have the last word,' she said quietly. 'I've noticed that about you. Why is that? Why is it so hard for you to accept anyone else's agenda? People *do* have them, you know—it's not just *you* living in a bubble.'

Was that how she really saw him? Was he really that blind to other people's feelings?

'It wasn't intentional,' he said. 'I'm sorry if it seemed that way to you. It was…' He groped for a way to explain that wouldn't sound totally crap. 'I like staying in control,' he said at last. 'Being the one that makes all the decisions. Perhaps it's become a bit of a habit.' He paused and added, 'A defence mechanism.'

The same one he'd used so successfully since childhood.

'If the only person you look out for is yourself, you can't be hurt.'

'I don't understand.'

He looked at the ceiling, at the blank white expanse of it.

'There was someone once,' he said. 'I'm not talking about one of the girls I see now. They're just dates. Nothing more to it than that. There was someone else a long time ago.'

He didn't look at her. It felt easier, not doing that.

'Maggie and I were housemates at college,' he said.

'There were six of us. Couple of girls, four blokes, each of us renting a room and sharing a kitchen and bathroom. You know the kind of thing. Student accommodation. For the first time I was living away from home.'

He remembered how liberating it had felt that his life was finally his own. An escape route.

'We were friends, Maggie and me, then one night after a party we ended up sleeping together. We kept it really casual, though. Both of us had big career plans. She was training to be a teacher. Primary school kids, you know?'

He glanced at Emma and she nodded acknowledgment, not interrupting. That was a good thing. If he stopped talking about this now he might never start again.

'And she lived up north, had a big family there, and she was going to be moving back once she'd finished her course. It wasn't serious. It was never *going* to be serious.' He laughed. 'Hell, I'd just got *away* from home life, finally tasted a bit of freedom. I wasn't about to get myself tied down to someone before I'd even finished my first year.'

She looked puzzled.

'But you did? You must have for her to have made such a big impact on you. What happened?'

He paused, gathering his thoughts. Who had he told about the baby? Anyone at all? He stormed ahead before he could think twice.

'Maggie got pregnant,' he said simply.

He felt the change in her posture as she shifted in his arms. She lifted herself on one elbow to look at him. He steeled himself to glance at her and read the response in her face, ready for the questions that he was sure would follow.

She said nothing. Her eyes were filled with gentleness but she didn't speak, didn't pry. She was letting him talk on his own terms.

'And that changed everything,' he said.

He took a sharp breath as he recalled the memory. It came back to him easily, in such perfect clarity that it made a mockery of his conviction that he'd done such a great job of putting it behind him.

'At first I was horrified. I thought it was the last thing I could possibly want. Maggie had strong views. She was going to keep the baby whether I was involved or not.' He sighed. 'She made it sound like she was offering me my freedom, but looking back I think to her I was dispensable even at the outset.'

'And were you? Involved, I mean?'

He could see the puzzlement in her eyes. She was wondering if he had a secret family stashed away somewhere.

'Once I got used to the shock I was more and more delighted. The longer it went on the more I bought into it. With every day that passed I had a clearer idea of what the future would be like. I was going to be the best bloody husband and father the world had ever seen.'

'You've been married?'

He gave a rueful smile and shook his head.

'It was my one and only brush with it, but, no, it never happened. I wanted it to be as different to my experience of family as I could make it. Proper commitment, hands-on parents with a strong, healthy relationship.' He paused. 'I probably envisaged a white picket fence somewhere. And a dog. Sunday roasts. All the stereotypes. I was right in there with them.' He took a breath. 'And then it all disappeared overnight because we lost the baby.'

The wrenching, churning ache deep in his chest made a suffocating comeback. Dulled a little at the edges over time, like an old wound, but still there, still heavy.

She was sitting up now, reaching for his hands, her eyes filled with sadness.

'Oh, bloody hell, Dan. I'm so sorry.'

He waved a dismissive hand at her, shaking his head, swallowing hard to rid his throat of the aching constriction.

'It was a long time ago,' he said.

In terms of years, at least.

'I'm over it.'

'I never imagined you being remotely interested in kids or family,' she said. 'I mean, it isn't just the way you keep your relationships so short or the fact you never see your own parents. You're the most un-child-friendly person I've ever known. You have a penthouse flat with a balcony and it's full of glass furniture and white upholstery. Your car is a two-seater.'

'Why would I need a family home or a Volvo?' he said. 'I have absolutely no intention of going down that road again. I gave it my best shot and it didn't work out.'

A worried frown played about her face and he gave her a reassuring *I'm-over-it* smile.

'That's why I didn't step straight up to the plate when Adam needed a helping hand. That's why I made it into the car before I realised I couldn't leave for London. I was trying to play things the way I always do. I don't get involved with people. I like keeping things simple.'

'At arm's length.'

'Exactly. Arm's length. After Maggie I decided relationships weren't for me. Family wasn't for me. I threw myself into work instead. After all, it had always worked at digging me out in the past. And it worked again.' He shrugged. 'But maybe it's become a bit of a habit. I never wanted to come across as selfish or unkind when I said you liked your comfort zone. It was a retaliation, nothing more.'

He pulled her back down from her elbow into a cuddle. Her head nestled beneath his chin. She shook her head slowly against his chest.

'Maybe it *was* just a retaliation but actually you might have had a point,' she said quietly.

He pulled away enough to give her a questioning look and she offered him a tiny smile.

'A *small* point,' she qualified. 'Did you ever know I had a crush on you for months, like some stupid schoolgirl?'

That flash of clarity kicked in again, the same as he'd felt the night before, as if something he wasn't seeing had been pointed out to him. A wood instead of a mass of trees, maybe.

'You did?'

'Why am I not surprised that you never noticed?' She sighed and rolled her eyes. 'I think maybe part of the reason I was so struck on you was because of what you're like. I knew you'd never look twice at me. I didn't fit your remit.'

'My *remit?*' He grinned and tugged her closer.

She snuggled into his arm. 'Blonde, bubbly, curvaceous. That's your type.'

'Dispensable, simplistic, inconsequential,' he said.

'Those were the real qualities I was aiming for. None of which apply to you.'

'That's exactly my point. I got to know you over months, I saw the kind of girls you went for and I knew none of your relationships lasted. I knew you'd never be interested in me and that made dreaming about the prospect from afar a very nice, safe thing to do.'

She held a hand up as if it was all suddenly clear to her.

'Plus it was a great reason not to get involved with anyone else, and it gave me the perfect way to fob off criticism from my parents when they asked about my life. So there you are, you see. When you said I was happy living in Adam's shadow, staying under my parents' radar, you kind of had a point. My choices were all about keeping an easy life.'

'You must have hidden it well,' he said, scanning his mind back over the last twelve months. Little signs jumped out at him now that he had that hindsight—the way she'd always been available for any work engagement, no matter how short the notice, the effort she'd always made with her appearance. He'd assumed those were things she did for everyone. Because that was what he'd *wanted* to assume. The alternative hadn't been allowed on his radar.

'Then again, I'm not sure I would have noticed unless you'd smashed me over the head with it,' he conceded. 'I had you filed very comfortably under "Work Colleague". That was what I needed you to be. I never intended things between us to be more than that.'

'Our plus-one agreement.'

He didn't respond, although the ensuing silence was heavy with the unspoken question. What would happen now with their ludicrous arrangement? He'd told her it would be over when they got this weekend out of the way and went back to their London lives. With every moment he spent with her, sticking to that decision and riding it out felt more and more difficult.

# CHAPTER ELEVEN

'YOU WANT TO try and get to breakfast?' he asked.

Emma felt the light brush of his kiss against her shoulder. Even after the night they'd spent, followed by the delicious intimacy of this morning, his touch thrilled her.

She wriggled against him. Her arms fitted around his neck as if they were meant to be there. She smoothed the dense spikes of his hair through her fingers.

'Let me think,' she said, smiling into his eyes. 'Would I rather sit opposite my parents and watch my father drool over a full English while my mother force-feeds him muesli, or would I rather stay here with you?'

He laughed and pulled her tighter.

'Adam's married now. I think he's grown-up enough to manage without me watching his back through one little breakfast.' She dropped her eyes briefly. 'And I think you've done enough for him. We can catch him before he goes.'

Was it just that? Or was part of it that she didn't want to leave this gorgeous little bubble where he was hers for fear that it might burst? After wanting him for so long, all the while convinced nothing would ever come of it, to actually have her crush requited made it seem all the sweeter.

Needling doubt lurked at the edge of her consciousness despite the gorgeous night they'd spent and the way
he'd opened up about his past. She knew Dan—knew
the way he played relationships. Despite his reassur-
ances there was no getting away from the fact that pretty
soon after you made it into Dan's bed you made it just
as quickly out of it, never to be heard of again. Was this
like some holiday romance? Would the magic be theirs
as long as they didn't leave? What would happen when
they got back to London?

She'd noticed that her mention of the old plus-one
agreement hadn't been picked up by him. His intention
to cut all ties with her after this weekend gnawed at the
edge of her consciousness as she tried to push it away.


Adam and Ernie stood at the hotel doorway, waving
madly. Those who had made it down to breakfast clustered in the lobby. Emma had dragged Dan downstairs
with moments to spare and eased her way through the
group of smiling friends and relatives, her hand entwined in his.

Emma's mother dabbed a tear from the corner of her
eye.

'Well, it wasn't the most traditional set-up,' she
sniffed, 'but still…it's been a lovely weekend.'

She kissed Adam's cheek and then leaned in to do
the same to Ernie.

'Tradition?' Ernie said. 'I think we can stretch to a
bit of that before we go.'

He grabbed at a bunch of yellow lilies standing in
a huge vase on the side table near the door, turned his
back on the gathered crowd of guests and lobbed them
high in the air over his head to the sound of claps and

squeals, showering the guests with drops of water. As the flowers plummeted, twisting and turning, faces turned to watch their progress.

Dan shot out a hand and caught them on autopilot, to prevent them from smacking him over the head.

He stared down stupidly at the bunch of flowers in his hand as cheers and mad clapping rang out all around them. Even Emma's mother was smiling.

'You're next!' Adam hollered from the doorway. 'Great catch, sweetie!'

Dan glanced at Emma and saw the look of delight on her face. Her eyes shone. Her smile lit up her face. She radiated happiness.

Shock flooded into the pit of his stomach.

*You're next!*

Was he? Was that where this led?

He'd had a game plan way back in London, before they'd even set foot in the West Country. A plan to be a last-time-pays-for-all fake boyfriend stand-in for Emma and then go back to London. Back to work. Back to what *worked*. And somehow he'd been caught up in the moment, had lost sight of what was important to him.

He'd ended up standing here with flowers in his hands to the sound of excited applause because the path ahead of him led down the aisle. Maybe not now, maybe not even in the next few years, but *that* was the destination.

*If* they made it that far.

That was the risk. A risk he'd vowed never to take again after the months of despair that had plagued him when Maggie left.

This was way off-plan. Yet the thought of losing Emma now made his heart plummet and misery churn in his stomach.

He followed the rest of the group outside to watch Adam and Ernie pile into a yellow Rolls-Royce. Maybe he could find another way forward. A way to keep her that still minimised risk. A compromise.

She'd been right.

There really was more between them than one of his casual flings. They'd been back from the wedding for nearly a week now and he was a different man. He was in touch with her daily, and with every phone call and text she felt more secure. Flowers arrived from him at her workplace, eliciting envious stares and buzzing interest from her colleagues. He hadn't so much as mentioned their old plus-one agreement, but that was because it was obsolete—right? Past history. OK, so she wasn't expecting him to propose...let's not get ahead of ourselves—although a girl could dream. But she'd been the one to change his behaviour. He really *was* different with her. They were a couple now—not just work contacts.

Dan didn't *do* flowers and phone calls. He did swift exits and dumping by text. And now she was seeing him tonight and her stomach was one big ball of excitement and anticipation. She couldn't wait.

The doorbell. On time.

She checked her appearance one last time. A new dress, a less austere one than usual, with a floaty, feminine skirt. Deep pink instead of her usual black or grey choice of going-out outfit. Because going out with Dan was about pleasure now, not business. About getting to know each other instead of working the situation for every career advantage they could get out of it.

She opened the front door and excitement at seeing him brought an instant smile to her face—one she couldn't have held back. He stood on the doorstep, leaning against the jamb, his crisp blue shirt deepening the tones of his eyes as he smiled at her, a perfectly cut business suit and silk tie sharpening the look.

Not the same relaxed designer look he'd had at the wedding weekend. Her mind stuttered briefly. *Business suit.*

From nowhere cautionary unease jabbed her in the ribs and a wave of disorientating *déjà vu* swept over her. She could have rewound to a couple of months before Adam's wedding, before Alistair had put a stop to their agreement, and Dan would have looked exactly like this when she'd opened the door for one of their business engagements.

He slid an arm around her waist and kissed her softly on the mouth, starting up all the latent sparks from the weekend.

She pulled herself up short.

Jumping at shadows—that was what she was doing. She was so used to being doomed to failure when she put herself out there that now she was pre-empting problems before they even happened. She'd ruin things herself if she wasn't careful. Already he had a puzzled expression on his face—no doubt because her first reaction on seeing him since their gorgeous weekend at the wedding was to hesitate.

He'd called her. He'd sent flowers. He'd texted. And now she was spooked because of the *suit* he wore? She really needed to go to work on her own insecurities if she was going to move forward with her life.

'Where are we going, then?' she asked when he started the car.

'Dinner first,' he said easily, putting it in gear and

moving smoothly into the early-evening traffic. 'I've got a table booked at La Maison.'

Another jab of unease.

'La Maison?'

It was Dan's choice of venue for work dinners. She'd been there with him too many times to count, always as his stand-in date, always with a work objective in mind. Maybe it would be a new contact to impress, perhaps a sweetener before he put in a tender for services. Whatever it happened to be, she'd been there to help smooth the path.

He glanced across at her.

'For starters, yes. If that's OK with you? Then maybe later we could go on somewhere else? End up at my place?'

'Of course.'

She smiled brightly at him and pressed her palms together in her lap. They were damp.

He parked the car and escorted her into the restaurant. The usual subtle piano music played in the background, and the usual perfectly dressed dark wood tables and soft lighting provided the perfect ambience for discussion, which had always been the point of coming here.

His usual table. She felt Dan's hand rest gently on her hip as he guided her between the tables towards it.

*Usual restaurant. Usual table.*

It didn't mean anything, did it? The restaurant was a good one after all.

*Usual quick run-through of background?*

'Roger Lewis and Barry Trent,' he said in a low voice at her shoulder. 'Medium-sized business providing bespoke travel packages specifically aimed at the over-fifties. Looking for advice on growing their business to the next level.' He gave her shoulder a squeeze. 'Could be in the market for a change in legal services, too— you could be in there!'

As they arrived at the table she turned to stare at him and he actually *winked* at her. It felt as if her heart was being squeezed in a vice.

'Table for four,' she said dully, stating the obvious.

He looked at her as if she might be mad. As if there was nothing spot-the-deliberate-mistake about this at all.

'Of course it is,' he said. 'Just a bit of business to discuss and then the evening's ours. They'll be along in a minute.'

The waiter pulled a chair out for her and fussed over her as she sat down hard, her mind reeling. Dan gave him the nod and he poured them each a glass of champagne, replacing the bottle in the ice bucket to one side of the table.

Her throat felt as if it might be closing up and she swallowed hard. She clasped her hands together on the table to stop them shaking.

'I thought we were going on a date,' she said, making her tone as neutral as she could manage when what she wanted to do was grab him by the shoulders and shake him. 'Just you and me. But this is basically the same old set-up, Dan.'

She waved a hand at the extra two table settings, at the surrounding quiet tastefulness of the restaurant.

'Is that it, then? Now we're back in London it's back to the same old routine? Were you actually going to discuss that with me, or did you just assume I'd go along with it?'

He reached for her hands but she removed them to her lap.

'I don't know what you mean,' he said.

'What this looks like to me is the same old plus-one agreement,' she said, forcing the words out, voicing her worst fears. 'Just with sex thrown in.'

He grimaced and leaned across the table to touch her cheek.

'This is *not* the same old plus-one agreement,' he said, 'and I really wish we'd never given the damn thing a name. It makes it sound like we signed something official when all we really did was get into a routine over time. Because it worked so well for *both* of us.'

*A routine?* She pressed her lips together hard and pushed a hand through her hair as anger began to course through her. It felt suddenly uncomfortably hot in here. She hadn't missed the emphasis there on the word *both*. No way was she letting him lump her in with this as if it were some joint bloody venture.

When he next spoke it felt as if he'd tipped the contents of the ice bucket over her head.

'But if we *have* to call it that,' he continued, holding out a hand, 'for what it's worth I don't think we should be too hasty about changing how we relate to each other when it comes to work. Why end something that's worked so well for us just because you and I have got closer? What do you think about varying it a little? Adding in a few amendments?'

His tone was jokey—teasing, even. As if he were proposing something exciting. As if she ought to be taking his arm off in her eagerness to say yes.

'Different rules this time—it'll be fun. We can still do work engagements together, give it everything we've got just like we always have, but without the need to limit it. There'll be no need to *pretend* we're a couple any more—no need to go our separate ways at the end of the night.'

He wanted to carry on seeing her but without any full-on legitimacy. Work would continue to come first with him, just the way it always had. He would expect her to carry on acting as his plus-one, smoothing the way for his business prowess at charity dinners and the like. The difference would be that this time she would get to share his bed, as well.

Well, *lucky, lucky* her.

All the pent-up excitement that had built this week as she'd looked forward to seeing him again had quit bubbling and dissipated like flat champagne. The flavour would still be there—the tang of white grape and the sharp aroma reminiscent of the effervescent drink it once was—but when you got right down to it, it was past its best. What you were really getting was the dregs.

And one thing she knew without a shadow of a doubt was that she was not going to be the dregs. Not for anyone.

Not even for him.

She stood up, a veil of calm slipping over her. She'd wanted him to be hers so much she'd believed she'd give anything to keep him.

But when it came to it she found that her self-respect just wasn't up for grabs.

He looked up at her, his expression confused, as she picked up her handbag and lifted her wrap from the back of her chair, making it obvious this wasn't just a visit to the ladies' room. She was leaving.

'Where are you going?'

'Home,' she said, not looking at him.

She pushed her chair back into place. Sick disappointment burned in her throat, blocking it. She wasn't sure she could stop it transforming into tears if she looked at him. She absolutely was *not* going to cry. No way.

He stood up immediately, his hand on her elbow.

'Why? What's wrong? Are you ill?'

The look of concern in his eyes touched her heart and she almost faltered. But this was just too bloody reminiscent of the last guy she'd met for dinner, thinking she was on her way to a happy ending. Dan was just like Alistair after all.

'No, Dan,' she said. 'I'm not ill. I'm stupid. Stupid for thinking there might actually be more between us than *work*.'

She made a move to leave and he grabbed her by the hand.

'Hey, we can talk about this. That's what this is about? You're annoyed because I factored a work dinner into our date night?' He shrugged. 'I'm sorry. Maybe I should have talked to you about it first. I just didn't think you'd mind. Before last weekend you were all for carrying on with the agreement, and you'd gone back to work instead of taking that sabbatical, so I just assumed you'd be all for it.'

'That was before the weekend,' she said.

She looked down at her hand, encased in his.

'This isn't what I want. Some half-arsed excuse for a relationship. I thought you understood that. I don't want some relationship where we both have our own agenda and factor the other person in wherever they happen to fit. You know where that kind of relationship ends up?' She didn't wait for his answer. 'It ends up with separate bedrooms and separate interests and separate bloody lives. If we can't even get that right now, what hope do we have? I want you and me to be the priority—not an afterthought to whatever work ambitions we might happen to have.'

'It never bothered you before,' he pointed out.

'Because it was all I *had* before,' she said. 'It was the only way I could have some level of relationship with you. But I want more than that now. And after last weekend I thought you wanted that, too.'

Two business-suited middle-aged men were being ushered between the tables towards them. The over-fifties leisure break people, she assumed.

'Don't go,' he said. 'Let's get this business discussion out of the way and then we can talk this through properly.'

She gave a wry laugh and flung her hands up.

'That's the problem, you see. Right there. You *still* think I might actually sit down and put your work meeting first—before we get to talk about what's happening between us. I'm not doing it. Whatever this is for you—plus-one bloody agreement, quick fling, friends with benefits—it's over.'

She'd raised her voice and some of the diners seated nearby rubbernecked to stare at them. She didn't give a damn. She had no intention of ever visiting this restaurant again. In fact, the way she felt right now, she might not go out socially again. Possibly ever. Maybe she'd embrace her inner workaholic and make senior partnership by thirty-five. A new goal. One that was attainable. One that relied solely on her and so wasn't doomed to failure.

She walked away from the table.

He moved after her as she passed the two businessmen, one with his hand outstretched. She heard Dan apologise briefly before he ran after her. He caught her near the door, took her arm, turned her to face him.

'You're dumping me?' A grin lifted the corner of his mouth.

Her heart twisted agonisingly in her chest.

'Yes,' she said.

'What? No champagne-throwing?' he joked, as if he still couldn't believe she was making such a fuss.

She didn't smile. It felt as if her veins were full of ice water.

'That was a *fake* break-up, Dan,' she said. 'All for show. This is the real thing.'

She walked out of the restaurant without looking back.

# CHAPTER TWELVE

DAN STARED AT the city skyline from the balcony of his flat. Grey today, misted in drizzle. The fine rain was the kind that coated and his hair and skin were slowly soaking; the boards were slick beneath his feet.

So she'd dumped him.

No one dumped him. *Ever.* And now she'd done it twice in the space of a couple of months.

The confused feeling of a loss of control which had buried him the first time, back at the art gallery, kicked right back into action. Had that really only been a month or two ago? It felt like years.

He wasn't going to make the same mistake again—grappling for control of the situation and leaving himself open to a second body blow.

Except it really hadn't been just a body blow, had it?

*Let it go.*

In the first defiant moments after she'd left him to sort out the embarrassment in the restaurant that had felt doable. He didn't need this kind of chaos in his life. That had been the whole point of keeping relationships distant. He'd had a lucky escape.

In the ensuing days it had become more and more difficult to keep himself convinced of that. It wasn't as if he'd let her have an access-all-areas pass to his life after all. Their paths crossed at work functions, they communicated via e-mail and the occasional phone call. Businesslike. At arm's length. She'd visited his flat on two or three occasions—never when it was just the two of them. So it wasn't as if her absence left a gaping hole in his life where she'd previously been. How could you miss something that you never had?

He knew that was possible better than anyone.

Somewhere in the depths of his consciousness he understood that what he was missing was the way she'd made him feel—the way she'd altered his take on life.

He'd spent so long making sure no one became important to him, but she'd somehow managed to get past that barrier. She'd done it so quietly that he hadn't realised how much he needed her until she was gone, so perfect had his conviction been that he had everything under control.

It had seemed like the perfect solution—the perfect way to keep things at the comfortable distance he'd thought he needed. Why not just reinstate the old social agreement? Keep their relationship grounded in something that was tried and tested? Keep some areas of his life untouched rather than investing his entire soul in something that might fail?

And in his stupid arrogance he'd just expected her to go along with his every whim, just to accept that their relationship had a work slant to it. Especially after her revelation about her age-old crush on him. She'd taken whatever he'd thrown her way for the last year, never asking for anything in return, and he saw now that he'd just taken that for granted.

If anything he admired her all the more for finally

standing up for what she wanted. She'd wanted out because she wasn't prepared to settle for second best. After years of playing second fiddle to Adam and then being trounced by that moron Alistair Woods she'd been ready to risk everything to be with him and he'd failed her. He'd been too afraid to reciprocate.

The flat that she'd barely visited now felt empty where it had always felt relaxing. So far removed from any family vibe, he'd been able to look around him and know he'd built a new life—one that was successful, one that couldn't collapse under emotional rubble. The prospect of living here now felt empty. He'd had a taste of a different life. He'd tried to keep it in check. But apparently a taste was all that was needed to suck him totally in.

He was in love with her. And it was too late now to guard against loss because the damage was done. He'd screwed up.

He glanced around the balcony—hot tub with its cover on in the corner, railings with a sheer drop below. What had she said—his life was child-unfriendly? It was. Deliberately so. Only now he began to question whether he still wanted that. Whether he ever truly had.

He moved back inside and slid the double doors shut. The flat was totally silent and devoid of character. No mess. No clutter.

He could let this go. See if he couldn't put it behind him. Hell, work had done the trick before—it might do it again. Perhaps if he ceased eating and sleeping and all other essential functions, doubled the effort with his business, he could crush her from his mind.

Or he could take a risk.

He glanced around him again. What, really, did he have to lose?

\* \* \*

'…and Adam and Ernie are heading back from Mauritius. Adam's already got a ton of interest in his new planned collection of pictures and there's talk of them being immortalised on table mats and coasters. Can you imagine?' Her mother paused a moment to let the enormity of that fact sink in. 'That's the kind of mass appeal he has.'

Emma held the phone briefly away from her ear. Dan should have held out for a share in Adam's business in return for helping him. He could have made a mint. Then again, it would have been another tie, another responsibility, another link to a family he wanted to keep at a distance. Of course he wouldn't have wanted that.

She gritted her teeth hard and forced Dan out of her mind, to which he seemed to return at the slightest opportunity.

She put the phone back to her ear.

'What about you? Any news?' her mother was saying. 'Is that Dan showing any signs of making an honest woman of you?' She gave the briefest of pauses, clearly believing the answer was a foregone conclusion of a no. 'Thought not. Work, then?'

How many times had Emma had varying versions of this same conversation? Made the right noises just to avoid interest and interference, just to keep her comfort zone comfortable? She never had any new successes to hold up to her mother's scrutiny, but she never had any epic failures, either. Comfortable, uncomplicated middle ground. And where exactly had it got her?

She opened her mouth to give her mother some stock fob-off—something that would buy her another couple of months below the radar before she had to repeat this whole stupid fake conversation all over again. Probably it would be something about her legal career boring enough to have her mother fast-forwarding onto her next gossip morsel before she could scrutinise Emma's life beyond the surface. It had worked like a dream these last few years.

For the first time in millions of conversations she hesitated.

She was the most miserable she could ever remember being and the hideous pain was sharpened to gut-wrenching level because she'd known that brief spell of sublime perfection before Dan had reverted to type. In actual fact there had been no reversion. He'd never left type. It had all been a façade.

Was there *any* aspect of her life left that was real or of value?

'Dan and I aren't together,' she blurted, then clapped a hand over her own mouth in shock at her own words. 'We never were.'

*Except for a week or two when I thought I was the stand-out one who could change him.*

'We work together and we had an agreement to stand in as each other's dates at parties and dinners.'

For the first time ever there was stunned silence on the end of the phone and Emma had the oddest sensation in her stomach. A surge of off-the-wall indignant defiance. She picked it up and ran with it.

She really had been wallowing in the role of Adam's underachieving sibling all these years, kidding herself about how hard that was, when in reality it had been the easy option. Pigeonholing herself as failure meant she had absolutely nothing to live up to.

She didn't need to define herself by her childhood inadequacies—she had known that for years—but knowing it really wasn't enough. The real issue was whether or not she'd truly bought into that. Or had a part of her remained that sweaty-palmed kid on the stage in spite of the passing years?

For the first time she took a breath and really did buy into it. Just how much of her inadequacy was she responsible for? Who had put Adam on a gilded pedestal and kept him there? Guilty as charged. It had been easier to live in his shadow than to prove herself in her own right.

Had it in some way been easier to accept the categorisation of herself as the clumsy one? The underachiever? The let-down? The singleton? No relationships for her, because that would lead to rejection. Just oodles of work, because that was the one thing she could feel good at, because it depended only on her. Had it been easier to blame her family for her failures instead of living an actual functional, healthy life?

'I'm taking a sabbatical from work,' she said. 'I'm going travelling.'

All that excitement she'd had about going away with Alistair, about escaping her dreary old life where everything was safe and secure and devoid of risk, made a cautious comeback. When she'd finished with him she'd finished with all of that, too. But now that Adam's wedding was over and the train wreck that was her friendship, relationship, romance with Dan was finished—she wasn't even sure what the bloody hell to call it—what exactly was there to keep her here? Why the hell did she need Alistair on her arm to have an adventure of her own?

She had absolutely no idea what she wanted in life any more, so why not take the time to find out?

* * *

She slid her bag from her shoulder and sat down at a pavement café overlooking the harbour. She ordered coffee and watched the bustle of tourists passing by, queuing for boat trips, browsing the local shops, fishing. The sun warmed her shoulders in the simple linen dress she wore. Just time for a coffee before her own boat trip departed—a day cruise around the island.

She looked up as someone snagged the seat opposite her with their foot, and her heart leapt as they pulled it out and sat down.

She must be seeing things. Maybe that was what happened when you missed someone enough—no matter how stupid and pointless missing them might be.

He took his sunglasses off and smiled at her, and she knew instantly that for all her telling herself she was way over him her thundering heart had the real measure of things.

'How did you find me?' she said.

He motioned to the waiter, ordered coffee.

'I had to ask your mother.'

Damn, he'd been serious about tracking her down, then.

'And how did that work for you?' She kept her voice carefully neutral.

'Well, it was no picnic, I can tell you.'

'She doesn't know where I'm staying,' she said. 'I've been picking up accommodation as I go along, depending where I want to go next.'

'I know. Didn't sound like you. What—no agenda? No travel itinerary?'

She grinned at that. At how well he knew her.

'My life's been one massive agenda these last few

years—all about what impression I want to give to this person or that person. I needed a change. My mistake was waiting for someone else to come along and instigate that instead of biting the bullet myself.'

'She told me you'd been e-mailing her, and she knew you'd booked a boat trip from here today. She just didn't know what time.'

She stared at him.

'You mean you've been hanging around here all day on the off-chance I'd show up?'

He shrugged.

'It was a good chance, according to your mother.' He paused. 'It was the best shot I had.'

Bubbles of excitement were beginning to slip into her bloodstream. She gritted her teeth and took a sip of her strong coffee. Nothing had changed. Nothing would. He might have jetted out to see her but it was still the same Dan sitting opposite her. He probably just wanted the last word, as usual. He earned a fortune. A plane trip to the Balearics was hardly going to break the bank. She wasn't going to get sucked back into this—not now.

'It wasn't particularly easy to persuade her to help me, actually,' he added. 'Since you told her our relationship was fake.'

She looked sideways at him, one eye squinting against the sun.

'It was, Dan,' she said.

He leaned forward, his elbows on the table, and for the first time she saw how strained he looked.

'Don't say that.'

'Why did you come here?' she said. 'To make some kind of a point? To finish things between us on your terms? Go ahead and have your say, if that's what you need for closure. Get yourself the upper hand. I've got a boat to catch. I've got plans.'

She moved her hands to her sides and sat on them to maintain some distance between them.

'I know that's how I've behaved in the past.' He held his hands up. 'I hated it when you met Alistair and pulled out of our stupid agreement. I've spent years making sure *I'm* in charge in every relationship I have. I've built a life on controlling everything around me. When you just dumped the whole thing without a moment's thought I just couldn't let it slide. I manipulated the situation until it worked in my favour—agreed to bring the agreement back just so that *I* could be the one to pull out of it. I thought I'd totally nailed why it bothered me so damn much. I thought it was about calling the shots. But really I think you've always meant more to me than I realised.'

He paused, held her gaze.

'I didn't track you down so I could make some kind of a point. I came to apologise and to try and explain.'

Her stomach was doing mad acrobatics and she moved one of her hands from underneath her legs and pressed it hard.

'Go on,' she said.

'I told you how things were with Maggie,' he said. 'The thing is, it wasn't just a break-up with Maggie— something that's tough but that you reconcile in time. There was this underlying feeling I've never been able to shake—that there was my one chance and I lost it. I never had that sense of belonging when I was growing up, and when Maggie got pregnant it felt like a gift. It was my opportunity to have a family and I would have done whatever it took to protect that.'

He sighed.

'Of course what it really boiled down to was an idea. I had this whole idealistic future mapped out in my head. Birthdays, holidays, where we were going to live. My family was going to want for nothing. I think Maggie understood the two of us better. If I'm honest, when she walked away, I think losing that whole dream future I'd been cultivating hurt a hell of a lot more than losing Maggie. I knew it, too, you see. It wasn't really working between us. If she hadn't got pregnant we might have carried on seeing each other for a few more months, then we would have gone our separate ways—wherever our work ambitions led us. We were fun. We were no-strings. It was never meant to be anything serious. Her pregnancy changed all of that. A baby on the way is one hell of a big string attached. Maggie didn't want me to look out for her. After we lost the baby it became very clear that for her any future we had together was gone. There was no alternative future—not for Maggie. She found it easier to cut all ties than to stick it out with me. And I knew that she was right. Because family hasn't exactly been my finest hour, has it?'

She held his gaze. She couldn't stop her hand this time as she reached across the table and touched his arm lightly.

'None of that means you're some kind of failure. It just means you haven't given yourself a proper chance.'

'I had absolutely no desire to give family a proper chance. Not when it ended up like that. It just seemed easier to accept that I'm not a family guy. And there were compensations.'

He gave her a wry smile. She smiled back.

'You mean your little black book of girlies?'

'I thought if I was going to cut myself off from family

life I might as well make the most of what the bachelor lifestyle has to offer. Don't get the idea that I've wallowed in misery for the last ten years or so, because I haven't. I've had a brilliant time. It's only very recently that...' He trailed off.

'What?'

He looked at her then and the look in his eyes made her heart flip over.

'That it began to feel...I don't know...hollow. Nothing seemed to give me the buzz that it used to. I kept trying to up the stakes—pitching for tougher contracts, brainstorming new business ideas. Dating just lost its appeal. I felt like I was doing the rounds—the same old thing, the same old conversations. I couldn't work out what it was I needed to fix that. And then you met Alistair.'

She glanced along the harbourside. The queue for her boat trip was gradually diminishing as people stepped into the boat. She should wrap this up...crack on with her plans.

But hearing him out suddenly felt like the most important thing in the world. She told herself it didn't mean her resolve was weakening, and for Pete's sake there were other boat trips.

'I don't think I'd considered you in that way before. I hadn't let myself. I'd conditioned myself to centre everything in my life on work. But suddenly you had all these big plans—you were buzzing with happiness, you were taking a risk—and I was stuck there on the same old treadmill. I didn't like it. I think I was fed up with my own life. But it's been so long. I've really typecast myself as bachelor playboy. I thought that was who I am. I didn't think I could be anyone else.'

She covered his hand with hers and squeezed it.

A sympathy squeeze. Not a leaping-into-your-arms-is-imminent squeeze. The hope that had begun to grow in his heart when she hadn't simply left the table at the get-go faltered.

'Alistair did me a favour,' she said. 'Until I met him I think I could quite easily have carried on in that same old rut I was in, pretty much indefinitely. Thinking one day you might come to your senses and show some interest in me—'

'Emma…' he cut in urgently.

She shook her head and held up a hand to stop him.

'The crazy thing about that was that I *knew* exactly what you were like. I'd seen it first-hand for months. Different women, same old short-term thing… You never changed for any of them. I used to think they were mad—couldn't they *see* what you were like? Didn't they *know* it was a recipe for disaster, getting involved with you? And then I went right ahead and did exactly the same thing.'

'It wasn't the same. You and I are different. *I'm* different.'

She was shaking her head.

'We don't want the same things, Dan. We're fundamentally mismatched. If I've managed to salvage one thing from the stupid mess with Alistair it's that I know I want to be with someone who puts our relationship first, above anything else. Above some stupid dream of a film career.' She paused. 'Above a crazy work ethic.'

'I want us to be together.'

'Back at the wedding…what you said about me and Adam…' She looked down at her fingers. 'You told me I *liked* living in Adam's shadow. That I was wallowing in always being the one who didn't measure up. And you were right. Knowing I'd be perceived as a failure was the perfect excuse for not trying things, for staying safe. All this time—right back since school, where it felt like nothing I did was right—I've been living in Adam's shadow, and somewhere along the way I learned to prefer it. It made everything easier. Doomed not to measure up, so why bother trying?'

'But you've done brilliantly at work. You're sought after. You do a great job.'

She shook her head, a rueful smile touching her lips.

'The one area I knew I could succeed at, yes. That was a safe bet, too. I made sure I picked a job that doesn't depend on other people's perception of you for success. And something as far removed from Adam's work as possible. I don't even think it was a conscious decision—it was more of an instinctive self-preservation thing that I've been cultivating since I was a stupid, oversensitive teenager.'

She looked up at him then and the look in her eyes wrenched at his heart.

'I even deluded myself, Dan,' she said. 'I thought the single most essential thing, if I was to find someone, was for them to put me first for once. That was my bloody dating criteria, for Pete's sake! Being important to someone. Anyone.'

She threw a hand up.

'Alistair would've done. An idiot like him! If he'd carried on treating me like a princess I'd probably still be there with him, feeling smug and telling myself I was happy with that self-centred moron. I was missing the point completely. The person I really want to be important to is myself. *I* never thought I was worthwhile, but it was easier to put that on other people. I thought I could get self-esteem by keeping away from my parents, moving to London, fobbing them off with a fake life of the sort I thought I should have. But all along that was part of the problem. I liked my fake life better than my real one, too. I never really wanted to be me.'

'I want you to be you,' he said. 'There's not one single thing I'd change about you. Not even your obsessive overpacking for one weekend, which fills me with horror at what you might be like to actually *live* with—how much *stuff* you might bring into my life. I've never wanted anything more. I was scared. Too scared to give our relationship everything I've got because I didn't want to risk losing it. My track record sucks. I couldn't afford to buy into it completely because I couldn't bear to lose you.'

He reached a hand out and tucked a stray lock of her hair behind her ear. She reached for his hand, caught it and held it against her face. But her eyes were tortured, as if she were determined to stick to her decision regardless of how much it hurt.

'What about kids?' she said quietly, and his heart turned over softly. 'What about your glass furniture and your bachelor pad and your determination never to have a family of your own? Because that stuff *matters,* Dan. I'm only just starting to find myself here, but what if I want to have kids in the future? Are you going to run for the horizon?'

A smile touched his lips at that, but her face was deadly serious. Inside his spirits soared.

'I never thought I'd have another chance at family,' he said. 'I know I've built a life that reflects that, but it's all window dressing—all peripheral stuff that I've built up to convince myself as much as anyone else that I'm living the bachelor dream. Truth is, the bachelor dream is pretty bloody lonely. I want to be with you—whatever that involves.'

The thought of a future with her by his side, the possibility of a family of his own with her, filled him with such bittersweet happiness that his throat constricted and he blinked hard and tried to swallow it away.

'So what are you suggesting?' she said, her eyes narrowing. 'Another crack at the plus-one agreement, just with a few more terms and conditions? Maybe with me living in?'

He shook his head, looked into her eyes in the hope that he could convince her.

'The agreement is dissolved,' he said. 'It's over—just like it should have been after that weekend. Months before that, even. I was just looking for a way to keep seeing you that held something back.' He paused. 'But by doing that I've undervalued you. I didn't know until I lost you that I'd taken that risk already. Trying to keep some distance couldn't change that. I love you, Emma. I'm *in* love with you.'

Silence as she looked into his eyes, except for the faint sound as she caught her breath. The guarded expression didn't lift.

'That's all very well, but you've got your business to think of. I'm going travelling. I'm doing something for *me* for a change. I want my life to go in a different direction. I don't want to end up some bitter, twisted woman trying to live my kids' lives for them because I've done such a crap job at living my own life that I'm totally dissatisfied with it. You can't just expect me to throw in the towel on all my plans because you've decided you want to give our relationship a proper go. Not after everything that's happened.'

'I don't expect you to back out of all your plans. I'll come with you.'

She laughed out loud at that and he realised just how entrenched his work ethic had seemed to the outside world.

She shook her head. 'That's never going to work and we both know it. What would happen to your business? You can't even leave it alone for a weekend without carting your laptop and your damn mobile office with you. You're the biggest work control freak in the universe.'

She stood up then and his heart dropped through his chest.

'I'll do delegation for you!' he blurted.

'You'll what?'

She looked back at him, her nose wrinkled, amusement lifting the corner of her mouth.

'I'll delegate. For you, I'll delegate. Give me a few weeks to promote someone to manager and do a handover and then I'll fly out and join you. Doesn't matter where you are—you choose the itinerary. We'll have a sabbatical together.'

A moment passed during which he was convinced he'd lost her, that there was nothing he could do or say that would persuade her.

He stood up next to her, took her hand in his, tugged her back down onto the seat beside him. The fact that she went willingly he took as a positive sign. At least she wasn't running for the boat without hearing him out.

'Please, Emma,' he said. 'I know how it sounds. I know I haven't got a great track record when it comes to taking time off work. But this is different. This isn't just some holiday. This is *you*. You're more important to me than the business. You're more important to me than anything.'

She looked down at his hand in hers, tentative happiness spreading slowly through her. He was ready to put her first. And she knew how much that must cost him after what had happened to him in the past. He'd spent the last decade not letting anyone or anything become important to him.

She laced her fingers through his, finally letting herself believe, and offered him a smile and a nod.

'You realise that if you take me, you take my family, too?' she said, and then he was kneeling in front of her.

'Your mother can organise the wedding,' he said, taking both her hands in his.

\* \* \* \* \*

# THE RETURN
# OF MRS JONES

## JESSICA GILMORE

*For Dan.*
*Thanks for giving me the time to write and always*
*believing that I would make it. I couldn't have done it*
*without you x*

*Special thanks must also go to my amazing critique*
*group, Jane, Julia and Maggie for three years of pep*
*talks, brainstorming and patience, to Merilyn for*
*making writing fun and to Fiona Harper and Jessica*
*Hart for all their encouragement and support.*

After learning to read aged just two, **Jessica Gilmore** spent every childhood party hiding in bedrooms in case the birthday girl had a book or two she hadn't read yet. Discovering Mills & Boon on a family holiday Jessica realised that romance writing was her true vocation and proceeded to spend her maths lessons practising her art, creating a Dynasty-inspired series starring herself and Morton Harket's cheekbones. Writing for Mills & Boon really is a dream come true!

An ex au pair, bookseller, marketing manager and Scarborough seafront trader selling rock from under a sign that said 'Cheapest on the Front', Jessica now works as a Membership Manager for a regional environmental charity. Sadly she spends most of her time chained to her desk wrestling with databases but likes to sneak out to one of their beautiful reserves whenever she gets a chance. Married to an extremely patient man, Jessica lives in the beautiful and historic city of York with one daughter, one very fluffy dog, two dog-loathing cats and a goldfish called Bob.

On the rare occasions that she is not writing, working, taking her daughter to activities or tweeting, Jessica likes to plan holidays – and uses her favourite locations in her books. She writes deeply emotional romance with a hint of humour, a splash of sunshine and usually a great deal of delicious food – and equally delicious heroes.

# CHAPTER ONE

'YOU CAN COME in, you know. Or do you city folk wear coffee patches and bypass the actual drinking process now?'

Lawrie Bennett jumped as the mocking tones jolted her out of her stunned contemplation of the ultra-modern building clinging to the harbour's edge. Turning, half convinced she had conjured up his voice along with her memories, she saw him lounging against the arty driftwood sign, the same crooked smile lurking in familiar blue eyes.

'Jonas?'

No, not a ghost. Subtle changes showed the passage of time: the surfer-blond hair was a little shorter, and a few lines round the eyes added new character to the tanned face.

Embarrassment, guilt, humiliation. Lawrie could take her pick of any of that ugly trio. Being caught hanging around outside her ex-husband's business like a gauche teenager with a crush was bad enough. To have been caught *by* her ex-husband really was a fitting end to what had been a truly terrible few weeks.

Trying to summon up an illusion of control, Lawrie switched on her best social smile—the one that had seen her through numerous meetings and charity balls. But her eyes hadn't got the 'cool and collected' memo, and flicked quickly up and down the lean body facing her.

The black tailored trousers and short-sleeved charcoal
shirt were a startling change from the cut-off jeans and
band T-shirt uniform of her memories, but the body underneath the sharp lines was as surfer-fit as she remembered.
He still looked irritatingly good. And even worse—judging by the smirk that flared briefly in the cool eyes—he
was fully aware of both her perusal and approval.

So much for control.

Jonas quirked an eyebrow. 'So, are you...planning to
come in?'

How, after all this time, could his voice be so familiar?
It was such a long time since she had heard those deep,
measured tones tempered with a slight Cornish burr. Yet
they sounded like home.

'I was just wondering if I was in the right place,' she
said, gesturing at the wood and glass building behind him;
so shiny and new, so unfamiliar. 'Everything's different.'

And *that,* Lawrie thought, was the understatement of
the century.

'I've made some changes. What do you think?' There
was pride in his voice underneath the laid-back drawl.

'Impressive,' she said. And it was. But she missed the
peeling, ramshackle old building. The picturesque setting
for her first job, her first kiss. Her first love. 'Did you de-
molish the boathouse?'

Her heart speeded up as she waited for his answer. It
mattered, she realised with a shock. She hadn't set foot in
the small Cornish village for nine years. Hadn't seen this
man for nine years. But it still mattered.

It was her history.

'I had it relocated. It was the start of everything, after
all. Demolishing the old girl would have been pretty poor
thanks. And we kept the name and brand, of course.'

'Everything?' Was he talking about her? *Get a grip,*

she told herself. Walking down the hill and along the harbour might have sent her spinning back in time, brought all those carefully buried memories abruptly to the surface, but by the look of the building in front of her Jonas had moved on long ago.

'So, are you coming in or not?' He ignored her question, pushing himself off the sign with the languid grace only hours balancing on a board in the rough Cornish sea could achieve. 'The coffee's excellent and the cake is even better. On the house for an ex member of staff, of course.'

Lawrie opened her mouth to refuse, to point out that the building wasn't the only thing to have changed—that, actually, she hadn't touched caffeine or refined sugar in years—but she caught a quizzical gleam in his eye and changed her mind. She wouldn't give him the satisfaction.

Besides, clean living hadn't got her very far, had it? This enforced time out was about new experiences, trying new things. There were worse places to start than a good cup of coffee brewed the way only Jonas could.

'Thank you,' she said instead.

'This way, then.' And Jonas moved to the double glass doors, holding one open for her with exaggerated gallantry. 'And, Lawrie,' he murmured as she walked past him, 'Happy Birthday.'

Lawrie froze. Just half an hour ago she had reached the sad conclusion that you couldn't get more pathetic than spending your thirtieth birthday on your own—not unless you were unemployed, single *and* alone on your thirtieth.

Lawrie was all three.

Adding an encounter with her ex really was the cherry on top of the icing on her non-existent birthday cake. She should have listened to her instincts and stayed indoors and sulked. Damn her conscience for pushing her out to get fresh air and exercise. Both were clearly overrated.

'This is where you say thank you.'

He had moved away from the door and was leading her towards a small table tucked away at the back, clearly at his ease.

'Sorry?' What was he talking about? Maybe she was in some surrealist dream, where conversation made no sense. Any second now she'd be viewing the world in black and white, possibly through the medium of mime.

'I know you've been in the city for a while…' there was an unexpected teasing note in his voice '…but back in the real world when someone wishes you a Happy Birthday it's usual to acknowledge them—often with a thank you.'

For the first time in over a week Lawrie felt the heaviness lift slightly, a lessening of the burden. 'Thank you,' she said with careful emphasis. 'Of course I *might* be trying to forget this particular birthday.'

'Oh, yes, the big three oh.' He laughed as she grimaced. 'It's really no big deal, once you get used to the back ache and the knee twinges.'

'I hoped it might be like the tree falling in the woods— if no one knows it's happening then is it real?'

'*I* know,' he reminded her.

'Thereby foiling my cunning plan.'

A smile curved the corner of his mouth but it didn't reach his eyes. They radiated concern. For her. She didn't need the stab of her conscience to tell her she didn't deserve his concern.

'Well, now it's out in the open you have to celebrate. How about a slice of my signature carrot cake with chocolate icing? Unless, now you're a Londoner, you prefer elaborate cupcakes? Pretty frosting but no real substance?'

Lawrie looked up sharply. Was that some kind of cake metaphor?

'Or would you rather wait till your fiancé joins you?'

And just like that the heaviness engulfed her again. Lawrie searched for the right words, the right tone. 'Hugo and I parted ways. It seemed time for a new beginning.'

'Again?'

There was a lifetime of history in that one word. More than Lawrie could cope with this day, this week. At all.

Coming back had been a mistake. But she had nowhere else to go.

Lawrie hadn't exactly spent the last nine years planning how she'd react if she bumped into her ex-husband, but if she *had* spent time imagining every possible scenario she doubted—short of falling at his feet—that she could have come up with a situation as humiliating as this.

She looked around, desperately searching for a change of subject. 'The café looks amazing.'

It really did. She was standing in an open-plan space, with the driftwood counter along its far end and the blue walls a reminder of the ever-present sea. The real thing was a stunning backdrop framed through dramatic floor-length windows. It was all very stylish—beautiful, even—but once again Lawrie felt a pang of nostalgia for the small, homespun bar she had known.

The season was not yet fully started, but the café was buzzing with mothers and small children, groups of friends and the ubiquitous surfers. There were no menus. The day's choices were chalked up on boards displayed around the spacious room and notices proclaimed the café's values—local, organic and sustainably sourced food.

A flare of pride hit her: *he's done it—he's realised his dreams.* Long before celebrity chefs had made local food trendy Jonas had been evangelical about quality ingredients, sourcing from local farms, and using only free-range eggs in his legendary fry-ups.

'I'm glad you approve. So, what will it be?'

For one second Lawrie wanted to startle him, order
something he wouldn't expect. Prove that actually she *had*
changed in nine years—changed a lot. But the temptation
to sink into the comfort of the past was too much. 'Skinny
latte with cinnamon, please. And if you have the carrot
cake in…?' She peered up at the menu board, running her
eyes over the long list of tasty-looking treats.

'Of course I have it in.'

Jonas turned away to deliver her order, but Lawrie could
have sworn she heard him say, 'It *is* your birthday after all.'

She was still there. Jonas tried to keep his concentration
on the screen in front of him but all his attention was on
the cake-eating occupant at the small table below.

The mezzanine floor that housed his office was situated directly over the kitchens, shielded from the café with
blue-tinted glass that gave him privacy whilst allowing him
to look out. Some days he was so busy that he completely
forgot where he was, and he would look up and notice the
chattering people tucking in below in complete surprise.
There were bigger offices at his hotel but he preferred it
here. Where it had all begun.

'Jonas? Are you listening to me?'

He jumped. 'Of course,' he lied.

'You didn't even hear me come in! Honestly, Jonas,
if I want to be ignored I'll stay at home and ask my husband to clean.'

'Sorry, Fliss, I was engrossed in this email.'

Fliss peered over his shoulder. 'I can see why. It's not
every day you get offered a million pounds just for letting
somebody borrow your bank account, is it?'

Damn spam. 'The spam filter should be picking these
up. I was just wondering why it's not working.'

She shot him a sceptical look. 'Delete that and turn you

formidable mind to a real problem for a change. Suzy has been ordered to keep her feet up for the rest of her pregnancy and won't be able to project-manage Wave Fest for us.'

'Pregnancy?' He looked up in shock. 'I didn't know Suzy was expecting.'

'I expect she was keeping it a secret from you, knowing your less than enlightened views on working mothers,' Fliss said drily.

Jonas raised an eyebrow for one long moment, watching her colour with some satisfaction. 'I have no view on working mothers—or on working fathers, for that matter, I just expect my employees to pull their weight at *work*— not be at home with their feet up. Damn! There's only a month to go and we'll never get anyone to take over at this short notice. Fliss, is there any way you can take this on?'

'I don't think so.' The petite redhead was contrite. 'I still have a lot to do with the last café you bought, and if you do take over The Laurels I'll need to start on the rebrand there too. I can help with the PR—I usually do most of that anyway—but I cannot project-manage an entire festival. Suzy has all the information written out and timetabled, so at least all we need is someone to step in and run it.'

Jonas acknowledged the truth of Fliss's statement. Her workload was pretty full-on right now. He pushed his chair back and swivelled round, staring down sightlessly on the room below. 'Think, Fliss—is there anyone, any summer jobber, who's capable of taking this on?'

She stood lost in thought, concentration on her face, then shook her head. 'Nobody springs to mind.'

Jonas grimaced. 'We'll just have to bite the bullet and get a temp in—though that's far from ideal.'

It had been hard enough handing the festival over to Suzy when it and the rest of the business had got too big for him to manage comfortably alone, even with Fliss's support. Letting a stranger loose on such an important event was impossible to imagine.

But he couldn't see another way.

Fliss was obviously thinking along the same lines. 'A temp? That will take at least a week, *and* cost a fortune in agency fees.'

'Bringing outsiders in is never easy, but it looks like we have no choice. You and I will have to keep it all ticking over until we find somebody. We managed the first three, after all…'

She flashed a conspiratorial grin at him. 'Goodness knows how. But we were young and optimistic then—and they were a lot smaller affairs; we are victims of our own success. But, okay, I'll let Dave know I'm working late so he'd better come here for dinner. Again. We were going to come back for Open Mic Night anyway.'

'Great. You drive straight over to Suzy's and go over all those lists and spreadsheets with her. We'll divvy up tasks later. Have another think about anyone internally, and if there really is nobody I'll call a couple of agencies later today.'

A sense of satisfaction ran through him as he made the decision. He was a hands-on boss—too hands-on, some said—but he liked to know exactly how everything was handled, from salad prep to food sourcing. It was his name over the door after all.

Fliss saluted. 'Yes, Boss,' she said, then turned round to leave the room, only to stop with a strangled cry. 'Jonas! Look—in that corner over there.'

'Why exactly are you whispering?' Although he knew exactly what—exactly *who*—she had seen. He cocked an eyebrow at her, aiming for a nonchalance he didn't feel.

Lawrie's unexpected presence was no big deal. He had no intention of letting it become one.

Fliss obviously had other ideas. Her eyes were alight with excitement. 'It's Lawrie. *Look*, Jonas.'

'I know it's Lawrie, but I still don't know why you're whispering. She can't hear you, you know.'

'Of course she can't, but...' Her voice turned accusatory. 'You knew she was here and didn't tell me?'

'It slipped my mind—and it's obviously slipped yours that we were discussing a rather pressing work matter.' His tone was cool. 'Don't you have somewhere to be?'

'Five minutes?' Fliss gave him a pleading look. 'I can't *not* say hello.'

To Jonas's certain knowledge Fliss hadn't seen or spoken to Lawrie in nine years. What difference would a few hours make? But his second-in-command, oldest employee and, despite his best efforts to keep her out, best friend was looking so hopeful he couldn't disappoint her.

He wasn't the only person Lawrie had walked out on.

'Five minutes,' he allowed, adding warningly, 'But, Fliss, we have a lot to do.'

'I know. I'll be quick—thank you.' Fliss rushed from the room, casting him a grateful glance over her shoulder as she did so. Less than a minute later she had arrived at Lawrie's table, falling on her in a breathless heap.

Jonas watched as Fliss sat down at the table. He saw Lawrie look up in slight confusion, her puzzled expression quickly change to one of happiness, and the mobile features light up with enthusiasm as she greeted her friend.

When they both looked up at the office he looked away, despite knowing that they couldn't see through the tinted glass; he had far too much to do to watch them catch up.

Jonas pulled up a report he had commissioned on the

small chain of restaurants in Somerset he was considering taking over and read it.

After ten minutes he was still on the first page.

He glanced over at the window. They were still yakking away. What on earth had they got to talk about for so long?

Typical Lawrie. Turning everything upside down without even trying.

When he had seen her standing outside, looking so uncharacteristically unsure, he had seized the opportunity. As soon as he'd known she was back—heard through the village grapevine that she was here to stay, that she was alone—their moment of meeting had been inevitable. Trengarth was too small for a run-in not to be a certainty, but when it came he'd wanted it to be on his terms.

After all, their parting had been on hers.

Inviting her in had felt like the right thing to do. The mature thing. Maybe he should have left her outside after all.

He looked back at the computer screen and started again on the first line. It was gobbledygook.

Jonas's jaw set in determination. If Fliss had forgotten that she had a lot to do, he hadn't—and he was going to go down there and tell her. Right now.

At first Lawrie hadn't recognised the small redhead hurtling towards her. Nine years ago Fliss had sported a pink bob and multiple piercings and wouldn't have been seen dead in the smart black trousers and blouse she was wearing today, but the generous smile and the mischievous twinkle in the hazel eyes were just the same. After five minutes' excited chatter it was as if they were still teenage waitresses, hanging out after work, although so many things had changed Lawrie could barely keep up.

'You've been working for Jonas all this time?' Try as she

might, she couldn't keep the incredulous tone out of her voice. 'What about acting and RADA?'

'Turns out I am a great amateur.'

Lawrie looked sharply at her but Fliss was still smiling, and there was no hint of disappointment in the candid eyes. 'I am also a great brand and marketing manager—who would have thought it?'

'But you wanted to do so much—had so many plans.'

'I *have* so much! Wait till you meet Dave. He moved here after you left, came for a week's surfing and never left.'

The two girls giggled conspiratorially.

'I have my drama group, and I love my job. I may not have done the travelling or the big city thing, but I have everything I need and want. I'm a lucky girl. But *your* plans sound exciting. New York! I have always wanted to live there—starring on Broadway, of course.'

So she might have made New York sound like a done deal rather than a possibility, but Lawrie had had to salvage pride from somewhere.

She was considering her reply when a shadow fell across the table. Glancing up, she saw a stern-looking Jonas standing there, a frown marring the handsome face. An unexpected flutter pulled at Lawrie's stomach, one she'd thought long dead, and she took a hurried gulp of her coffee, avoiding both his eye and Fliss's sudden speculative gleam.

'I thought you were off to see Suzy?' His attention was all on Fliss.

'I am,' Fliss protested. 'But I have just had a brainwave. How about Lawrie?'

Lawrie's grip tightened on her cup. She could feel her cheeks heating up.

'How about Lawrie, what?' Jonas asked impatiently.

It was odd, being back with the two of them and yet apart, now an outsider. Lawrie took a deep breath and leant back in her chair, affecting a confidence she was far from feeling.

'For Wave Fest, of course. No—listen,' Fliss said, jumping to her feet and grabbing Jonas's arm as he turned dismissively away. 'She's on gardening leave for the rest of the summer.'

'Gardening *what*?' He stopped and looked back at the table, catching Lawrie's eye, a sudden glint of a humour in the stern blue eyes.

She knew exactly what he was thinking—knew that he was remembering her ability to kill every plant with a mixture of forgetful indifference and remorseful over-watering.

'Is this some sort of corporate environmental thing? Time to learn how to garden?'

'No, it's a set period time to serve out your notice away from the office,' Lawrie said, her own eyes warming in response to his and her pulse speeding up as his amused gaze continued to bore into her. 'I'm on paid leave until the end of September.'

'And she's planning to stay in Cornwall most of that time,' Fliss interjected.

'Well, yes. I am. But I'm arranging my next move. I'll be travelling back and forth to London a lot—possibly overseas. What's Wave Fest, anyway?'

'Oh, Lawrie, you remember the festival Jonas and I started, don't you?'

'Actually, Fliss, Lawrie was never at Wave Fest. She was on work placements for the first two.'

The humour had left Jonas's face. It was as if the sun had unexpectedly disappeared behind a cloud. He didn't say the words she knew he was thinking. She had left before the third.

'I know we're desperate, but Lawrie's a solicitor, not a project manager—and she knows nothing about festivals.'

'But we need someone organised who can get things done and she can do that all right. Plus, she's here and she's available.'

'Fliss, you said yourself that at this time of year organising Wave Fest is a full-time job. If Lawrie's got to sort out a move—' the sharp blue eyes regarded Lawrie for an intent moment before flicking away '—she won't be able to dedicate the time we need to it.'

'Yes, for *me* it would be full time, because I have a neglected husband and the work of three people to do anyway, but Lawrie's used to city hours—this will be a relaxing break for her!'

It was almost amusing, listening to them bicker over her as if she wasn't there. Lawrie took another sip of her coffee, letting the words wash over her. After the shock of the last week it felt nice to be wanted, even if it was for a small-time job she had no intention of doing.

Suddenly she was aware of an extended silence and looked up to find two pairs of eyes fixed on her expectantly.

'What?'

'I was just asking why you are on leave?' Jonas said, with the exaggerated patience of somebody who had asked a question several times already. 'If "gardening leave" means you're serving out your notice then you must be leaving your firm—why?'

The all too familiar sense of panic rose up inside her, filling her chest with an aching, squeezing tension. None of this was real. It was some kind of terrible dream and she would soon wake up and find Hugo snoring beside her and her pressed suit hung on the wardrobe door opposite, ready for another day at work, doing a job she was darned good at.

'I felt like a change,' she said, choosing her words carefully. 'They were offering good severance deals and I thought, what with turning thirty and everything, that this could be a good opportunity for a new start. After all, it seems silly to specialise in international law and never spend time abroad. I have lots of contacts in New York, so that seems like the logical choice.'

She had repeated the words so often to herself that she almost believed them now.

'That sounds amazing,' breathed Fliss, but Jonas looked more sceptical.

'You deviated from that all-important ten-point plan? Wasn't thirty the year you should have made partner?'

He remembered the plan. Of *course* he remembered it— she had gone over it with him enough, been teased about it enough. *'Lawrie needs to make a plan before we go out for a walk,'* he used to tell people.

She took a deep breath and forced a casual tone into her voice. 'People change, Jonas. I followed the plan for long enough, and it was very successful, but I decided that now I'm single again it might be time to see something of the world and enhance my career at the same time. It's no big deal.'

He raised an eyebrow but didn't pursue the point.

'But you won't be able to start your new job until after September so you *are* free to help out with Wave Fest.' Fliss wasn't giving up.

'Fliss, Lawrie isn't interested in the festival; she has a job to find. Plus, if she's still being paid by her firm then she won't be able to work for us—will you?'

'I'm not sure,' she said. 'It's not law, so it's not a conflict of interest, but I don't think I can take paid work whilst on gardening leave. I'll have to check the contract, but it would be unusual if it was allowed.'

'Volunteer! We could pay your expenses and it would look great on your CV, using your time to help out with a charity event. Come on, Lawrie. It's total serendipity, you being here just when we need you. You can't argue with fate!'

'Fliss!'

Jonas was sounding annoyed, but the word 'volunteer' had struck a chord with Lawrie. She tuned the pair out.

She liked to keep busy, and the thought of spending the forseeable future with nothing to do but job-hunt terrified her. Besides, her CV was already with the best recruiters in the business, so there was little she could do until they got in touch. Most importantly she had been racking her brains, searching for a likely explanation for her sudden departure from Forrest, Gable & Garner that prospective employers would find acceptable—laudable, even. If she could tell them that she'd taken the opportunity of severance to help out with a charity festival surely that would stand her in good stead? Every company liked a bit of free CSR in these straitened times.

Okay, it wasn't part of the ten-point plan, but which part of the last few weeks *had* been? Not finding Hugo labouring over his naked secretary, not watching the senior partners close ranks as they took his side and forced her out with a nice settlement and a good reference for keeping her mouth shut.

She had returned to Trengarth to lick her wounds, to regroup. Why not wring something positive out of her situation?

'Please?' Fliss looked pleading. 'Come on, Lawrie, you'll be perfect.'

'I'll do it.' The words left her mouth before she knew exactly what she was going to say.

Fliss squealed and flung her arms around Lawrie, but Jonas took a step back, his mouth tight, his eyes unreadable.

*What have I done?*

'If that's okay with you, of course, Jonas,' she added, not entirely sure what she wanted his answer to be—whether he would give her a get-out clause she didn't even know she needed. But he didn't answer—just continued to look at her with the same cool, steady regard.

Fliss jumped in before the silence stretched too far, got too awkward. 'It's fine, isn't it, Jonas? This is *fantastic*! I was going to get all the stuff from Suzy today, but why don't you come with me and meet her? Is tomorrow okay? Oh, Lawrie, it'll be just like old times, us working together.'

Fliss beamed at Lawrie, who couldn't help but smile back. Her old friend's joy was infectious.

'It looks like that's settled, then.' Jonas's face was still blank, his voice cool and professional. 'Lawrie, I'll chat to you tomorrow and go over the work involved, discuss how this will work as a volunteering role. Be sure this is something you can take on, though. Wave Fest raises tens of thousands for local charities. If you can't manage it it's imperative you let us know sooner rather than later.'

He sounded dismissive—as if he was expecting her to fail, to walk away.

How dared he? She'd negotiated million-pound contracts, painstakingly going over every single word, scrutinising each clause, routinely working sixty-hour weeks, often on short notice. One month sorting out a small local event would hardly tax her.

She lifted her head and looked straight at him, matching him cool glance for cool glance, every bit the professional, well-trained lawyer. 'I'm sure I'll manage. I like to see things through.'

He kept her gaze, scorn filling the blue eyes, turning them ice-cold. 'I'm sure you've grown up,' he said. 'But if there's a chance you'll get a job and leave before the contract ends I need to know. Promises aren't enough.'

She swallowed down her rage. If she had learnt anything from long hours of negotiating complex contracts it was how to keep her temper, no matter what the provocation. If he wanted to judge her on events that had happened nine years ago, so be it.

But she *had* promised to love him till death did them part. And that promise she had broken.

Did she actually need this hassle? The sensible thing would be to walk away, right now, lock up the cottage and go back to London. But then what? She had nowhere to live, nothing to do. At least in Cornwall she had a house, and now a way to occupy her time whilst finding the perfect job, getting her life back to the calm, ordered way it was supposed to be. And if that meant showing Jonas Jones that he was wrong—that the past wasn't as clear-cut as he obviously thought—well, that was just a bonus.

She smiled sweetly into the freezing eyes.

'I'll need to take time to sort out my move, of course,' she said, proud that her voice was steady. 'And there is a chance that I may need to travel abroad for interviews. But there will be plenty of notice. There shouldn't—there *won't* be a problem.'

'Then I'll see you tomorrow.'

The interview was clearly over.

'Enjoy the rest of your birthday.'

Fliss looked up in shock. 'It's your *birthday*? Here I am, thinking about spreadsheets and emails and offices, and what I should be doing is ordering you a cocktail to go with that cake. What are you doing later? I'm sure you have plans, but we could meet here for cocktails first?'

Lawrie's first instinct was to lie—to claim company, plans, unavailability. But Jonas had stopped, turned, was listening, and she couldn't let him know she was ashamed of her lone state. 'Actually, Fliss, I was planning a quiet one this year. I have a nice bottle of red and a good book saved up.'

It was the truth, and she had been looking forward to indulging in both. So why did it feel like a confession?

'A good book? I know you've been gone a long time, but nobody changes *that* much. Of *course* we're going to celebrate. I'll see you here for cocktails at seven, and then there's Open Mic Night later. Perfect! Jonas, you can pick her up. We don't want the birthday girl to be late.'

'Honestly—' Lawrie began, not sure what panicked her more: Jonas picking her up like old times, the chance that she might let her guard down after a cocktail, or spending her thirtieth birthday with the same people who had celebrated her eighteenth. 'I'll be fine.'

'Don't be silly.' Jonas's expression was indecipherable, his voice emotionless. 'Fliss is right. You can't spend your birthday alone. Besides, you used to enjoy singing. It'll be just like old times.'

And that, thought Lawrie, was exactly what she was afraid of.

# CHAPTER TWO

'So THIS IS where you're hiding.'

Jonas looked far too at home as he rounded the corner of Gran's cottage. And far too attractive in a pair of worn jeans that hugged his legs in all the right places, and a plain grey T-shirt emphasising his lean strength. 'I thought you had run away.'

'I thought about it,' Lawrie admitted, tugging at the hem of her skirt self-consciously.

It shouldn't take a grown woman two hours to get ready for a few drinks and some badly played guitar, and yet Lawrie had found herself paralysed by indecision. Her clothes were too conservative, too expensive, more suited to a discreet yet expensive restaurant or a professional conference than a small Cornish village.

In the end she had decided on a dress that was several years old—and several inches shorter than she usually wore.

Taking a deep breath, she pulled her hands away from the skirt and tried to remember the speech she had painstakingly prepared earlier, rehearsed at length in the shower.

'Thanks for coming to collect me—it's very nice of you. I know Fliss kind of forced your hand—' Lawrie stopped, her cheeks warm, the speech gone. 'Actually, she forced your hand in several ways earlier, and I should have thought… If you don't want me around—if it's awkward, I mean—then I'll tell her I can't do it.' She stumbled to a stop.

Great—in her former life fluency had been one of her trademarks. It looked as if she had lost that along with everything else.

'Fliss thinks she gets her own way, but if I didn't want you working for us you wouldn't be.' The blue eyes held hers for a moment. 'She's right. You'll do a good job—and, let's face it, we are a bit desperate. Beggars can't be choosers.'

Charming. It wasn't the most ringing endorsement she'd ever heard.

'I just don't want our past relationship to be an issue.' Lawrie was aware of how pompous she sounded. She'd been trying for offhand. A smirk at the corner of his mouth confirmed she had failed.

'We're both mature adults,' Jonas pointed out. 'At least I am. And it's your significant birthday we're celebrating, so hopefully you are too. I'm sure we can work together without too much bloodshed. In fact…' He moved away from the cottage and sauntered gracefully over the lawn towards her, a flat tissue-wrapped square in his hand. 'Happy Birthday.'

Lawrie stared at the proffered parcel in shock.

'Take it. It won't bite,' he teased. 'I promise. Think of it as a peace offering and a birthday present in one.'

He moved closer until he was standing next to her, leaning against the balcony, looking down on the curve of beach and sea below.

After a moment's hesitation Lawrie took the present, taking a moment to enjoy the thrill of the unknown. It was her only present, after all.

'Your gran always had the best view in the village,'

Jonas said. 'It's so peaceful up here.' He shot her a glance. 'I meant to write after she died, send a card… But I didn't really know what to say. I'm sorry.'

She turned the parcel round in her hands. 'That's okay. I think people were upset we had the funeral so far away, but she wanted to be buried next to Grandpa…' Her voice trailed away and there was a sudden lump in her throat. It had been six months since the funeral but the pain of loss still cut deep. 'I wish I had telephoned more, visited more.'

'She was very proud of you.'

Lawrie nodded, not trusting herself to speak. Swallowing back the tears, she turned her attention to the present, wanting to change the subject.

She slid her finger along the fold in the tissue, pulling the tape off slowly as she went, carefully opening the paper out to reveal a silk scarf the colour of the sea below. 'It's beautiful!'

His voice was offhand. 'It always used to be your favourite colour.'

'It still is.' She looked over at him, ridiculously overcome despite his casualness. *He'd remembered.* 'You really didn't need to, but thank you, Jonas.'

'No problem.' The blue eyes swept over her assessingly. 'It matches your dress.'

'I'll go and put it on. I won't be long.'

Walking through the back door, Lawrie felt yet again as if she had gone back in time—as if she was once again her sixteen-year-old self, skipping in to say goodbye to Gran before heading out on a date, full of possibilities, full of life and desperately, achingly in love.

Only there was no Gran.

And the world no longer felt full of possibilities. She was all too aware of her limits.

Oh, to be sixteen again, walking on the beach at night after her shift ended, unable to believe that her handsome boss had asked her if she fancied a stroll. She still remembered the electric shock that had run through her when his hand had first bumped against hers. The tightness in her stomach when his long, cool caressing fingers had encased hers. The almost unbearable anticipation drying out her throat, weakening her knees, setting every single nerve-end ablaze as she waited for him to kiss her. And, *oh...!* The almost unbearable sweetness when he finally, oh so slowly, lowered his mouth to hers as the waves crashed against the shore.

It had been Lawrie's first kiss and for five years she hadn't thought she would ever kiss anyone else.

*I haven't thought about that in years.* She pushed the memory of vivid, haunting dreams filled with waves, passion and familiar blue eyes firmly to one side.

She glanced up at the wall, where a framed photo hung. A much younger Lawrie looked out from it, her hair whipped by the wind and framing her face in a dark, tangled cloud, laughing, her eyes squinting against the sun. Jonas had taken it twelve years ago, on her eighteenth birthday—their wedding day.

It was all such a long time ago. Who would have thought then that they would end up like this? Apart, near-strangers, exchanging polite remarks and stiff smiles. If she'd known what lay ahead would she have made the same choices...the same mistakes?

Lawrie shook her head wildly, trying to clear the questions from her mind. She couldn't allow this temporary setback to derail her, to make her question her choices, her past. It was time to face her future—and if the plan had gone awry...well, she would tweak it.

But first her birthday. She needed—she *deserved* some

fun. Maybe she could relax—just a little, just for a short while. Maybe Lawrie Bennett was allowed to let go for just one evening.

It was one of Jonas's favourite things, watching the Boat House being transformed from a family-friendly, light and airy café to an intimate bar. It was more than the deepening dusk outside the dramatic picture windows, more than the tea lights on the tables, more than the bottles of beer and wine replacing the skinny lattes, the tapas in place of cream teas.

It was the way the atmosphere changed. Grew heavier, darker. Full of infinite possibilities.

Tonight was the monthly Open Mic Night—a tradition carried through from the earliest days. Before he'd held a bar licence he used to invite friends over to the café after-hours to jam; he'd always fancied himself as a pretty mean guitarist. Once he'd licensed the premises it had become more of an organised event, yet still with a laid-back, spontaneous feel.

Folk violinists rattling out notes at an impossible speed, grungy rock wannabes, slow and sweet soul singers—there were no exclusions. If you had an instrument and you wanted to play, you could sign up. There was a magic about Open Mic Night, even after all these years. The room might be full of regulars but there were usually one or two surprises.

And yet tonight he was wound tight, the tension straining across his shoulders and neck. Even the familiar feel of the sharp strings under his fingertips, the crowded tables, the appreciative applause, the melding and blending of notes and beats and voices couldn't relax him.

His eyes, his focus, were pulled to the small table in the corner where Lawrie perched, toying with a glass of cham-

pagne, her head resting on her hand, her eyes dreamy as
she listened. The dim lighting softened her; she looked like
his teen bride again, her dark hair loose, curling against
her shoulders, her huge grey eyes fixed unseeingly on
the stage.

On *him*.

A reluctant tug of desire pulled deep down. It was definitely the memories, the nostalgia, he told himself grimly.
Why was she back? Why had Lawrie Bennett, the girl who
put her work, her career, her plans before everything and
everyone, given up her job and moved back?

And why did she look so scared and vulnerable?

It was none of his business—*she* was none of his business. She had made that clear a long time ago. Whatever
trouble Lawrie was in she could handle it herself. She always had.

Resolutely he tore his gaze away, focussed on the room
as a whole, plastering on a smile as the song ended and the
room erupted into applause. Jonas exchanged an amused
look with his fellow musicians as they took an ironic bow
before vacating the stage for the next musicians—a local
sixth form experimental rock band whose main influences
seemed to be a jarring mixture of eighties New Romanti-
cism and Death Metal.

Maybe he was getting old, Jonas thought as he made
his way back to the bar. It just sounded like noise to him.

'I should be getting home.' Lawrie got to her feet and began
automatically to gather the glasses and bottles. Just like
old times. She stilled her hands, looking around to see if
anybody had noticed.

'Don't be silly—the night is just beginning,' Fliss said
in surprise.

Lawrie looked pointedly at the people heading for the

door, at the musicians packing away their instruments, at vaguely familiar faces patting Jonas on the back with murmurs about babysitters, getting up for work and school runs. Since when had most of his friends had babysitters and office hours to contend with? The surf-mad mates of his youth had matured into fathers, husbands and workers. The night might feel like a step back in time, but everything had changed.

'This is the fun bit,' Fliss said, grabbing a tray filled with lurid-coloured drinks from the bar and handing a neon blue one to Lawrie. 'We get to hog the stage. What do you want to start with?'

Several pairs of eyes turned expectantly to Lawrie and she swallowed, her mouth dry. She took a sip of the cocktail, grimacing at the sweet yet almost medicinal taste. 'You go ahead without me. I don't really sing.'

'Of *course* you sing! You always used to.'

'That was a long time ago. Honestly, Fliss, I'd rather not.'

'But...'

'I thought all lawyers sang,' Jonas interceded.

Lawrie shot him a grateful glance. Fliss was evidently not going to let the point go.

'Didn't you have a karaoke bar under your office?'

'Sadly I didn't work with Ally McBeal.' Lawrie shook her head, but she was smiling now. 'The only singing I have done for years is in the shower. I'd really rather listen.'

'You heard her. And she *is* the birthday girl.'

'Which is why she shouldn't be sitting there alone,' Fliss argued. She turned to Lawrie pleadingly. 'Just do some backing vocals, then. Hum along. This is the fun part of the night—no more enduring schoolboy experiments or prog rock guitar solos. Thank goodness we limit each act to fifteen minutes or I reckon *he* would still be living out his Pink Floyd fantasies right now. There's only us here.'

Lawrie hesitated. It had been such a long time—part of the life she had done her best to pack away and forget about. Small intimate venues, guitars and set lists had no place in the ordered world she had chosen. Could she even hold a tune any more? Pick up the rhythm?

Once they had been a well-oiled machine—Fliss's voice, rich, emotive and powerful, trained for the West End career she had dreamed of, filling the room, and Lawrie's softer vocals, which shouldn't really have registered at all. And then there had been Jonas. Always there, keeping time. There'd been times when she had got lost in the music, blindly following where he led.

The thought of returning there was terrifying. Lawrie shivered, goosebumps rippling up her bare arms, and yet she acknowledged that it was exciting too. On this night of memory and nostalgia, this moment out of time.

And how lost could she get if she stuck closely to backing vocals? Stayed near Fliss, away from Jonas and that unreadable expression on his face? Did he wish she would just leave? Stay? Or did he simply not care?

Not that there was any reason for him to care. She had made sure of that.

She took another sip of her cocktail, noticing with some astonishment that the glass was nearly empty. She should be thinking about Hugo, Lawrie told herself. Mourning him, remembering their relationship so very recently and brutally ended—not mooning over her teenage mistakes. If she was going to work here, survive here, she couldn't allow her past to intimidate her.

'Okay,' she said, putting the now empty glass down on the table and reaching for another of Fliss's concoctions— this time a sickly green. 'Backing vocals only. Let's do it.'

* * *

She was seated on the other side of the stage, angled towards the tables, so that all he could see was the fall of her hair, the curve of her cheek.Not that he was attracted to her—he knew her too well. Even after all this time. It was just that she seemed a little lost, a little vulnerable...

And there had been a time when Jonas Jones had been a sucker for dark-haired, big-eyed, vulnerable types.

He'd learned his lesson the hard way, but a man didn't want to take too many chances—not on a night filled with ghosts. He looked around, half expecting to see the creamy painted wooden slats of the old boathouse, the rough floorboards, the mismatched tables. But a twinge in his fingers brought him back to the present, reminding him that he was no longer nineteen and that, although thirty-two was certainly not old, he was too old to be playing all night on a work night.

His mouth twitched wryly. Once a work night had meant nothing. His hobbies and his job had blended into one perfect hedonistic existence: the bar, the music, the surf. He didn't know what had infuriated his parents more. How successful his beach shack had quickly become or how effortless he had made it look.

But in those days it *had* been effortless.

It wasn't that easy any more. Would his parents be proud or smug if they knew how many of the things he loved he had given up for success? Or would they still think it was not enough.

Maudlin thoughts. A definite sign that it was late, or that he'd allowed Fliss to make the cocktails again.

Time to wrap things up.

Only Fliss had started another song, carefully picking out the tune on her guitar. The breath caught in his throat. His heart was a painful lump blocking its passage.

Not this song. Not this night. Not on what could have been, *should* have been, their twelfth wedding anniversary.

There was only so much nostalgia a man could take.

And then Lawrie picked up the tune and he was plunged into a whole other level of memory. Her voice wasn't the strongest—nothing in comparison to Fliss's—yet it had a true, wistful quality that tore at him, hooked him in, wringing truth out of the plaintive words.

Despite it all Jonas found himself playing the harmony, his hands surely and smoothly finding the right notes. They hadn't forgotten. He still knew—still felt every note, every beat, every word. How long was it since he had played this song? Not since Lawrie had left. Not even in the last desperate year of their marriage as he had watched her retreat further and further away, her eyes, her focus, firmly fixed on the gleaming spires of Oxford.

Suddenly simple folk tunes hadn't been her thing at all. Yet she still knew all the words.

It was as if her whole body thrummed with the music. Her blood, her heartbeat, the pulses at her neck and her wrists. Long after the guitars had been packed away, the last few glasses cleared, the final lurid cocktail poured away—no one had felt able to risk the neon orange, not at past one in the morning—the beat still possessed her.

How had she managed to spend the last nine years without music? Had they even had music in the house? Music to listen to simply for the thrill it evoked deep down inside? There had been a stylish digital radio permanently tuned in to Radio Four, occasionally switched to Classic FM when they entertained. And Lawrie had attended concerts for corporate purposes—just as she had been to countless sporting events, black tie galas, charity auctions.

After a while they all blended together.

There was so much she had expunged from her life. Colour, impulsiveness, walking along a beach at dusk with the wind blowing salt-tinged tendrils of hair into her face. Enjoying the here and now.

She might have chosen a controlled, sleek, beige, stone and black existence. It didn't mean that she hadn't occasionally hungered after something a little more *vibrant*. But vibrancy had a price she hadn't been prepared to pay.

In the end control was worth it. It allowed you to plan, to achieve.

But, *damn*, the music had felt good. The right here, right now felt good. Even those ridiculously bright cocktails had been—well, not *good*, exactly but surprisingly palatable. Maybe coming back wasn't such a terrible thing after all.

'How are you getting back?'

Lawrie jumped, every sense suddenly on high alert. She didn't want to look Jonas in the eyes in case he read the conflicting emotions there. There had been a time when he'd been able to read her all too easily.

'I was planning to walk,' she said.

'Alone?'

'Unless there are suddenly bloodthirsty smugglers patrolling the dark streets of Trengarth I think I'll manage the mile home okay.'

'There's no lighting on your gran's road. I'd better walk you back.'

Lawrie opened her mouth to refuse—then shut it again, unsure what to say. Whether to make a joke out of it, point out that after negotiating London streets for the past few years she thought she could manage a few twisty Cornish lanes. Whether to just say thank you.

Jonas took her silence for acquiescence and strode off towards the door. Lawrie stood indecisively, torn between a childish need to stand her ground, insist she was fine, and a sudden hankering for company—any company—on the walk back up the steep hill.

She had been all too alone these last weeks.

Without thought, almost impulsively, she followed him.

The night was warm, despite the breeze that blew in from the sea and the lack of cloud, and lit up by stars shining so brightly Lawrie could only stand and stare, her neck tilted back almost to the point of pain as she tried to take in the vast expanse of constellation-strewn night sky.

'Have you discovered a new planet?'

Lawrie ignored the sarcastic tone. 'I'm not sure I'd realise if I had,' she said. 'It's just you never see the sky like this in London. I had almost forgotten what it was like.'

Another reclaimed memory to add to the list. Just how much had she shut out over the last nine years?

And how much could she bear to remember? To feel?

The shocking ache of memory—the whispers of 'what might have been'. If she hadn't walked in on Hugo she would still be in London, with Trengarth a million miles away from her thoughts, her ambitions, her dreams.

It was all so familiar. The dimly lit windy street, the harbour wall on one side and the shops on the other—a trendy mixture of surf-hire, arty boutiques and posh grub for the upmarket tourists who sailed or stayed in the village throughout the summer.

As they turned up the steep, hilly road that led to Lawrie's gran's house the shops became more prosaic: post office, grocer's, buckets and spades and souvenirs.

She stole a glance at the man strolling along by her side, walking up the hill with ease. He too was still the same in so many ways, and yet there was something harder, edgier. His very silence was spiky, and she had an urge to break it. To soften the mood.

'So…' Was that her voice? So tentative? She coughed

nervously and tried again—this time loud, abrasive. More suited to a confrontation than casual conversation. 'Are you married? Any children?'

He didn't break stride or look at her. Just gave a quick shake of the head. 'Nope.'

'Anyone special?'

'Not at the moment.'

So there had been. *What did you expect?* she asked herself fiercely. *That he's been living like a monk for the last nine years? Would you even want that?*

She wasn't entirely sure of her answer.

'A couple of times I thought maybe that there was potential. But it was never quite enough. I'm an old-fashioned guy.' He slanted a glance at her, cold, unreadable. 'Marriage should be for ever. Failing once was bad enough...'

'We didn't fail.' But her words had no conviction. Lawrie tried again. 'We just wanted different things.'

'If that's the way you want to remember it.'

Now this *was* familiar. The flush of anger, the ache of frustration as they stood on either side of a very deep chasm. *No,* Lawrie told herself. *Don't say anything.* What was the point in dredging up old arguments, conflict that should be dead and buried?

Only she had never been able to resist the opportunity to fight her corner.

'It's the way it was.' Cool, calm. As if it didn't matter. And of course it didn't. It was history.

Only it was *her* history. Theirs.

It was her job, knowing when to argue a point, knowing when to let it lie. There was nothing to gain from rehashing the same old themes and yet she felt compelled to go on.

'There's no shame in admitting something isn't working, in moving on,' she persisted as they reached the top of the hill and turned down the hedge-lined lane that led

to the cottage. The bumpy road ahead was hard to make
out, lit just by the brilliant stars and the occasional light
marking out driveways and gates. 'I couldn't stay here, you
wouldn't move—what else could we do? It all seems to
have worked out for you, though. You seem to have done
well for yourself.'

'Surprised?' The mocking tone was back. 'You always
did underestimate me, Lawrie.'

'I didn't! I never underestimated you!' Her whole body
flushed, first with embarrassment, then with indignation.
'We grew apart, that's all. I didn't think…'

'Didn't think what?'

How could those smooth, cream-rich tones turn so icy?

'That I was too naïve, too small-town for your new Ox-
bridge friends?'

'Wow—way to rewrite history! You hated Oxford, hated
London, disliked my friends, and refused to even consider
moving away from Cornwall. It wasn't all me, Jonas. You
wouldn't compromise on anything.'

He laughed softly. 'Compromise suggests some kind of
give and take, Lawrie. Remind me again what *you* were
willing to give up for *me*?'

'That's unfair.' She felt tired, defeated. She had just pre-
sided over the death of one relationship—did she really
have to do the post mortem on this one too?

'Is it?'

The worst part was how uninterested he sounded. As if
they were talking about complete strangers and not their
hopeful younger selves.

'Actually, I should thank you.'

She peered at him through the star-lit darkness. 'Thank
me?'

'For forcing me to grow up. To prove you, my parents,

everyone who thought I was a worthless, surfing bum wrong.'

'I never thought that,' she whispered.

An image flashed through her head. A younger, softer Jonas, his wetsuit half peeled off, moulded to muscular thighs. Naked broad shoulders tapering down to a taut, perfectly defined stomach. Water glistening on golden tanned skin. Slicked-back wet hair. Board under one arm, a wicked smile on his mouth, an invitation in his eyes. A sudden yearning for the carefree boy he had been ran through her, making her shiver with longing. How had he turned into this cold, cynical man? Had she done this to him?

He laughed again, the humourless sound jarring her over-wrought nerves.

'Oh, Lawrie, does any of it matter? It was a long time ago—we were practically children. Getting married in our teens…we must have been crazy—it was always going to end in tears.'

'I suppose it was.' Her voice was tentative.

Was it? Once she'd thought they would be together for ever, that they were two halves of one whole. Hearing him reduce their passion to the actions of two irresponsible teenagers nearly undid her. She fought against the lump in her throat, fought for composure, desperate to change the subject, lighten the mood which had turned as dark as night.

'Here you are.'

He stopped at the gate that led into the small driveway and Lawrie skidded to an abrupt stop—close, but not touching him. She was achingly aware of his proximity, and the knowledge that if she reached out just an infinitesimal amount she would be able to touch him made her shiver with longing, with desire, with fear. She wanted to look away but found herself caught in his moonlit gaze, the blue eyes silvered by the starlight.

'It wasn't all bad, though. Being a crazy teen.'

The cream had returned to his voice. His tone was low, almost whispered, and she felt herself swaying towards him.

'No, of course not. That was the happiest time of my life.'

*Damn*, she hadn't meant to admit that—not to him, not to herself. It must be the cocktails talking. But as the words left her mouth she realised their truth.

'The happiest time,' she whispered, so low she hoped he hadn't heard her.

Just one little step—that was all it took. One little step and she was touching him, looking up at him. Her breasts brushed against his chest and just that one small touch set her achingly aware nerves on fire. She felt the jolt of desire shock through her, buzzing through to her fingers, to her toes, pooling deep within her.

Jonas's head was tilted down. The full focus of his disconcertingly intense eyes on her. Lawrie swallowed and licked suddenly dry lips, her nails cutting into her palms as she curled them into tight fists. The urge to grab him and pull him close was suddenly almost overwhelming.

'Jonas?'

An entreaty? A question? Lawrie didn't know what she was asking him, what she was begging him for. All she knew was that it was her birthday. And that she hadn't felt this alive for a long, long time.

'Jonas…'

He stayed still for a long second, his eyes still fixed on hers, their expression unreadable.

And then he took a step back. The sudden space between them was a yawning chasm. 'Goodnight, Lawrie.

I'll see you in the morning. Don't be late—there's a lot to go through.'

Lawrie suppressed a shudder. It was suddenly so cold. 'I'm never late.'

'Good.'

She stood by the gate, watching as he turned and began to stride down the path, ruthlessly suppressing the part of her that wanted to call after him, run after him. Yet she couldn't ignore the odd skip her heart gave as he stopped and looked back.

'Oh, and, Lawrie… Happy Birthday.'

And then he was gone. Swallowed up by the velvety blackness like the ghost of birthdays past.

Lawrie sagged against the gatepost, an unwelcome mixture of frustrated desire and loneliness pulsing through her. If this was how one night with Jonas could make her feel, how on earth was she going to manage a whole summer?

She forced herself upright. She was vulnerable right now, that was all. She would just have to toughen up even more—harden herself.

And stay as far away from Jonas Jones as she possibly could, boss or not.

# CHAPTER THREE

LAWRIE WAS DETERMINED to be early.

'Don't be late' indeed.

Even if she *had* gone to bed long after one a.m., and
even if she *had* spent half the night lying awake in a frustrated tangle of hot sheets and even hotter regrets, there
was no way she was giving him the satisfaction.

Besides, she might be in Trengarth, not Hampstead, and
in her old, narrow single bed and not the lumbar-adjusted
super-king-size one she had shared with Hugo, but it was
nice to retrieve a little of her old routine from the wreck-
age of the last week.

She'd been up at six sharp, showered and ready to go
by seven.

So why was she still standing irresolutely in the kitchen
at ten past seven, fingering the scarf Jonas had bought
her? It looked good teamed with her crisp white shirt and
grey pencil skirt, softening the severe corporate lines of
her London work wardrobe, and yet she didn't want to
give Jonas the wrong idea—come into work brandishing
his colours.

She began to unknot it for the third time, then caught
sight of herself in the mirror. Face drawn, anxious.

*It's just a scarf,* she thought impatiently, pulling the door
shut and locking it behind her. *Not an engagement ring.*

She looked down at her left hand, the third finger bare—bare of Hugo's exquisite princess cut diamond solitaire, of Jonas's antique amethyst twist.

Two engagement rings before turning thirty. Not bad for someone who had vowed to remain independent. Her mother had been married three times before thirty; maybe Lawrie wasn't doing so badly after all.

It was another beautiful day, with the sun already shining down from a deep blue sky completely undisturbed by any hint of cloud, and the light breeze a refreshing contrast to the deepening heat. This was Cornwall at its best—this was what she had missed on those dusty, summer days in London: the sun glancing off the sea, the vibrancy of the colours, the smell of grass, salt and beach. The smell of home.

*Don't get too used to it,* Lawrie told herself as she walked along the lane—a brighter, far less intimate and yet lonelier walk in the early-morning light. *This is just an interlude.* It was time to start focussing on her next step, giving those recruitment agencies a quick nudge. After all, they'd had her CV for nearly a week now. She should have plenty of free time. How much work could organising a few bands be?

Five hours later, after an incredibly long and detailed handover by the sofa-bound Suzy, Lawrie was severely revising her estimate of the work involved. Just when had Wave Fest turned from a few guitars and a barbecue on a beach to a three-night extravaganza?

Walking back into Jonas's office, files piled high in her arms, her head was so busy buzzing with the endless stream of information Suzy had supplied that Lawrie had almost forgotten the ending to the night before—forgotten the unexpected desire that had flared up so hotly, despite thinking about nothing else as Fliss drove her through the narrow country lanes to Suzy's village home.

But walking back into the Boat House brought the memory flooding back. She had wanted him to kiss her.

It wasn't real. This was Jonas Jones. She had been there, done that, moved on. Besides, Lawrie told herself firmly, she couldn't afford any emotional ties. She was already mentally spinning this volunteer role into a positive on her CV. This could be the way to set her aside from all the other ambitious thirty-somethings hungry for the next, more prestigious role.

Volunteering to manage a high-profile project raising money for charity—an environmental charity, at that— would add to her Oxford degree and her eight successful years at an old City firm and she would be a very promising candidate indeed. She might even have her pick of jobs.

Only, Lawrie thought as she clasped the large, heavy files more firmly, negotiating contracts was a very different skill from organising a festival. She was used to representing multiple companies who thought they had first dibs on her time *all* the time, but at least there was uniformity to the work, making it simpler to switch between clients. This was more like running an entire law firm single-handed, handling everything from divorces to company takeovers.

There didn't seem to be an aspect of Wave Fest that Suzy hadn't been in charge of—that Lawrie was now in charge of—from budgets to booking bands, from health and safety forms and risk assessment to portaloo hire.

And there was a file for each task.

Jonas was hard at work as she staggered into the office, but he swung his chair round as she dumped the heavy pile on the round conference table with a bang. His face was guarded, although she could have sworn she saw a fleeting smirk as he took in the large amount of paperwork she had lugged in.

'Changed your mind now you know what's in store?'

It was said lightly, but a muscle beating at the side of his jaw betrayed some tension. Maybe he wasn't as indifferent to her as he seemed. Or maybe it was another dig at her lack of commitment.

*Stop trying to second-guess him, Lawrie.* It was probably just a throwaway comment.

'No, but it's more daunting than I imagined,' she admitted honestly. 'This lot—' she gestured at the files behind her '—is just invoices, purchase orders, health and safety certificates, insurance documents. The actual work is being emailed as we speak.'

'Can you do it?'

'It's different to my usual line, and my secretary would have taken care of most of the admin-related work—but, yes, I can do it. I'll need to spend a couple of days reading this lot, though.'

'Here?'

'Sorry?'

'Are you intending to work *here*?'

Lawrie looked up, confused. Where else would she work?

Her eyes caught his. Held them. And for several long seconds she was aware of nothing but the intense blue, the flicker of heat at the heart of his gaze. She caught her breath, an ache suddenly hollowing in her chest, need mingling with the excitement clenching at her stomach. She dragged her eyes reluctantly away, loss unexpectedly consuming her as she stepped back, self-consciously pulling at a folder, looking anywhere but at him, doing her best to ignore the sudden flare of desire, her total awareness of every inch of him.

His shirt matched his eyes, was open at his throat, exposing a small triangle of tanned chest; his long legs were encased in perfectly cut charcoal trousers.

She smiled at him, making it light, trying to keep her sudden nerves hidden, her voice steady. *For goodness' sake, Lawrie, you're a professional.* 'I was planning on it. I could work at home, but it will be easier to get answers to my questions if I'm on site.'

He nodded shortly. 'I agree. That's why I thought you might be better off based at the hotel.'

'The hotel?' For goodness' sake, she sounded like an echo.

'Coombe End. I appreciate it's not as convenient as here—you won't be able to walk to work—but as it's the venue for Wave Fest it makes a lot of sense for you to spend most of your time there.'

His smile was pure politeness. He might have been talking to a complete stranger.

Lawrie shook her head, trying to clear some of the confusion. 'You hold the festival at Coombe End? Your parents *let* you?'

She knew things had changed, but if Richard and Caroline Jones were allowing rock music and campers through the gates of Coombe End then she hadn't come back to the Trengarth she remembered. She had entered a parallel universe.

'No.' His eyes caught hers again, proud and challenging. 'They don't. *I* allow it. Coombe End belongs to me. I own it now.'

She stared at him, a surge of delight running through her, shocking her with its strength. So his parents had finally shown some belief in him.

'They gave you Coombe End? Oh, Jonas that's wonderful.'

He shook his head, his face dark, forbidding. 'They gave me nothing. I bought it. And I paid handsomely for every brick and every blade of grass.'

He had *bought* Coombe End? Lawrie looked around at the immaculately styled office, at the glass separating them from the café below, at the smooth polished wooden floor, the gleaming tiles, the low, comfortable sofas and designer chairs and tables. The whole building shouted out taste, sophistication. It shouted investment and money. She knew things had grown, changed, but how much? Whatever Jonas was doing now it was certainly more than serving up coffee and cakes to friends.

A lot more.

'That's great,' she said lamely, wanting to ask a million questions but not knowing where to start.

Besides, it wasn't any of her business. It hadn't been for a long time.

'I was planning to head over there this afternoon, so I could show you around, introduce you to the rest of the office staff. It'll probably be a couple of hours before I'm ready to leave, though, is that okay?'

Lawrie shook her head, her mind still turning over the 'rest of the office staff' comment. How many people did he employ?

'No problem. I want to go through this lot and make some notes, anyway.'

'If you're hungry just pop downstairs. Carl will make you anything you want.'

And he turned back to his computer screen, instantly absorbed in the document he was reading.

She had been dismissed. It shouldn't rankle—this was hard enough without his constant attention. But it did.

Lawrie sat down at the table and pulled the first file towards her, groaning inwardly at the thick stack of insurance documents inside. Deciphering the indecipher-able, crafting the impenetrable—those were the tools of her trade and she was excellent at it—but today her eyes were skidding over each dense sentence, unable to make sense of them. She was trying to focus all her attention on the words dancing on the page in front of her but she was all too aware of Jonas's every move—the rustle as he shifted posture, the tap of his long, capable fingers on the keyboard.

Despite herself she let her eyes wander over to him, watching him work. She tried to pull her gaze away from his hands but she was paralysed, intent, as his fingers caressed the keyboard, pressing decisively on each key.

He had always been so very good with his hands.

'Did you say something?'

'No,' she lied, hoping he hadn't turned round, hadn't seen her blush.

*Please,* she prayed silently, she hadn't just moaned out loud, had she? For goodness' sake she was a grown woman—not a teenager at the mercy of her hormones. At least she'd thought she was.

It was coming home. She had been away too long and this sudden return at a time of stress had released some sort of sensory memory, turning her back into the weak-kneed teenager crushing so deeply on her boss that every nerve had been finely tuned to his every word and movement. It was science, that was all.

Science, but still rather uncomfortable.

'I'm thirsty,' she announced. 'I'll just go and get some water.'

His satirical gaze uncomfortably upon her, she slid out of the door, heading for the kitchens beneath, relieved to be released from his proximity. If she didn't get a handle

on her hormones soon then she was in for a very uncomfortable few weeks.

Walking down the stairs, she pulled her phone out of
her pocket, automatically checking it for messages. Just
the simple act of holding it created a much-needed sense
of purpose, of control.

Nothing. Not from her old colleagues, not from her
friends in London, not from Hugo. It was as if they had
closed the gap her absence had created so seamlessly that
nobody knew she had gone. Or if they did they simply
didn't care. Yesterday had been her thirtieth birthday. She
was supposed to have been having dinner with twenty of
their closest friends. Other professional couples. How had
Hugo explained her absence?

Or had he taken his secretary instead? His lover. After
all, they had been *his* friends first.

This was the year she had been going to get around to
finally organising their wedding.

This was the year they'd been going to discuss children.
Not *have* them yet, obviously, but start timetabling them in.

They were supposed to have been spending the rest of
their lives together, and yet Hugo had let her go without a
word, without a gesture. Just as Jonas had all those years
ago. Just as her mother had.

She just wasn't worth holding on to.

Lawrie leant against the wall, grateful for the chill of
the tiles on her suddenly hot face. *Don't cry*, she told herself, willing away the pressure behind her eyelids. *Never
cry. You don't need them—you don't need anybody.*

A large glass of iced water and some fresh air helped Lawrie recover some of her equilibrium and she returned to
the office feeling a great deal better. Turning her back
determinedly on Jonas, she called on all her professional

resources and buried herself in the insurance folder, finding a strange calm in returning to the legalese so recently denied her. Pulling a notebook close, she began to scribble notes, looking at expiry dates, costs, and jotting down anything that needed immediate attention, losing herself in the work.

'Lawrie...? *Lawrie?*' Jonas was standing behind her, an amused glint in the blue eyes. 'Fascinating, are they?' He gestured at the folders.

'A little,' she agreed, pulling herself out of the work reluctantly. 'I'm sorry—do you need me?'

'I'm heading off to Coombe End. Do you still want me to show you around?'

Did she? What she really wanted was more time alone—more time to get lost in the work and let the real world carry on without her.

But it would be a lot easier tomorrow if she knew what to expect.

'Oh, yes, thanks.' She pushed her chair back and began to pile the folders and her closely covered sheets of paper together. 'I'll just...' She gestured at the files spread all over the table and began to pull them together, bracing herself ready to scoop them up.

'Here—let me.'

Jonas leant over and picked up the large pile, his arm brushing hers and sending a tingle from her wrist shooting through her body straight down to her toes. She leapt back.

'If you're ready?'

'Absolutely, I'll just get my bag—give me two minutes.'

'I'll meet you at the car; it's just out front.'

'Okay.'

The door closed behind him and Lawrie sank back into her seat with a sigh. She had to pull herself together. Stop acting like the gauche schoolgirl she'd outgrown years ago.

* * *

Jonas pulled his car round to the front of the restaurant, idling the engine as he waited for Lawrie. Their first day working together was going well. He'd had a productive two hours' work just then, not thinking about and not even noticing the exposed nape of her neck, her long, bare legs, not at all aware of every rustle, every slight movement.

Well, maybe just a little aware. But they were just physical things. And Cornwall in summer was full of attractive women—beautiful women, even.

And yet during the last two hours the room he had designed, the room that had evoked light and space, had felt small, claustrophobic, airless. How could someone as slight as Lawrie take up so much space?

Jonas looked over at the Boat House impatiently, just as Lawrie emerged through the front door, a carefully blank, slightly snooty look on her face—the expression that had used to mean she was unsure of the situation. Did it still mean that? He used to be able to read her every shifting emotion, no matter how she tried to hide them.

Then one day he simply couldn't read her at all.

She stopped at the gate, peering down the road, puzzled.

What was she looking for? He half raised one hand to wave at her, then quickly lowered it, leaning on the horn instead, with a little more emphasis than needed. He allowed himself a fleeting moment of amusement as she jumped at the noise and then, obviously flustered, crossed the harbour road, walking slowly towards the car.

He leant across to open the passenger door, sitting back as she slid in, looking straight ahead, trying not to watch her legs slide down over the seat, her round, firm bottom wriggling down over the padded leather, the sudden definition as the seatbelt tightened against her chest.

'Nice,' she said appreciatively, putting a hand out to

stroke the walnut dashboard as Jonas pulled the low, sleek car away from the kerb. 'I have to say I hadn't pegged you as a sports car man. I was looking for the camper van.'

'Oh, this is just a runabout. I still have the camper. There's no way I could get a board in here.'

He laughed as she grimaced.

'You and your boards,' she said. 'If they're that important you should have gone for a sensible people carrier rather than this midlife crisis on wheels.'

'Midlife crisis?' he mock-huffed. There was no way he was going to admit the secret pride he took in the car.

Jonas didn't care too much what people said, what people thought of him, but he allowed himself a little smirk of satisfaction every time he passed one of his parents' cronies and saw them clock the car and the driver and, for one grudging moment, admit to themselves that that no-good boy had done well.

'At least this has a real engine in it. I've seen that dainty little convertible you call a car. Do you actually put flowers in that holder?'

She shook her head, smiling. 'You have to admit it's convenient for parking. But I can see why you like this— she goes like a dream,' she said as he turned the corner onto the main road and the car began purring up the steep climb. 'And at least she isn't red, so not a total cliché! I'm glad that you kept the camper, though. I was always fond of the old girl. What?' she asked as he slid her a sly smile.

'I'm glad you've finally acknowledged that she's a she— you'll call her by her name next,' he teased.

'I will *never* call a twenty-year-old rusty van by such a ridiculous name—by *any* name. A car is not a person,' she said with a haughty flick of her ponytail.

But Jonas could hear the laughter in her voice as he

deftly swung the car round the corner and along the narrow lanes that led to the hotel, just two coves away.

'Go on—say it,' he coaxed her.

It had been a long time since he had seen Lawrie laugh. Judging by the wounded, defensive look in her eyes it was a long time since she *had* laughed.

'I'll help. Bar… Barb…'

'No!' But she was definitely trying not to laugh, and there was a dimple at the corner of her lush, full mouth. 'What about this one? What have you named her?'

'Nice escape, Ms Bennett. But I will get you to say her name before you leave.'

'We'll see.'

The words were dismissive but she still sounded amused. Jonas sneaked a glance at his passenger and saw her face was more relaxed, her posture less rigid.

'So go on—surprise me. What's she called?'

'Ah,' he said lightly. 'This baby doesn't have a name. It'd be disloyal to the camper.'

This time she did laugh—slightly croaky, as if she were unused to making the sound, but as deep and rich, as infectious as Jonas remembered.

'We wouldn't want to hurt the feelings of a rusting old van, would we?'

'I assure her every day that I only bought this to spare her tired old axles, but I'm not sure she believes me.'

'Nobody likes being replaced by a younger model.'

There was a dark undercurrent to her tone and he glanced at her sharply, but her face was as impassive as ever, the laughter gone as if it had never been, replaced by that cool mask she always put on.

It had been her coolness that had first attracted him— the innocent look on her face as she said the most outrageous things a stark contrast to the noisy beach bums he'd been surrounded by. It had been the unexpected moments when she'd opened up that had made him fall head over heels in love with her—the moments when her mask had dropped and she'd lit up with laughter, with indignation, with passion.

Dangerous memories. His hands tightened on the wheel as he navigated the narrow bends, the hedgerows high beside them as if they were driving through a dark, tree-lined tunnel.

'I'm glad you're driving. I'm not sure I'd find my way by road,' Lawrie said conversationally, as if she were discussing the weather.

As beautifully mannered as ever, Jonas thought.

'It's been a long time since I've been to Coombe End. I can't imagine it without your parents there—how are they?'

There were a million and one responses he could give to that. Jonas settled for the most polite. 'Retired.'

Lawrie made an incredulous noise. '*Retired?* Seriously? I didn't think the word was even in their vocabulary.'

'It wasn't. It took a heart attack to make them even talk about it, and a second one to make them do it.'

'I'm sorry to hear that. What are they doing now?'

Jonas's mouth twisted wryly. Making sure he knew just how much they regretted it. Just how much it hurt to see their profligate son undo all their hard work. Not that any of that was Lawrie's business. Not any more.

'Living in a respectable villa, in a respectable village in Dorset, and taking an inordinate amount of cruises—which they mostly complain about, of course. Still, every retiree needs a hobby.'

Lawrie looked at him, concern in the deep grey eyes. Of course she knew more about his relationship with his parents than anyone else. He wasn't used to that—to people seeing behind his flippant tone. He made damn sure that nobody did.

'I can't imagine it—your parents, of all people, taking it easy on cruise liners. How long since you bought them out?'

'Coming up to four years.' Jonas kept his answer short, terse.

'Are they still involved?'

'Now *that*, Lawrie dear, would mean them communicating with me.' All this talk of his parents—his least favourite subject. It was time to turn the tables. 'Talking about difficult relations,' Jonas said, 'how is your mother? Still in Spain?'

Lawrie twisted in her seat and stared at him. 'How did you know she was in Spain?'

Jonas grinned to himself, allowing his fingers to beat out a tune on the leather of the steering wheel. *Nice deflection, Jones.* 'I met her when she was over from Spain, introducing her new husband…John, isn't it? He seemed like a nice bloke. Didn't she come to London? She said she wanted to see you.'

Lawrie's mouth had thinned; the relaxed posture was gone. Any straighter and he could use her back as a ruler.

'I was busy.'

Jonas shrugged. 'I think this one might be different. She seemed settled, happy.'

Lawrie was radiating disapproval. 'Maybe five is her lucky number.'

'People make mistakes. Your mother certainly did. But she's so proud of you.'

'She has no right to be proud of me—she doesn't know me. And if she was so keen to see me she should have come back for Gran's funeral.'

'Didn't she?'

He should have been at the funeral too. He'd said his own private goodbye to Gran on the day, alone at the cottage. But he should have gone.

'She was on a retreat.' It was Lawrie's turn to be terse.

Maybe it had been too successful a deflection. Jonas searched for a response but couldn't find one. Lawrie had every right to be angry, but at least her mother wanted to make amends.

*His* parents wouldn't have known what they were expected to make amends *for*—as far as they were concerned any problems in their relationship were all down to him.

He was their eternal disappointment.

There was an awkward silence for a few long minutes, with Jonas concentrating on the narrow road, pulling over several times as tractors lumbered past, and Lawrie staring out of the window.

'I'm sorry,' she said suddenly. 'I'm glad she's happy— that five husbands and goodness knows how many boyfriends later she's settled. But it's thirty years too late for me.'

'I know.'

And he did. He knew it all. He knew how bitter Lawrie was about her mother's desertion, how angry. He knew how vulnerable years of moving around, adapting to new homes, new schools, new stepfathers had made her.

He knew how difficult it was for her to trust, to rely on anyone. It was something he couldn't ever allow himself to forget.

When it all got too much Lawrie Bennett ran away. Like mother, like daughter. Not caring who or what she left behind.

This time he was not getting to get left in her destructive wake.

# CHAPTER FOUR

'WHAT HAVE YOU done with the helipad? And didn't the ninth hole start over there? I'm not sure your father ever recovered from that lesson. Or your mother…although I *did* offer to pay for the window.'

Lawrie would have bet everything she owned that a country house hotel catering for the rich was not Jonas's style. But now she was here it was hard to pinpoint the changes she instinctively knew he must have made. Coombe End *looked* the same—a tranquil Queen Anne manor house set in stunning acres of managed woodland at the back, green meadows at the front, running into the vivid blue blur of sea on the horizon—and yet something was different. Something other than the change in owner and the apparent loss of a golf course and helipad.

Maybe it was the car park? There were a few high-end cars dotted here and there, but they were joined by plenty of others: people carriers, old bangers, small town cars and a whole fleet worth of camper vans, their bright paintwork shining brightly in the sun. Last time she had been here the car park had been filled with BMWs and Mercedes and other, less obviously identifiable makes—discreet and expensive, just like the hotel.

Lawrie hadn't seen many camper vans in London, and the sight of their cheery squat box shape, their rounded curves and white tops, filled her with a sudden inexplicable sense of happiness. Which was absurd. Camper vans were for man-boys who refused to grow up. Ridiculous, gas-guzzling, unreliable eyesores.

So why did they make her feel as if she was home?

As Jonas led Lawrie along the white gravelled path that clung to the side of the graceful old building her sense of discombobulation increased. The formal gardens were in full flower, displaying all their early summer gaudy glory—giant beds filled with gigantic hydrangea bushes, full flowered and opulent—but the gardens as a whole were a lot less manicured, the grass on the front lawns longer than she remembered, with wildflowers daring to peek out amongst the velvety green blades of grass.

And what was that? The rose garden was gone, replaced by a herb garden with small winding paths and six wooden beehives.

'You've replaced your mother's pride and joy?' she said, only half in mock horror.

'Doesn't it all look terribly untidy?' Jonas said, his voice prim and faintly scandalised, a perfect parody of his mother.

Lawrie shook her head, too busy looking around to answer him, as they walked up the sandstone steps that led to the large double doors.

The old heavy oak doors were still there, but stripped, varnished—somehow more inviting. The discreet brass plaque had gone. Instead a driftwood sign set onto the wall was engraved with 'Boat House Hotel'.

'Come on,' Jonas said, nudging her forward. 'I'll show you around.'

He stood aside and ushered her through the open door. With one last, lingering look at the sun-drenched lawn Lawrie went through into the hotel.

She hadn't spent much time here before. Jonas had left home the day he turned sixteen—by mutual agreement, he had claimed—and had slept above the bar or in the camper van before they were married. He'd converted the room over the bar into a cosy studio apartment once they were. It had always felt like a royal summons on the few occasions when they were invited over for dinner—the even fewer occasions she had persuaded Jonas to accept.

They had always been formal, faux-intimate family dinners, held on the public stage of the hotel dining room. Jonas's parents' priority had clearly been their guests, not their son and his wife. Long, torturous courses of beautifully put together rich food, hours full of polite small talk, filled with a multitude of poisoned, well targeted barbs.

Her memories made the reality even more of a shock as Lawrie walked into the bright, welcoming foyer. The changes outside had been definite, but subtle; the inside, however, was completely, obviously, defiantly different. Inside the large hallway the dark wood panelling, the brocade and velvet, had been stripped away, allowing the graceful lines of the old house to shine through in colours reflecting Jonas's love of the sea: deep blues and marine greens accentuating the cream décor.

'It's all reclaimed local materials—driftwood, recycled glass, re-covered sofas,' Jonas explained. 'And everything is Cornish-made—from the pictures on the walls to the glasses behind the bar.'

'It's amazing,' Lawrie said, looking about her at the room at once so familiar and yet so new, feeling a little like Alice falling into Wonderland. 'I love it. It's really elegant, isn't it? But not cold. It feels homely, somehow, despite its size.'

'That's the effect I wanted.' His voice was casual but his eyes blazed blue as he looked at her. 'You always did get it.'

Lawrie held his gaze for a long moment, the room fading away. That look in his eyes. That approval. Once she'd craved it, looked for it, yearned for it. Like the perfect cup of tea at the perfect temperature. A slab of chocolate exactly the right mixture of bitter and sweet. A chip, crisp and hot and salty on the outside, smooth and fluffy as you bit down.

Of course the only tea she drank nowadays was herbal, and she hadn't had a chip—not even a hand-cut one—in years.

And she didn't need anyone's approval.

'Some of my clients own hotels,' she said, injecting as much cool professionalism into her voice as she could. 'I've seen some great examples of décor, and some fairly alarming ones too. This is really lovely, though, Jonas.'

The approval faded, a quizzical gleam taking its place, but all he said was, 'I'm glad you approve. Let's hear your professional opinion on the rest of the place. This way.'

And Jonas turned and began to walk along the polished wooden floor towards the archway that led into the main ground floor corridor.

Lawrie heaved a sigh. Of relief, she told herself sternly. Job done—professional relationship back on track.

So why did she feel as if the sun had just disappeared behind a very black cloud?

Lawrie followed Jonas through the foyer and down the corridor, watching him greet both staff and guests with a smile, a quick word, a clap on the shoulder—evident master of his empire. It was odd... He used to be so unhappy here, a stranger in his own home, and now he appeared completely at ease.

Jonas led her into the old dining room. A large, imposing space, dominated by the series of floor-to-ceiling windows along the far wall matched by a parade of pillars reaching up to the high ceiling. This room too had been extensively remodelled, with a similar look and feel to the café on the seafront, all the lace and delicate china replaced with light woods and cheerful tablecloths.

A long table ran along one end, filled with large jugs, chunky earthenware mugs and plates of small cakes and biscuits.

'Wouldn't want the guests to get hungry,' Jonas explained as he grabbed a pair of large mugs and poured coffee from one of the jugs, automatically adding milk to them before handing one to Lawrie.

She opened her mouth to decline but closed it as she breathed in the rich, dark aroma.

Why had she given up coffee? she wondered as she took a cautious sip. It was delicious, and the creamy Cornish milk was a perfect companion to the bitter nectar. Two milky coffees in two days—she was slipping back into bad habits.

The coffee was the least of it.

Jonas carried his cup over to the nearest window, which stood slightly ajar, allowing the slight summer breeze to permeate the room with the sweet promise of fresh warmth. The breeze ruffled his dark blond hair, making him look younger, more approachable.

Like the boy she had married. Was he still there, somewhere inside this ambitious, coolly confident man, that impetuous, eager boy?

Lawrie had promised herself that she wouldn't probe. The last nine years, Jonas's life, his business... None of it was relevant. Knowing the details wouldn't help her with her job. Or with the distance she needed to maintain between them. And yet curiosity was itching through her.

She wandered over to the window and stood next to him, every fibre acutely aware of his proximity. Of the casual way he was leaning against the window frame. The golden hairs on the back of his tanned wrists. The undone button at his neck and the triangle of burnished skin it revealed.

Lawrie swallowed, the hot clench at her stomach reminding her of her vulnerability, of the attraction she didn't want to acknowledge.

She looked out, following his line of sight as he gazed into the distance. The sea was clearly visible in the distance, calm and unruffled, the smell of it clear on the breeze. And the urge to know more, to know him again, suddenly overwhelmed her.

'Why here?' There—it was said.

Jonas looked mildly surprised. 'Where else? This room works well as a dining room, has good access to the kitchens. It would have been silly to change it just for change's sake.'

Lawrie shook her head. 'I didn't mean the room. I meant the whole thing,' she said, aware she was probing deeper than she had any right to. 'I mean here. You hated this place. I couldn't get you to set foot inside the gates without a massive fight. I could understand it if your parents had gifted the place to you, but if you paid full value for and then remodelled it? It must have cost a *fortune*!'

Jonas quirked an eyebrow at her. 'Oh, I get it. You're wondering about how much I'm worth. Regretting the divorce after all?'

Heat flooded through her. She could feel her cheeks reddening. 'That's not what I meant,' she protested. 'You know I wouldn't have taken a penny.'

'That's my Lawrie—still so serious.'

Jonas let out a laugh and Lawrie swatted him indignantly, trying to repress the secret thrill that crept over her at the possessive word 'my'.

'Oh, ha-ha. Very funny.'

Jonas leant back against the window pane, still grinning, and took a sip from the chunky Cornishware mug. 'You always were so easy to wind up. Good to know some things don't change.'

'So?' she pressed him, taking advantage of his suddenly companionable mood. 'How come you ended up at Coombe End?'

Jonas didn't reply for a long moment, and the mischievous glint in his eyes faded to annoyance. When he spoke his tone was clipped. 'This was my home once, Lawrie. It wasn't a big conspiracy or takeover, no matter what the village gossips say.'

Lawrie winced. She hadn't considered the inevitable fall-out the change of ownership must have caused. The whole of Trengarth—the whole area—knew how things stood between Jonas and his parents. And there were few without definite opinions on the matter.

'Since when did you care about what the gossips say?' They had always been different in that regard. She so self-conscious, he proudly indifferent.

His eyes were cold. 'I don't. My decision to buy Coombe End was purely a business one. I always knew this place could be more. Yes, it was successful—very successful—if that kind of thing appealed: a little piece of the capital by the sea. You could drive straight here, fly your helicopter here, use the private beach, play the golf course and return home without ever experiencing what Cornwall is about,' he said, his lip curling as he remembered. 'The kind of place your fiancé probably took you.'

'Ex-fiancé,' Lawrie corrected him. She shook her head, refusing to take the bait, but there was an uncomfortable element of truth to his words. Hugo had liked the luxury hotel experience, it was true, but they'd been so busy that just snatching a night away had been enough. There had never been time to explore local culture as well.

'Of course,' Jonas said, putting his mug down decisively and stepping away from the window. 'Ex. Come on. There's a lot to go through.'

No wonder she felt like Alice, being constantly hustled from place to place. She half expected Jonas to pull out a pocket watch. If there were croquet lawns she was in serious trouble.

Lawrie took a last reluctant gulp of the creamy coffee and placed her mug onto the nearest table before following Jonas once again. He led her back down the corridor, through the foyer and outside, along the winding path that led to the woods that made up most of the outside property.

One of Coombe End's winter money-makers had been shooting parties. Lawrie had hated hearing the bangs from the woods and seeing the braces of poor, foolish pheasants being carried back to the house, heads lolling pathetically.

Jonas was walking fast, with intent, and she had to lengthen her stride to keep up with him. It took her by surprise when he came to a sudden halt at the end of the gravelled path, where a long grassy track snaked away ahead of them up the small wooded hill that bordered the hotel gardens.

Lawrie skittered to an undignified stop, clamping down on the urge to grab onto him for support. 'A bit of warning would be nice,' she muttered as she righted herself cautiously.

Jonas ignored her. 'I never hated this place, Law,' he said after a while, gesturing out towards the woodland, its trees a multitude of green against the blue sky.

A secret thrill shuddered through her at the sound of the old pet name.

'I love it here. I always did. But I wanted a different way.'

He resumed walking, Lawrie kept pace with him, wishing she was wearing flatter, sturdier shoes. He had a fast, firm tread; she had always liked that. Hugo was more of a dawdler, and it had driven her mad—as had his admonishments to 'Slow down…it's not a race'.

Jonas didn't look at her as she reached his side but continued as if there hadn't been any break in the conversation. It was as if he was glad he had the chance to explain. And why shouldn't he be? The boy had done well. *Very* well. He hadn't needed her at all. It must be *satisfying* to be in his position. Successful, in control, magnanimously helping out your ex.

Lawrie clenched her fist, digging her nails deep into the palm of her hand. This wasn't how her life, her return to Trengath, was supposed to have been.

'By the time my father had his second heart attack I'd managed to expand the Boat House into twenty-seven seaside locations in the South-West and people were buying into the whole experience—branded T-shirts, mugs, beach towels. So, from a business point of view, expanding the dining experience into a holiday experience made sense.'

Lawrie pulled her mind away from her introspection. Self-pity had never been her style anyway. It didn't get you anywhere.

'I guess,' she said slightly doubtfully. 'But I don't go to my favourite coffee shop and think what this place needs is somewhere for me to sleep.'

'But your favourite coffee shop is near where you live or work,' he pointed out. 'Sure, we're popular with the local population, but in summer especially seventy per cent of our customers are tourists—even if just a small percentage of those people want to take the experience further and holiday with us then that's already a good deal of our marketing done.'

She looked at him in fascination. He sounded like one of her clients.

'I was writing the dissertation for my MBA on brand expansion at the time. Fascinating to put the theory into practice.'

An MBA? Not bad for a boy who'd left school at sixteen. Not that she hadn't known he was capable of so much more. But, truly, had she ever thought him capable of all this? Shame crept over her, hot and uncomfortable. Maybe he was right. She *had* underestimated him.

He flashed her a smile, warm and confiding—a smile that evoked memories of long late-night conversations, of dreams shared, plans discussed. Had she and Hugo ever talked like that? If they had, she couldn't remember.

'Luckily I had been planning what I would do with this place if I were in charge since I was a kid. I've left the hotel itself as pretty high-end, with the rooms still aimed at the luxury end of the market, but I've utilised the woods and the golf course more effectively and I began to reap the rewards almost straight away.'

They were near the top of the small hill. He reached it first and paused, waiting for her to catch up, an expectant look on his face.

She looked down and gasped. 'What on earth...?'

Set beneath them were the woods, which opened almost immediately into a large glade, easily seen from the top of the bank on which they were standing. Inside the glade were eight round white cotton objects that looked a little like mini circus tents.

'Glamping' he said, his voice serious. His eyes, however, had warmed up and were sparkling with amusement at her expression. 'Oh, come on—you're a city girl. Isn't this how the London middle classes enjoy the great outdoors?'

She found her voice. 'You've put *tents* into the woods?

Do your parents know? Your dad will have a third heart attack if he sees this.'

'Ah, but these are luxurious, fully catered tents,' he assured her. 'Perfectly respectable. People can enjoy all the hotel facilities, including their own bathrooms and food in the hotel—although there are barbecues if they want to be pioneer types. They arrive to fully made-up camp beds, there's space to hang clothes, armchairs, rugs, heating. Not what I call camping, but it's hugely popular. The traditional bring-your-own-tent-type campers are on what used to be the golf course, and there are lots of shower and toilet blocks for their use there. According to one review site they are the best camping loos in Cornwall.'

'Well, *there's* an accolade.'

'I'm hoping for a certificate.'

'Anything else?' she asked. 'Tree houses? Yurts? A cave with hot and cold water laid on?'

He chuckled softly, and the sound went straight to the pit of her stomach.

'Just a few stationary camper vans dotted around here and there.'

'Of course there are.' She nodded.

He looked at her, his blue eyes darkening, suddenly intense. 'They're very popular with honeymooners—complete privacy.'

She felt her breath catch as she looked at him, and a shiver goosed its way down her spine. 'A bit cramped,' she said, hearing the husky tone in her voice and hating herself for it.

'They're customised cosy getaways for two—big beds, good sheets and baskets of food delivered.'

'You've thought of everything.'

So different from the two of them, with a sleeping bag and a couple of blankets, a bottle of champagne, the moon, the stars, the sound of the surf. And each other—always each other. Bodies coiled together, lips, hands, caresses... She swallowed. How did these memories, buried so deep, resurface every time this man spoke?

'I had long enough to plan it, watching my parents cater for rich idiots who didn't give a damn where they were,' he said, his mood changing instantly from dangerously reminisce to businesslike again. 'This place is so beautiful, and yet only a handful of people ever had the opportunity to enjoy it—and once they were here they had no idea what was outside the estate walls. Opening it up to campers and glampers means anyone can come here, whatever their budget. We make sure they have all the information they need to go out and explore, hire them bikes, provide transport. All our food is sourced locally, and we recruit and promote locally whenever possible.'

Lawrie laughed, shaking her head in disbelief. 'It's inspired,' she said honestly. 'Utterly inspired, Jonas.'

Without thinking, without even realising what she was doing, she put a hand on his arm, squeezed softly.

'Amazing.'

The feel of his arm was warm and firm under her hand, and the fine cotton of his shirt bunched up under her fingers. How many times had she slid her hand up this arm, admired the strength inherent in the toned muscles as he emerged, sleek and shiny, from the sea? Felt their gentleness as he pulled her in close, encircling her in the safety of his embrace?

'I'm glad you like it.'

Jonas stepped back. Stepped away from her hand, her touch.

'The hotel isn't just the base for the festival—it sets the tone. It's important you understand that. Shall we?'

He gestured back towards the hotel. She shivered, suddenly cold despite the balmy warmth of the day and the wool of her suit jacket. If only she was still with Hugo. If only she were secure in her job. Then seeing Jonas, speaking to him, would have meant nothing apart from a certain nostalgic curiosity. She was feeling vulnerable, that was all.

'You're right—this is the perfect setting for the festival. I see how it works now.' She could do businesslike as well. She'd practically invented it.

He registered the change, a querying eyebrow shooting up as she adjusted her jacket again, smoothing her hair back away from her face, plastering a determinedly polite smile onto her face.

'So, what other changes have you made?' Lawrie kept up a flow of light conversation as Jonas led the way back to the hotel, barely knowing what she was saying, what his answers were.

Thoughts tumbled around her brain. Coming back wasn't easy, starting again was hard, but she had expected that. What she *hadn't* expected, she admitted honestly to herself, was that anything would have changed.

Walking back into Gran's cottage had been like entering a time warp, and for the first couple of days as she'd holed herself up and licked her wounds it had looked as if Trengarth had stayed the same as well.

She had walked down to the harbour on her birthday looking for the safety and comfort of her past. She had truly expected to see the Boat House in its original incarnation—Jonas behind the bar, a little older, a little more thick-set, his mind firmly fixed on waves, on guitar chords, on fun.

She had wanted to validate her choices. To know that even if her present was looking a little shaky at least her past choices had been right. She had been so convinced, once, that Jonas was holding her back, but what if she had been the one holding *him* back?

He was obviously better off without her. Which was *good*, she told herself defiantly, because despite everything she was definitely better off without him.

Or she would be once she had decided exactly what she was going to do.

The familiar niggle of worry gnawed away at her. She had just a few weeks left of her gardening leave—just a few weeks to get a job so much better than her old one that to the outsider it would look like a planned move. Just a few weeks to show Hugo and the senior partners that she was better than their firm. Just a few weeks to get her plan back on track.

They had reached the front of the hotel again and she turned to face Jonas, her features deliberately smooth, matching his. 'This has been fascinating, Jonas, and I can't wait to get started. If you show me where I am to work I'll get set up.'

And then Jonas smiled. A slow, intimate, knowing smile. A smile that said he knew exactly what she was doing. A smile that saw right through her mask. It crinkled the corners of his eyes, drew her gaze to firm lips, to the faint shadow on the sculpted jawline.

It was the kind of smile that offered comfort, acceptance. The kind of smile that invited a girl to lean in, to allow those broad shoulders to take the strain.

It was almost irresistible.

But Lawrie Bennett was made of sterner stuff. Just.

She straightened her shoulders, met his eyes with a challenge. 'After all, you must have a lot to be getting on with.'

The smile deepened. 'Good to see work is still your priority, Lawrie.'

It was. And it evidently was a priority for him as well. So why did he sound so amused?

'The staff entrance is round the back, but you can use the front doors. Just this once.'

Once again Lawrie was following Jonas, moving behind the stylish reception desk and through a door that led to the offices, kitchens and staff bedrooms.

'I have an office here, of course,' he said. 'But I do prefer to work at the Boat House—whether it's because I designed the office there, or because it's where this all began I don't know.' He shrugged. 'A business psychologist would probably have a field-day, trying to work it all out, but I'm not sure I need to know as long as it works and the business keeps growing.'

'You don't live in your parents' apartment?'

He looked surprised at the question. 'Oh, heavens, no. This place needs a whole team of managers and some of them live in. The general manager and his family have the apartment. I bought a place on the seafront a few years ago. One of the old fishermen's cottages by the harbour. You'd like it.'

She nodded, maintaining her cool, interested air even as a stab of pain shot through her. It had always been her ambition to own one of the stone-built cottages clustered around the harbour. On moonlit nights she and Jonas had strolled along, hands entwined, as she'd pointed out her favourites, and they had laughingly argued over decorating plans, colour schemes, furniture.

Now he lived in one of those cottages, without her.

It was ridiculous to feel wounded. To feel *anything*. After all she had spent the last five years living in a beautiful flat with another man; very soon she fully intended to be in an apartment of her own somewhere completely new. Yet the thought of Jonas living in the dream house of their youth filled her with a wistfulness so intense she could barely catch her breath.

He had opened a door to an empty office and held it open, motioning her to move inside. Swallowing back the unexpected emotion as she went through, she saw the office was a large room, distinguished by two big sash windows, each with a cushioned window seat, and furnished with a large desk, a small meeting table and a sofa.

'This is supposed to be my office,' he explained. 'I never use it, though, so you may as well have it while you're here. As I said, it'll be useful for you to be based on site. I'm sure it's all in your notes, but the hotel itself usually hosts the bands, VIPs and essential staff, and most festival-goers camp in the grounds—although quite a lot book out the local B&Bs and caravan parks too.'

She nodded. Of course she had read all this yesterday, but it was still hard for her to comprehend.

Jonas had started this festival during her first year at Oxford, getting local rock and folk bands to play on the beach for free, raising money for a surfing charity that campaigned against marine and beach pollution. The first ever festival had been a one-night affair and the festival-goers had slept on the beach…if they'd slept at all. Food had, of course, been provided by the Boat House. Lawrie was supposed to have returned to Cornwall for it, but at the last minute had decided to stay in London, where she'd been interning for the summer.

Her refusal to promise that she would attend the third festival had led to the final argument in their increasingly volatile relationship. She had packed her bags on the eve of her twenty-first birthday and gone to London for another summer of interning. At the end of that summer she had returned to Oxford for her fourth and final year. She had never returned to Cornwall.

Not until a week ago.

And now that little beach festival had grown—just like the Boat House, just like Jonas's business. Everything was so much bigger, so different from the small, comforting life she remembered. Three nights, thirty-six bands, family activities, thousands of festival-goers, raising substantial funds for charity—yet still local, still focussed on the best of Cornish music, food, literature. It was daunting.

Not that she was going to confess that to the imposing man standing before her.

Lawrie had never admitted that she needed help before. She wasn't going to start now.

'This is great, Jonas,' she said. 'I can take it from here.'

His mouth quirked. 'I have complete faith in you,' he assured her. 'You know where I am if you need me.'

She nodded, but her mind was completely made up. She did not, *would* not need Jonas Jones. She was going to do this alone. Just as she always did.

# CHAPTER FIVE

JONAS LOVED THIS drive. The winding lanes, the glimpses of
sea through the dense green hedgerows. If he put the top
down he could smell the intoxicating scent of sweet grass
and gorse, feel the sea breeze ruffling his hair.

And he loved the destination. The hotel *he* owned. The
hotel *he* had bought. The hotel where his ex-wife was right
this moment sitting at his desk, taking care of his festival.

It had been an unexpected couple of days. Of course
the village gossips were having a field-day. Again. What
would they do without him? He should start charging a licence fee for the resurrection of their favourite soap opera.
He would always be that no-good boy who'd broken his
parents' hearts, and she would always be the no-better-
than-she-should-be teen bride, flighty daughter of a flighty
mother. Their roles had been set in stone long before no
matter how they tried to redefine them.

Well, the viewers were doomed to disappointment. Re-
union episodes were always a let-down. He had no intention of allowing this one to be any different.

Pulling into the gates of the hotel, he felt the usual spark
of pride, of ownership, zing through him. Who would have
thought the prodigal son would return in such style?

It would be nice, though—just once—to drive through
the gates and not be assailed by memories. By the dis-

approving voices of his parents and their disappointed expectations.

When he'd failed his exams at sixteen his parents had wanted to send him away to boarding school—ostensibly to do retakes, in reality to get him away from his friends. It showed a lack of character, they'd thought, that rather than befriend the other boys from the private school they'd sent him to he preferred to hang around with the village kids.

His hands tightened on the steering wheel. Yes, he probably should have studied rather than sneaking out to swim and surf. Taken some interest in his exams. But his achievements—his interest in food, his surfing skill, his hard-won A* in Design and Technology—had meant nothing. His father couldn't, or wouldn't, boast about his son's perfect dovetailed joints on the golf course.

His parents hadn't ever lost their tempers with him. Cold silence had been their weapon of choice. There had been weeks, growing up, when he could swear they hadn't addressed one word to him. But they'd come close to exploding when Jonas had refused to go to the carefully selected crammer they had found.

Some parents would have been proud, Jonas thought with the same, tired old stab of pain, proud that their child wanted to follow in their footsteps. He had thought his plan was a winner—that he would finally see some approval in their uninterested faces.

He'd been so keyed up when he'd told them his idea to run a café-bar on the hotel's small beach. One that was aimed at locals as well as tourists.

He had even offered to do a few retakes at the local college before studying Hospitality and Tourism.

It hadn't been enough. Nothing he did ever was.

In the end they had reached a grudging compromise. They'd given him the old boat house they hadn't used, preferring to keep their guests—and their guests' wallets—on the hotel grounds, and they'd cut him loose. Set him free.

They'd expected him to fail. To come back, cap in hand, begging for their forgiveness.

Instead, twelve years later, he'd bought them out.

And it had been every bit as satisfying as he had thought it would be. It still was.

And, truth be told, Jonas thought as he swung his car into the staff car park, it was quite satisfying having Lawrie here as well. Working for him once again. Seeing just how much he had accomplished. Just how little he needed her.

Whereas she definitely needed him. She was doing her best to hide it, but he could tell. Her very appearance in Trengarth. Her acceptance of the job. None of it was planned.

And Lawrie Bennett didn't *do* spontaneous.

There were just too many ghosts, and Jonas felt uncharacteristically grim as he walked through the foyer—although he did his best to hide it, playing the jovial host, the approachable boss. If growing up in a hotel, then running a café at sixteen, had taught him anything it was how to put on a mask. Nobody cared about the guy pouring the coffee—about his day or his feelings. They just wanted a drink, a smile and some easy chat. Funny how he had always accused Lawrie of hiding her feelings. In some ways they were exactly the same.

Walking along the carpeted corridor that led to his office—now Lawrie's—he felt a sense of *déjà vu* overwhelm him. Once this had been his father's domain. He had never been welcome here—summoned only to be scolded. Even stripping out the heavy mahogany furniture and redecorating it hadn't changed the oppressive feeling. No wonder he preferred to base himself at the harbour.

He paused at the shut door. He didn't usually knock

at his employees' doors, but then again they weren't usually shut. And this was *his* office, after all. Jonas felt his jaw clench tight. Nothing was simple when Lawrie was involved—not even going through his own damn door in his own damn hotel.

He twisted the heavy brass door and swung it open with more force than necessary, striding into the room.

Then he stopped. Blinked in surprise.

'You've certainly made yourself at home.'

There was a small overnight bag open on the floor. Clothes were strewn on the table, chairs and across the sofa—far more clothes than could ever possibly fit into such a small case. Jeans, tops, dresses, skirts—all a far cry from the exquisitely tailored suits and accessories that in just two days Lawrie was already famous for wearing to work.

If Jonas had to hear one more awed conversation discussing whether she wore couture, high-end High Street or had a personal tailor, then he would make all his staff—no matter what their job—adopt the waiting staff's uniform of bright blue Boat House logo tee and black trousers.

Lawrie was on the floor, pulling clothes out of the bag with a harassed expression on her face.

'Have you moved in?' he asked as politely as he could manage, whilst making no attempt to keep the smirk from his face.

Lawrie looked up, her face harassed, her hair falling out of what had once, knowing Lawrie, been a neat bun. She pushed a tendril of the dark silky stuff back behind an ear and glared at him. 'Don't you knock?'

'Not usually. Are you going somewhere?'

'Road trip,' she said tersely. 'And I have nothing to wear.'

Jonas raised an eyebrow and looked pointedly at the sofa. And at the table. Finally, slowly, he allowed his gaze to linger on the floor. A pair of silky lilac knickers caught

his eye and held it for one overlong second before he pulled
his gaze reluctantly away.

'Half this stuff is mine. Only it's about fifteen years
old—whatever I still had at Gran's. The rest is Fliss's, and
as we aren't the same height or size it's not really much
use. The truth is I don't really know how to dress down.
Where I live it's all skinny jeans and caramel knee-length
boots, with cashmere for shopping and lunch or yoga pants
at home. None of that is very suitable at all,' she finished,
with a kind of wail.

'Suitable for what?' Jonas decided not to ask why she
was packing here and not at home. He wasn't sure she
even knew.

'The road trip,' she said.

He cocked an enquiring eyebrow and she rocked back
on her heels and sighed. Irritably.

'*You* know! Suzy always gets a couple of local bands
to come and play Wave Fest. They send in their CDs, or
links to their downloads or whatever, and she whittles them
down to a shortlist and then goes to see them play live. At
a *gig*,' she said, pronouncing the word 'gig' with an odd
mixture of disdain and excitement. 'I haven't been to a gig
in years,' she added.

'Not much call for yoga pants at Cornish gigs.'

'Or cashmere,' Lawrie agreed, missing his sarcasm completely, or just ignoring it. 'Three of the shortlisted bands
are playing over the next three nights so I'm going to see
them all. Two of them are in the county, but tomorrow's gig
is in Devon, so it made sense to plan a whole trip and do
some mystery shopping at some of the caterers and cafés
we've got tendering as well. We're behind in letting them
know. Only that means a three-day trip and I don't have
anything to wear. Why do you have to be so inclusive and
get other people to provide the food?' she ended bitterly.

'Because we couldn't possibly feed thousands of people, and it's good publicity to make the festival a celebration of local food as well,' Jonas said, his mouth twitching at Lawrie's woebegone expression.

She looked like somebody being dragged to a three-day conference on dental drills—not like someone heading out for a long weekend of music and food, all on expenses.

He took pity on her.

'Right, unfortunately packing light may not be an option,' Jonas said, gesturing to the small bag. 'Three gigs in three nights? You'll need to be prepared for beer-spills,' he clarified at her enquiring expression.

Lawrie pulled a face. 'I'm not planning to *mosh*.'

'You did once.'

Lightly said but the words evoked a torrent of memories. Lawrie, so small and slight. Vulnerable. Hurling herself into the mass of bodies right at the front of the stage. It had taken him a long time to make his way through the tightly packed, sweaty mass to find her, jumping ecstatically to the beat of the music, eyes half closed. He'd liked staying near her, to protect her from the crush as the crowd moved to the music.

Lawrie's eyebrow furrowed. 'What did I wear?'

He looked at her incredulously. 'How am I supposed to remember? Probably jeans…' A memory hit him, of thin straps falling off tanned shoulders, a glimpse of skin at the small of her back. 'And a top?' he added. 'Was there a green one?'

Her eyes lit up. 'Hang on!' She jumped up and ran over to the table, where she sifted through a pile of brightly coloured tops. 'Do you remember this?' She held up a light green floaty top.

Jonas wouldn't have said he was a particularly observant man, especially when it came to clothes. His last girlfriend

had claimed that he said, 'You look nice…' on autopilot.
And it was true that he generally didn't notice haircuts or
new outfits. He knew better than to admit it, but he preferred his women laid-back and practical. Jeans, trainers,
a top. Even a fleece if they were out walking. There was
nothing less sexy than a woman stumbling along the cliff-
tops in unsuitable shoes and shivering because her most
flattering jacket proved useless against a chill sea breeze.

But the sight of that green top took his breath away,
evoking the beat of a drum, the smell of mingled beer, sweat
and cigarettes in the air. Not the most pleasant of smells,
yet in the back room of a pub, a club or a town hall, as guitars wailed and people danced, it fitted. Dark, dirty, hot.
The feel of Lawrie pressed against him in the fast-moving,
mesmerised crowd.

He swallowed. 'I think so,' he managed to say, as normally as he could.

Lawrie regarded it doubtfully. 'I guess it will fit. I'm the
same size, and luckily Gran had them all laundered.' Now
it was her turn to swallow, with a glint in her eye.

Had she grieved properly for her gran? For the woman
who'd brought her up? The woman who had provided him
with a sanctuary, a sympathetic shoulder and a lot of sound
advice?

Had helped him become the man he was today.

'There you go, then,' he said. 'Three tops like that, some
jeans for the gigs, something similar for the day, and pyjamas. Easy.' He tried not to look at the lilac silk knickers.
'Plus essentials. Where are you staying?'

'I'm not sure. Fliss was supposed to have sorted out accommodation. Wherever I can get in last-minute, I guess.'

She didn't look particularly enthusiastic and he didn't
blame her. Three nights alone in anonymous, bland rooms
didn't sound like much fun.

'I'm looking into buying a small chain that covers the whole of the South-West,' he said. 'We could see if any of those are near where you need to be and you can do some evaluation while you're there. Let me know what you think of them.'

She nodded. 'I'm near Liskeard tonight, then over to Totnes tomorrow, and back towards Newquay on Saturday. I could drive straight back from there, but there are several food producers I want to sample around that area so it makes sense to stay over.' Her eyes darkened. 'I wish Fliss hadn't bailed, though. It would be nice to have a second opinion.'

'Isn't she going with you?'

'She was supposed to be—we were going to road-trip. Like Thelma and Louise—only without guns or Brad Pitt. But Dave has tickets for some play she really wanted to see and I think he wants to make a weekend of it. It's fine. I'm quite capable. Only she was going to sort out the accommodation and didn't get round to it.'

Her face said exactly what she thought of such woeful disorganisation.

Jonas suppressed a chuckle. He'd have liked to see them set off—Fliss laid-back and happy to wing it, Lawrie clutching a schedule and a stopwatch. 'I'll have a word with Alex and get him to find you some appropriate rooms. What time are you off?'

'After lunch, I think. If I can get packed by then.' She cast a despairing look at the clothes-strewn room.

'I'll let you know what Alex says. Let him arrange your bookings—he knows all the good places. That's why I employ him.'

'Thanks.' She was trying to hide it, but there was still uncertainty, worry in the dark eyes.

'No need to thank me; it's his job. I'll see you later.'

Jonas needed some air. The room suddenly felt hot, claustrophobic. He'd been working too hard, that was the problem. Head down, losing himself in spreadsheets and figures and meetings. He hadn't been near a board for days, hadn't touched a guitar.

He needed a break. Lucky Lawrie. A road trip sounded perfect.

Good food, music, and some time on the road.

It really *did* sound perfect.

If only he had known earlier he could have offered to go instead. A trip was just what the doctor had ordered.

Lawrie checked her watch. Again. This was ridiculous. She had planned to be on the road fifteen minutes ago. Nothing was more irritating than being behind schedule.

Even worse, she was hungry. It must be the Cornish air, because far from acting like a normal jilted bride, and existing on tears alone, for the first time in years Lawrie had a real appetite. Every day she went to the staff dining room promising herself she would just have the soup. A *small* bowl of soup. Because she strongly suspected it was made with double cream.

Yet every day she would find herself drifting over to the bread. Carbs, wheat, gluten. Things that Lawrie had been depriving herself of for so long she had completely forgotten why. Bread covered with real butter, with rich, creamy cheese…sharp, tangy cheese. Even worse, she sometimes had crisps on the side, and the handful of lettuce and tomatoes she added to her heaped plate went no way to assuaging her guilt.

Only—as the pang in her stomach reminded her all too well—she was skipping lunch today. The first stop on her schedule was a baker's, and she had an Indian restaurant and an ice cream maker to fit in today. She might be the same size as her teen self right now but, she thought, the chances of her remaining that slender were looking very, very slim.

She checked her watch again and shook her head. She couldn't wait. Her schedule was packed. Alex would just have to leave her a message and let her know where she would be staying that night. She swallowed. That was okay. He would hardly leave her to sleep in the car. So what if she hadn't checked out the hotel website and printed out directions in case the sat nav didn't work? This was a road trip, not a military manoeuvre.

Lawrie grabbed her handbag and moved towards the door, picking up the stuffed overnight bag and the shopper she had quickly bought in the hotel shop to carry the overspill as she did so. She averted her eyes from the mass of clothes on the sofa. She had tried to tidy up but it still looked as if a whole class of fifteen-year-olds had done a clothes-swap in the normally tidy office.

'Okay, then,' she said out loud, but the words sounded flat in the empty room and her stomach lurched with the all too familiar panic she'd been trying to hide since Fliss had pulled out last night.

Lawrie was no stranger to travelling alone, to making decisions alone, but usually she was clothed with the confidence of her profession. Sharp suits, intimidating jargon, business class flights. This time it would just be Lawrie Bennett, unemployed and jilted. Alone.

She dropped her bags, pressing a fist to her stomach, trying to quell the churning inside. For goodness' sake, she dealt with CEOs all the time. How could standing in a dark room listening to music be scarier than walking into a hostile boardroom?

But it was.

It had been so long. Gigging belonged to a younger, more

naive Lawrie. A Lawrie she had said goodbye to many years
before. Still, she thought grimly, it would all make an amusing anecdote one day—possibly even at a job interview.
An example of how she was prepared to go the extra mile.

The trill of her desk phone made her jump. Good—Alex
at last. Walking over to it, she prayed for a reprieve. There
were no hotel rooms left in the whole of Cornwall…. She
was needed elsewhere…

'Sorted out your sartorial crisis?'

Not Alex. Warm, comforting tones, as caressing as a
hot bath on a cold night. A voice she wanted to confide her
fears in—a voice that promised safety. Sanctuary.

'I'm running late,' she said, more sharply than she had
intended. The last thing she needed was for Jonas to guess
how relieved she was to hear his voice, to know how scared
she was. 'Did your guy manage to sort out a place for tonight? I really can't hold on any longer.'

'Everything's organised. Come and meet me in the car
park.'

Was that laughter tinting the deep tones? 'Fine. I'm on
my way.'

Laden down, it took Lawrie a few minutes to make her
way along the corridors and through the staff door that led
to the car park.

The weather had cooled suddenly, and the sky was a
mixture of grey and white with occasional glimpses of
hopeful blue. It meant nothing. Cornwall was full of micro
climates, and she had packed for every eventuality bar bliz-
zards.

Her convertible Beetle was tucked away in the far corner of the car park. Hugo had laughed at it—told her that
she was obviously still a hippy surf girl at heart—although
she had eschewed all the pretty pastel colours for a sensible
metallic grey. She had thought of it as the perfect choice

for a city car: small and compact. But its rounded lines and
cheerful shape fitted in here. Maybe Hugo had been right
about that part of her at least.

She pushed Hugo from her mind. He didn't belong here,
in this world dominated by the sea and the open country.
In the new life she was trying to make for herself. She
looked around for Jonas but he wasn't by her car or by the
hotel entrance.

'Lawrie?'

There he was, predictably enough standing by one of the
camper vans that were always dotted around the car park,
several of them staff vehicles. She was pretty sure ownership of one guaranteed you a job here.

This van was freshly painted a minty green, its contrasting white trim bright. Jonas leant against it, arms folded,
one long leg casually crossed over the other, a look of en-
joyment on his face. The same feeling of safety she had
experienced on the phone rushed over her as she walked
towards him.

'I'm behind schedule, so this had better not take long,'
she said as she stopped in front of him, dropping her bags
at her feet.

She wasn't going to give in to temptation, to allow her
eyes to flicker up and down the long, muscled legs, the
firm torso that broadened out in exactly the right place.
She wasn't going to pause at the neck—what *was* it with
this man and his unbuttoned shirts? One button lower and
it would look sleazy, but as it was he managed to show just
enough chest to tantalise. And she wasn't going to linger
on the perfectly defined jawline, on the cheekbones wasted
on a mere man—even on this one. She certainly wasn't
going to step closer and allow her hand to brush that lock
of dirty blond hair back from his forehead, no matter how
much her hand ached to.

'You have a schedule?' He shook his head. 'Of course you do. A timetable, printed maps, telephone numbers all printed out. I bet there's a clipboard.'

Hot colour crept over her cheeks. 'There's nothing wrong with being organised.'

He raised an eyebrow in pretend surprise. 'I didn't say there was. It's an excellent quality in a festival-planner and an equally excellent one in a navigator. Come on—hop in.'

Confusion warred with panic and a tiny, unwanted tendril of hope. 'What do you mean?'

Jonas gestured to the van. 'She doesn't know whether to be pleased or offended that you don't recognise her, even though she spent a good six months being restored.'

'They all look the same,' Lawrie replied automatically, but her eyes were searching the camper van, looking for the tell-tale signs, looking for the rust, the dents. 'That's not Bar…? Not your old van?'

'You nearly said her name.' A smirk played around the firm mouth. 'Not looking so old now, is she? A facelift—well, an everything lift, really—new custom interior, new engine. She's never been in better shape.'

'Boys and their toys,' Lawrie scoffed, but secretly she was impressed.

The old van did look amazing—a total change from the ancient rust bucket whose tattered interior might have been original but had definitely seen better days. The same magic wand that had been waved over the Boat House, over the hotel, even over Jonas himself had been hard at work here.

'She looks good, but I still don't get what that has to do with me.'

The blue eyes gleamed. 'You said yourself you needed a second opinion.'

The tiny tendril of hope grew larger, bloomed. Lawrie

stamped down on it. Hard. 'I said Fliss was going to *give* me a second opinion—not that I needed one.'

'And I realised that I need to recharge my batteries.'

He carried on as if she hadn't spoken, pushing himself away from the van and sauntering slowly towards her. Lawrie fought an instinctive urge to take a step back. With his unhurried grace he reminded her of a predator, blue eyes fixed on her, hypnotic.

Lawrie swallowed, her mouth suddenly dry, her heart pounding so loudly she was sure he could hear it. 'I'm not sure it's a good idea. Working together is one thing, but spending time alone after everything...' Her voice trailed off. Lost for words again. It was becoming a habit around him.

Jonas paused in his tracks. 'But we *will* be working. Second opinions, remember?'

'Alone—we'll be working together alone,' she snapped.

He quirked an eyebrow. 'Oh, I'm sorry. I totally misread the situation. I thought you were totally over me, what with the divorce and the fiancé and the nine years apart, but if this is awkward for you maybe I had better keep my distance.'

He stood grinning at her. He obviously thought he had the upper hand.

Lawrie could feel her teeth grinding together. With a huge effort she unclenched her jaw, forcing a smile onto her face. 'I hate to burst your highly inflated opinion of yourself,' she said, as sweetly as she could, 'but I was only thinking of you. If this isn't awkward for you, then great— by all means join me.'

He moved a step closer, so close they were nearly touching. She could see the smattering of freckles that dusted the bridge of his nose, the tops of his cheeks. They gave him a boyish air, emphasised by the hair falling over his forehead, the impish grin.

But he was no boy. Jonas Jones was all grown up.

'Ready?' he asked, eyes locked on hers.

She stared straight back at him, channelling every ounce of cool professionalism she had right back at him. 'Of course.'

'Then let's go.'

'Did Alex book the hotels? I can plot out the best routes for the entire weekend once I know where we're staying.'

Jonas had to hand it to her. Lawrie was never knocked down for long. He could have sworn that his decision to crash her trip had completely thrown her but she was hiding it well. The road atlas open on her lap, clipboard and pen in hand, she was seemingly back in control.

For now.

Of course she had a point. A very good point. Spending three days on the road with any colleague would be testing. Make that colleague the person you'd once thought was the love of your life and things got a little more difficult.

But this was purely business. Lawrie had been thrown in at the deep end, after all. She might be a whizz with a spreadsheet and able to decipher the finer points of contracts in the blink of an eye, but Jonas was prepared to bet good money that she hadn't been anywhere near a tent or a crowded gig in years. This was his festival—his reputation at stake. He might agree that in the circumstances Lawrie was the right person to help them out, but she still needed hand-holding. Metaphorically, of course.

Of course he *might* be playing with fire. But what was life without a little danger? He'd been playing it safe for far too long.

Time to light the fireworks.

Jonas nodded towards a folder on the dashboard. 'Our accommodation is in there.'

Concealing a smile, Jonas watched out of the corner of his eye as she slid the folder onto her knee and pulled out the sheaf of paper from inside.

Her brow crinkled. 'These aren't hotels.'

'Excellent opportunity to check out some of the competition,' he said.

'You own a hotel.'

'And a campsite,' he reminded her.

'But I'm not set for camping. I don't camp—not any more.' Her voice was rising. 'I don't even own a sleeping bag.'

'Relax,' Jonas said easily. 'I'm not subjecting you to a tent. Barb has everything we need. You won't even need a bag. I have sheets and quilts. Even pillowcases.'

'We're sleeping in *here*? Both of us?'

'She's a four-berther, remember?' He flashed a grin over at her, looking forward to her reaction. 'Do you want to go on top or shall I?'

'I'm not nineteen any more, Jonas.'

Lawrie's face was flushed, her eyes dark with emotion. Anger? Fear? Maybe a combination of both.

'This really isn't acceptable.'

Jonas raised an eyebrow appraisingly. What was she so scared of? 'I'm sorry, Lawrie, I didn't think this would be a big deal. I really do want to see how the facilities at the sites compare with mine. Look, if you feel that strongly about it I can drop you at a motel or a B&B after tonight's gig. But I promise you you'll get a better night's sleep here than in some anonymous hotel chain bedroom.'

'Call me old-fashioned, but I like en-suite facilities.'

But his conciliatory tone seemed to have worked as she

sounded more petulant than angry. He decided to push it a little.

'I promise you we won't be roughing it. Barb's newly sprung and very comfortable. All these sites have electric hook-up and plenty of shower blocks. The place I have picked out for tonight has a very well-regarded organic restaurant too. I thought it would be good to compare it with the Boat House. And Saturday's site prides itself on its sea views, which is one thing we're lacking. I really would value your opinion.'

'But I thought you had the best toilets in Cornwall? I won't settle for less.'

Was that a small smile playing around the full mouth?

'If I didn't think every single one of these toilets weren't a serious contender I promise you I wouldn't have dreamt of bringing you along. Come on, Lawrie, it'll be fun. Food, music and the stars. I know I need the break. And…' he slid his eyes over to her again, noting the dark shadows under her eyes, the air of bewildered fragility she wore whenever her professional mask slipped '…I'll bet everything I own that you do too.'

'This isn't a break—this is work,' she reminded him primly.

'True,' he conceded. 'But who's to say we can't have fun while we're working?'

She wound a tendril of hair around her finger, staring out of the window, lost in thought. 'Okay, then,' she said finally. 'I'll give it one night. But if it's cold or uncomfortable or you snore—' she gave him a dark look '—then tomorrow we're in a hotel. Deal?'

'Deal,' he said. 'Okay, then, woman-with-clipboard, which road do you want me to take?'

# CHAPTER SIX

'THIS IS SO good.'

'Better than your Pinot Noirs and Sauvignon Blancs?'

Lawrie took a long sip of the cool, tart cider and shook her head. 'Not better—different. I'm not sure I'd want to drink it in a restaurant. Too filling, for a start,' she finished, turning the pint glass full of amber-coloured liquid round in her hands, admiring the way it caught the light.

'They have a micro-brewery on site.' Jonas was reading the tasting cards. 'Rhubarb cider—that sounds intriguing. I wonder if they would want a stall at the festival? Talking of which, have you made a decision on the bands yet?'

Lawrie pulled a face. 'It's so hard,' she said. 'They were all good, and so different. Seriously, how do you compare punk folk with rock with acoustic?' She shook her head. 'Who would have thought punk folk even worked, and yet they were fab. Can I ask them all?'

'You're the organiser; it's up to you,' Jonas said. He gave her a mock stern look. 'Not last night's support, though. We want people to *enjoy* their festival-going experience.'

'Oh, I don't know.' Lawrie smiled at him sweetly. 'I thought the part where she read out poetry to a triangle beat was inspiring. Especially the poem about her menstrual cycle.'

'Stop!' Jonas was covering his ears. 'Those words are

seared onto my brain. As is that triangle. I swear I could hear it in my sleep. *Ting, ting ting.*' He shuddered.

Lawrie laughed and took another sip. 'I think the triangle represented her feminine aura.'

It was amazing, how comfortable she was. How comfortable *they* were. Having him around, driving, tasting, listening, bouncing ideas—it had made the whole trip easy, fun. And it hadn't been awkward. Well, hardly at all. Lying in the upper berth listening to his deep breathing had been a little *odd*. A little lonely, maybe. But nothing she couldn't shake off.

And he'd been a perfect gentleman. Which was good, obviously.

'It was a good idea of yours to stay an extra night,' she said with a small, happy sigh.

Jonas had been right about the views. The final campsite was perfectly placed in the dip of a valley, with the beach and sea clearly visible from their sheltered pitch. Lawrie wriggled back in her chair and closed her eyes, savouring the feel of the late-afternoon sun on her face.

'It seemed a shame to get a pitch with these views and then not be around to enjoy them,' Jonas said. 'Besides, we deserve some relaxation. And we discovered this cider.' He held up his pint with a satisfied smile. 'And that crêperie this morning. I think you should consider that patisserie too—their croissant was a work of art.'

'Hmm…' Lawrie opened her eyes and reached down to the folder at her feet. Picking it up, she flicked through it thoughtfully. 'They were good, weren't they? And the bakers near Liskeard were superb. I think that's enough pastries and bread though, don't you? We need some diversity. Two ice cream suppliers, four breweries, one Indian, one Thai and an Indonesian takeaway. Paella, the baked potato stall…'

'Stop right there.'

Jonas held his hand up and, startled, Lawrie let the folder slip shut.

'Lawrie Bennett, it is Sunday afternoon. You have been working day and night all weekend. Relax, enjoy the view, and drink your cider.'

A warm glow spread through her at his words. Nobody else had ever cared about how hard she worked, told her to slow down. She needed it. Somehow, when brakes were being handed out Lawrie had been last in line.

They lay side by side, sprawled out in the deckchairs, united in a companionable silence. That was another thing, she thought drowsily. He was easy to talk to but she didn't *have* to talk to him, to entertain. She was free to be lost in her own head if she wanted.

It was nice to be sitting here with no plans, nothing to tick off on her physical or mental to-do list. It was just… Lawrie shifted in her seat. What were they going to do tonight? At least her schedule had meant there were no awkward gaps to be filled. Their conversation had revolved around the food they were tasting, the music they were listening to. But tonight stretched ahead—empty. Maybe there was another band playing locally. Or another restaurant to check out. A seafood stall might be an interesting addition to the mix.

'Stop it.'

Lawrie turned her head in surprise. 'Stop what?'

'Timetabling the evening.'

How did he know? 'I'm not,' she said. Then, a little more truthfully, 'I was just thinking about later. Wondering what we were going to do.'

'We haven't stopped for three days,' Jonas pointed out. 'Do we have to do anything?'

'No…' she said doubtfully. 'Only what about food? Or

when it gets dark? Not that I'm not enjoying the sun and the view, but it will start to cool off in an hour or so.'

'Good thing we packed jumpers, then.'

The teasing tone was back in his voice and Lawrie squirmed, hot with embarrassment. It was unfair of him to make her feel uptight. Just because she liked to know what was coming next. Hugo had liked her organisational skills. Maybe that was what had attracted him to his secretary? Not the leopard print thong but the way she organised his diary.

'Okay.'

Jonas was sitting up in his chair and she could feel his eyes fixed on her, despite the sunglasses shielding them.

'I haven't made notes *or* a list, and I don't own a clipboard, but I had vaguely thought of a walk, finishing up at the farm shop for cheese and bread and more of this excellent cider. Then back to the van, where I can finally take cold-blooded, nine-year-old revenge for *quilling* on a triple word score. If you're up to the challenge, that is?'

That sounded really pleasant. In fact it sounded perfect. Almost dangerously so.

'Misplaced confidence was always your problem,' Lawrie said, adjusting her own sunglasses, hoping he couldn't see just how much the evening he had outlined appealed to her. 'There have been many high-scoring words since then, Mr Jones. But if you are willing to risk your pride again, I am more than willing to take you down.'

Jonas leant forward, so close his face was almost touching hers, his breath sweet on her cheek. 'I look forward to it.'

'That is *not* a word!'

'It is.' Lawrie couldn't hide the beam on her face. Ah, the sweet smell of victory. 'Check the dictionary.'

'I don't care what the dictionary says,' Jonas argued. 'Use it in a coherent sentence.'

Foolish, foolish boy. He should know better than to challenge Lawrie Bennett at Scrabble. Or at any game.

'How many *exahertz* are these gamma rays?' she said, sitting back and enjoying his reaction.

'You have never, ever used that sentence in your whole life!'

'No,' she conceded. 'But I could. If I went to work at CERN, for instance, or had a physics laboratory as a client. Besides, the rules don't specify that you have to have used the word in everyday conversation.'

'They should do,' Jonas grumbled, staring at the board in some dismay.

As he should, she thought, looking at the scores neatly written down on the pad in front of her. There was no way he could win now. And if she could just prevent him from narrowing the gap too much…a two-hundred-point lead was so satisfying.

Leaning back against the bench, she began to add up her points. They were both sitting on the floor of the camper van, the amost full board between them. The van doors were slid fully open, giving the scene a dramatic backdrop as the sun sank into the sea, leaving a fiery path on the top of the calm waves.

'That is thirty-one tripled, plus fifty for getting all my letters out. It's a shame it's the H on the double letter score, but all in all not a bad round. Okay, your turn.'

'I don't think I want to play any more,' Jonas said, disgust on his face as he surveyed his letter tiles. 'Not even *you* could manage to make a word out of three Is, a U, two Os and an R.'

Lawrie bit back a smile as she surveyed the board. 'Oh, dear,' she said, keeping her face completely serious.

'I think the official Scrabble term for your situation is screwed. *Ow!* What was that for?'

'Excessive smugness.' Jonas held up a second cushion. 'Don't think I won't,' he threatened.

Retrieving the cushion he'd already lobbed in her direction, Lawrie held it up in front of her, half shield, half offensive weapon. 'You just try it, Jones.'

He eyed her. 'A challenge? Really, Lawrie? You may, on this occasion, have won on brains, but I am always going to win on brawn.'

'Brawn,' she scoffed, uneasily aware of a tightening in her abdomen—a kind of delicious apprehension uncoiling—as she brandished her pillow. 'At your age?'

'In the prime of my life,' he said. 'Never been in better shape. What?' He laughed indignantly as Lawrie collapsed into giggles. 'It's true.'

'Says the man sat on a caravan floor, unshaven and holding a cushion!' It was hard to get the words out.

'It's not a caravan, you blasphemer. This is a classic and you know it. Besides, *you* can't talk. If only all your fashion admirers could see you now they would be totally disappointed. Nothing chic about leggings and a sweatshirt—even I know that.'

Swallowing back the laughter, Lawrie hugged her knees to her chest. 'Yoga pants and cashmere, actually.'

It felt good to laugh. Free.

Trying hard not to think about how long it had been since she had laughed like that, Lawrie fastened onto Jonas's last words. 'Hang on—what do you mean, fashion admirers?'

Jonas shook his head and pushed the Scrabble board away, sliding down so only his head and shoulders were propped up against the bench seat, the rest of his long, lean body sprawled comfortably along the floor.

He took up a lot of room. A lot of air. Lawrie swallowed and adjusted her gaze so that she was looking straight ahead, at the glorious sunset, at fresh air. Not at the denim-clad legs lying close to her. Close enough to touch.

'I dress really conservatively for work,' she said, probing for an answer as Jonas seemed disinclined to speak. 'And my only night out was on my birthday.'

'Apparently West London's "conservative" is Trengarth's cutting edge,' Jonas said, swirling the Scrabble tiles around on the board and mixing up the words. 'It's all about the cut, or so I've heard. Definitely not High Street, they say.'

'I *do* get my suits made for me by a tailor who specialises in women's clothes.' Why did it feel like an admission of guilt? 'They fit better, though I wouldn't call them fashionable. But I don't know why I am explaining this to you.' She rounded on Jonas. 'If your suits aren't handmade I'll eat a Scrabble tile.'

He grinned, picking up an *I* and holding it out to her. 'Here you go—there are too many of these anyway.' Lawrie raised an eyebrow at him and he palmed the tile. 'Okay, you win. I *do* frequent an establishment in Plymouth run by a gentleman who trained on Savile Row.'

'I knew it!' The moment of triumph was shortlived as the impact of his words hit. Lawrie's chest tightened painfully and she breathed deeply, slowly. 'Why do people care about what I wear?'

Jonas looked surprised. 'They don't—not really. Only you're new, have history with me, and you look smarter than anyone else. It was bound to make a bit of a stir. It's not a big deal.'

But it was. 'I don't like being talked about. No one even noticed my suits in the City. Maybe I should get some new clothes for the rest of the summer.'

'What on earth for?' He sounded incredulous.

A wave of irritation swept over her. 'To blend in. The last thing I want is to be noticed for anything but my work.'

'People aren't exactly staring at you as you walk down the street,' Jonas pointed out. 'Wait...' He pulled his legs in and sat up, facing her. Blue eyes studied her face intently. 'Is this why you were so stressed about what to bring on this trip? You wanted to blend in?'

'There's no reason to sound so judgmental.' Lawrie could feel her face heating up, a prickly and uncomfortable warmth spreading down her neck and chest. 'I'm not comfortable standing out from the crowd. No big deal.'

He was still looking at her. Looking into her, as if he could see her soul. As if he was unsure about what he was seeing there. It took every bit of self-control that she had not to squirm or pull away.

'Is it, Law?' he said softly 'Is it just about blending in?'

'I don't know what you're talking about.' She wanted to pull away, look away, but it was as if his eyes had a hypnotic effect on her. She was paralysed, stuck to the spot, as he stared at her searchingly.

'You didn't sing in London. Not once in nine years.'

'For goodness' sake, Jonas, I was busy!'

'What *did* you do? Apart from work.'

She tried to remember but it was all fog. It seemed like a lifetime ago. 'We had dinner with friends. Went to the theatre, to museums and exhibitions. The usual things.'

'Usual for who? West London professionals like you?' His gaze sharpened. 'You're a tribal animal, aren't you, Lawrie? You like to dress the part, act the part—whatever that part might be. What is it you really want? You like? Do you even know?'

'What do you care?' The words were torn from her. 'As soon as my life diverged from yours you gave up on me.

So don't you dare be so damn superior—don't act like I'm letting you down by trying to fit in.'

'But you're not.' He looked surprised. 'Why would you be letting me down? But are you letting yourself down, Lawrie? If you spend your whole life hiding your own needs and wants away can you ever be really happy?'

'Happiness is not about *things*.' The words snapped out of her, surprising her with their fierceness, their certainty. 'Clothes, hobbies, food—they're just trappings, Jonas. I don't care about any of them. All I want—all I have ever wanted—is to be successful, to be independent. To stick to the plan.'

'Is this the plan? To be here with me?'

It was like a punch straight to the stomach, winding her with its strength. 'No,' she said after a long pause. 'No, this wasn't in the plan. But I'm adaptable, Jonas. I'm strong. Don't ever mistake a desire to fit in with weakness. Lions blend in with the Sahara, you know.'

He threw his head back and laughed. The sound jarred with her jangled nerves.

'Weak is the last word I'd use to describe you. Lioness, on the other hand…'

It was his turn to duck as she threw a cushion at him.

'I was just agreeing with you,' he protested.

'If you had lived with my mother you'd have learned to fit in as well,' Lawrie said. She didn't know why she was telling him this—why she needed him to understand. But she did. She needed him to know that she wasn't shallow or weak. 'One moment I'm living in Stockbrokerville in Surrey, learning French and pony-riding, the next we're in a commune near Glastonbury and my mother is trying to make me answer to the name of Star. She changed completely, depending on who she was with, and she never went for the same type twice.'

'I know,' Jonas said, pity softening the keen eyes. 'It was hard for you.'

Lawrie shook her head. 'I don't need you to feel sorry for me. I'm just explaining. What I wore, ate, did, the friends I had—they were interchangeable, dependent on her whims. If I had cared, had tried to hang on to *things*, it would have been unbearable. So I kept my head down, I worked hard, and I vowed that I would be so successful that I would never have to be dependent on anyone. And I'm not.'

'Is that why you and the fiancé split? Because you didn't need him?'

'No.' Of course it wasn't. Hugo had *liked* her independence. Hadn't he? 'It was…complicated.' That was one word for it. 'Is that why you wanted out? Because I didn't need *you*?'

'Oh, Lawrie.' There was no lightness in his voice, in his face, at all. 'I was used to that. Not being needed. And, if you remember, in the end you were the one that walked away.'

'Maybe…' Her voice was low. 'Maybe I was afraid that I did need you.'

'Would that have been so bad?' He examined her face, searching for answers behind the mask.

She shook her head and another lock of hair fell out of the loose ponytail, framing her face. 'Bad? It would have been terrible. I was barely started on my path. Oxford, an internship at one of the best City firms… And I seriously, *seriously* considered giving it all up. For you. For a man. Just like my mother would have. Just like she did again and again. I *had* to leave, Jonas.' She turned to him, eyes wide, pleading for understanding. 'I had to hold on to me.'

And in doing so she had let go of him. Jonas closed his eyes for a second, seeing a flash of his heartbroken younger self frozen in time. He hadn't wasted a single emotion on his parents' rejection, pouring all that need, all his love, into the slight girl now sitting beside him. It had been far too much for someone so young to carry.

He reached out and cupped her cheek. Her skin was soft beneath his hand. 'I guess I needed you to choose me. I needed *somebody* to choose me. I still needed validation back then. It was a lot to put on you. Too much.'

'Maybe you were right. We were too young.' Her eyes were filled with sadness and regret. 'I didn't want to agree with you, to prove all the *I told you so* right, but we had a lot of growing up to do. We weren't ready for such a big step.'

He nodded. Suddenly he didn't feel any anger or contempt towards her or towards their shared past. Just an underlying sadness for the idealistic kids they had once been. For their belief that love really was all they needed.

He was still touching her cheek. She leant into him trustingly and he turned his hand to run the back of it down the side of her face, learning once again the angle of her cheekbone, the contours of her chin, the smoothness of her skin.

Jonas had made some rules for himself before he came on this trip. No talking about the past, no flirting, and definitely, absolutely no touching.

But sometimes rules were meant to be broken.

Slowly, deliberately, he let his fingers trail further down her face, brushing her full mouth before dipping down to her chin. He let them linger there for one long, agonising moment, tilting her face towards him, giving her ample time to pull away, to stop him, before he leant in slowly— oh, so slowly.

It was a butterfly kiss. So light, so brief, their lips barely touching. Jonas pulled back, searching her face for consent. Her eyes were closed, her face angled towards his, lips slightly parted. Expectant. It was all the agreement he needed.

He shifted closer to her, closing the space between them as he slid one arm around her slender shoulders. The other hand moved from her chin to the sweet spot at the nape of her neck. She moved in too—an infinitesimal shift, yet one that brought her body into full contact with his. Her face lifted, waiting, expecting. Jonas looked down at her for one moment—at the face at once so familiar and yet so strange to him, at the dark eyelashes, impossibly long, improbably thick, the creamy skin, the lush, full mouth waiting for him.

And a gentleman should never keep a lady waiting.

Another fleeting kiss, and another, and another. Until, impatient, she moaned and pressed closer in, her mouth opening under his, seeking, wanting. She tasted of cider, of sunshine. She tasted like summer, like coming home, and he deepened the kiss, pulling her even closer until they were pressed together, her arms wound around his neck. His own arms were holding her tightly to him, one bunching the silky strands of her hair, the other caressing the planes of her back through the lightness of her top.

It was like being a teenager again, entwined on the floor of the camper van, mouths fused, hands roaming, pulling each other closer and closer until it seemed impossible that they were two separate bodies. There was no urgency to move, no need to start removing clothes, for hands to move lower. Not yet.

Seconds, minutes, hours, infinities passed by. All Jonas knew was the drumming of his blood in his ears, the fierce heat engulfing him. All he knew was her. Her touch, her taste, her mouth, the feel of her under his hands. When she pulled back it was as if she had been physically torn away from him, a painful wrench that left him cold. Empty.

She looked at him, eyes wide, dark with passion, her pupils dilated, mouth swollen. 'I think…' she began, her voice husky, barely audible.

Jonas readied himself. If she wanted to be the voice of common sense, so be it. He looked back at her silently. He might not argue, but he wasn't going to help her either.

'I think we should close the doors.'

Her words were so unexpected all he could do for a moment was gape. The van doors were still open to the night sky. The sea breeze floated in, bringing the taste of salt and the faint coconut-tinged smell of gorse.

Then the meaning of her words hit home. Anticipation filled the air, hot and heavy, making it hard to breathe as excitement coiled inside him.

'There's no one out there.'

They were in a secluded spot, parked at the very edge of the field. As private as you could be in a campsite full of tents and caravans. Not as private as they could have been if he'd planned for this.

'Even so…'

She smiled at him, slow and full of promise, and slowly, as if he were wading through treacle, he got to his feet and swung the sliding door firmly closed. The outside world was shut out. It was just the two of them in this small enclosed space. The air was heavy with expectation, with heat, with longing.

'Satisfied?' He raised an eyebrow and watched her flush.

'Not yet.' She was turning the tables on him. 'But I'm hoping to be.'

Passion jolted through him, intense and all-encompassing. In swift, sure steps he closed the space between them, pulling her in tight. 'Oh, you will be,' he promised as he lowered his mouth to hers once again. 'I can guarantee it.'

# CHAPTER SEVEN

'Ooof!' WHEN HAD breathing got so *hard*? Bending over to catch her breath, the tightness of a stitch pulling painfully at her side, Lawrie conceded that a ten-mile run might have been a mite ambitious.

Of course, she reassured herself, running outside was harder, what with all those hills and the wind against her, to say nothing of no nice speedometer to regulate her stride. Straightening up, one hand at her waist, Lawrie squinted out at the late-afternoon sun. On the other hand, she conceded, although her late, lamented treadmill came with TV screens and MP3 plug-ins it was missing the spectacular views of deep blue sea and rolling green and yellow gorse of her current circuit. It was definitely an improvement on the view of sweaty, Lycra-clad gym-goers that her old location had provided her with.

Taking a much needed long, cool gulp of water, Lawrie continued at a trot, looping off the road and onto the clifftop path that led towards the village. If she continued along to the harbour she could reward herself with a re-fuelling stop at the Boat House before walking back up the hill home. No way was she going to try and run up that hill—not unless her fitness levels dramatically improved in the next half an hour.

*Just keep going,* she thought fiercely. *Concentrate on that latte...visualise it.* It was certainly one incentive.

And if Jonas just happened to be working at the Boat House today then that, just possibly, could be another incentive. The pain in her side was forgotten as the night before flashed through her mind, her lips curving in a smile as she remembered. Another night of heat, of long, slow caresses, hot, hard kisses, hands, tongues, lips. Bodies entwining.

Lawrie's pulse started to speed up as her heartbeat began racing in a way that had nothing to do with the exercise.

She upped the trot to a run, her legs pumping, her arms moving as she increased her pace. She wasn't going to think about it. She wasn't going to dwell on the delicious moment when day turned into evening. She wasn't going to remember the tingle of anticipation that ran through her as she sat on the terrace in the evening sun, an untouched book and an iced drink before her, pretending not to listen for the purr of his car. Pretending not to hope.

She was most certainly not going to recall the thrill that filled her entire body, the sweet jolt that shot through her from head to toe, when he finally appeared.

Time was moving so fast. She had less than a month left in Trengarth. So she wasn't going to question what was going on here. She was going to enjoy the moment. And what moments they were. She couldn't remember the last time she and Hugo had made love twice in a week, let alone in a night, whereas she and Jonas... Well...

Sure, she hadn't planned for this, and for once she was being the exact opposite of measured and sensible. But wasn't that the point? She had to make the most of this enforced time out. It would all get back to normal soon enough.

Starting with today. Her first interview.

It was all happening so fast. Just a few days since the initial approach, the phone call, and now a face to face interview. In New York.

It was perfect. This would show Hugo and the partners. She could just imagine the gossip. *Lawrie Bennett? Out in New York, I believe. A most prestigious firm.* Anticipation shot through her. It was as if a load had been lifted. To be approached for such a role meant that her reputation was intact. It should be, but sudden departures were responsible for more scurrilous gossip in the legal world than any tabloid could imagine.

Lawrie slowed her pace as the cliff path began to wind down towards the harbour and the pretty stone cottages clustered beneath her. Which was Jonas's? He hadn't asked her over and she was certainly not going to invite herself, to admit she was curious.

Even if she was.

Was it the one overlooking the harbour, with the pretty roof garden situated in exactly the right place for the afternoon sun? The three-storeyed captain's house, imposing its grandeur on the smaller houses around? The long, low whitewashed cottage, its yard covered in tumbling roses?

*What did it matter anyway?*

Despite herself she slowed as she jogged along the harbour-front, looking into the windows, hoping for some clue. She didn't care, she told herself, but she still found herself craning her neck, peeking in, searching for a sign of him.

*Beep!*

A car horn made her jump. The follow-up wolf whistle which pierced the air brought her to a skidding halt.

Lawrie turned around, hands on hips, ready for battle, only to find her mouth drying out at the sight of Jonas

Jones in that ridiculous low-slung sports car, top down.
She coloured, looking around to make sure nobody had
heard, before crossing the narrow road and leaning over
the car. 'Shush. People will hear you,' she hissed.

He raised an eyebrow mockingly and Lawrie clenched
her hands, controlling an irresistible urge to slap him. Or
kiss him. Either would be inappropriate.

'Let them,' he replied nonchalantly, that annoying eyebrow still quirked.

She wanted to reach out and smooth it down, caress
the stubble on the strong jaw, run her fingers across the
sensual lips. She clenched her hands harder. She wouldn't
give him or the curious onlookers openly watching them
the satisfaction.

Jonas leant closer, his breath warm and sweet on her
cheek. 'They all think they know anyway.'

'Let them think. There's no need to confirm it.' She was
painfully aware of people watching them—many openly.
How many times had she seen neighbours, parents at the
school gates, people in the local shop watch her mother in
the same way as her latest relationship began to disinte-
grate? 'I hate gossip, and I really hate being the focus of it.'

'Just a boss having a chat with his festival-organiser—
nothing to see…move it along,' he said, an unrepentant
grin curving the kissable mouth.

She bit her lip. She was *not* going to kiss him in public,
no matter how tempted she was. But how she wanted to.

Her eyes held his, hypnotised by the heat she saw in
the blue depths. The street, the curious onlookers faded
away for one long moment. She didn't know whether to
be relieved or disappointed when he leant back, the grin
replaced with a purposeful businesslike expression.

'I was on my way up to collect you—thought you might
appreciate a lift to the airport. Yet here you are.' He ran

his eyes appreciatively over her and she fought the urge to tug her running top down over her shorts. 'You're not really dressed for flying, though. And I don't mean to be offensive, but...'

Lawrie snorted. 'That will be a first,' she muttered.

'But I'm not sure eighties aerobics is really the right look for business class *or* an interview. You might want to get changed,' he continued, ignoring her interruption. 'I could give you a lift up—or, if you really want to finish your run, I can pick you up in ten minutes.'

'If you're in such a hurry I'd better take the lift,' Lawrie said, opening the door and sliding in, her pride refusing to admit to him that she'd had no intention of running up the hill. 'I was planning to drive myself, though. I do appreciate the offer, but can you spare the time?'

She sounded cool enough—shame about her hair, pulled high into a sweaty bun, the Lycra shorts, the sheen of sweat on her arms and chest.

'Actually, it's on my way—that's why I'm offering. I'm heading over to Dorset to look at some potential sites. I'll be passing Plymouth so I might as well drop you off.'

'Oh.' He wasn't making the journey especially. Of course he wouldn't—why would he? Her sudden sharp jolt of disappointment was ridiculous. 'Well, it's very kind of you.'

There was a long silence. She sneaked a look over to see him pushing his hair out of his eyes, his face expressionless.

'It's nothing,' he said. 'As I said, I was passing the airport anyway.'

Neither of them spoke for the two minutes it took to drive back to the cottage, and as soon as the car pulled up in the driveway Lawrie was ready to leap out. The atmosphere was suddenly tense, expectant.

'I'll be five minutes,' she called as she hurried over the lawn and round to the back door. 'Make yourself at home.'

She fumbled with the key, breathing a sigh of relief as she finally pushed the door open, almost collapsing into the sanctuary of the kitchen, then heading straight to the bathroom to peel off her sweaty clothes and get into the welcome coolness of the shower.

The same peculiar feeling of disappointment gripped Lawrie as she lathered shampoo into her hair and over her body. What did it matter if he was dropping her off in passing or making the journey especially? Either way she ended up where she needed to be. Her trip to New York would be short—just a few days—but it meant time away from Cornwall, from the festival, from Jonas. Which was good, because their lives were already re-entangling, boundaries were being crossed. This interview was a much needed reminder that there was an end date looming and neither of them could or should forget that.

It had been a sweet kind of torture, watching her Lycra-clad bottom disappear around the corner. Jonas had to hold onto every ounce of his self-control to stay in the car and not follow her right into the shower, where he would be more than happy to help her take off those very tight and very distracting shorts.

He grabbed his coffee and took a long gulp.

This was temporary. They had always had an undeniable chemistry, even when nothing else between them had worked. And now they were both single, available, it was silly to deny themselves just because of a little bit of history.

Besides, they both knew what this was. No messy emotions, no need to prove anything. No need for words. It was the perfect summer fling.

It was all under control.

She'd said five minutes so he settled in for a half-hour wait, roof down, coffee in hand, paper folded to the business pages. But in less than fifteen minutes she reappeared, wheeling a small suitcase, laptop bag and handbag slung over her shoulder. She looked clean, fresh, so smooth he wanted nothing more than to drag her back inside and rumple her up a little—or a lot.

His hands clenched on the steering wheel as his pulse began to hammer, his blood heating up.

Damn that chemistry.

He dragged his eyes down from freshly washed, still-wet hair, combed back, to creamy skin—lots of it. Bare arms and shoulders, with just a hint of cleavage exposed by the halter-necked sundress, skirting her waist to fall mid-thigh.

He stifled a groan. He had a couple of hours' driving ahead of him and it was going to be hard to concentrate with so much skin nestled next to him.

'Is that suitable for flying? You'll need a cardigan,' he bit out, wrenching his gaze from the satisfied smile she gave him as she pulled a wispy wrap from the bag hung over her shoulder. 'Hurry up and get in. There's bound to be a lot of traffic.'

The powerful sports car purred along the narrow, winding lanes connecting Trengarth to the rest of the county. Lawrie leant back in the low leather seat, feeling the breeze ruffle her hair and watching the hedges and fields flash by. The blue glint of the sea was still visible in the distance, but soon the road would take them through the outskirts of Bodmin Moor, its rolling heathland and dramatic granite tors a startling contrast to her coastal home.

Home? She felt that pang again. Home was a danger-ous concept.

'Lawrie?'

She jumped as Jonas repeated her name.

'Sorry, I was just daydreaming.'

'I know. I recognised that faraway look in your eyes,' he said wryly. 'Where were you? Round some boardroom table in New York?'

'Actually, I was thinking how beautiful it is round here.' That felt uncomfortably like a confession. 'No moors in New York.'

'No.'

Now it was his turn to stay silent, a brooding look on his face, as he navigated through open countryside and small villages until they met the main road. Suddenly the silence didn't feel quite so companionable, and after one uncomfortable minute that seemed to stretch out for at least five Lawrie began to search desperately for a topic of conversation.

It felt like a step backwards. Things had been so easy between them for the last few days—since the road trip, since that last night in the van. They had fallen into a pat-tern of colleagues by day, lovers by night—professional and focused at work, equally focused in the long, hot eve-nings.

Now she suddenly had no idea what to say.

'Will you be visiting your parents when you're in Dor-set?'

Whatever had made her say that? Of all the topics in the world.

His face darkened. 'I doubt I'll have time.'

'You'll pass by their village, though, won't you? You should just pop in for a cup of tea.'

He didn't say anything, but she could see the tanned

hands whiten as he gripped the steering wheel. She tried again, despite the inner voice telling her to back off, that it was none of her business. 'They must know the areas you're looking into. It might be interesting to hear their thoughts. Seems silly not to canvas local opinion, even if you don't take them into account.'

He was silent again. Lawrie sneaked a quick glance over, expecting to see anger, irritation in his expression. But he wasn't showing any emotion at all. She hated it—the way he could close himself off at will.

'I just think it's worth one more chance,' she said hesitantly. Why did she feel compelled to keep going with this? Because maybe this was one relationship she could fix for him? 'If they understood why you work the way you do—understood that you love Coombe End, that your changes are an evolution of their work, not a betrayal—maybe things would be better.'

He finally answered, his face forbidding. 'What makes you think I want things to be better?'

Lawrie opened her mouth, then shut it again. How could she tell him that where his parents were concerned she understood him better than he understood himself? That she knew how much he was shaped by his parents' indifference, how much he craved their respect?

'You're going to be in the area,' she said at last. 'Is popping in to see your parents such a big deal?'

He didn't answer and they continued the drive in silence. Lawrie stared unseeingly out at the trees and valleys as they flashed past, relieved when Jonas finally turned into the airport car park and pulled up at the dropping-off point.

'That's great—thank you.'

He didn't answer. Instead he got out of the car and walked round to the boot, retrieved her bag and laptop case as she smoothed her dress over her thighs and pushed herself out of the low seat.

It was hard to be dignified, getting out of a sports car.

'What time is your connection?'

She stared at him, wrenching her mind away from her thoughts to her surroundings. Back to her plans, her flight, her interview, her future. 'Oh, two hours after I get to Heathrow—which is plenty of time for Security, I hope.'

'Should be. Let me know if there are any changes with your flight back, otherwise I'll see you here.'

He was going to pick her up? Her heart lurched stupidly. 'You don't have to.'

'I know.'

'Okay, then.' She picked up her bags and smiled at him. 'Thanks, Jonas.'

'Good luck. They'd be mad not to offer you the job.'

'That's the hope.' She stepped forward and gave him a brief, light kiss, inhaling the fresh, seaside aroma of him as she did so, feeling an inexplicable tightening in her chest. 'Bye.'

He stood statue-still, not reacting to the kiss. 'Bye.'

She paused for a split second but she had no idea what she was waiting for—why she had a sudden leaden feeling in the pit of her stomach. Taking a deep breath, she picked up the bags and, with a last smile in Jonas's direction, turned and walked away towards the sliding glass doors.

'Lawrie?'

She stopped, turned, unexpected and unwanted hope flaring up inside her.

'I'll make a deal with you. I'll go and visit my parents if you email your mother.'

The familiar panic welled up. 'I don't have her email address.'

'I can forward it to you.'

'Oh.' She searched for another excuse.

'Scared?' His voice was low, understanding, comforting.

'A little.' Not that she wanted to admit to fear—not to him. 'I don't know, Jonas. I feel safer with her not in my life.'

'I know.' His mouth twisted. 'It's just one step. It doesn't have to be more.'

Just one email. It sounded like such a small gesture and yet it felt so huge.

'One step,' she echoed. 'Okay.'

'Good. I'll see you here in four days.'

And he was gone.

Five hours later Lawrie was ensconced in a comfortable reclining seat, her laptop already plugged in on the table in front of her, her privacy screen blocking out the rest of the world.

Wriggling down into her seat, Lawrie squared her shoulders against the plump supporting cushions. She loved business class! The firm's willingness to pay for it boded well.

Ostensibly her ultra-comfortable journey should ensure she arrived in New York both well rested and prepared, but although her research on the firm was open on the laptop she had barely glanced at it.

Instead she had spent an hour composing an email to her mother. Lawrie reread the few short lines again and sighed. For goodness' sake, how hard could it be? She was aiming for polite, possibly even slightly conciliatory, but she had to admit the tone was off. The words sounded snooty, accusatory, *hurt*.

Exasperated, she deleted the lot and typed a few stiff sentences as if she were addressing a stranger.

She supposed she was. Would she even recognise her mother if she sat next to her? Her early teens were so long ago. Had it hurt her mother, leaving her only daughter in Trengarth? Never seeing her again?

Did she ever wonder if she had done the right thing? Regret her past?

She wondered how Jonas was doing with his parents—if his efforts were any more successful than her own.

She shook herself irritably. For goodness' sake! She was supposed to be preparing for her interview. This was it—her big chance.

So why did she feel so empty?

Lawrie slid a little further into the plush seat and looked out of the small window at the wispy white clouds drifting lazily past. What was wrong with her? Surely she hadn't let a blue eyed surfer derail her the way he had done twelve years ago?

Hot shame flushed through her body. She couldn't—wouldn't repeat the mistakes of her past. *Because let's face it*, she thought, *ambitious little Lawrie Bennett wanted many things*. She had planned her whole life through, and getting married the year she left school, before she'd received her A-level results, going to university as an eighteen-year-old bride had not been part of that plan.

*Yet she had still said yes.*

Lawrie pulled a piece of hair down and twizzled it around her finger. That moment—the utter joy that had suffused her whole being the second he'd asked her. Had she felt like that since? Not when she'd graduated with a first, not when she'd got hired at a top City firm.

And certainly not when Hugo had proposed.

She shook herself irritably, tucking the strand of hair back into her ponytail. Joy? 'For goodness' sake, grow up,' she muttered aloud. She was in business class, flying to be interviewed for the job of her dreams, and—what? It wasn't enough?

It was everything.

She had to remember that. *Everything.*

Jonas pulled over and typed the address into his phone, but he knew long before the icon loaded that he was in the right place. Looking around the tree-lined lane, he saw a row of identikit 1930s detached houses, all painted a uniform white, every garden perfectly manicured, every drive guarded by large iron gates, every car a sleek saloon. There wasn't a plastic slide or football goal to be seen.

The quiet, still road was crying out for bikes to be pedalled along it, the wide pavements for chalk and hopscotch. But there was no one to be seen.

Jonas sighed. What was he doing here? How many times could a guy set himself up for disappointment? He wouldn't be welcome. Even if his parents liked surprises his unheralded appearance wasn't going to bring them any joy.

But he had made a deal. And he might not know much about Lawrie Bennett any more, but he did know that there was something lost at the heart of her.

That desperate need to fit in, to be in control. To follow the plan...

He'd tried to fill that void once. Maybe someone in New York could, if she could just let go of her fears. And if he could do that much for his ex-wife—well, maybe their marriage wouldn't have been such a disaster after all.

A sharp pain twisted inside him at the thought of her with someone else but he ignored it. One of them deserved to be happy; one of them should be. And himself? Well... He smiled wryly. There were moments. Moments when a deal went well, when a chord was played right, when he looked around at a café full of content customers, when a wave was perfect.

Those moments were gold. He didn't ask for more. He wasn't sure he was capable of more.

Sighing, Jonas looked down at the icon on his phone, busily flashing away, signalling a road just to the left. He was pretty sure the next few moments were going to be anything but gold. But he'd promised.

And he always kept his word.

Why did his parents favour cups that were so damn small? And chairs that were so damn uncomfortable? And wallpaper that was so very, very busy? And, really, would it hurt them to smile?

The silence stretched on, neither side willing to break it. Side? That, thought Jonas, was a very apt word. Somehow—so long ago he had no idea when or why—they had become entrenched on opposite sides of a chasm so huge Jonas didn't think there was any way across it at all.

'So…' he said slowly. Speaking first felt like giving in, but after all he *had* intruded on them. 'I was just passing…'

'Where from?'

Did he just imagine that his mother sounded suspicious? Although, to be fair, he hadn't been 'just passing' in four years—not since the day he had told them that he had bought their beloved hotel.

'I was dropping Lawrie off at the airport.'

'Lawrie? You're back together?'

Now *that* emotion he could identify. It was hope. Even his father had looked up from his teacup, sudden interest in his face. Lawrie was the only thing he'd ever done that they'd approved of—and they hadn't been at all surprised when she'd left him.

'She's working for me this summer. Just a temporary

thing before she moves to New York. And, no, we're not back together.' It wasn't a lie. Whatever was going on, they weren't back together.

'Oh.'

The disappointment in his mother's voice was as clear as it was expected. Jonas looked around, desperate for something to catch his eye—another conversation-starter. A spectacularly hideous vase, some anaemic watercolours… But something was lacking—had always been lacking. And it wasn't a simple matter of wildly differing tastes.

'Why don't you have any photos?' he asked abruptly.

The room was completely devoid of anything personal. Other people's parents displayed their family pictures as proudly as trophies: bald, red-faced babies, gap-toothed schoolchildren, self-conscious teens in unflattering uniforms.

The silence that filled the room was suddenly different, charged with an emotion that Jonas couldn't identify.

His mother flushed, opened her mouth and shut it again. 'Dad?'

Jonas stared at his father, who was desperately trying to avoid his eye, looking into the depths of the ridiculously tiny teacup as if it held the answer to the secret of life itself.

'Dad,' he repeated.

The anger he had repressed for so long—the anger he'd told himself he didn't feel, the anger that was now boiling inside him—was threatening to erupt. He swallowed it back, tried to sound calm, not to let them know that he felt anything.

'I know I'm not the son you wanted, but—really? Not even one photo?'

'Leave it, Jonas,' his father said loudly, putting his cup down so decidedly it was a miracle the thin china didn't break in two.

'Why?' he persisted.

He would not leave it. For so many years he had endured their disapproval and their silence, their refusal to engage with him. He'd listened to their instructions, to their plans for his life—and then he'd gone ahead and done what he wanted anyway. But suddenly he couldn't leave it—didn't want to walk away.

He wanted answers.

'I appreciate that I don't live my life the way you want me to, that I didn't make the most of the opportunities you gave me, and I admit that failing my exams at sixteen wasn't the smartest move.'

He tried a smile but got nothing back. His father was still trembling with some repressed emotion; his mother was pale, still as stone.

'But,' he carried on, determined that *this* time they would hear him, *this* time he would have his say, 'I have an MBA, I have a successful business, I own a house, I'm a good boss, I give to charity.' Despite himself, despite his best intentions, his voice cracked. 'I just don't know why I have never been good enough for you.'

There. It was said.

The silence rippled round the room.

His mother got to her feet, so pale her carefully applied make-up stood out stark against her skin. 'I can't do this, Jonas,' she said.

He stared at her in astonishment. Were those tears in her eyes?

'I'm sorry, I just can't.' She laid one, shaky hand on his shoulder for an infinitesimal second and then was gone, rushing out of the room.

What the hell…? He'd expected indifference, or anger, or some lecture about what a waste of space he had always been, but this tension strung as tight as a quivering bow was unexpected. It was terrifying. Whatever was going on here was bigger than the fall-out of some adolescent rebellion.

Jonas glared at his father, torn between utter confusion and sudden fear. 'Dad? What *is* going on? I think I deserve the truth, don't you?'

# CHAPTER EIGHT

IT WAS HORRENDOUSLY hot, and the airport was overcrowded as families, couples, grandparents waited anxiously, pressing close to the gate, necks craning for the first glimpse of a loved one.

Some had even brought signs—handwritten, decorated. Jonas looked over at the young man barely out of his teens, standing at the very end, as close as he could get to the gate without crossing the yellow line. He had love hearts all over his sign. The poor sap.

He even had flowers, Jonas noted. A bouquet so big it almost obscured the sign.

Whereas it was all Jonas had been able to do to turn up at all. He was still processing the afternoon he had spent with his parents. He wasn't sure he could share it with anyone, and Lawrie was bound to ask.

After all they had a deal.

'Hey.'

He hadn't even seen her come through the gate. 'Hey, yourself. Good trip?'

She beamed. 'The best. They're a really exciting firm, with some great projects, so fingers crossed they liked me.'

'I bet they loved you.' He took her bag from her and led the way out of the airport to the short-stay car park. Suddenly, despite everything, the day seemed brighter, the clouds drifting away. It was too nice to be shut away in an office—even his office.

'Are you exhausted?' he asked.

Lawrie shook her head. 'I might have had a red-eye flight, but I was spoiled enough to spend it tucked up in business class. I feel fresh as a daisy! I swear those seats are comfier than my bed.'

'I was thinking a picnic,' he said. 'There's a nice farm-shop about twenty minutes away where we could grab some supplies. Unless you want to get back?'

Lawrie looked down at herself and pulled a face, although Jonas thought she looked immaculate, in dark skinny jeans that clung to her legs in a way he definitely approved of.

'I need a shower at some point in the next few hours,' she said. 'No matter how air-conditioned the airport and plane are, I still land feeling completely grubby. But fresh air sounds good, and I guess I could eat. My business class freshly cooked breakfast seems a long time ago now.'

'Nice subtle reminder of your exalted status.' Jonas nodded approvingly. 'You'll need to up the stakes when you get to New York, though, I believe lawyers on the Upper East Side only travel by private jet.'

'Ha-ha.' Lawrie stuck her tongue out at him as they reached the car and he opened the door for her before stowing her cases in the boot.

'Your post is on your seat,' he called over. 'I knew you would want to look through it before you relaxed properly.'

'Thanks,' she called back.

Closing the door, he saw she was already engrossed, flipping through the pile and sorting the mail into order. She was up to date with her emails too, he knew. Lawrie wouldn't allow a little thing like the Atlantic Ocean to stand between her and her work.

A good reason to make sure she had the afternoon off. And it would probably do him good too. He'd barely left his desk these last two days. Sometimes hard work was the only way to cope.

He slid into his seat and looked over at her. She was staring at an envelope, her cheeks pale. He recognised it: a thick, expensive cream envelope with the name of her old firm stamped on the back. It was probably her P45 or something.

It didn't explain the pallor in her cheeks, though.

'Everything okay?' He turned the key and felt the engine purr into life.

She didn't answer.

'Law?'

She looked across, a dazed expression on her face. 'Hmm? Yes, I'm fine.'

But she didn't sound convincing.

'Are you going to open that?' He nodded towards the envelope. She was turning it over and over, as if she could read the contents through touch alone.

'Yes, of course. It's probably some HR stuff.'

But she looked anxious as she tore the envelope open, pulling out a handwritten letter with another slip of paper clipped to the outside. It looked like a cheque.

'What on earth…?'

'Redundancy?' he suggested.

She shook her head. 'That will get paid with my last month's salary, and not until my notice is completely served,' she said, unfolding the letter and slipping the cheque out. Her eyes widened. 'My goodness—how many noughts?' Then, her voice seemed strangled with what sounded suspiciously like tears. 'It's from Hugo.'

The ex.

Jealousy, ugly and hot, seared through him. What was he doing writing to her? Sending her cheques?

Grimly he set his eyes on the road ahead, concentrating on the exit from the airport, trying to give Lawrie the space she needed as she fought for control.

'It's for my share of the house,' she said after a while, her voice a little croaky. 'He didn't have to. I mean, yes, I contributed to the bills, of course—paid for decorating and stuff. But it was his house. Legally I'm not entitled to anything. My name wasn't on the mortgage.'

Was she regretting leaving him? A man who made such generous gestures? Thoughtful? 'Will you accept?'

There was a pause.

'Yes,' she said finally. 'My pride tells me to shred it and return it to him, but he's right. If I hadn't moved in with him I'd have bought my own place, made money on that. This cheque is enough for a reasonable deposit so I can buy in New York, or wherever I end up. I'd be a fool to turn it down. And I guess morally I do deserve it.'

She was silent again as she read the rest of the letter, all her attention on the closely written lines until an exclamation burst out, her voice high with shock 'He's getting married! In September. His fiancée is pregnant so they're rushing it through.'

Indignation replaced the jealousy.

'He has a *fiancée*? A *pregnant* fiancée? How on earth did he manage that? You've only been apart a couple of weeks! Unless he was cheating on you?'

The colour in her cheeks gave him the answer.

Jonas whistled softly. 'What a bastard!'

Lawrie didn't answer for a bit, turning the letter over to read it again. 'No. He isn't—not really.'

It was odd, listening to her defend another man. A man she had lived with.

'Okay, that's not entirely true. He behaved horribly, but I think it was my fault—at least partly.' She whispered the last part, tears choking her voice again.

Jonas's first instinct was to pull over, to pull her into his arms and comfort her. But one look at her rigid face as she fought for control dissuaded him. She was so private, so secretive, he instinctively knew she'd clam up if he offered sympathy.

He kept his voice impersonal. 'Your fault how? Because you left?'

'Because I didn't love him. Not in the way he deserved to be loved. I see that now.' She looked away, out of the window, and when she spoke again her voice was level. Composed. 'I wasn't entirely honest with you. It was just too humiliating. I didn't leave Hugo. I didn't change the plan. It was changed for me the day I found him with someone else. If it had been up to me I'd still be there, working towards making partner, putting off planning my wedding, engaged to someone I couldn't admit I didn't love.'

'He didn't deserve you.' Jonas knew that absolutely. If he had he would have been faithful.

She shook her head. 'He really did love me once. And I wanted to love him, I thought I did, but...' She faltered. 'Ouch—honesty hurts, doesn't it? Truth is, I think it was the lifestyle I wanted—the package. He should have someone who doesn't care about the package, who wants him because he is kind and decent.' She sniffed. A slight sound that almost broke his heart. 'I hope he's found that.'

'That's big of you. Really.'

When Lawrie had left him the last thing he'd wished for was her happiness. It shamed him to remember how bitter he had been.

'There was a point when I could happily have castrated

him with a spoon,' she admitted. 'And strangled *her* with her own leopard print thong.'

Jonas's eyebrows rose at the extraordinary visual and he tried his best to control a smirk. A watery giggle next to him confirmed his failure.

'But I was more unhappy about having to leave the firm than about the infidelity. I think, if he'd offered I would have allowed him to grovel and pretend I hadn't seen anything. Wow, I'm pitiful.'

'That *is* a little sad,' he agreed. 'But why did you have to be the one to go?'

'Because his grandfather founded the firm. Oh, my payoff will be good, my reference glowing—as it should be!—but it was made clear that they would prefer me to pack up, get out and keep my mouth shut. And I was too embarrassed to fight.' She sighed. 'So there you are—the big, ugly truth. The real reason I turned up at the Boat House alone on my thirtieth. Do you hate me?'

'I think you're amazing,' Jonas said.

He honestly did. This woman was strong—a survivor.

'And I'm glad you found your way home to Trengarth. Even if it's just for the summer.' He reached over and put his hand on her knee. 'I'm glad I've had this opportunity to know you again. And,' he added with a teasing smile, 'you're a great project manager!'

'So…' Lawrie lay back on the picnic blanket, looking up at the sky. 'I did it. Are you proud?'

'Did what?'

Jonas knew exactly what she was talking about. He still didn't know what he was going to say—if he could be honest.

He opted for diversionary tactics. 'Ate your own body

weight? Because I have to say that was a pretty impressive amount of food.'

'I blame the sea air,' Lawrie said thoughtfully. 'I never ate like this in London. It's a good thing I'm off soon—there isn't enough exercise in the world... But, no, that's not what I meant. I emailed my mother. Proud?'

'Mmm,' he said noncommittally. Aware of her sudden keen scrutiny, Jonas tried for more enthusiasm. 'That's great. Did she reply?'

It was Lawrie's turn to sound less than enthusiastic. 'Oh, yes—a great long stream of consciousness that was all about her.' She pulled a face. 'Not one question about me or what I'm doing.'

Jonas propped himself up on an elbow and looked down at her. 'I'm sorry.'

'Don't be.' Lawrie sat up, wrapping her arms around her knees and staring out to sea. 'Of course she *is* monumentally self-centred—I knew that. What kind of woman ditches her teenage daughter to go trekking? Doesn't come to her own mother's funeral? Truth is, I've spent my whole life hating her and at the same time wanting her to put me first, you know? But reading that email I just felt sorry for her. Which is an improvement, I guess. And I know she isn't capable of more. I just have to accept that.'

She turned to him, her face alight with interest.

'So…?'

'So?'

Here it was. And he still didn't know what to say.

'Did you go?'

The sand suddenly felt lumpy, hard beneath his elbow, and Jonas lay down. It was his turn to look up at the clear blue sky, the wisps of cloud lazily bobbing overhead. The weight of his newly acquired burden pressed down on him. Maybe sharing would help.

If anything could.

And Lawrie would be going soon. She wouldn't be there to constantly remind him, asking him how he felt, looking at him with sympathy or pity. And if she recoiled from him in disgust—well, maybe he deserved it.

'Yes,' he said slowly. 'I went.'

'And…?'

She seemed to sense the turmoil in him, was looking down at him in concern.

'Jonas, what is it? What did they say?'

He took a deep breath. 'I asked them why they had no photos of me—not one anywhere.' The words were almost dragged out of him, yet the very act of saying them relieved some of the almost unbearable load his father had bequeathed to him.

Lawrie was utterly still, her concentration all fixed on him. 'And…?'

'At first? Nothing. Then finally my father admitted they couldn't bear to—couldn't bear to have pictures of their only son. It was too painful a reminder.' He exhaled noisily. 'My presence, my *existence*, is too painful a reminder.'

He turned his head to look at her, to see her reaction as he finally said the words.

'There were two of us, Law. I had a twin—a sister. But we were early…too early. I was a lot bigger than her, so when we were born I had a better chance. She was too small.' He paused, remembering the utter look of desolation, of loss, on his father's face as he'd stumbled through the family secret.

'The doctors said if I hadn't taken up so much of the blood supply things could have been different—they might have saved us both. But as it was I killed her, Law. I killed my twin sister.'

For an agonisingly long time Lawrie didn't say anything. Was she horrified at him? By him? By what he had done? Because *he* was. This explained everything, and suddenly he couldn't blame his parents at all.

She was bolt upright, one hand covering her mouth, tears swimming in her eyes. One was falling and rolling unheeded down her cheek. With a muffled sob she turned to him, her arms reaching out, enfolding him, pulling him close, pulling him in.

'You poor boy,' she whispered, her tears soaking into his hair. 'It wasn't your fault—you hear me? Don't let *any-one* put this horrible thing onto you. It wasn't your fault.'

Jonas knew he should pull away, that the temptation to sink into her and never let go was too strong right now— that letting her go might be the hardest thing he had ever had to do. But the relief of another person's touch, another person's warmth, was too much, too intoxicating for a long, blissful moment, and he bathed in her warmth, in her understanding, before pulling back, reaching for her hand, lacing her fingers into his.

'If I had been a different kind of boy it might all have been easier,' he said after a while, caressing the soft smoothness of her hand. 'If I had been more like them… quieter…maybe they could have accepted me. But I was so boisterous, so energetic—always wanting to be different. I was always showing them how strong I was, how healthy. A constant reminder that if I had been a little *less* strong then she might have made it too.'

'No.'

The strength in her voice surprised him, her conviction ringing true.

'No. You mustn't ever think that. What happened was horrible—*horrible*. Your poor parents…I can't even imagine…' She shuddered. 'But it was no one's fault. Especially not yours.' She shook her head. 'And although I feel desperately sorry for your parents I could also shake them. Pushing you away, rather than thanking God every moment that they were blessed with one healthy, amazing boy? That's their tragedy. And they have to live with it. But you...' Her fingers tightened on his. 'You let this go.'

They sat, hands entwined, staring out to sea, neither of them speaking, and gradually, slowly, Jonas felt some of the darkness lift. He would always have to carry this knowledge, this loss, with him, but Lawrie was right. He didn't have to let it define him—even if his parents had allowed it to define their lives, their relationship with him.

There was nothing he could do about that. His card had been marked from the moment of his birth. He just had to live with that and move on—properly this time.

'At least...' he said slowly. 'At least I know it wasn't me—some terrible defect in me. I used to wonder, you know...wonder why they couldn't love me...why I was so damn unlovable.'

'Lots of people love you.' Lawrie leant in close, her hair soft on his cheek. 'Gran loved you—she adored you. When I left—when we split up—she told me I was a fool, that there was no finer man out there. Who knows? Maybe she was right.'

'She was definitely right,' he said, and was rewarded with a low laugh. 'Thank you,' he said. 'For listening.'

She turned to him, eyes serious. 'You know, I thought coming back here was going to be the most humiliating experience—facing you again, no job, no Hugo.' She shook her head. 'And it was pretty awful at first, but in a way I'm glad. That we got the chance to reconnect. To be friends again.'

'Is that what the kids call it nowadays?'

She smiled, moving her hand up to push the hair from

his eyes in an old, intimate gesture. 'I believe the phrase says "with benefits".'

He stared deep into her eyes, watched her pupils darken, grow, heard her breath quicken. His hand caressed hers, moving down to circle the delicate skin at her wrist. Right now all he wanted, needed, was to lose himself in this person who believed in him, who had once needed him.

'I, for one,' he said, 'am a great fan of benefits. I think they should be explored in much greater detail.'

Her pulse leapt at his touch. 'How great?'

'Let's go home,' he said. 'And I'll show you.'

# CHAPTER NINE

DAMN, SHE WAS daydreaming again.

It was this office. Too much space, too many large windows with far too beautiful views. It just wasn't conducive to concentration. She'd choose her old windowless, airless, tiny internal office over this spacious luxury any day. At least she'd never been distracted there.

And it *was* the view, the sun, the come-hitherness of the summer's day that was the problem. It was not—most certainly *not*—the last few days.

Lawrie gazed unseeingly at the complicated document in front of her, detailing band schedules, riders, accommodation, entourage lists, her mind churning.

After the initial awful shock, the sudden grief and guilt, Jonas had seemed freed, unburdened. And hellbent on getting as much benefit out of their newfound friendship as he possibly could.

And she was matching him every step of the way.

She told herself it was because she was worried about him, because he seemed to be coping too well, because she could still see the hurt behind the playboy smile, but the selfish truth was that the benefits were working both ways.

Working really well.

It was no good. For once work was letting her down. Maybe she needed to take a break.

Sitting up, she grabbed her phone and flicked to her personal emails—belated birthday greetings from friends who didn't even know she'd left London, the usual deluge of sales emails offering her shoes, spa days, holidays, clothes. None of it mattered. Not any more.

'That's rather a scary grimace. Planning some street theatre?'

She looked up with a start. 'Some warning would be nice. You shouldn't sneak in like that.' It was the shock that had made her heart leap—not the sight of Jonas, immaculate in tennis whites, legs bronzed and muscular, hair damp with exertion pushed back off his forehead.

After all, *any* passable man looked good in tennis clothes.

Still, despite herself, she let her gaze travel from the dark blond tip of his head down over broad shoulders to his chest, clearly outlined through the fine white material, down past the shorts that clung to his narrow hips far too comfortably for her peace of mind and down those rather magnificent legs.

Lawrie swallowed, desperate to moisten her suddenly dry mouth as a jolt of desire pulsed through her, as a sweet, persistent ache settled in the pit of her stomach.

'You look like you've been busy.'

'Got to make sure all the facilities are in perfect working order.' He grinned at her boyishly. 'It's a hard job, but someone has to do it.'

Sauntering across the room, Jonas perched next to her on the edge of her desk.

Lawrie swallowed, the spreadsheet, her emails all forgotten. There was so *much* of him, and it was all so close. So much toned, tanned flesh, perfectly set off by the white fabric. Too much of the overwhelmingly male scent evoking grass, sun and sea. She licked her lips nervously, unsure whether she wanted to push the self-assured interloper off the desk or push him back and straddle him.

'And are they? In working order?'

Goodness, why did everything sound like a *double entendre*?

'Of course.' He smiled at her, slow and sweet. 'Want to find out?'

'No, I haven't played in years.' And she looked away from his knowing grin, feeling the heat spreading downwards, pooling in the pit of her belly. She tried again. 'I don't really have time to play. I watch a little, though. The firm had a corporate box at Wimbledon.'

He pulled a face. 'Wining and dining clients, hospitality boxes—it's all right for some, I suppose. It's not the real deal, though, is it?'

'It's different,' she said, ruthlessly pushing aside memories of being trapped in conversation with CEOs who knew nothing and cared less about the top-quality tennis being played out before them, who were there solely because it showed that they were *somebody*.

'But not better?' He was still sitting by her, disconcertingly close, one trainer-clad foot swinging. 'Although I hear the queuing facilities are much better now, and people have proper tents and loos and everything.' He put on a quavery voice. 'People today don't know they're born. In my day a couple of fold-up chairs and a sleeping bag did us.'

'Men's quarter-finals day,' she remembered. The sound of the racket hitting the ball, the smell of grass mingling with traffic fumes and sun cream, the taste of sweet, succulent strawberries, rich cream, and Pimm's fizzing on her tongue. 'Seems so long ago. We saw Agassi!'

He laughed. 'You can keep your Seychelles and your Maldives. A dusty pavement and top-quality tennis is the perfect honeymoon destination in my book. You wanted me to buy you an Agassi T-shirt!'

She laughed with him, couldn't help it. 'Well, I *was* eighteen,' she defended herself. 'Have you been since?'

He shook his head. 'June and July are such busy times for me. Pete, our pro, usually goes—takes some of the local kids he coaches—but I haven't joined them yet. One day.'

She nodded her agreement and tried to think of something else to say. Hard to think with him so close, so casual, so overpowering, so very male. Her mouth was dry, her mind suddenly empty. *Say something, damn it,* she thought. She opened her mouth but no sound came out.

'I was going to go for a swim,' Jonas said, seemingly unaware of her awkwardness.

Didn't he feel the uncomfortable silence? The weight of their past happiness?

'Fancy it?'

'Oh, I…well…' She fumbled desperately for the right words. If she was finding Jonas hard to cope with when he was semi-respectably clad in tennis whites then how would she manage with him wearing nothing but swim shorts? 'I haven't brought anything suitable to swim in,' she finished.

'Good thing we have a shop,' he said, and his eyes took on a disconcerting gleam. 'Or you could just wear nothing at all…'

For a long second Lawrie couldn't breathe. All she could do was stare at him, hypnotised by the heat in his eyes, the way the blue deepened until she was drowning in their azure depths. The ache in her stomach intensified, moved even lower, and for one hot, blazing moment all she was aware of was him.

*Zzzzzzzz.*

Lawrie jumped. The buzz of her phone as it signalled

the arrival of a text message broke the spell. Blinking her way slowly into reality, she realised in one mortifying moment that she was leaning forward, moving closer to him. With an effort she wrenched her gaze away, leaning back and looking intently at her computer as if all the answers were to be found there.

She summoned up a light, amused tone. 'I thought this was a respectable family hotel?'

Jonas still looked ridiculously at ease, seemingly unaware of her struggle to stay focused. 'It is—and I have something a bit more refreshing in mind than a pool full of overtired toddlers and harassed parents. Ready?'

Sensible Lawrie, clipboard-touting, plan-making Lawrie, knew it was a bad idea. She glanced at the spreadsheets still open on her desk. The safe, easy option. The right option.

But not the only option.

Just a couple of weeks left. A short while to be someone else. Someone less measured, less careful, less controlled. Someone free.

And then she would go to New York, Sydney, Toronto—wherever—and this summer would be a dream, a memory.

Someone else.

A smile curved her lips. She took a deep breath, kicked the chair back, away from the desk, and swivelled it towards Jonas, still sitting there on the desk, one bare leg idly swinging, watching her with an impenetrable gaze.

'Let's go,' she said.

Lawrie felt like a schoolgirl playing hooky as Jonas led her across a field at the back of the hotel garden towards the path that led down to the cove bordering the hotel property. It wasn't a private beach, but as there was no public right of way to it, it was used solely by hotel guests and anyone with access to a boat.

'Feels good doesn't it?'

'What does?'

'Being outside when you should be at work.'

'But you're my boss,' she pointed out as they slowed to a jog. 'And as I'm not being paid I'm not sure this technically counts as skiving.'

He shook his head, a mischievous smile playing around the sensual lips. 'Admit it—you still feel half guilty, though, I bet this is the first time you've ever bunked off work.'

She didn't answer, increasing her pace so that she sprinted past him, enjoying the sun on her face, the slight breeze ruffling her hair, the unusually giddy feeling of being free. Jonas gave a startled shout as she raced ahead, before also breaking into a fast run, catching her up with long-legged strides, elbowing his way past her to reach the stile first.

'Aren't you glad I made you get changed?' he asked, glancing down at her shorts and vest top appreciably. 'Those power heels of yours wouldn't have lasted five minutes.'

She pulled a face before darting round him and jumping over the stile onto the path that wound round the cliff, sniffing appreciatively. Gorse—how she loved it.

Jonas leant against the stile post, watching her. 'You look like a Labrador off after a scent.'

'It just smells so good,' she explained, knowing how idiotic she sounded.

It was funny… She'd read that smell was the best sense to evoke memories but she had never really noticed it personally before. Yet ever since she had returned to Cornwall she'd found herself reliving, remembering, her memories triggered by the very air about her. A primal creature after all, despite her veneer of city sophistication.

Jonas stepped up beside her and his hand brushed against hers. Such a small touch to provoke such intense memories. Long, lean, capable fingers entwined round hers. She felt the coolness of his palm, the slight roughness of his skin. She was preternaturally aware of every tiny square millimetre where their flesh touched, of little trickles of desire rippling up her arm. Her breasts suddenly felt full, heavy, aching, and an almost painful pressure behind her ribs echoed the intensified beating of her heart. Did he know? Was he aware of the effect his slightest touch had on her?

She didn't speak. Didn't look down at their hands. Didn't acknowledge him in any way. But she didn't pull away either.

Lost in a haze of feeling, Lawrie was unaware of where they were walking, knowing only the heady joy of touch, smell, sensation until they reached the top of the cliff.

'Where are we?' she asked looking about her in some confusion. 'This isn't the hotel beach.'

'Nope, this is the next cove along,' he explained. 'The hotel beach will be full of guests and their families, and mini-tot surf schools, sandcastle-building. All perfectly lovely, but a little more crowded than I had in mind.'

He looked back and flashed her a grin of such pure, seductive wickedness that her knees weakened and she nearly stumbled, steadying herself against the sparsely covered cliff-face with one trembling hand.

*He means swimming,* she told herself. *Get a grip.*

'Careful,' he called back as she picked her way down the dirt track. 'There're lots of little stones—it's easy to slip.'

'I do know how to walk down a cliff path,' she told him, but she slowed down a little, dragging her mind away from his earlier comments and her own overheated imaginings until she reached the bottom and looked about her.

It was a tiny little cove—a perfect little semi-circle of fine sand leading down to lapping waves, hidden from the rest of existence by the tall cliffs whose arms reached out into the sea on either side. A few rocks clustered at the foot of the cliff.

Jonas was standing by a large flat one and had laid the small rucksack he was carrying on top, was already shaking out the tartan blanket and laying out a couple of towels.

'It's beautiful,' Lawrie said, looking around in delight. 'I can't believe I've never been here before.'

'You can't access it from Trengarth,' Jonas said. 'With the hotel so close nobody ever comes here. Which is why I like it.'

Having taken care of the contents of the rucksack he was kicking off his trainers, pulling his T-shirt over his head. She stared, fascinated, at the still slim but perfectly toned chest, at the smattering of golden hair over his well-formed pecs turning into a fascinating line running down his taut stomach and disappearing into the top of his swim shorts.

Lawrie swallowed, an insistent pulse of desire throbbing through her entire body.

'Come on,' he teased her, moving from foot to foot.

Reluctantly she tore her eyes from his torso and looked out at the sea. Yes, it was calm, blue, inviting, and it was August, but even so...

He followed her gaze and sighed. 'Wimp,' he said. 'Honestly, when we were kids we swam in just our costumes Easter to October—now it's wetsuits all year round. Does no one like the feel of water on their skin any more?'

'You always liked your wetsuit well enough,' she retorted. But, stung by his words, she reluctantly pulled off her vest top, glad that she had bought a modest one-piece from the hotel shop and not the skimpy bikini he had picked out for her.

'I like my wetsuit for surfing, when I'm in the water for hours at a time, not for a good swim. The cold's half the fun.' He eyed her as she slipped the shorts off, an appreciative glint in his eye. 'That's not the itsy-bitsy polka-dot bikini I picked out, but it's rather nice.'

She looked down at herself. The fifties-style swimsuit suited her, she thought. The nipped in waist added curves to her leanness; the halter-style neckline lifted her breasts. He was still looking at her, his eyes lingering on the hint of cleavage, the exposed tops of her breasts. Feeling suddenly, unaccountably shy she took a step back, towards the sea.

'Last one in is a rotten egg,' Lawrie said, and took off, running towards the sea.

Jonas stood still for one disbelieving second before he took off after her, running up behind her, swinging her into his arms and running them both headlong into the sea until he was waist-high when, despite her laughing entreaties, he dropped her straight into the cold, clear water.

It was freezing. Like little shards of ice on her overheated skin. She sank beneath the surface, spluttering with outrage, with laughter, with cold. Her feet found the sandy bottom and she steadied herself and stood up, revenge on her mind.

Jonas had already anticipated her mood and was swimming away from her, widthways across the bay, reaching out with sure, sharp strokes. She stood for a minute, pushing her wet hair away from her face, blinking the water out of her eyes and watching him—sleek, strong, completely at home in the marine environment he loved. He turned, floating onto his back, and gave her a little ironic wave.

*Right.* She set out across the water. Goodness, it was

hard work swimming against the waves; a flat gym pool
was no substitute for the sea. Forgetting Jonas for a second, she stopped swimming, treading water and allowing
the waves to bob her up and down, closing her eyes and
enjoying the sensation of the hot sun contrasting with the
cold sea, the sound of the waves, the seagulls overhead—
until a splash of sea water on her face brought her back to
the present with a startled cry.

'You…' she threatened scooping up some water and
flinging it at him.

Laughing, he dodged out of the way. Lawrie pursued
him, pushing more and more water at him, until with a
triumphant yell she doused him, moving in, holding him
back whilst she thoroughly dunked him, enjoying the feeling of power, the play of muscles in his shoulders as she
held him down, enjoying the way their bodies entwined
as they play-fought. The hardness of him, the strength…
She shivered.

He stopped fighting her, suddenly still, waist-deep in
the sea. Her hands stilled on his shoulders as he straightened, and her wet body was close to his as one of his arms
came to rest loosely round her waist. The other was at
the nape of her neck until he drew a slow, tantalising line
down her bare spine, his hand coming to rest on the small
of her back, his long, oh, so capable fingers drawing a slow
circle. Every sense she had seemed to be centred in that
small area of sensitised skin.

'Jonas?'

It was such a small sound—a question, an entreaty? She
couldn't have said. She just knew that she needed something—something more, something only this man could
give her. She moved in closer, leg against leg, her aching
breasts pressed against the tautness of his chest, her face
raised pleadingly to his. This was why they had come here,

wasn't it? For this…for the sheer sweetness of the moment as he finally lowered his mouth to hers.

Light kisses, delicate kisses, lips against lips, murmured endearments and still such restraint. One of his hands was still caressing the small of her back, the other was lightly on her waist as she held onto his shoulders, pressing herself closer against him, trying to get more of him, to deepen the kiss, to lose control.

Just for a while. Just for now, for this moment.

He picked her up again, swinging her up as if she weighed no more than a child, his arms tight around her. Without saying a word he strode towards the shore.

Lawrie felt a dreamlike calm mixed with an almost unbearable anticipation as she wound her arms around his neck and snuggled in, pressing small butterfly kisses onto the side of his neck. Her tongue flicked out, tasting the salt, and he gave a groan. Emboldened, she carried on exploring the wet, golden flesh, following drops of water with her lips, enjoying the effect she was clearly having on him.

He reached the picnic blanket and knelt down, placing her carefully onto it. She lay there waiting, welcoming, wanting, rolling towards him as he lay beside.

She needed this…she *deserved* this.

'Lawrie?'

His eyes were dark with desire, and the fire she saw in them elicited a primal response in her. The ache pulsating between her thighs was insistent, strong, powerful. She didn't answer. Words were beyond her. She was all instinct, all desire. She rose to her knees and leant over, pressing her mouth to his, her arms on either side of him supporting her weight.

With a groan he grabbed onto her, rolling her on top of him, deepening the kiss as his hands finally moved away from her waist, roaming over her body, touching, caressing, lighting sparks everywhere they travelled. She was aware of nothing but him, the planes of his body, the sensations his oh, so skilled fingers were inducing in her, his kiss, the taste of him, the feel of his lips, his tongue.

Sun, sea, salt, sensation overwhelmed her, whisking Lawrie away to some faraway place where all that existed was this. All that existed was them, just as it had used to be. She closed her eyes, allowing his touch, his mouth, his body to take her away, to soar over the cliffs and spiral up into the sky.

Jonas lay stretched out on the blanket, Lawrie curved into his side, one arm flung lightly across his chest. She was dozing, almost asleep but not quite, her eyes closed, her breathing even. Despite the lateness of the hour the air was still warm, sticky. He felt...*content*. That was the nearest word for the relaxed laziness of his body and mind.

For once Jonas didn't want to jump up, make his excuses and leave, break the intimate silence with meaningless small talk designed to keep a clear distance between his companion and himself. He wanted to stay here, holding Lawrie Bennett, and just *be*.

Although he really ought to think about getting dressed. He had been to this cove many times, and had yet to see another living soul beyond the gulls, but there was always a first time, and he'd rather not be naked when that time came. He ran a hand along the length of Lawrie's body, shoulder to hip, feeling the slight curves, marvelling at the silkiness of her skin. Even now, unclothed, half-asleep, there was a quiet dignity to her—a dignity that had been noticeable by its absence during the last hour.

He smiled to himself as he ran his hand back up her body, feeling her quiver under his touch. Passionate, unguarded, fiery, tender—she had been many things but not dignified.

'Lawrie?'

'Hmm?'

'Wake up, honey, it's getting late.'

She muttered something indistinguishable, rolling over away from him. He flicked his eyes down her graceful back, lingering at her curved behind, before trying again.

'Come on, Lawrie, time to get dressed. You wouldn't want some ramblers copping an eyeful, would you? Though it'd probably make their day—do wonders for the local tourist economy.'

She muttered again but rolled back, pushing herself up until she was sitting, legs drawn close to her chest as she flicked her hair out of her still sleepy eyes. 'What time is it?'

He held up his bare arm. 'No watch…no phone,' he teased. 'Can you cope with being so far from communication and order?'

She smiled, but warily. 'Good thing I brought my bag,' she said. 'I think I should probably get dressed, though. Erm…could you possibly…?' She gestured at her clothes, neatly folded on top of the rock.

'Of course,' he said, getting to his feet and noticing how her eyes were drawn towards his body before she lowered them, a faint blush staining her cheeks. Taking pity, he threw her shorts and T-shirt to her before retrieving his, unable to keep from watching her as she wriggled into her clothes in as discreet a style as possible.

'Don't mind me,' he said, and grinned as her head came up and she glared at him.

'A gentleman would turn his back.'

'Poor gentleman—he'd miss out.'

She stood up slowly, stretching out her arms and legs

with a lithe grace. 'Do you want a hand?' She gestured at
the blanket and towels.

'Do you want to rush off? I brought food and wine.'

She eyed him nervously. 'You said it was getting late,
that we should get back.'

'It is, and we should,' he agreed. 'But we can stay a
little longer if you want—or do you have plans tonight?'

'No, but if I drink that I won't be able to drive home,'
she pointed out as he reached into the rucksack and drew
out a bottle of wine encased in a cooling holder.

'I own a hotel. Finding a bed for the night is never
a problem.' He unscrewed the top and handed it to her.
'You're not too posh to drink from the bottle, are you?'

'Seriously?'

Her face spoke volumes but at his amused nod she
screwed up her nose and raised the bottle to her lips. Only
Lawrie Bennett could make drinking from a bottle look
refined. And sexy.

'I, however, don't own a hotel.'

'We may have a spare tent somewhere—*ow!*' This as
she flicked his shoulder smartly. 'What was that for?'

'Seriously, Jonas. What are you suggesting? That I stay
at the hotel tonight with you? People are already talking…'
Her voice trailed off.

'So what?' People always talked. They'd been talking
since the second she'd sashayed back into town. Let them.
'Come and eat something. I brought all of this for you. I'm
not lugging it back up the cliff.'

Lawrie flopped down onto the blanket next to him and
took the paper plate he was holding out to her, loading it
daintily with a selection of breads, cheeses and salads.
She began to build a towering sandwich of cheese, salad,
grapes and coleslaw.

Jonas watched, fascinated. 'That's quite some sandwich,' he said.

'Hmm, I'm not quite sure how I'm going to manage to bite into it,' she admitted. 'Maybe sandwiches could be my thing?'

'What thing?'

'Well, you said it yourself—I'm a blender. I don't have an interest that's really mine,' she said, reassembling the sandwich into several smaller parts. 'Maybe it's time I did. In New York they asked me what I liked to do in my spare time and I told them about going to museums and exhibitions. But of course that was Hugo's interest, not mine. I enjoyed them, but would I go by myself? And then I said singing, but I only do that when I'm with you. I don't know *what* I like to do apart from work.'

'And sandwich-making is your new hobby?'

'Being a foodie might be. I've had a lot of practice. Or I might take up art? What?' she asked as he shook his head.

'I've played Pictionary with you. Believe me when I say that art is *not* your thing.'

'Good point. Well, maybe quilting, or distressing furniture.'

'You could… But you don't have to decide right now, do you?'

'But if I decide before I go then I can research,' she said, taking a bite of the newly assembled sandwich. She chewed, then swallowed. 'I'll tell you what I'm not going to do, though. I am not going to date anyone I work with. Especially not my boss. Twice bitten, three times shy. Or something.'

Jonas grinned. 'Interesting statement, considering I am kind of your boss now.' His smile grew wider, more wicked, as he saw the blush colour her pale cheeks, the answering smile in her eyes. 'And, considering how you've been spending your nights lately, I have to conclude that you haven't started to enforce that rule too strictly.'

She laughed and her colour was high, her lips reddening, full, inviting. 'Ah, but we're not dating.'

'No?'

'No.'

'Then...' He leant in, close. Took her hand in his, turning it over to slowly trace a circle on her palm. 'What *are* we doing late at night, Miss Bennett?'

She swayed towards him, her hand closing onto his. Jonas slid his thumb over the plump flesh of her palm, every sense suddenly heightened. The brightness of the sun illuminated the scene in honey-coloured light: her glorious hair, the creaminess of her skin, the crash of the waves onto the shoreline, the call of the birds swooping high above, the distant coconut smell of gorse mingling with her light, fresh perfume, the silky smoothness of her hands in his. The anticipation of taste. The so very sweet anticipation...

He pulled her closer, sliding his hands out of hers and up her bare arms, then down her back, where they rested on the soft skin of her shoulderblades. His thumbs moved in small circles. She shivered under his touch, her breath speeding up, coming in small gasps, as one finger slid leisurely down her spine and then up to the nape of her neck. She swayed towards him, her face tilted up, eyelids half closed, desire and need in her expression, her eyes, her mouth. He leant in, brushed her mouth with his oh, so slowly, before trailing kisses along her jaw, down the side of her neck, to the soft pulse beating insistently in her throat.

She sighed, leaning against him as his tongue flicked out, tasted her warm skin. His hands were still playing up and down her spine, enjoying her uninhibited response to his touch, his kiss, the feel of her quivering beneath him.

'Jonas…' she began, one hand coming up to clutch his T-shirt, the other to encircle his neck.

But whatever she'd been going to say was interrupted by the shrillness of a ringtone from her bag, flung carelessly at his feet. Lawrie pulled back slowly, her expression clearing, releasing him. Reluctantly he let her go, his hand lingering against her back as he did so.

She gave him an apologetic smile. 'I should get this.'

Jonas nodded, standing up and taking a step away to recover himself as she rooted in her bag and pulled out the insistently shrieking phone.

He closed his eyes, inhaling the sea air deeply. He felt so alive. At some point in the last few days his eagerness for life, his zest, had returned—and yet he hadn't even noticed that it was gone

'Yes…yes. Absolutely. That sounds great—thank you. Yes, okay. I will. Bye.' Lawrie switched the phone off and stood still, a dazed expression on her face.

He looked over at her enquiringly. 'Bad news?'

'Huh? Oh, no.' She looked a little dazed. 'No, it was the agency.' A wide smile broke out on her face. 'The New York firm want me! They were really impressed with my interview and want me to start the day my gardening leave finishes. Isn't it wonderful?'

'Yes, wonderful.' Jonas forced a smile onto his face, made himself move over to her, pull her close into a hug. 'Of course they want you. They'd be mad not to.'

She returned the embrace, then stepped back, excitement filling her vivid dark eyes. 'New York…' Her face glowed. 'It's all coming together, Jonas.'

'Of course it is. You've made it come together.'

She had. She'd worked hard for it, picked herself up when it all had been snatched away from her. She deserved this.

So why did it feel as if the bottom had dropped out of his world?

'So?' She was tugging at his hand, playfully. 'You were saying before we were interrupted…?'

'I think we should head back,' he said, still with that forced smile on his face. 'News like this calls for champagne.'

She looked slightly surprised, a little disappointed, but didn't demur, helping him pack up, chattering about New York, the firm, the work she hoped to be doing. He listened, agreed, asked questions, and the topic lasted them all the way home.

Her eyes were firmly fixed on the bright lights of a big city once again.

# CHAPTER TEN

THE FIELDS WERE full of life. Families, couples, groups of friends, were laughing, chattering, wandering into one of the myriad teepees, tents and yurts to enjoy theatre, story-telling, music or poetry readings. Food stalls offered local beers and ciders, and every type of food, from traditional Cornish cream teas to Indian street food. Meanwhile over on the main stage one of Cornwall's best-known folk bands was entertaining a large crowd. It was exhausting. It was exhilarating. Lawrie was loving every minute of it.

When she had a chance to stop and think about it, that was.

She reached up a hand to check the earpiece that kept her connected to the main radio network bleating out security breaches, lost children, petty theft, missing artists. She was aware of every single incident taking place on the festival site. Even last night, when she'd stayed in Jonas's camper van, parked backstage so she was in the midst of the activity at all times, she'd kept it switched on. Her bulging file and her phone had been close by the bed, ready to be snatched up at a moment's notice.

She hadn't slept a wink.

But here they were: Day Two. The sun was still mirac-ulously shining, no musician so lost he couldn't be found and shoved out on stage on time, every sobbing child reunited with grateful parents. No food poisoning—yet, she thought anxiously—no serious crimes or marauding youths. Just a happy, laid-back vibe. Like a swan, with the festival-goers the body, floating serenely along, whilst she and the other members of staff paddled furiously to keep the whole thing afloat.

Goodness, what an overblown simile. She must be tired.

'When did you last eat?'

She jumped as a pair of hands landed on her shoulders, squeezing lightly.

'Have you even sat down once in the last two days?' Jonas continued mock severely. 'Taken time to listen to one of the bands you booked?'

'They were mostly booked before I started,' she protested, resisting the urge to lean back against him, to surrender the worries, the responsibilities into his oh, so capable hands for just a few seconds.

'It's on; we're live; it's all good,' he said, turning her round to face him. 'You should relax and start enjoying it.'

Lawrie hugged the black file that had been her constant companion over the last month closer to her chest. 'I'll enjoy it in twenty-four hours' time,' she told him. 'Once I know the last bands have turned up and that tonight has run smoothly.'

'Or once you've picked the last piece of litter up from the campsite in a week's time?'

She smiled. 'Maybe.'

Like her, Jonas was dressed casually. There was no sign of the successful businessman in the cut-off denims and orange T-shirt, a baseball cap covering the blond hair subtracting years from him.

'Well, at least let me buy you some lunch.'

'I'm not really hungry,' she demurred.

But, too tired to make a fuss, she allowed him to lead

her to a falafel stand and order her a humus salad wrap. The smell of fried onions and spicy chickpeas hit her as she stood there; they smelt like summer. A hollow feeling in her stomach reminded her that actually she had barely touched her breakfast that morning, nor supper the night before.

'Part of the fun of Wave Fest is the food,' he scolded her as she nibbled at the edges of the wrap, trying to avoid spilling what was inside down her top. 'You should be getting out there, experimenting.'

She licked humus off the top of the wrap. 'I'm not really the experimenting type.'

He leant in close. 'I don't agree.'

His breath tickled her ear, soft, tantalising, like a soft summer breeze. The faint brush of air on her sensitive earlobe spread through her body, warming her right down to her toes. She was almost paralysed with a sudden stab of desire—hotter, needier, more intense than ever. She swallowed, willing her knees to stay up, her stomach to settle, trying to control her traitorous body. It was the hunger, the lack of sleep, the craziness of the day. She couldn't still want him—not this much.

Her time here was almost over.

The thought was a short, sharp shock. The sweet, languorous need that had enveloped her fled as quickly as it had come. Their time together was nearly at an end—as it should be…as she wanted.

Autumn was coming. By the time the leaves had turned she would be across the ocean, beginning her new life. Jonas would be here.

They both knew long-distance didn't work. They had failed so spectacularly before.

Lawrie plastered a bright smile on her face, turning

to look at him, hoping that no trace of her thoughts remained visible.

'Have you seen many of the bands?' she asked, before taking a bite of the wrap. She nearly moaned out loud. Maybe it *was* lack of food that had caused her earlier weakness, because the combination of crisp wrap, rocket, humus and freshly made falafal was sensual overload.

'Is that good?'

Amusement was written all over his face as she nodded mutely, cramming another mouthful in.

'Maybe I was hungry,' she mumbled as she swallowed it down.

'Maybe.' His eyes were bright with laughter. 'You'll be admitting you need a nap next.'

She shook her head. 'Try coffee—caffeine might help,' she allowed.

He took her elbow, steering her effortlessly through the partying crowds. 'At least come into the hotel and sit down while you drink it,' he said, and the thought of a comfy armchair was too tempting.

She allowed him to lead her away, finishing off the wrap hungrily as they walked back to the hotel.

'Are your parents still here?' she asked as they mounted the steps and made their way through the crowded foyer to the desk. The hotel itself was strictly VIP for the duration of the festival, but it was no less hectic than outside, with staff, guests and the bands not camping backstage all based there.

'No, they left after a seafood lunch.'

His voice was non-committal. She sneaked a peep at his face but it was expressionless. Her heart sank. Getting his parents to agree to visit the hotel during the festival had seemed like a major coup; she hoped it hadn't backfired.

'That's a shame,' she said carefully. 'I would have liked to see them again.'

'Maybe it's for the best.' He flashed her a warm smile. 'My mother, despite thinking that you are far, far too good for me, has not-so-secret hopes that we may get back together and she can have her dream daughter-in-law again. Don't worry—I warned her that you're off again soon.'

He could at least sound a little regretful about it.

If only she wasn't so tired, could think more clearly. Where was that coffee?

She followed Jonas into her office and curled up thankfully on the large squishy sofa.

He cast her a concerned look. 'You are done in.'

'Not at all,' she protested. 'A coffee will sort me out.'

He looked unconvinced, but made her promise not to try and get up, no matter what, and then disappeared off to fetch her a drink. Lawrie leant back against the cool, plumped-up cushions and sighed. She *had* hoped that seeing the festival in full swing would help his parents appreciate all that Jonas had achieved, but maybe she'd been wrong.

Maybe she needed to accept that some things were best left alone. If she had kept to her original plan and stayed clear of Jonas then she would be in such a different frame of mind as she contemplated her life changing move.

She sighed. She should be much more excited, optimistic. This was what she wanted.

And yet it was as if her life had been beige and grey for the past nine years and colour had suddenly returned to it. It was bright, and it hurt sometimes, but oh, the difference it made. She just had to figure out how to keep the Technicolor when she left. When she started again.

'I managed to get you carrot cake as well.' Jonas returned to the room, carefully carrying a tray holding a cafetière of deliciously pungent coffee and a large slab of spicily fragrant sponge cake. 'Sugar and caffeine should sort you out.'

He placed the tray onto the small coffee table and poured out a cup of coffee, adding cream and handing it over to Lawrie, who sniffed ecstatically.

'I can't believe you've got me addicted to coffee again,' she said accusingly as she took a sip of the bitter brew.

'You are moving to New York,' he pointed out as he poured a cup for himself and sat next to her on the sofa. 'You don't want to be seen as a strange tea-drinking Brit who spends the whole time complaining that she can't get a proper brew, do you?'

'Well, no,' she conceded, leaning forward to hook the plate of cake off the tray. She forked a small portion of frosting and sponge and sat looking at it for a second.

'Are you going to eat that or just study it?'

'Eat it,' she retorted, and suited her action to her words. She sucked the fork appreciatively, her mind still whirling.

'Did you serve them the shellfish special or the fried fish platter?' She attempted to keep her tone light, nonchalant, and licked the last bit of frosting off the cake fork.

'Huh?'

Jonas's eyes were glued to the fork, to her tongue flicking out and licking it. She coloured, forking up some more cake casually, as if she hadn't noticed his intense gaze, the disconcerting gleam in the blue eyes.

'Your parents? I think they're more shellfish people myself, but the whitebait on the fried platter is so delicious.' She was on the verge of babbling, but her words had the desired effect. Jonas pulled his eyes away from her mouth distractedly.

'My parents? Oh, the shellfish. They like big, extravagant gestures so it had to be lobster, really.'

'And did they see any bands?'

'Oh, yes. They had the full guided tour.'

'And...?' she prompted him.

He gave her a rueful grin. 'They didn't throw themselves on my neck with tears of apology for neglecting me all these years and promises of a brighter tomorrow,' he said.

His words were light, almost jocular, without the slight undercurrent of disappointment or the hint of bitterness talk of his parents usually brought out in him.

'On the other hand they didn't criticise, cry with disappointment or walk out in disgust. They stayed for lunch and even said it was "rather nice" so overall a success, I think.'

'A complete success,' she agreed.

He reached out his hand, tucking back a lock of her hair. She sat frozen, aware of nothing but his touch, the unexpectedly tender look in his eyes, the sound of her own heartbeat hammering.

Their eyes continued to hold. Her mouth was dry, she flicked her tongue out nervously to moisten her lips. They had been alone, been intimate, so many times—every night for the last few weeks—but this...this felt different. It felt *more*. But even as part of her welcomed it, thirsted for it, another, larger part of her shrank from it. It was too much.

Because they had been here before.

'I should go.' Was that really her voice? So hesitant, so unsure? She pushed herself up, legs wobbly. 'Wave Fest won't run itself, you know.'

He was still seated, still looking at her with that disconcertingly knowing gaze, as if he could see right inside her. He was so close. He just needed to reach out, pull, and she would be in his lap.

But if she allowed herself to settle there she would never want to leave.

He didn't. Didn't move, didn't pull, didn't try and dissuade her. He just watched her as she drank down the rest of her coffee, grabbed her file and walked out of the office. He didn't say a word.

Work. It was always the answer. And this was a workaholic's dream. The second she left the office Lawrie was pounced upon to sort out some problem with the evening's line-up, and by the time she'd pacified the disgruntled artist who expected a higher billing she'd managed to push all thoughts of Jonas to the back of her mind—where, she told herself sternly, he had better stay until she felt more like herself again.

Whatever and whoever herself might be. She certainly wasn't the brittle London girl who had arrived here just over a month ago, but she wasn't the Cornish girl in vest top and shorts she appeared to be either. She was only playing at her role here.

But, playing or not, there was a lot to do.

Eight hours later her lunch was just a distant dream. She had barely had the opportunity to grab any water, despite the heat of the sun, and must have walked miles. Next year she would recommend golf carts, she thought.

'There you are.'

Lawrie turned around, blinked blearily. Everything was suddenly amplified. The light was almost blinding; people and objects were a mingled blur. The sounds were an amalgamated cacophony of discordant notes and loud voices.

She swayed, pressing a trembling hand to her head.

'Lawrie! Are you okay?'

Jonas. How broad he looked...how comforting. She took

a small step towards him, then stopped, trying to summon up the energy to reply. 'Yes, just tired still. I'll be fine.'

It had been such a warm day. And yet now she was shaking with cold, wrapping her arms around herself, trying to press some warmth into her bones.

A touch on her chin tilted it upwards. She tried to meet his probing gaze but had to close her eyes.

'I told you to take a proper rest. There are another twenty-four hours of this festival, and you are not going to last,' Jonas said grimly and, disregarding her protests, whirled around, taking her elbow and pulling her along.

'What are you doing?' she said, trying unsuccessfully to pull her arm out of his grasp.

'Taking you home for the night. If you are on site you won't switch off,' he said pulling out his handset. 'Fliss, you are in charge for the next twelve hours. Lawrie is taking a few hours off.'

Lawrie could hear Fliss's voice floating up from the handset, worrying, agreeing, admonishing Lawrie to get some rest.

She wanted to argue, to tell them she was fine but the words wouldn't come. 'Are you all ganging up on me?'

'If that's what it takes.'

She felt as if she should fight harder but she didn't have the strength. 'Just a short nap,' she conceded.

'You are having the whole night off. You can come back tomorrow morning, but not a second before.' There was no trace of humour in his voice, just worry. 'And I'll see how you are then.'

'Yes, boss.'

But it was an effort to form the words, and she didn't demur as Jonas led her through the crowds and round to the staff car park, where he gently helped her into his car.

Lawrie sank into the seat and closed her eyes. Half

asleep, she didn't notice the route Jonas took until he stopped the car with an undignified squeal of brakes. She prised her eyelids open and looked about her. They were in the tiny old town, amongst the fishermen's cottages that clustered around the harbour.

'This isn't home,' she murmured sleepily.

'This is my house,' Jonas told her, and he unbuckled her seat belt before getting out and coming round to open her door and help her out. 'I don't trust you not to be logging on and fussing if I let you go back to yours.'

'Too tired to log on,' she protested, but obediently followed him along the street.

They were at the very top of the old town, with the cliffs towering above them and views over the rooftops down to the harbour below. Jonas came to a stop by a long crooked house that lurched drunkenly along the street and opened the door. Lawrie stopped on the doorstep and stared at him, suddenly more awake.

'The crooked house? You bought it?'

'Yep. Come in.'

She looked at him. Didn't he remember? That this was *the house*—the one that every time they played the 'one day when we are rich' game they had decided they would buy. Some were bigger, others more imposing, cuter, older, quainter, but something about this last house in the old town had appealed to her the most. The funny little corners, the different levels, the roof garden… It had always drawn her in, and now it belonged to Jonas.

'Lawrie, are you all right?'

'Yes, I'm coming.'

Slowly she stepped into her dream house. Inside it was just as she'd imagined. The hall that bisected the mismatched halves of the house was covered in grey flagstones, a wooden bannister curved around the crooked staircase.

She didn't have time to see more as Jonas ushered her straight upstairs. He turned down the winding passage to his left and stopped at the first door, pausing with his hand on the handle, a look of slight embarrassment on his face. 'I haven't made the other beds up but my sheets are clean on...' He trailed off.

She stared at him incredulously, then laughed. 'Jonas, we have been sleeping together most nights for the last month—plus, I am so tired I wouldn't care if your sheets hadn't been changed in weeks.'

He grinned. 'Good point,' he said and, turning the handle, ushered her inside.

It was a large, rectangular room, with two small windows cut into the deep walls, the stone window seats covered in plush cushions. An oak bedstead dominated the room and was made up in a rich, dark chocolate linen. It was the most inviting thing Lawrie had ever seen.

'Right...' He still stood at the door. 'I will leave you to...ah...make yourself comfortable. There's a bathroom just there.' He gestured at a door set in the far wall. 'I'll be back in the morning with some clean clothes and a meal, so just sleep, okay?'

''kay...' She nodded, but her eyes were already fixated on the plump, cool-looking pillows, the king-size comfortable bed.

Jonas had scarcely pulled the door shut behind him before she'd started to undress, kicking off her shoes, slipping off her shorts and unhooking her bra, manoeuvring it off under her vest top. Clad just in her top and knickers, she climbed into the bed and closed her eyes.

As she drifted off to sleep the events of the day replayed themselves. Why had Jonas been so funny about her sleeping in his bed? Of *course*, she thought drowsily as sleep began to overtake her. They had only shared a bed to have sex—sometimes sleeping together afterwards, sometimes he would leave her and go home. But this—this letting her into his bed, into his home—this was intimacy.

It scared her…it comforted her.

Lawrie drifted off to sleep.

It wasn't worth going back to the hotel, Jonas decided. After all, Fliss could cope for a few hours, and if she couldn't he was just fifteen minutes' drive away; it could take longer than that to walk from one side of the site to the other.

Dropping by Lawrie's to pick her up a change of clothes had taken him far longer than he'd anticipated. Choosing an outfit had felt almost uncomfortably intimate— which, considering some of the truly intimate actions he had been performing with and to her on a nightly basis, was just too weird.

He hadn't wanted to dwell on why that might be, choosing a dress and cardigan almost at random and plucking underwear out of her drawer with his face averted.

Well, maybe he'd had a little peek. But not a long one— he wasn't one of *those* guys.

Back at his house, he wandered into his sitting room, falling onto the leather corner sofa with a sigh, his mind fixated on the room above, where Lawrie slept. He had avoided bringing her here, to his home, to the house she had once loved so much.

He dragged his eyes away from the ceiling he was staring at as if he had X-ray vision—as if he could see through to the room, to the bed, to the sleeping girl above—fixing his gaze instead on the large watercolour portrait that hung above the open fireplace. It was a sea scene, of course—

every work of art he owned reflected the coast in some way—in which a girl sat on a rock, staring out to a wild sea, her hair whipped and blowing. She was turned away from the artist, so only a small part of her face could be seen.

Lawrie. A portrait painted by a summer visitor years ago. Jonas had tracked it down and bought it several years ago.

He didn't really like to examine his reasons why. Just as he didn't like to examine his reasons for buying this house in particular. The house he and Lawrie had play-furnished in their dreams time and time again. He could easily afford something bigger, fancier, more luxurious, but he felt grounded here—at home.

In the house she'd loved, with her portrait on the wall.

He sat bolt upright, adrenaline running through him. What was he *doing*? What had he been doing these last nine years?

He was pathetic. All these years he had prided himself on how independent he was, how he needed no one but himself, and look at him.

No wonder he was still single. How could any real woman compete with the ghost at the feast? They had never had a chance, had they? No matter how fun or accomplished or sexy they were, they had always been missing something very important.

They weren't Lawrie.

Maybe part of him had held on, hoping for her return. And here she was. Back in his life and back in his bed.

About to leave again.

He could try and change her mind. He could ask her to stay, beg her to stay. Rush up there now and tell her how he felt.

And then what?

Jonas got to his feet and walked over to the painting. There she was, her eyes fixed on the horizon, on the future. She had always dreamt big.

Right now she was vulnerable, more scarred by the loss of her job and her fiancé than she would ever admit. He could play on that fear and she might stay.

And then what?

He knew too well how *that* scenario played out. He would watch her feel more and more confined and constricted. Watch her start to blame and resent him. Again. Watch her walk away, walk out of his life, and this time never come back.

Or he could let her go and then move on himself. Finally, *properly* move on.

He looked at the clock sitting on the mantelpiece. Eight hours before he needed to wake her. It wouldn't hurt if he just stretched out for a while himself. The sofa was long enough, wide enough, comfortable enough... And yet he couldn't relax.

This was ridiculous. He had a perfectly good bed upstairs. Lawrie wouldn't mind.

She was fast asleep, the covers kicked off, exposing long, lean legs. The curve of her bottom encased in sheer black silk was a stark contrast to the cream of her skin. The strap of her vest had fallen down, showing a rare vulnerability in the usually self-possessed, contained, organised Lawrie. Looking down at her, he felt a tenderness creep over him for his beautiful, intelligent wife.

*Ex*-wife. Just two letters made such a difference.

Jonas kicked off his shoes and quietly slipped his shorts off, hanging them on the chair before crossing the room to get into bed beside her. He fitted his length against her, pulling her in close, one arm holding her tight.

'I love you,' he whispered. 'I'll always love you.'

Eyes open, thoughts racing, Jonas lay there, holding Lawrie close, willing time to slow, wishing that the night would last for ever.

# CHAPTER ELEVEN

IT WAS THE campfire's fault. If Lawrie hadn't attended the end-of-festival campfire—hadn't met up with old friends, hadn't found herself singing songs she had forgotten she had ever known, hadn't cooed over babies and admired stroppy, tired toddlers, hadn't met new couples and heard one hundred stories about how they'd met...

If she hadn't spent the evening watching Jonas, golden in the flickering firelight, laughing, relaxing, looking over at her with laughter, with tenderness in his eyes.

If after the campfire they hadn't sneaked back to the camper van. If they hadn't made love with an intensity she couldn't remember having ever experienced before.

She should have left the minute the festival finished—packed her bags and disappeared without a word.

Then she wouldn't need to find the words to say goodbye. Find the will to turn and walk away.

'You're very quiet.'

Jonas was once more driving her to the airport.

Only this time there would be no return trip.

She forced a smile. 'I'm a little apprehensive,' she admitted.

He raised an eyebrow. 'Lawrie Bennett, lawyer, festival-organiser, campfire chanteuse...apprehensive? I don't believe it.'

He was so calm, so *cheerful*. As if her leaving didn't matter at all.

And, although she couldn't handle a scene, a little regret might be nice—a sign that their time together had meant something to him.

*What if he asked you to stay?*

Where had that thought come from?

She pushed it to one side, searching for something to say. 'Do you think I'm like my mother?'

As soon as she asked the question she regretted it, not sure she could bear to hear the answer.

Jonas looked surprised. That was good, right?

'I can't imagine you abandoning your teenage daughter while you go and party in Goa, no,' he said finally. 'Why?'

Immediately Lawrie wanted to backtrack. What could she tell him? That she wasn't sure about leaving? Didn't know if she could do this alone?

She fell back on an old conversation. 'I don't even know what I like, for goodness' sake. Is festival-going, shorts-wearing, beach-loving Lawrie more real than the suited and booted City lawyer? I worry that I'm a chameleon, Jonas, just like she is.'

Excuse it might be, but there was truth there. She had always defended her need to blend in. Maybe it was time to learn to stand out.

He was silent for a moment. 'Your mother spent her life searching—you've spent yours *doing*. You have spent your life trying to achieve something, Law. You have been working for it since I knew you. You're dedicated, single-minded. That's nothing like her. You never wasted your time on dreams and fairytales.'

That was true, but not enough. 'But I don't even know whether I like the stuff I like because of me, or because of you or Hugo. See? Chameleon!'

He laughed, and the warm humour caressed her taut nerves.

'We're back to this, are we?'

She nodded, slightly shame-faced.

'You're not a chameleon, I promise. Maybe you've just found it easier to adapt to other people's interests as that gives you more time to concentrate on what really matters to you.'

He was silent for a moment, concentrating on overtaking, and Lawrie took his words in, a warmth stealing over as she did so.

He understood her. In some ways better than she understood herself.

He spoke again, quiet and serious. 'For what it's worth, I think you're both of those people. Even city slickers are allowed to be beach bums occasionally. You don't have to choose. Okay—we're here.'

Looking up with a start, Lawrie realised Jonas was taking a left hand turn—the one that led to the airport short-stay car park. He was planning to come in.

Panic clawed at her chest. She couldn't handle a long, protracted goodbye. Memories flashed through her of tearful train station farewells, clutching desperately on to Jonas as the train drew in, suitcase at her feet.

She'd never been good at goodbyes.

'You don't need to stay, honestly. Just drop me off.'

He flashed her a quick glance. 'You sure?'

She put on her brightest smile. 'Goodness, yes. You don't want to waste an hour hanging out at the airport, and I don't have much luggage—most of my stuff was shipped out last week. I'll head straight to the departure lounge and read there. You go.'

There was a slightly desperate tinge to her voice as she

finished speaking but Jonas didn't seem to notice—he just turned the car around to drive into the drop-off area.

He pulled up to the kerb and they sat there. Silent. Lawrie stared at her hands, twisting them nervously together.

'Okay, then, this is it.'

'Yep.'

'I'll get your bag.'

Once again he was walking round the car to fetch her bag. Once again she was sliding out of the low-slung seats, stepping onto the grey paving slabs, ready to walk through the sliding glass doors.

Once again she was leaving.

'Right—you have your suitcase, laptop, handbag, jacket, tickets, passport?'

She nodded. 'I'm all good.'

'Okay, then.' He was moving away, the few steps back towards the car. It was just Lawrie and her bags, alone on the pavement. Just as she wanted. *Fight me on this,* she thought desperately. *Come in with me. See me off. Ask me not to go.*

The need was getting louder, harder to ignore.

Lawrie picked up her bag, testing its weight. This was it. She shot a look over at him, leaning against the bonnet, oblivious or uncaring of the cars lined up behind, waiting for a drop-off spot. His face was calm, set. Inscrutable.

'Law…?'

She paused, a fizz of hope bubbling up inside her, shocking her with its intensity.

'Just remember: tea is drunk hot, not iced, and jelly wobbles and is always eaten with ice cream.'

And just like that she was flat.

She attempted a smile. 'I thought you wanted me to fit in?'

'Fit in? Yes. Go native? No.'

The world had fallen away. All she was aware of was him. The foot between them seemed an ocean already—that solid, comforting presence a continent away. It was up to her. Only her.

And it terrified her.

Lawrie took a deep breath. 'I could stay if you wanted me to. If you asked me I would consider it, definitely.' *Ask me,* she begged silently. *Tell me you need me...you can't live without me. Tell me it will be better this time. Tell me we can make it.*

His expression didn't change. 'Why?'

Lawrie didn't know what she had expected him to do. To regretfully but politely turn her down and send her on her way? To run over to her, swoop her up, twirl her, like a montage of every rom-com she had seen? To be embarrassed?

But she hadn't expected that one-word question. She hadn't expected the warm blue eyes to turn to steel.

'Last-minute nerves,' she said as brightly as she could, pulling the tattered shreds of her pride around her, trying to match his cool expression. 'You know I hate saying goodbye. It's been a good few weeks. I got carried away, sorry. Forget I said anything.'

'What if I did ask?'

How could she have thought him calm? His voice reverberated with suppressed emotion. But not the emotion she'd hoped for. It wasn't warm, comforting, loving.

'Would you make it till the end of the year? Till next summer? How long before you blame me because you're stuck here and not in New York?'

*Wow.* Lawrie had never really believed that words could hurt before, but that hit deep—painfully deep. 'I can't believe you said that...' she almost whispered, torn between hot tears and plain old-fashioned anger. 'I only asked you...'

'You asked me to make a decision for you. *Again*. You want to stay, Lawrie?' The words whipped through the air, taut and clear. 'You stay. *You* make the decision and *you* live with the consequences. Don't ask somebody else to shoulder the responsibility for you so you can blame them the second it goes wrong.'

'I'm not!' All her verbal skills had deserted her. She was defenceless against the unexpected onslaught.

'No?' His laugh had no humour in it. 'You didn't blame me for keeping you here before? For getting married so young?'

The warmth of the summer's day had disappeared and a chill wind goosepimpled her bare arms, making her shiver. 'We were young!'

'You said yourself you would still be with your ex, making wedding plans, if he hadn't forced your hand. Now you want me to force it again?' Jonas shook his head. 'I don't think so, Lawrie. Take some responsibility for yourself, decide what the hell you want—what you *really* want—and then maybe we can talk.'

'I don't need to talk.' Lawrie's uncertainty and shock had disappeared, been replaced with a burning anger. How dared he speak to her like that? 'I made a mistake. Clearly. Thanks for pointing that out. Message received.'

And, picking up her bag, she turned and strode away as confidently as she could, his steel-blue gaze burning into her back as she did so.

No one had warned her how cold New York could be. It was barely autumn—fall, she corrected herself—and already the temperatures were dropping, the wind was howling through the island city, and the rain lashed down in great dramatic storms.

Not that Lawrie had much time to concentrate on the weather. New York prided itself on being the city that never slept and its standards were high. She was no shirker, but it was taking everything just to keep up.

And keeping up wasn't enough. She needed to excel. Others might skate in Central Park, go for coffee wrapped up in giant jumpers and cashmere scarves and hats; Lawrie worked. She had found a small studio flat close to the office, but spent so much time at her desk it really was just a base to sleep, shower and eat. Ostensibly she was apartment-hunting, looking for a place of her own to buy. In reality her attempts mirrored her wedding-planning with Hugo. Non-existent.

Hugo was now married to his secretary, Helen—happily, she assumed. His social media pages certainly painted that picture, showing a beaming Hugo—he had put on weight, she thought critically—with one arm possessively around his blooming bride. Every detail of Helen's pregnancy was detailed, along with scans, possible baby names and more information about her physical symptoms than Lawrie was entirely comfortable with.

On the surface she was cynically amused, but buried deep down inside—*very* deep down—she was touched and a little jealous. Not of Helen and Hugo, exactly, but of the absolute patent happiness that glowed out of every sentimental update. No amount of completed contracts, of senior partner compliments could compete with that.

And Jonas didn't get in touch. Not one word. No apology.

And she didn't contact him.

His last words reverberated around her mind, echoing at unexpected times. Not just when she was alone, and not just in the dead of night as she lay sleepless in an unfamiliar bed in a strange city, but in meetings, at the gym, as she walked down the street.

*Take some responsibility.*

And then the anger flared up again, but it was getting weaker as the days slowly passed.

And at the same time that unwanted voice was whispering insistently, *What if you could do it again? Would you ask him or would you tell him? Would you tell him you were staying and want to be with him?*

*Would you tell him that you love him?*

'Are you having a party this year?'

Jonas looked up irritably. 'What?'

'I asked,' Fliss repeated equably, 'if you want to have a birthday party again this year?'

As Jonas's birthday coincided with the final weekend of the season—the start of autumn proper—he usually had a big party at the Boat House. A chance for the locals and the villagers to let their hair down and reclaim their home after months of incomers.

He couldn't imagine anything worse, but the speculation if he missed a year would be unbearable.

'I haven't really thought about it. I suppose so.'

'Oh, great!' Fliss was obviously annoyed. 'Masses of preparation for "I suppose so". What you mean is, *Thank you, Fliss, I would love to—and, yes, I will of course be leaving the grumpy expression and the grunting at home and try to enjoy myself for once in my miserable life.*'

That was a little too close for comfort. 'That's enough,' he snapped.

Fliss looked anxious. 'Honestly, Jonas, you've been the proverbial sore-headed bear for weeks. Even *I* am finding you pretty difficult, and I have a much higher Jonas tolerance than most.'

Jonas swung his chair round and stared at her. 'Oh, come on. I know I've been a bit short—'

'A *bit*?' she interjected.

'Busy—'

'A reclusive workaholic.'

'And I don't suffer fools gladly.' He shot her a look as she opened her mouth and she snapped it shut. 'There has been a lot happening, as I am sure you have noticed: new cafés, two new hotels, getting the clothes line launch ready for next year.'

'I know,' she said. 'I work here too, remember?'

'Well, then, life isn't all surfing. Sometimes it is pure, hard, exhausting work.'

'But a balance is always good. When did you last take a board out? Not since the day after Lawrie left.'

'Don't say her name!'

It was involuntary, and he cursed himself for revealing so much—for revealing everything. But Fliss didn't look shocked or horrified. She looked knowing. She looked… heck…she looked *sorry* for him. Jonas gritted his teeth.

'Just because L… Because her departure coincided with a busy period does not mean that my present mood has anything to do with her.'

Fliss looked apologetic. 'But we've been here before,' she reminded him. 'That summer she left, before the third Wave Fest, you changed. You went curt and mean and nearly drove all your staff away. You worked twenty-four-seven and a year later—*voilà*—five more cafés and a mini-chain.'

'And a career for you.'

'And a career for me,' she agreed. 'But I bloody earned it, Jonas. And I am earning it now, acting as a buffer between you and the staff, trying to keep up with your break-neck speed, going along with the vision whilst making sure that we don't over-expand—and that we don't lose all our staff while we do so.'

His voice was icy. 'I know what I'm doing.'

'Well, yes, we all know what you're doing. You're throwing yourself into work to forget about Lawrie. After all, it worked once before. Is it working now?'

*Not really.* His mouth twisted. 'She wanted me to ask her to stay.' The words were out before he could stop them.

Fliss didn't look surprised 'Did you?'

Jonas stared at Fliss. 'No,' he said bleakly. 'No, I told her to go.'

'Why?'

The same question he'd asked Lawrie. The question that had swept the hope out of her eyes and left her looking broken.

He shook his head, trying to clear her stricken face from his mind. 'Because it's not my decision to make. If she wanted to be with me she would. I shouldn't need to ask.'

'Jonas, I love you, and I love her too, but you—you're my best mate as well as my boss and I'm worried about you. So I am begging you, for everybody's sake, win her back or get over her once and for all.'

*Win her back.* The words reverberated around Jonas's head as he walked along the harbour wall back home—back to the house that no longer seemed so cosy, no longer a sanctuary. She had spent less than twelve hours there, yet memories of her permeated every corner, every shadow. Lying there at night he could remember how her body fitted against his, the sound of her breathing, the silky texture of her hair as he stroked it.

How could he win her back when she'd never been his

to start with? He had tried marrying her, binding her close to him with legal ties, but she had left anyway.

He stopped and looked into the inky black water broken up by the reflected light from the street lamps.

*If you love someone set them free.* What kind of crazy thinking was that? If you loved someone you should never let them go.

Or, just possibly, you could go with them.

He had never done that. Never supported her, taken the journey with her.

He circled slowly, looked at the village that was his only home, his whole life.

It felt like a prison.

Slowly he began walking again, his brain whirring, reliving the past once again. And it wasn't comfortable viewing. He had only visited Oxford a handful of times. The beach-bred boy had been uncomfortable with the city of dreaming spires, and he had flat out refused to go to London at all the first summer she had interned there.

Shame flooded through him. He had been her husband and he had let her down. Badly. What must it have been like for her alone, renting a room in a far-flung suburb, travelling for an hour every morning in her one good suit to work twelve hour days in a city where she knew no one? She must have been so lonely. And yet he had never visited, never surprised her by showing up unexpectedly at her door. What kind of husband did that make him?

It was cold, with a chill wind whistling in off the sea, but he barely felt it wrapped in his ski jacket—a jacket that had never seen snow because he rarely took time off work. He'd blamed her workaholic nature for their inability to stay together; he was just as bad. If he couldn't survive outside of Cornwall, away from the comfort of his home seas, then was he any kind of success at all?

And if he was destined always to live alone then probably not much of a success at all.

If he had taken a chance, moved to be with Lawrie all those years ago, would they still be together now? He'd always thought that would have spelled disaster, that she would have been embarrassed by her non-professional husband and he would have struggled to find work. Jonas shook his head. He had underestimated her. Even worse, he had underestimated himself.

He looked out into the darkness, listening to the eerie voice of the wind, the crash of his beloved surf against the harbour wall. The wind blew spray up and over and he flinched as the icy drops flicked his skin, tasted salt. His beloved home. He'd always thought his heart was right here. But, if so, why did he feel so empty?

He turned his back to the sea and with a heavy heart made his way back to the cottage, alone.

'Lawrie, we're heading up to the Hamptons this weekend. My wife would love you to come. We can introduce you around.'

The older man's expression was sincere and Lawrie felt a rush of gratitude as she shook her head.

'Honestly, Cooper, I am fine,' she assured him. 'I've worked through every weekend since I arrived, and I think it's time I got to know the city a little. Some other time, maybe, if you'll ask me again?'

'Any time,' he assured her. 'Have a lovely weekend.'

'I will,' she promised.

And she meant to—or to try at least. She had been here nearly a month; it was time to put down some roots. Buy an apartment of her own, get a cat—she'd never had a pet. Pets were a sign of belonging.

Then she'd get out more, make some friends, date. Okay,

dating was a slightly terrifying prospect for an English girl
who might have been married once and engaged twice but
had never dated—especially New York style, whereby
men seemed to think nothing of chatting to you in book-
stores, in coffee shops, in lifts—*elevators*: she was a New
Yorker now—and asking you out. She might have been
with Hugo through most of her London life, but she was
fairly sure men didn't behave like that there. It was most
disconcerting.

But if dating was what it took to make her a native of
New York then date she would.

But not yet.

Pulling her long cream coat on and wrapping her cashmere scarf securely round her neck, Lawrie left the office.
It seemed that the whole city was heading out this weekend, and at almost seven on a Friday night the building
was eerily empty. The Friday before she had worked until
after ten. The Friday before that the same. The evening
stretching ahead of her seemed very long and very empty.

*This is the city that never sleeps*, she reminded herself.
*I am going to have some fun.* She could shop, she thought.
Go to Barneys or Saks, buy an outfit. Go for a cocktail. A
small stirring of interest reared its head in her breast. Yes,
shopping. How long since she had done that?

An hour later Lawrie was feeling a little bit better. A
beautiful wool wrap dress and a pair of designer leather
boots had helped. *Maybe clothes will be my thing,* she
thought, admiring her reflection one more time. *I'm well
paid, single, and living in New York. Dressing well is a
duty.*

Walking through the ground floor of the store, watching
the sales assistants as they got ready to close, she found
her eye caught by the displays of men's accessories. But-
ter-soft wallets, discreet briefcases, exquisitely cut gloves.

It wasn't just the women who knew how to look stylish in this city.

And then she saw it. A beautiful cashmere scarf. Dark greys, velvety blacks and inky purples combined in a pattern that reminded her irresistibly of a winter's night in Cornwall. Lawrie came to a sudden halt and, almost against her will, reached out to caress the soft wool. The feel of it filled her with a sudden yearning for wind, waves and the tang of salt. On autopilot she picked up the scarf and took it to the desk to be gift-wrapped, managing not to gasp when the assistant asked for a truly exorbitant amount of money.

It was Jonas's birthday in just a couple of days. It would be polite to send him a gift, surely.

Lawrie stood stock still, clutching the gift box, sudden homesickness hitting her like a punch to her stomach. She needed to snap out of it. Once New York felt like home it would all be easier. A cocktail was definitely next on the list. Possibly two.

Heading out of the store, she flung her arm out as a yellow cab cruised by. 'Taxi!'

Sometimes, no matter how good the intention, it was impossible to get in the right frame of mind. She was trying. But being perched on a high stool in the plush bar, reading the cocktail menu, watching the chattering, laughing clientele, was strangely distancing—as if she were in the audience of a play. She looked like them, these young, affluent, attractive people with designer clothes and salon-dried hair, but she was apart. Not just because she was on her own, but because she knew that all this was a charade....

Take away the dress and the heels, the artfully done make-up and the professionally glossy hair, and who was she? Lawrie Bennett, daughter of a teen mum, stepdaugh-

ter, granddaughter, young bride, divorcee. All those links
and yet she was completely, utterly alone. She could disappear here and now and nobody would know until the
office opened again on Monday morning.

Lawrie smiled to herself with bitter humour, imagining their shock if she wasn't at her desk by seven-thirty,
skinny latte in hand, freshly showered after a half-hour
session in the gym.

It didn't have to be like this. She could do anything,
grab a flight, go anywhere. Be impulsive. Of course the
last time she was impulsive she had ended up kissing Jonas
Jones, and look where *that* had got her.

Well, it had got her some pretty amazing sex. It had got
her fun and laughter and time spent with a man who understood and accepted her.

Maybe being impulsive wasn't such a bad thing after all.

Looking up, she caught the bartender's eye and beck-
oned her over. No, she wouldn't have one of the more obvious cocktails.

'A gin gimlet, please,' she ordered. She wasn't entirely
sure what a gin gimlet was, but it made her think of in-
trepid bohemian flappers, drinking gin on safari, quite
possibly in the middle of a thrilling adventure.

When was she going to have *her* thrilling adventure?

She took a sip and grimaced, but the second sip was
strangely refreshing and led quite naturally to a third. She
leant back and looked round. Opposite her was another
lone drinker—a woman. Perfect hair, discreetly expensive
clothes, sipping a cocktail while she typed busily on her
laptop. It was hard to tell but she looked ten years older
than Lawrie—although this *was* New York. She probably
had an excellent surgeon.

As Lawrie watched her the woman looked up from her
laptop and stared out at the laughing throng. An expression

of such desolation, such loneliness, such sadness swept over her face that Lawrie quickly averted her eyes, embarrassed to be looking at such unvarnished pain. When she looked back the woman looked calm again, blank, coolly professional.

*That could be me,* Lawrie thought. *That could be me in ten years if the dates and the cat and the making an effort don't work. If I keep doing nothing but working I could make partner, be respected, be admired—and find myself drinking alone every Friday night, watching the happiness but being apart from it. Just like I am today.*

Panic caught her chest and for one horribly long second she couldn't breathe. The rush in her ears was drowning out the chatter and the laughter; her heart was swelling and aching. Was this what she wanted? Was this what she was working towards? Dinner for one and a taxi home?

Was this *living*?

She pulled out a crumpled note and put it on the table with shaking fingers, downed the rest of the cocktail—a drink that no longer seemed reckless and fun but tart and bitter—grabbed her bags and hurried out of the bar.

She managed to flag a taxi straight away and, after giving the driver her address, sat back, staring out of the window as the city changed. Shoppers and workers were making way for the partygoers, the theatregoers, the young and the beautiful, the wealthy and the stylish. The atmosphere had subtly changed to one of excitement, anticipation. It was Friday night and the city was truly waking up.

When was *she* going to wake up?

Almost panicking, Lawrie pulled her phone from her pocket and brought up her emails. Selecting an address, she began to type, jabbing at the keys in her anxiety to get it written and sent. She had to make a decision. She had to make a change. She had just seen her future, sitting across from her, and it hadn't been a pretty sight.

The clothes, the cocktails, the success. None of it mattered if she was this empty inside.

And she *was* empty. Without Jonas she had nothing.

It had only taken her nine years to work that out.

He was just relieved it was over. Spending the first Sunday lunch with his parents for twelve years had been challenging. The fact it was his birthday hadn't made it any easier.

But it had been the right thing to do. They had even smiled a couple of times.

It was odd, but it was the first time they'd ever had a celebratory dinner with just the three of them. Before, every holiday, Easter, Christmas, birthday had been spent in the hotel dining room, publicly celebrating with the hotel guests. Their whole family life played out in a public arena.

No wonder Jonas liked to be alone. He couldn't wait to get home, to relax.

But there was a party waiting for him at the Boat House, whether he wanted it or not.

It was a beautiful autumn night, although a definite chill in the air heralded the change of seasons. A perfect night for a stroll. If he parked the car back at his house he could walk along the harbour, clear his head, think about his plans one more time.

The streets leading from the harbour were narrow, twisting, but navigating them was second nature to him. On autopilot he reversed his car into a parking space and thankfully unfolded himself from the driver's seat, taking a deep breath of the cold sea air.

He stood still for a moment, gazing down the hill at the sea, lit only by the moon and stars. It was his favourite view. It made him feel alive, grounded.

He would miss it.

For one moment he stood indecisively. Home was so close. A glass of his favourite single malt, music, a good book… But he had promised Fliss.

He took a few steps down the hill, coming to a stand-still as a car swung round the bend. Automatically Jonas pressed himself against the rough stone wall. Not every driver was as careful as he. The headlights were blindingly bright, sweeping up the hill as the car drew to a stop outside his house.

Who on earth could be visiting him at this hour?

A figure got out and shut the door, standing still as the car revved up and watching it drive away. A slim, grace-ful figure, a bag over one shoulder, another in her hand, shoulder-length hair silhouetted against the street lamp on the corner.

His heart sped up as the figure crossed to his door. And stood there.

'Lawrie?'

Rich as Cornish cream, deep as the Cornish sea.

She jumped. 'Happy Birthday.'

'You came all this way to wish me a Happy Birthday?'

'No, actually I came to bring you a present. I left it too late to post it, so here…'

She held out the box she had kept on her knee for the six-hour flight. 'Open it.'

'Out here?'

She shrugged, her eyes drinking him in as he stood lit up by the street light.

Jonas Jones. His face grey with tiredness, his hair ruf-fled, but so handsome, so alive, so close that her heart nearly flooded. And he was grinning as he opened the box, the corners of his eyes creased—grinning that same wicked grin she had been banishing from her thoughts, from her dreams, over and over again.

'It's a scarf,' Lawrie said shyly.

'I can see that. You really bought it for me?'

'It reminded me of you. Do you like it?'

His heart was in his eyes, so blue, so warm, so full she couldn't meet them, looking down at the dark, uneven flagstones instead.

'I love it. Is this what we do now?'

'What do you mean?'

'Buy each other scarves?'

She looked up, startled, laughed. 'Looks like it.'

'I like traditions. I think we should have one.'

'We should?'

He nodded, his eyes fixed on hers. 'A long-standing tradition. The kind grandkids find amusing and cute.'

'Grandkids?'

'I'm in favour, are you?'

Her palms were clammy, her stomach tense. Surely he didn't mean what it sounded as if he meant?

'I've never really thought about it,' she lied. Because the alternative life she could have had with him was something she liked to torture herself with on long, sleepless nights.

'Of course to have grandkids you need to have kids,' he continued, still in that calm, conversational voice whilst his eyes burned with passion. 'Shall we have kids, Lawrie?'

'We?'

Damn it, why was she croaking?

He stepped forward, took her trembling hands in his, looked down at her, and his face was filled with so much tenderness, so much hope, so much love, that she was bathed in it, suddenly calmer, suddenly braver, suddenly ready to hear whatever it was he had to say.

'I love you, Lawrie. I have loved you since you were

sixteen and I have never stopped—not for a day, for a second. I was a fool to let you go once, but to let it happen twice...? If you will just let me I promise to spend every second of our future making it up to you.'

The lump in her throat had doubled in size and her chest tightened even more. She could hardly see his face through the tears in her eyes.

'I...'

His grip tightened. 'I'm too hands-on. I know that. I don't need to interview every damn gardener, every cook, source every piece of fabric, every spoon. I pay people to do that. Obviously I would need to travel back and forth, but I could be based anywhere, really. I could be based in New York. Or Sydney, Kuala Lumpur. I can be based wherever you are—if you want me to be, that is.'

The tears were spilling, falling down her face as her hands returned his grip. 'You'd move for me?'

'Anywhere. I should have it done nine years ago, but if it's not too late I will now. Please tell me I'm not too late.'

The crack in his voice nearly undid her. She was crying openly now, but laughter mingled with the tears, breaking out into a smile as she stepped into him, pressed herself against his glorious, solid strength.

'Okay.'

He put his hands on her shoulders, pushing her back to look into her eyes. 'Okay?'

'Okay, kids, grandkids, traditional scarves. I'm in,' she said. 'I'm in for the whole crazy ride. I love you, Jonas. I missed you too. There I was in this amazing place, doing my dream job, and I was so *empty* I couldn't bear it. When you didn't email, didn't call, I thought I'd missed my chance with you again. And I didn't know where to go. I thought I'd go crazy. I missed you so much. I had to come home.'

His smile, his kiss, his arms were tender as he pulled her in. 'You came home.' He grinned at her, boyish and unafraid. 'Seems only fair—after all, I see a lot of flying in my future.'

Lawrie raised her head, pressing close, lips trailing sweet, teasing kisses across his jaw, towards the corner of his mouth. 'It might not be necessary,' she whispered in between kisses.

His hand tightened possessively around her waist, drawing her closer, loosening her belt, undoing her coat buttons with his capable hands.

'Hmmm?' he breathed as he slid his hands inside her coat and under her cardigan, one hand sliding underneath her top to draw circles on her bare tummy.

She shivered.

She arched back to allow his mouth access to her throat, to the pulse beating so insistently, desperate for his attention. 'I spoke to my firm.'

The hands stopped, the mouth moved away, and she gave a little moan of loss. 'And…?'

Damn, he wanted to talk. Talking was very overrated. 'We talked about setting up a European office. I'd still need to travel: London a couple of times a month at least, Paris, Berlin pretty regularly. But I could be based anywhere. I could be based here.'

His face lit up, love and happiness shining out. 'You'd be based here? You're coming home?'

*Home*. The word sounded so good.

She looked away, suddenly shy. 'If you want me to.'

'If I want? Lawrie, without you nothing works, nothing fits. If I *want*? I don't want anything else. Are you sure?'

'All this time I thought my job defined me, was all I needed. All this time I was wrong.' She stood on her tiptoes, nestled in close, seeking his warmth, his strength.

'All I need is you. You were right. I needed to be strong enough to admit it.'

Jonas shook his head, his expression rueful. 'That day at the airport I was harsh. I'm sorry.'

'You were a little harsh,' she conceded, allowing her mouth to find the strong lines of his jaw, to travel slowly towards his throat. 'But you were right too. It was unfair of me to ask.'

He looked over to the harbour at the lights shining brightly in the Boat House. 'There's a party going on at the café,' Jonas said, dropping a kiss onto the top of her head as his arms circled her. 'Or—and I would just like to point out that this is my preferred option—we could go into the cottage, barricade the doors and not come out for a week.'

'I like the idea of barricading ourselves away,' Lawrie said, smiling up at him suggestively. 'But I was hoping we could celebrate your birthday the old way: you, me, a sleeping bag and Barb, parked up on a headland somewhere? What do you say?'

His eyes were blazing with laughter, love and a promise so intense she could barely breathe.

'You said her name! I guess that means you really are back.'

'And this time it's for good,' she promised him. 'I've come home to you.'

\* \* \* \* \*

# The World of
# MILLS & BOON®

With eight paperback series to choose from, there's a
Mills & Boon series perfect for you.  So whether you're
looking for glamorous seduction, Regency rakes or
homespun heroes, we'll give you plenty of inspiration
for your next read.

*Cherish*™

*Experience the ultimate rush
of falling in love.*
12 new stories every month

*Romantic Suspense*
INTRIGUE

*A seductive combination of
danger and desire*
8 new stories every month

*Desire*™

*Passionate and dramatic
love stories*
6 new stories every month

nocturne™

*An exhilarating underworld
of dark desires*
2 new stories every month

For exclusive member offers go to
**millsandboon.co.uk/subscribe**

# The World of
# MILLS & BOON®

## HISTORICAL

*Awaken the romance of the past*
6 new stories every month

## MEDICAL ROMANCE

*The ultimate in romantic medical drama*
6 new stories every month

## MODERN™

*Power, passion and irresistible temptation*
8 new stories every month

## By Request

*Relive the romance with the best of the best*
12 stories every month

WORLD_ M&B2b